THE
SEA
PRIESTESS

THE
SEA
PRIESTESS

DION FORTUNE

SAMUEL WEISER, INC.

York Beach, Maine

A NOTE FROM THE PUBLISHER

In her Introduction, Dion Fortune remarks that "this book has not got the imprint of any publishing house." This statement refers to the first edition of The Sea Priestess which was published privately in England in 1938.

First published in 1978 by
Samuel Weiser, Inc.
Box 612
York Beach, Maine 03910

Reprinted, 1991

First published in 1938
Published in England in 1957

ISBN 0-87728-424-5
Library of Congress Card Number: 83-159136
MV

Printed in the United States of America

INTRODUCTION

IF one wishes to write a book that is not cut according to any of the standard patterns, it appears to be necessary to be one's own publisher; therefore this book has not got the imprint of any publishing house to lend it dignity, but must stand upon its own feet as a literary Melchizedek.

I once had the entertaining experience of receiving one of my own books for review, but if I were called upon to review this one, I should find it difficult to know how to set about it. It is a book with an undercurrent; upon the surface, a romance; underneath, a thesis upon the theme: "All women are Isis, and Isis is all women," or in the language of modern psychology, the anima-animus principle.

Various criticisms have been levelled at it by those who have read it in manuscript, and as they will probably be repeated by those who read it in print, I may as well take the opportunity of a preface to deal with them, especially as there is no production-manager to say to me: "You must cut fifty pages if we are to get it out at seven-and-six."

It was said by a reviewer of one of my previous books that it is a pity I make my characters so unlikeable. This was a great surprise to me, for it had never occurred to me that my characters were unlikeable. What kind of barber's blocks are required in order that readers may love them? In real life no one escapes the faults of their qualities, so why should they in fiction?

There are many drawbacks to my hero as a son, a brother, a husband and a business partner, and he makes no attempt to

5

minimise them; nevertheless I retain my affection for him, though I am quite alive to the fact that he could not compete with the creations of the late Samuel Smiles. But then I do not know that I particularly want him to. It has often seemed to me that as one cannot please everybody, one may as well please oneself, especially as I have, God be thanked, no publisher to consider, who would naturally expect my book to contribute its quota towards his overhead expenses and errors of judgment.

It was said of this book by a publisher's reader, who ought to know what he is talking about, that the style is uneven, rising to heights of lyric beauty (his expression, not mine), and on the same page descending to colloquialisms.

This raises a pretty point in technique. My story is written in the first person; it is therefore a monologue, and the same rule applies to it that applies to dialogue—that the speakers must speak in character. As my hero's mood changes, his narrative style therefore changes.

Any writer will agree that narrative in the first person is a most difficult technique to handle. The method of presentation is in actuality that of drama, though maintaining the appearance of narrative; moreover everything has to be seen not only through the eyes, but through the temperament of the person who is telling the story. A restraint has to be observed in the emotional passages lest the blight of self-pity appear on the hero. He must, at all costs, keep the reader's respect while evoking his sympathy, and this he cannot do if he wallows in his emotions. Consequently in the most telling scenes, where an author would normally pull out the tremolo stop and tread on the loud pedal, only curt, brief Anglo-Saxon may be used, for no one employs elaborate English when *in extremis*. All effects have to be obtained by "noises off". Therefore unless the reader has imagination and can read constructively, the effects are lost.

And this brings me to the question of constructive reading. Everybody knows how much the audience contributes to the performance of a play, but few people realise how much a reader must contribute to the effect of a work of fiction. Perhaps I ask too much of my readers: that is a point I am not competent to judge, and can only say with Martin Luther: "God help me, I can do no otherwise." After all, the style is the man, and short of castration, cannot be altered. And who wants to be a literary eunuch? Not me, anyway, which is perhaps the reason why I have to do my own publishing.

People read fiction in order to supplement the diet life provides for them. If life is full and varied, they like novels that analyse and interpret it for them; if life is narrow and unsatisfying, they supply themselves with mass production wish-fulfilments from the lending libraries. I have managed to fit my book in between these two stools so neatly that it is hardly fair to say that it falls between them. It is a novel of interpretation and a novel of wish-fulfilment at the same time.

Yet after all, why should not the two be combined? They have to be in psycho-therapy, where I learnt my trade. The frustration that afflicts my hero is the lot, in some degree at any rate, of a very considerable proportion of human beings, as my readers doubtless can confirm from their own experience.

It is too well known to need emphasis that readers, reading for emotional compensation, identify themselves with the hero or heroine as the case may be, and for this reason the writers who cater for this class of taste invariably make the protagonist of the opposite sex to themselves the oleographic representation of a wish-fulfilment. The he-men who write for he-men invariably provide as heroine either a glutinous, synthetic, saccharine creature and call the result romance, or else combine all the incompatibles in the human character and think they have achieved realism.

Equally the lady novelist will provide her readers with such males as never stepped into a pair of trousers; on whom, in fact, trousers would be wasted.

It is difficult for me to judge of my own characters; naturally I think the world of them, but such partiality is probably no more justified than that of any other doting parent. The late Charles Garvice was convinced he wrote literature and was bitterly jealous of Kipling.

How far my creations are wish-fulfilments is a matter on which I am the last person to be able to express an impartial opinion. It has often been said of me that I am no lady, and I have myself had to tell the secretary of a well-known club which craved my membership that I am no gentleman, so we will leave the mystery of sex wrapped in decent obscurity, like that of the parrot.

Nevertheless, I think that if readers in their reading will identify themselves with one or another of the characters according to taste, they will be led to a curious psychological experience—the experience of the therapeutic use of phantasy, an unappreciated aspect of psycho-therapy.

The psychological state of modern civilisation is on a par with the sanitation of the medieval walled cities. Therefore I lay my tribute at the feet of the great goddess Cloacina—

"In jesting guise, but ye are wise,
Ye know what the jest is worth."

DION FORTUNE

THE SEA PRIESTESS

CHAPTER I

THE keeping of a diary is usually reckoned a vice in one's contemporaries though a virtue in one's ancestors. I must plead guilty to the vice, if vice it is, for I have kept a fairly detailed journal for a good many years. Loving observation but lacking imagination, my real rôle was that of a Boswell, but alas, no Johnson has been forthcoming. I am therefore reduced to being my own Johnson. This is not my choice. I would far rather have been the chronicler of the great, but the great never came my way. Therefore it was myself or nothing. I am under no delusion that my journal is literature, but it served its purpose as a safety-valve at a time when a safety-valve was badly needed. Without it, I think I would have blown the lid off on more than one occasion.

They say that adventures are to the adventurous; but one can hardly go seeking adventure with persons dependent upon one. Had I had a young wife to face the adventure of life with me, it might have been a different story, but my sister was ten years my senior and my mother an invalid, and the family business only just enough to keep the three of us during my salad days. Adventure, therefore, was not for me, save at a risk to others which I did not feel was justifiable. Hence the need for a safety-valve.

These old journals, volume upon volume of them, lie in a tin trunk in the attic. I have dipped into them occasionally, but they are dreary reading; all the pleasure lay in the writing of them. They are an objective chronicle of things seen through the eyes of a provincial business man. Very small beer indeed, if I may be allowed to say so.

But at a certain point there comes a change. The subjective becomes objective. But where, and exactly how, I cannot say for certain. It was in an endeavour to elucidate the whole business that I began to read through the later journals systematically, and finally to write the whole thing out. It makes a curious story, and I do not pretend to understand it. I had hoped it would come clear in the writing, but it has not. In fact it has become more problematical. Had I not had the diary-keeping habit, much would have safely disappeared into the limbo of things forgotten; the mind could then have arranged matters in a pattern after its own liking, to suit its pre-conceived ideas, and the incompatibles would have slipped into the discard unnoticed.

But with things down in black and white, this could not be done, and the affair had to be faced up to as a whole. I record it for what it is worth. I am the last person to be able to assess its value. It appears to me to be a curious chapter in the history of the mind, and as such, to be of interest as data if not as literature. If I learn as much from the re-living of it as I learnt from the living of it, I shall be well repaid.

The whole thing began with a dispute over money matters. Our business is an estate agent's business which I inherited from my father. It has always been a good business, but was heavily embarrassed by speculation. My father had never been able to resist the temptation to pick up a bargain. If a house which he knew had cost ten thousand to build were going for two, he had to have it. But nobody wanted these great sprawling mansions, so I fell heir to a stableful of white elephants. All through my twenties and well into my thirties I

wrestled with these brutes, peddling them piecemeal, till finally
the business assumed a healthy complexion once more and I
was in a position to do what I had long wanted to do—sell it
and be rid of it—for I hated it and the whole life of that dead-
alive town—and use the money to buy a partnership in a London publishing company. That, I thought, would give me the
entrée into the life that fascinated me; and it did not seem to
me a particularly wild-cat scheme financially, for business is
business, whether you are selling bricks or books. I had read
every biography I could lay my hands on that dealt with the
world of books, and it appeared to me that there was scope for
someone accustomed to business methods. I may be wrong,
of course, having no first-hand experience of books and their
makers, but that was how it looked to me.

So I mooted the idea to my mother and sister. They were
not averse, provided I did not want them to come to London
with me. This was a boon I had never expected, for I had
quite thought I should have to get a house for them, as my
mother would never have put up with a flat. I saw the way
opening up before me in a manner I have never dared even to
dream of. I saw myself leading a bachelor life in Bohemian
circles, a club-man, and God knows what not. And then the
blow fell. The offices of our firm were part of the big old
Georgian house in which we had always lived. You couldn't
sell the business without the premises because it was the best
site in the town, and they wouldn't agree.

I suppose I could have forced it through and sold the house
over their heads, but I didn't like to do that. My sister came up
to my room and talked to me, and told me that it would kill my
mother to have her home broken up. I offered to set them up
in any house they fancied that was within my means, but she
said no, my mother would never settle. Surely I would let her
live out her old age in peace? It couldn't be for long now.

(It is five years ago, and she's still going strong, so I think she would probably have transplanted all right if I had been firm.)

Then my mother called me into her room, and said that to give up the house would completely disorganise all my sister's work, for all her meetings were held in our big drawing-room, and the Girls' Friendly had their headquarters in the basement, and my sister had given her whole life to her work, and it would all collapse if the house were given up, because then there would be nowhere where she could do it. I did not feel justified in going my own way in the face of all that, so I made up my mind to stick to the estate agenting. Life had its compensations. My work took me about the country in my car, and I have always been a great reader. It was the lack of congenial friends that had really been my trouble, and the prospect of making them had attracted me to the publishing idea. Still, books are no bad substitute, and I dare say I should have been pretty badly disillusioned if I had gone to London and tried to make friends. In fact, as it turned out, it was a good thing I did not make the venture, for it was just after this that my asthma started, and I should probably not have been able to stand the racket of life in London. The firm I should have sold to set up a branch office in the town, and after that the opportunity for a good sale was over, so the choice was no longer mine.

All this does not sound much like a row over business matters. Neither was there any row over the actual decision. The row came after everything was settled and I had written turning down both offers. It was at Sunday evening supper. Now, I dislike cold suppers in any case, and the vicar had preached a particularly silly sermon that evening; so I thought, at any rate, though my mother and sister liked it. They were discussing it, asked my opinion, which I would not have volunteered, and I, being a fool, said what I thought and got sat on, and then, for no reason that I have ever been able to discover, I went in off the deep end, and said that as I paid for the food on the table, I could say what I pleased at the table. Then the fun began. My womenfolk had never been talked to like that in their born days, and they didn't like it. They were both experienced parish workers, and after the first burst I was no match for them. I walked out and slammed the door, shot up the stairs three at a time, with that dreadful cold Sunday supper inside me, and had my first go of asthma on the half-landing.

They heard me, and came out to find me hanging on to the banisters and were scared. I was scared too. I thought my last hour had come. Asthma is an alarming thing, even when one is used to it, and this was my first attack.

However, I survived; and it was to the time I was lying in bed after the attack that I can trace the fountain-head of all that followed. I suppose I had been pretty drastically drugged; at any rate I was only semi-conscious and seemed to be half in and half out of my body. They had forgotten to draw the blind, and the moonlight was blazing in right on to the bed and I was too weak to get up and shut it out. I lay watching the full moon sliding across the night-sky through a light haze of cloud, and wondering what the dark side of the moon was like, that no man has ever seen, or ever will see. The night-sky has always had an intense fascination for me, and I never grow used to the marvel of the stars and the greater marvel of inter-stellar space, for it seems to me that in inter-stellar space must be the beginning of all things. The making of Adam from the red clay had never appealed to me; I preferred that God should geometrise.

As I lay there, doped and exhausted and half hypnotised by the moon, I let my mind range beyond time to the beginning. I saw the vast sea of infinite space, indigo-dark in the Night of the Gods; and it seemed to me that in that darkness and silence must be the seed of all being. And as in the seed is infolded the future flower with its seed, and again, the flower in the seed, so must all creation be infolded in infinite space, and I along with it.

It seemed to me a marvellous thing that I should lie there, practically helpless in mind, body and estate, and yet trace my lineage to the stars. And with the thought there came to me a strange feeling, and my soul seemed to go forth into the darkness, yet it was not afraid.

I wondered if I had died as I thought I should die when I clung to the banisters, and I was glad, for it meant freedom. Then I knew that I had not died, and should not die, but that with the weakness and the drugs the bars of my soul had been loosened. For there is to every man's mind a part like the dark side of the moon that he never sees, but I was being privileged to see it. It was like inter-stellar space in the Night of the Gods, and in it were the roots of my being.

With this knowledge came a profound sense of release; for I knew that the bars of my soul would never wholly close again, but that I had found a way of escape round to the dark side of the moon that no man could ever see. And I remembered the words of Browning—

"God be thanked, the meanest of His mortals,
  Has two soul-sides, one to face the world with;
  One to show a woman when he loves her."

Now this was an odd experience; but it left me very happy and able to face my illness with equanimity, for it appeared to be going to open strange gates to me. I had long hours lying alone, and I did not care to read lest I should break the spell that surrounded me. By day I dozed, and as it came towards dusk I waited for the Moon, and when she came, I communed with her.

Now I cannot tell what I said to the Moon, or what the Moon said to me, but all the same, I got to know her very well. And this was the impression I got of her—that she ruled over a kingdom that was neither material nor spiritual, but a strange moon-kingdom of her own. In it moved tides—ebbing, flowing, slack water, high water, never ceasing, always on the move; up and down, backwards and forwards, rising and receding; coming past on the flood, flowing back on the ebb; and these tides affected our lives. They affected birth and death and all the processes of the body. They affected the mating of animals, and the growth of vegetation, and the insidious workings of disease. They also affected the reactions of drugs, and there was a lore of herbs belonging to them. All these things I got by communing with the Moon, and I felt certain that if I could only learn the rhythm and periodicity of her tides I should know a very great deal. But this I did not learn; for she could only teach me abstract things, and the details I was unable to receive from her because they eluded my mind.

I found that the more I dwelt on her, the more I became conscious of her tides, and all my life began to move with them. I could feel my vitality rise and ebb and flow and ebb again. And I found that even when I wrote of her, I wrote in time to her rhythms, as you may have noticed; whereas when I write of everyday things I write in the staccato rhythms of everyday life. At any rate, be things as they may, I lived in time to the Moon in a very curious manner while I lay ill.

Presently, however, my illness ran its course, as illnesses will, and I crawled downstairs again, more dead than alive. My family were very attentive, having had a thorough scare, and everybody made a great fuss of me. However, when it began

to be realised that these performances were going to be a regular
routine, everybody began to get a bit tired of them, once the
novelty wore off and they ceased to be so spectacular.   The
doctor assured them that I was not going to die in these attacks,
however much I looked like it, so they began to take them more
philosophically, and left me to get on with it until I had
finished.   All except me.   I am afraid I never took them philosophically, but panicked afresh every time.   One may know in
theory that one will not die, but there is something very alarming in having one's air-supply cut off, and one panicks in spite
of oneself.

Well, as I was saying, everybody got used to it, and then
began to get a bit sick of it.   It was a pretty long haul with
a tray from the basement to my bedroom.   I began to get a bit
sick of it myself, as those stairs took a lot of managing when I
was wheezy.   So the question arose of changing my room.
The only other choice seemed to be a kind of dungeon looking
into the yard—unless I dispossessed someone else—and I must
say I viewed that dungeon with disfavour.

Then it suddenly occurred to me that down at the bottom of
the long narrow strip of what we called by courtesy a garden
were the old stables, and that it might be possible to rig up
a kind of bachelor flat there.   The minute I thought of it, the
idea took hold of me, and off I went, down through a wilder-
ness of laurels, to see what could be done about it.

Everything was abominably overgrown, but I shoved my way
through, following the track of a long-lost path, and came to
a small door with a pointed arch like a church door, set flush
with the wall of ancient brick.   It was locked, and I had no
key, but a shove with the shoulder soon disposed of that, and I
found myself in the coach-house.   On one side were the horse-
stalls, and on the other the harness-room, and in the corner a
corkscrew staircase led upwards into cobwebs and darkness.

I climbed this cautiously, for it felt pretty rickety, and came out into the hayloft. This was all in darkness save for chinks of light that came through the shuttered windows.

I opened one of the shutters, and it came away in my hand, leaving a broad gap through which sunlight and fresh air streamed into the musty gloom. I leant out, and was amazed at what I saw.

I knew from the name of our town, Dickford, that it must stand on a stream of some kind; presumably the stream which came out at Dickmouth, a seaside resort of sorts ten miles away. Well, here was the stream, presumably the River Dick, whose presence I had never suspected though I was born and bred in the place. Down in a little overgrown ravine it ran, and quite a considerable stream too, from what I could see through the bushes. It evidently entered a culvert a little higher up, and the old bridge, which crossed it a little lower down, had houses built on it, so that it had never occurred to me that Bridge Street was an actual bridge, as it must be. But here was a perfectly genuine stream, some twenty feet broad, overhung by authentic willows like a Thames backwater. I had the surprise of my life. Who would have thought that anyone, especially a boy, could have lived his whole life within stone-throw of a stream and never known it was there? But I had never seen a stream so completely hidden, for the backs of all the long narrow gardens abutted on the ravine and were full of trees and old overgrown shrubs, like ours. I expect all the local urchins knew it, but I had been nicely brought up, and that cramps one's style.

Anyway, there it was, and one might have been in the heart of the country, for not even a chimney was visible over all the heavy-leaved trees that lined both banks as far as eye could see, leaving the water to run in a tunnel of greenery. It was probably just as well I had not discovered this stream in the days of my youth, for I should certainly have been so fascinated by it that I would have fallen in.

I had a look round the place. It was a solidly-built, Queen Anne affair, like the house, and it would be no great job to fix up the roomy, dormered loft as a couple of rooms and a bath-room. There was already a chimney at one end, and I had seen a tap and a drain downstairs. Full of my discovery I returned to the house, to be met with the usual douche of cold water. It was out of the question to expect the servants to trail down there with trays if I were ill. It had got to be the dungeon or nothing. I said: damn the servants and damn the dungeon (since my illness my temper has got pretty short), got the car out, set off on a round of nominal business and left them to stew in their own wrath.

The business was not altogether nominal. We had to see about getting possession of a row of cottages that were to come down to make way for a petrol-pump, and one old dame had declined to turn out and had got to be talked to. I rather like to do those jobs myself, as bailiffs and suchlike bully abomin-ably, and I dislike hauling these old folk to court if it can be helped. It is an unpleasant job for all concerned.

They were what had been country cottages, and the town had grown round them, and in the last of them was a little old dame, Sally Sampson by name, who had been there since the year dot, and move she wouldn't. We had offered her alternative accommodation and all the rest of it, and it looked as if we should have to make a court case of it, which I very much dislike with these old folk who cling to their bits of sticks. So I knocked on Sally's little green door with her little brass knocker, and made up my mind to harden my heart, which I am not very good at; but it was better me than the court bailiff.

Sally opened the door about half an inch on a terrible clanking chain by which one could have pulled her whole cottage over, and demanded my business. I fancy she had a poker in her hand. As luck would have it I was so breathless after having walked up her rather steep garden path that I couldn't get a word out, I could only lean against her door-post and gasp like a fish.

That was enough for Sally. She opened the door, and put down the poker, and hauled me in, and sat me down in her one armchair and made me a cup of tea. So I had tea with Sally instead of evicting her.

And we talked things over. It came out that she had nothing but her old age pension; but in this cottage she could make a bit by doing teas for cyclists, and in the one we offered her she couldn't; and if she couldn't make a bit, she couldn't keep body and soul together, and it was her for the workhouse. So no wonder the old dame jibbed.

And then I had another brain-wave. If the trouble over my bachelor flat was going to be the servant problem, here was the solution. I told Sally my ideas, and she wept copiously from sheer joy. It appeared that her dog had died recently, and that she had been very lonely by day and very nervous by night since it had gone, and she seemed to think that I would be just what she wanted to fill its place. So we fixed things up then and there. I was to get the place put into shape, and Sally and I would move in and set up housekeeping as soon as it was straight, and the petrol-pump could go up in peace.

So I went home in triumph and told the family. But even that didn't please them. They said it would cause gossip. I said an old age pension was the next best thing to marriage lines, and there was no one to gossip if they didn't, as the place was invisible from the road and no one need know I had shifted my digs. They said the servants would gossip, and I said: to hell with the servants. They said, which was true, that I wouldn't have to do the housework if the servants gave notice, or I wouldn't consign them to hell so readily. I said that servants never gave notice on account of scandal, as they always wanted to stop on and see the end of it. There was no better way of keeping servants than to have a skeleton in the cupboard. My sister said she couldn't have the Friendly Girls there if I were living in all the appearance of sin with Sally at the end of the garden, even if I refrained from the actuality. I said: to hell with the Friendly Girls, and we left it at that. However, when my sister saw Sally in her best black bonnet covered with bugles, she agreed that she had been rather far-fetched in her innuendoes. So we settled down. Sally had the horse-stalls and I had the loft—a kind of urban garden of Eden before the serpent.

CHAPTER II

I MUST say I loved that place. My sitting-room had four
dormer windows, full south, and my bedroom faced east and
the sun called me every morning. I fixed up a wide brick
hearth and burnt peat from the marshes; and had the space
either side of it shelved, and began to collect the books I had
always wanted. I had never been able to do that before because
there wasn't room in my bedroom and I disliked the idea of
having my books about the house. There is something very
intimate and personal about one's books. They reveal so much
of one's private soul. I had no mind to wear my books on my
sleeve for my sister to peck at. Besides, they would probably
have corrupted the Friendly Girls and set the servants talking.

I am afraid it was rather mean of me, but I very much disliked the idea of my sister visiting my stable. I suppose she is a
decent creature in her way, in fact she is very highly thought of
in the town, but we have got nothing in common. My mother
always called me the changeling; God knows how I came to be
born into our family. My sister and I have always been like
cat and dog, and since I developed my asthma and my temper
got short, I have been the cat. Anyway, I didn't want her. All
the same, I knew it was hopeless to try and keep her out; all I
could do was to put a Yale lock on the door and make her
knock for admission.

Things turned out better than I expected, however, for she
fell foul of Sally right away by pulling her up over her work.
Sally, I admit, was not a good duster, but she was a champion

cook. My sister, on the other hand, was a good cleaner but a foul feeder. Sally told my sister that she worked for me, and wasn't taking orders from anybody but me. My sister came to me and demanded Sally's head on a charger. I said that Sally suited me and I wasn't going to sack her. I liked dirt. It made the place more homely. My sister said she wouldn't enter the place again while Sally was there, even if I lay on my death-bed. I said Right-o, that suited me fine. So we left it at that, and she kept her word.

So it ended that my partner Scottie and the doctor were the only folk who ever set foot in the place. And they loved it. The trouble was that when they got in, they couldn't be got out, but just sat yarning. Now they were very good chaps in their way, especially Scottie; in fact there were plenty of decent chaps in the town and round about, fellows you could go to in a difficulty. I knew them all and was friendly with everybody, as it was my business to be; but all the same, I had no real friends, except perhaps, Scottie, in his queer way. He and I have nothing in common, and we each go our own way, but I can trust him in any emergency; there are worse foundations for a friendship than that.

He is an odd bird with an odder history. His parents were on the stage; and when they were here with a touring company, they went sick with the flu, and died of it, first one, and then the other, and little Scottie ended up in the workhouse. But even at the tender age of three his Scotch accent was well established. It has never been eradicated, and whatever came after was budded on the parent stock. He picked up the local dialect from the paupers, and God willed it that the master and his wife should be Cockneys; the result is a regular plaid of an accent. Fortunately he is a man of few words.

But what with his portentous silences and my disinclination to drive a hard bargain, we built up a terrific local reputation for probity, which in the long run paid us better than larger profits on the individual deals, though my sister foamed at the mouth when she heard of some of them. If everybody had their rights, she would have been running the business and I the Girls' Friendly.

Scottie's education was the usual, but the Scotch came out in him and he made the most of it. If there had been anyone to see about scholarships for him, he would probably have got on; but there was no one, and as soon as he finished school age, they got him a job with us as office boy and made him self-supporting.

My education was also the usual. I was sent to the local academy for the sons of gents, and that just describes us. It was a debilitating establishment for both mind and body. I got no good from it that I know of; but then, on the other hand, I don't know that I took any particular harm. It closed down when the head ran away with the damsel from the local sweet-shop. An appropriate end, for it was an establishment that combined saccharine and muck in an amazing manner—impractically high precepts in the class-rooms, and unbelievably low practices in the dormitories. Even at that tender age I used to wonder if the head had ever been a boy himself, and doubted it. I gathered such worldly wisdom as falls to the lot of adolescent louts under such circumstances, which I suppose is better than nothing. I never went away from home except for short holidays.

When I arrived at the office under my father, Scottie was already well established and had developed the most extraordinary air of an elderly clerk who has been with the firm for generations. He always spoke of my father as Mr. Edward after my arrival, as if he had held his position under *his* father. But even when he is sitting on my bed he never calls me anything except Mr. Wilfred. We were just about the same age, but whereas Scottie was already a circumspect business man, I was a callow hobbledehoy.

I liked old Scottie from the first, but my father put his foot down on any sort of personal friendship owing to his work-house origin. However, when my father's death threw every-thing into confusion, it was Scottie who steadied things. Our old head clerk just wept. Scottie and I had to shore him up, youngsters though we were. Everyone thought it was he who steered me through, and so you would have thought it was to hear him talk after the troubles were over, but as a matter of fact, it was Scottie.

When my asthma began I soon saw that I was going to be a very uncertain quantity in the business. It was no good relying on me for routine work. I never have been a good auctioneer even at the best of times. A good auctioneer is the gift of God. Moreover, I am slightly short-sighted, and I either get myself accused of favouritism by indignant females because I miss their bids, or else knock things down to people who don't want them. I once sold five lots to an unfortunate individual with a running cold before I realised that he was repressing sneezes and not bidding. My speciality is valuing. I'll value anything except pictures.

When the doctor saw the way I was shaping, he told me I ought to take a partner. I asked him to break it gently to my family that a partner would have to be taken into the business. He did, and they agreed. They still had their original wind-up over me. What they didn't agree to, though, was the partner I chose, which was Scottie. They had hoped we should get something County that wanted to mend its fallen fortunes.

They raised a terrific yelp, as I knew they would. I admit he is horribly common; that his taste in clothes is deplorable and his H-s uncertain; but he is honest and shrewd and kindly, and a dashed good worker, so I persevered.

I cannot see that I have let the business down, as our sort of clients don't call on their house-agents in any case. They never have on us, anyway, and I have never cherished any illusions that they ever would, even if my sister has. To want workers for a flag-day is one thing : to want the pleasure of your company is another. There is no one I would sooner have come and sit with me after a go of asthma than old Scottie, and that is a pretty good test. He sits like a hen and says not a word, but is uncommon matey all the same. So I took him into partnership, and I think I had the best of the bargain. It is a curious characteristic of my family that they will oppose a thing tooth and nail even when they have nothing to put in its place.

Scottie got married soon after he was made a partner. I suppose that is bound to make a difference to a friendship, even if you like the wife, and I didn't. She was all right in her way. My sister thought her a very worthy girl. She was the daughter of the local undertaker. Now auctioneers are a cut above undertakers—I don't quite know what undertakers pair off with—so I should have thought she would have considered that that was letting the business down still further, but apparently not. Odd, isn't it, that Scottie's commonness doesn't worry me, but I can't stand his wife's; and her commonness doesn't worry my sister, but she can't stand his. Scottie's marriage left a gap in what had never been very densely populated. He wasn't much of a companion, but he was a friend all right.

After Scottie had settled down to the partnership I took no part at all in the routine, but stuck altogether to valuing. That was the part of the business I liked. It took me about the country and I met interesting people, especially when the assizes were on, for I was often wanted as an expert witness, which is a great lark if you have a sense of humour. Sometimes one barrister had me to give evidence, and sometimes another, and the fellow who had held me up as the last word at one assize would be trying to make out I was mud at the next. Then after it was all over I would dine with them at the "George", and the landlord, who was a pal of mine, would set to work to make us all tight. He never managed it with me, not unduly, at any rate, because I knew his stock, for I used to pick the stuff up for him at the auctions—and jolly good some of it was, too—but we generally fixed *them*, between us.

Now all that sort of thing is very good fun, and I thoroughly enjoy it; but the barristers were here to-day and gone to-morrow, and though I enjoyed them enormously while I had them, it never ripened into friendship.

However, in the end I settled down, more or less, with Sally and my books and the wireless; everybody said I was damned unsociable, but God knows I wasn't unsociable if I could have got the sort of society I liked. I am afraid I played my asthma for all it was worth.

So I read variously, and I read queerly. I read a lot of Theosophical stuff, for one thing, which I couldn't have done, not in comfort, anyway, if I had still been at the house. Some of it I liked, and some I didn't. I accepted reincarnation; it was the best thing of its kind I had ever come across and helped me a lot. This life looked like being a wash-out, so I pinned my hopes to the next. When I had nothing better to do, I used to think about the last.

I always had to lay up for a day or two after a bout of asthma; one gets rather fed up with books after a bit, and I had never encouraged visitors at the best of times, and these were not the best of times with me. I probably could not have talked if they had come. So I used to lie and think and wonder, and amuse myself by reconstructing my past lives.

Now it is an odd thing that I, who cannot piece together a plot for a novel to save my life, much as I like observing people, could construct the most elaborate and fantastic past incarnations for myself. Moreover, after I had been working at them all day, as I would be when I was getting over a bout of asthma, I would begin to dream about them, and on the occasions when I had to be doped I would dream of them with extraordinary vividness. I used to lie between sleeping and waking, and I don't suppose I should have stirred if the house had gone on fire under me. In that state my mind seemed to possess a power of penetration it possessed at no other time. In the ordinary way I skated about over surfaces, and saw no further through a brick wall than most, and my own feelings were an obscure muddle to me, overlaid by what I ought to be, and honestly tried to be. But when I lay doped like this, I had no delusions.

Now the odd thing about this state was its curious inverted sense of reality. Normal things were far away and remote and didn't matter: but in the inner kingdom, as I called it, to which I had been transported by the prick of a syringe, my wishes were law, and I could create anything I wanted by just thinking about it.

I have a pretty good idea why people take to dope to escape from reality, and abandon life for pipe-dreams and never miss it. I dare say I owe a good deal to the Dangerous Drugs Act. I can best compare my life to a vitaminless diet—plenty of nutritive bulk, but the little something that meant health was lacking. I suppose my trouble was really spiritual scurvy. They say that badly-managed horses develop stable vices, such as crib-biting. What with my dope dreams and Theosophical reading, I began to get on to Peter Ibbetson's idea of "dreaming true". I gradually learnt the knack of day-dreaming, and although I could not obtain the same reality as I got when I was doped, I got quite a bit, and every now and again a day-dream would carry over into a night-dream and I got something really worth while.

What I was doing, was, I suppose, really a very superior sort of novel-reading. For after all, we read novels as a kind of supplement to daily life. If you look over the shoulder of the mildest man in the railway carriage, you will find he is reading the bloodiest novel. The milder the man, the bloodier the novel—and as for maiden ladies——! Any particularly tough-looking individual, with overseas tan still on his skin, is probably reading a gardening paper. Thrillers are, it seems to me, an attempt to vitaminise our spiritual diet. Of course the difficulty is to get exactly the thriller prescription you want. One may be able to identify oneself with the hero for vicarious adventure, but the heroines are always so piffling. I gradually got more and more expert at compounding my own romantic prescriptions, and less and less dependent on the ready-made kind. Almost I came to look forward to my bouts of asthma because I knew it meant a dose of dope; for then the phantasies would become real and take charge, and I would "see life" in the most extraordinary fashion.

I also developed my power of "feeling-with" nature things. I had had my first experience of this when I accidentally got in touch with the Moon during my first attack; later I read some of Algernon Blackwood's books; also *The Projection of the Astral Body*, by Muldoon and Carrington. These gave me ideas. Muldoon had poor health, and when he was lowered by illness he found he could slip out of his body. Asthma is also a lowering thing at the time. Mystics who want visions always fast; any asthmatic who wants a night's sleep always sleeps on an empty stomach. Put the three together, the asthma, and the drugs, and going supperless to bed, and you have all the conditions for slipping out of your body, or so it seems to me. The only drawback is that it was odds-on as to whether one slipped back again. To be perfectly honest, I should not have minded very much if I hadn't—in theory anyway, though on the one or two occasions when I nearly put it to the test I fought like a fiend. I hope this doesn't bore you, but it amused me enormously at the time. And anyway, one cannot please everybody, so one may as well please oneself.

CHAPTER III

WELL, to continue. I said my power to build up my reincarnation phantasies developed gradually. That is true in a way, and in a way it isn't. It developed in a series of jerks. I would go for some time and get nothing, and then I would get a sudden step forward. Then I would go on again for another blank patch, and then another step.

I had read in the Theosophical literature that the best way of remembering your past incarnations was to go over the day backwards every night when you got to bed. I tried that, but I don't think there is anything in it. You do not actually think backwards, you think in a series of disconnected pictures arranged in the reverse order, which is not the same thing. At least, I did, and if anybody does anything different, I should be interested to hear what it is. Personally, I think a lot of that stuff is eye-wash.

I had always been fascinated by ancient Egypt, and as in these realms of fancy there is no extra charge for anything, it amused me to think that in a past incarnation I had been an Egyptian. That left rather a long gap between now and then, during which I slept with the worms, a boring occupation, so I decided that I had also been an alchemist who, needless to say, discovered the Philosopher's Stone.

Then, one Sunday evening, I went to church with the family, as I do occasionally for the sake of peace and quietness and the business, for one must do these things when one lives in a small place. There was a visiting parson who read the lessons, and he read them rather well. I had never realised before what magnificent literature the Authorised Version is. We had the part about the Flight into Egypt, and the gold, and frankincense and myrrh, and the Three Wise Men who were led of a star, and I was fascinated by it. When I got home I hunted up the Bible that had been given me when I was christened, and that I had never looked at since, save under compulsion, and read it all up.

I also read about Moses being trained in all the wisdom of the Egyptians, and Daniel in the wisdom of the Babylonians. We hear a lot about Daniel in the lions' den, but we hear nothing at all about Daniel in his official capacity as Belteshazzar, head magician to the king of Babylon and satrap of Chaldea. Another thing that interested me was that curious business of the battle of the kings in the valley, four against five—Amraphel, king of Shinar; Arioch, king of Ellasar; Chedorlaomer, king of Elam, and Tidal, king of nations. I knew nothing whatever about them, but their names were magnificent and sang in my head. Then there was the even odder incident of Melchisedek, king of Salem, priest of the most high God, who went out to meet Abraham, bearing bread and wine after the fight was over and the kings were all sunk in the slime-pits. Who was this priest of a forgotten worship whom Abraham honoured? I admit candidly that there is a great deal about the Old Testament worthies that I do not find admirable, but these I found fascinating. So I added a Chaldean incarnation in the days of Abraham to my collection.

Then my efforts met with a set-back. I saw a lecture on re-incarnation advertised at the local lodge of the Theosophical Society, so I went to hear it, and it sounded good to me. But in the question-time at the end a lady got up and said that she was the reincarnation of Hypatia, and the chairman got up and said she couldn't be, as that was Mrs. Besant; then the lady started to argue, and they played a tune on the piano to drown her voice, and I went home with my tail between my legs and dropped Chedorlaomer and Co. into the discard.

I was a bit shy of reincarnation fantasies for some time after that, and took up my old interest in communing with the Moon. The little river under my windows was tidal, and one could tell by its voice what the tide was doing away on the coast. Just above our garden was a weir that marked the end of the tide-water. When the tide was high it was silent, but when the tide was low, there was a lovely silver waterfall effect. There was also a distinct smell of the sea at such times that I rather liked, though I believe it was supposed to be very unwholesome. It always puzzled the doctor why I, an alleged asthmatic, could bear to live over water like that, and he put it down to its being salt water. But as a matter of fact, I think my asthma started over the hell of a shindy with my family, and I got the first relief from it when I cleared out into the stables and slammed the door behind me. After all, asthma is not the same as bronchitis. There is nothing actually wrong with the works. It is simply that your extensors and flexors cannot agree to differ and jam the bellows.

Anyway, I liked the seaweedy smell that came up to me when the tide was low; the mist that rose from the water lay in the deep ravine and never got as far as my windows, but looked like a series of pools and lagoons with the moonlight on it and the trees rising out of it like ships in full sail. And when the tide was making away on the bay, and the salt water pushing back the fresh water and banking it up against the weir till the sluices at the mouth should open at the turn of the flood, there was a curious voice in the water as it gurgled and eddied; a restless, contending voice, as if sea and land were at loggerheads.

I used to listen to the land-water trying to push back the sea-water, and remembered what I had read of our local archaeology, for this part of the world was all drowned land. There were knolls that rose like islands in the salt marsh, and sea-ways through the slime when the tide was high, for all the earth about here is estuary silt, brought down from the hills of Wales. If the sea-banks went on the bay, the saltings would be six feet deep in flood-water. Dutch William made the banks, and they burst once, and the water came up to our church. That is why there are sluices at Dickmouth that only open at half-tide.

It is all salt marsh between us and the sea, and the town stands on the first of the rising ground. Behind the town is a wooded ridge that carries the road, and coming home along it in the dusk one can see the marshes full of mist, mile after mile, and when the moon is bright, it looks like water, and one could believe that the sea had come again to drown the land.

There has always been a strange fascination for me in the story of the lost land of Lyonesse, with its drowned churches whose bells ring fathoms deep. I have been out in a row-boat off Dickmouth and seen distinctly through the clear still water of a neap-tide the walls and towers of an old monastery that was drowned when the river shifted its bed one night of storm.

I have often thought, too, of the Breton legend of the lost city of Ys and its magicians; and how treachery delivered the keys of the sea-gates one night, and the sea came in and whelmed it. And I wondered what was the riddle of Carnac, and our own Stonehenge, and who were the men who built them, and why? And it seemed to me that there were two worships, one of the sun, and one of the moon; and that my love of the moon and the sea was the older and was to the other as the other is to us. And I could believe that the druids, priests of the sun-cult, must have looked upon the strange sea-fires of a forgotten worship as we look upon the barrows and dolmens.

For it came to me, I do not know why, that those who wor-shipped the moon and the sea built great fires at the uttermost neap, and as the tide came in, it took them. I could see the flaming pyre of drift on the rocks laid bare but once a year. Black rock, covered with deep-sea slime and giant fucus and great thriving shell-fish that fear no fisher. There was the pyramidal pyre of burning drift, blue-flamed from the salt. And the slow waves licked towards it as the tide rose, and it hissed and blackened below, till at last the high fiery crest fell sparkling into the water, and all was still save for the slow quiet wash of the dark waves on the rocks again, taking back to their depths the giant fucus and great shell-fish. Sometimes these visions of the inward-looking eye had a strange reality and validity for me. In them I could do what is very seldom done in a dream—I could smell the peculiar, acrid smell of burning wood extinguished by salt-water.

CHAPTER IV

WELL, things went on with me much as usual, no better, and no worse; in fact I think on the whole a little better, after one diabolical bout of asthma, and it came towards spring again, and round about March quarter-day, when of course we were particularly busy in the office, I had a very curious experience. The doctor had seen fit to shoot me full of dope without waiting for me to get into *extremis*, having had the wind put up him by my last performance, and I was lying in my usual moribund condition, not caring if the skies fell in on me, when I had a queer vision between sleeping and waking.

I seemed to go out of my body and leave it behind me after the manner that Muldoon describes, and I found myself out in the saltings towards Bell Head. I remember noting with a feeling of surprise that it was all firm level yellow sand-banks instead of the dark alluvial mud we have nowadays. Obviously there were no sea-dykes, but apparently when it was water, it was water, and when it was land, it was land, instead of the marshy mixture we have nowadays.

It seemed to me that I was standing on a rocky outcrop with nesting sea-birds all around me, and above my head, on a high pole, was a fire-basket. Behind me, on the scanty beach, a small row-boat, or rather paddle-boat, was drawn up, and it was exactly like the picture of coracles in the history books. I was waiting beside the beacon ready to light it when a ship should be coming up the channel through the marshes, and we had been waiting and watching for days for that ship, for it

35

came from a far sea-voyage, and I was getting pretty sick of it. Then, unexpectedly close, I saw the ship through the sea-mist and the dusk. And she was a long low craft, undecked amidships where there were rowers, and she had a single mast with a great purple sail, and on the sail were embroidered the faded remains of a crimson dragon.

As she drew close I shouted—it was too late to fire the beacon. They dropped the sail with a run, and backed water with the oars and just kept her off the sand-bank. And as they drifted past within a stone's throw, I saw, sitting high on the stern poop, a woman in the carven chair. She had a great book in her lap, and at the commotion with the sail she raised her head, and I saw that she had a pale face and scarlet lips, and long dark hair like seaweed in the tide. Round her hair, binding it, was a gold and jewelled band. For those few moments as the boat wore off the sand-bank I looked into her face, and she into mine; and her eyes were strange eyes, as of a sea-goddess. I remembered that the boat we were awaiting was bringing a strange priestess from the land beyond the sunset who was needed for our worship, for the sea was breaking the dykes and drowning the land and it was said that she had the magic that could master it. Now this, I thought, is the sea-priestess we have been awaiting. And I looked at her, and she looked at me.

Then she passed in her boat and disappeared in the mist and the dusk, and I knew that she was going to the high knoll that rose from the estuary some miles inland. On its crest was an open temple of stones and a perpetual fire, sacred to the sun; but underneath was a sea-cave where the water rose and took the sacrifices bound alive to the rocks. It was rumoured that the sea-priestess would require many sacrifices for her goddess, and when I remembered her cold strange eyes, I believed it.

Then I had to pull myself together and help Scottie with the quarterly accounting, and there was no more time for day-dreaming of sea-priestesses or anything else.

Now it so happened that back in my grandfather's time there had been an old gentleman of the name of Morgan who had owned a lot of land around these parts, and as he got ancient he put it in the hands of our firm as agents to manage it. Then he departed, and left an old sister to carry on. And the old sister had a companion, supposed to be a niece, a foreign-looking woman, reputed to be of French extraction. The Morgans themselves must have been Welsh at some time, as the name indicates; anyway, they never really seemed to belong round about, though they had been here for countless generations. Well, the old lady made a will leaving everything to the companion, which was not unreasonable, as she had neither kith nor kin, being the last of her line; and she left it on condition that the companion took the name of Morgan, which she did, calling herself Le Fay Morgan, she having originally been a Miss Le Fay. Of course the neighbourhood never managed the Le Fay Morgan, and when the generation that had known her as Miss Le Fay died out, the next generation called her Miss Morgan, *toute courte*.

My father, acting for old Miss Morgan the First, had hocked all the agricultural land to which old Colonel Morgan had pinned his faith, and bought plots at Dickmouth, believing it to be a rising seaside town, for the railway had got as far as us, and was expected to go on to the coast. But as luck would have it, there came a slump in railway-building at that moment, and the railway stopped where it was. Consequently he had sold everything that was worth having and bought what wasn't, and luckily for him the old lady died or I should imagine he would have heard about it.

In anticipation of the expected seaside boom he had put up

rows and terraces of pretentous family mansions in every direction at Dickmouth. There were shops and a dreadful mangy
arcade where the station ought to have been but wasn't, and
there was a site for a pier, which, thank God, was never built.
With the coming of motors, Dickmouth had perked up a bit,
and in the end we had got practically everything let—at a
price; but there was precious little profit on that estate by the
time we had finished propping it up and sticking it together,
for the pater had been the prophet Jeremiah of all the jerry-
builders. Consequently the companion, who ought to have
been well off if she had had what the old lady had intended
her to have, only got just about enough to hold body and soul
together and keep her in black bombazine.

Then, after we had fixed up all the twenty-one year leases at
knock-out prices, the railway pulled itself together and did the
last lap, and our seventy-five pound leases commanded pre-
miums of four or five hundred when they changed hands.
However, all things come to an end in time, even leases, and it
was our turn now. I had been able to send Miss Morgan the
Second some quite decent cheques for the last few quarters, so
it looked as if she would have a bit of prosperity in her declining
years to make up for the uncommon lean time she must have
had in her middle ones.

A lot had to be done about that estate now that the leases
were falling in. I didn't think it was the slightest use patching
up my father's white elephants any more. In fact, some of
them had forestalled the leases by falling in on their own
account. The rest were coming home to roost, or whatever it
is white elephants do when their day is over. I had got her a
decent figure for the site of the pier, and a really handsome one
for that dreadful arcade, which had been boarded up as a dangerous structure for the last five years. But I thought it was a
pity to sell any more sites as I happened to know from inside

information that the railway was going to be electrified. So I thought I would see if I couldn't do a deal with Miss Morgan, and we would find the money for rebuilding and share the proceeds with her. It would be a dashed good deal for her, and we should pick her up a bit at every corner and turn in the proceedings. That is how house-agents live—nibble, nibble, nibble, all down the line.

My father had let these blessed white elephants on repairing leases as far as possible. A repairing lease is a curious arrangement whereby one man spends money on another man's property. Towards the end of the lease he just naturally doesn't spend it. My father had also believed in using a thin layer of cement as a facing for cheap brick. This is all right if you use a good cement that sticketh closer than a brother; but if you don't, and the pater just naturally wouldn't, it comes up like gumboils on the first frosty night and then blows off on the first windy one. The poor devils who took those houses on repairing leases got a dashed thin deal.

Well, the houses and leases were all falling in together, and something had to be done about it. Scottie was going up to London to give evidence in some lawsuit of a client of ours, and I suggested to him that he should call on Miss Le Fay Morgan and put before her my idea for rebuilding instead of selling sites. It is my experience that women take things in much better when they are told than when they are written to. As a matter of fact, being out of their depth when it comes to house property, they judge the man and not the scheme. I knew that Scottie was bound to make a good impression with his overwhelming air of prudence and probity, so I sent him along.

In due course he came back, like Noah's dove, but it wasn't an olive branch he had in his mouth, not by a long chalk. He had met with scandal. It appeared that he had gone to the address we had on our books, and it turned out to be a kind of converted mews that had become a studio. Old Scottie had toiled up a chicken-ladder to what should have been the hayloft, and found that all the chairs had the legs sawn off, so that one was practically sitting on the floor, and round all the walls were divans made by the simple expedient of putting box-mattresses on the floor and throwing Persian rugs over them. Scottie knew they were box-mattresses because he turned up their skirts and had a look. Mattresses were inextricably associated in Scottie's mind with beds, and he was shocked. I pointed out that there was safety in numbers, but it did no good. I said I was shocked myself at him lifting their petti-coats and looking at their legs. That did still less good. He said that as soon as ever he came in and saw those sawn-off chairs, he knew there was something wrong, and when the lady came in, he knew he was right.

"How long have we done business with the leddy?" said he.

"God knows," said I. Scottie sniffed; he never gets used to hearing me take the name of the Lord in vain.

"Her name was on the books when I joined the furrm," he said.

"Her name was on the books when I was born," I said.

"Weel, what age would ye say she was?" said Scottie.

"Getting on," said I. "I'm thirty-six, and she was pasting into my parent properly from the earliest I can remember."

"Aweel," said Scottie, "a leddy came into the room, if room ye call it—I should call it a barrn myself—and I said to her: 'I wish to see Miss Le Fay Morgan.' And she said: 'I am Miss Le Fay Morgan.' And I said: 'Ye are verra weel-presairved, madam, if ye will pardon my sayin' so.' And she went a verra bright pink and said: 'I think ye had better do yer business by letter,' and I said: 'I think I better had.'"

From all which I gathered that the lady with whom we had

been doing business for years as Miss Le Fay Morgan jolly well wasn't Miss Le Fay Morgan, whoever else she might be.

Well, that put us in rather a queer position. Was it our business to rout out the genuine Miss Le Fay Morgan? We had a look at the correspondence, which was as bulky as the family Bible, and the signature never varied, right down through the ages. I took the first and last and a selection of intermediates, and went over to see the bank-manager; he and his cashier had a look at them and pronounced them perfectly O.K. I came back to Scottie, and we scratched our heads. At that moment the afternoon post came in, and we scratched our heads still further, for there was a letter from Miss Le Fay Morgan to say she was at the Grand Hotel, Dickmouth, and would the senior partner go over and take her round the property, "as she had always transacted her business with his father".

"A preecocious bairn," was Scottie's comment. "Will ye go?"

"You bet I'll go," said I.

"Don't parrt with any money," said Scottie.

CHAPTER V

I DROVE over to Dickmouth, and went to the Grand Hotel, and asked for Miss Le Fay Morgan. The page parked me in the enormous palm court, and I amused myself by watching the people; Dickmouth was becoming distinctly posh, and they were worth watching. It is always a marvel to me why women wear things that are intrinsically ugly in an effort to appear beautiful.

Then a woman came in. She was tall and slight, and she had got a black velvet tam o' shanter on her head with a diamond clip in it, and a black fur coat with enormous collar and cuffs. I thought she looked well in it, though she was quite different from the others, as she had long, straight, draped lines, whereas they had bits stuck on here and there. I could not see her face because her tam was pulled down over the ear that was towards me and her huge collar was up, but I could tell by the way she moved that she was a beautiful woman.

She looked round as if looking for someone, called a page, and the page pointed at me.

"Oh," said I to myself. "So you're the lady who saws legs off chairs, are you?"

She came over to me, and I rose to greet her. I couldn't see much of her face because of her collar, but I saw quite enough to know why Scottie had come home hastily. She had fine eyes, and her lips were heavily painted. That, of course, would have been enough for Scottie any dark night.

It is a curious thing to look back on the first meeting with a person who subsequently plays an important part in one's life, and see whether one had any premonition of what was to come. I can honestly say that although I hadn't seen that woman's face, I should never have looked at anyone else while she was in the room.

She gave me her hand, and we did the polite, and I stared at her. Her eyes looked into mine very steadily. She had come down to grip a nettle, if I was not very much mistaken. Scottie had evidently made no secret of *his* view of the situation. It was not difficult to guess why she had come. Scottie, duly espoused to the undertaker's daughter, was highly uninflammable and Miss Le Fay Morgan, very wisely, had not tried anything on with him. I might prove different material, however, if I took after the old man; he had led my mother the devil of a dance.

"Mr. Maxwell?" she said.

"Yes," said I.

"I knew your father," said she.

I didn't know what to say. I couldn't very well tell the woman to her face she was a liar—and I didn't want to. I once heard Sarah Bernhardt give a scene from *L'Aiglon* as a music-hall turn. She was old, as this woman must be old—if she were to be believed, and I was more than half inclined to believe her at that moment—and she had had the same kind of golden, throaty voice. King Lear said that a low voice is an excellent thing in women, but I doubt if he had this kind of low voice in mind when he spoke.

I took her out to my car. She didn't speak again. She was evidently a woman who knew how to be still, a very potent thing if anyone really knows how to do it. As I put her into the car I observed her ankles.

"You're no hag-beauty," I said to myself as I looked at those ankles. She had very fine dark stockings on. Stockings are very revealing of a woman's status.

She sat silent in the car. I felt I had to speak. I made some trite remark about the place. She said: "Yes," and that was all, but I was getting more conscious of her with every minute I sat beside her.

I had planned out a circular tour, and we parked the car at a strategic spot and began to visit the houses. And then I learnt something else about Miss Le Fay Morgan. There was not much about house property she did not know. Moreover she knew not only a builder's terms—and all his little tricks— but she also had a sound grasp of first principles. That is not a thing that everyone acquires, even with experience; but the thing that had always struck me about Miss Morgan's correspondence with us, even that which dated back a quarter of a century, was her remarkable grasp of first principles. I was glad my companion had her collar up; I did not particularly want to see her face; in fact, I definitely preferred not to.

We had worked our way down to a house at the end of the esplanade, and had some distance to walk back to the car. It was a small detached villa residence, standing in its own grounds, much gone to seed, and from the back windows one could see right out over the marshlands round the estuary. I looked out and I saw the devil's own squall coming up over the levels.

"We had better wait till that has blown over," said I.

She looked out, saw the distant hills rapidly disappearing, and agreed.

We were in a small kind of back study with a gas-fire. I had noted a shilling-in-the-slot meter in the scullery, so I slipped a shilling into it and put a match to the fire. There was, however, nothing to sit on. Miss Morgan solved the problem by sitting down on the floor, putting her back against the wall, stretching her long, slender legs straight out in front of her and crossing her ankles. I had another view of her very nice stockings.

"I like sitting on the floor," she said.

"Is that why you saw the legs off your chairs?" I asked, without thinking what I was saying, for hitherto I had been most carefully professional with her.

She laughed—that deep, golden, throaty laugh, that gave me a queer feeling even the first time I heard it.

"I am afraid I was altogether too much for your partner," she said.

"Yes, I am afraid you were," said I, not knowing what else to say.

"He is not the kind of person one can explain things to," said she.

"Am I?" said I, with a sudden revulsion of feeling at being vamped.

She considered me. "You are better than he is—but not much," she added as an after-thought, and we both laughed. It flashed into my mind that she had shifted her ground very quickly and cleverly when she sensed my reaction—or else that she had never meant to vamp me, and I rather inclined to the latter view; I felt instinctively that there was something fine about Miss Le Fay Morgan. Anyway, she was distinctly a personality, and one can forgive a lot to that.

The storm struck the windows with a swish and distracted our attention, for which I was not sorry, for I wanted to scramble back to the safety of professionalism, if that were possible while one was sitting cross-legged on the floor with a person. But Miss Le Fay Morgan wasn't having any. She had come down to grip a nettle, and she laid hold of it.

"I want to talk to you," said she.

I pulled my face together and made it as blank as I knew how, and stood on guard.

"Your partner made no bones about calling me a thief," she said. "And if I am not very much mistaken, he had it in his mind to call me a murderer too."

"We should certainly like to know what has become of Miss Le Fay Morgan."

"I am Miss Le Fay Morgan."

I did not answer. It was raining like liquid Hades, and neither of us would want to walk out and slam the door in weather like that.

"Don't you believe me?" she asked.

"I am not in a position to judge," said I. "I can't see much of you behind that collar."

She raised her hands and loosened her coat at the neck, and it fell back revealing face and breast.

She was a dark woman, brown-eyed, black-browed, slightly aquiline, and her skin was a very pale olive, more creamy than olive, in fact. Her eyes were not darkened with mascara—they did not need it—but her lips were pillar-box scarlet. She had long slender white hands, too, and the nails were filed to a point and looked as if they had been dipped in blood. So altogether, what with the black furs and white face and splashes of scarlet at the mouth and nails, she was a pretty startling figure to let loose on a bachelor from a one-eyed hole like Dickford. As she opened her coat a whiff of scent, aromatic and spicy, not sweet, came across to me. It was a very queer scent, and I think there was a good deal of musk in it. I took a reef in my backbone and thought hard of estate agenting.

"What age do you suppose I am?" she asked.

I looked at her. Her skin was perfectly smooth and unlined, just like ivory-white velvet. I have never seen such a lovely skin, it was as different from my sister's as chalk from cheese. All the same, the eyes were not the eyes of a girl. There were no pouches round them, the skin was quite taut, like a young woman's, but the eyes themselves had the peculiar expression of quiet watchfulness that goes with experience. She certainly was not a young girl, despite her figure, I was quite prepared to concede that; but would Miss Le Fay Morgan be so—I could think of no other word than Scottie's dreadful expression—well-preserved?

She seemed to guess my thoughts.

"So you do not believe in the power of beauty-parlours to preserve one's youth?" she said.

"Not to the extent to which you have preserved it," I said frankly.

"Not even with glandular treatment?"

"Frankly, no."

"But supposing all this were backed up by a knowledge of mind-power?"

I hesitated, and there suddenly came to my memory another face I had seen, a face uncommonly like hers—the face of the sea-priestess of my vision, who had sat in the great carved chair on the high stern-poop reading the book with the heavy clasps.

The effect on me was extraordinary. For a moment I was back on the estuary in the sea-mist and dusk. All sense of time and place was gone and I had slipped into timelessness. I suppose my face must have shown what I felt, for I saw Miss Le Fay Morgan's dark eyes suddenly glow like lamps.

I came back to normal and looked at her. It was a queer situation. There was she in her handsome furs, and there was I in my old raincoat—and yet there was something between us that was very queer. I thought of that marvellous scene in Rider Haggard's story, where "She's" hand comes through the curtains. It was as if the woman opposite me had laid her hand on a curtain, and could, if she chose, draw it back and reveal something very strange indeed.

Then she spoke. "I am very far from being a young

woman," she said. "I was not a young woman when I joined Miss Morgan. If you look closely, you will see that. I have cared for my skin, and my figure has taken care of itself, that is all."

Her ways were certainly not the ways of a young woman, but we had had her name on our books getting on for half a century. At the very least she must be rising seventy. It took a lot of swallowing.

"Well, Miss Morgan," I said, "I really don't know that it is any business of ours what your age is. We shall send the cheques to the address we have always sent them to, and we shall be satisfied with the receipts we have always had. I don't suppose I am particularly competent to form an opinion. You look very young to me; but if you say it is the result of taking care of yourself, I am not in a position to dispute it."

"I thought you were an authority on antiques," said Miss Le Fay Morgan with a mischievous smile, and made me laugh, which I had not meant to do. However, she let the curtain fall back again, and I think we both breathed more freely.

She got up and walked over to the window.

"How much longer do you suppose this downpour is going on?" she asked.

"Not long like this," I said. "As soon as it lets up a bit, I will slip out and get the car."

She nodded negligently, and stood gazing out of the window with her back to me, lost in thought. I wondered what she had to think about. If she really were Miss Le Fay Morgan, she must have had plenty. She probably remembered the Franco-Prussian War, if not the Crimea.

I was trying to sum up how far we were involved if we kept our mouths shut and did nothing about it. Of course she wasn't Miss Morgan the First's antiquated companion. I may be pretty green about women, but I am not as green as all that.

I wondered what had become of the original Miss Le Fay Morgan. I had read a detective story once where a wealthy old dame had died on the Continent and the companion had impersonated her. There was no reason to presuppose murder, even if Miss Morgan the Second were not forthcoming. Miss Morgan the Third might have ministered to her last moments most dutifully, and then planted her perfectly respectably. It was not improbable that Miss Morgan the Second had followed the example of Miss Morgan the First, and having no little nephews and nieces, left everything to her faithful companion —a very decent thing to do, in my opinion, and infinitely better than organised charity. Then there might have been some hitch in the will, it wasn't witnessed, or something, and the faithful companion saw what she had been promised going to some fourth cousin twice removed who already had more than he needed, and had taken the will for the deed, literally as well as metaphorically, forgotten to inform us of the funeral, and traced the signature on the receipts.

I suppose all this reasoning was pretty specious if one looked at it closely. One thing was quite certain, however, I had no mind to turn private detective and put my head in a hornets' nest from purely altruistic motives. I will not go so far as to say I had taken a liking to Miss Le Fay Morgan, I distrusted her too much for that, but I found her decidedly stimulating. This was the sort of thing I had wanted to go to London for; I had hoped that writing women would be of this type; but I expect if I had got there, I should have found out my mistake. The only authoress I ever saw looked like Ophelia in the Mad Scene, and you couldn't tell where the hair ended and the straws began.

Miss Le Fay Morgan seemed to have forgotten my existence, and I was very anxious not to commit myself in any way till I had talked things over with Scottie and Headley, our solicitor.

We did not want to be let in as accessories after the fact if any-thing fishy had been afoot. I could not imagine anything more likely to make you commit yourself than being shut up alone with Miss Le Fay Morgan in an empty villa during a thunder-storm, so I sidled quietly across the room without drawing attention to myself, turned up my coat-collar, and slipped out of the door. The rain was coming down in sheets, with a wind behind it that drove it down my neck, but that couldn't be helped, so I put my best foot foremost and legged it for the car. Then I collected Miss Morgan and drove her to her hotel. She blew me up in a most motherly manner for having gone out in the rain, and if I looked half as sheepish as I felt, I must have looked a prize sheep. She wanted me to stop and have tea with her, but I wouldn't, saying I must get home and get changed, which was the sober truth; but even if it hadn't been, I should have said it, for I had had quite enough of Miss Le Fay Morgan for one afternoon.

CHAPTER VI

O F course the inevitable happened, and I developed a feverish cold and went down with a go of asthma.

Miss Le Fay Morgan rang up the office to make another appointment, as she hadn't finished her business with me. Scottie told her I was ill, and offered himself. She waved him aside and demanded details of my symptoms, which Scottie wouldn't give, disapproving of her thoroughly. Finally one of them hung up on the other, but I was never able to find out which.

Scottie went and saw Headley and put the worst possible face on everything; but Headley told him to shut his mouth and look the other way, as he couldn't prove anything, and had better not try. You can't have an inquest unless you have a corpse, and there wasn't any corpse, so far as we knew; or at any rate, if there were, Miss Le Fay Morgan was walking about inside it. I have a suspicion that Scottie also consulted Headley about the possible effect Miss Morgan might have on my morals, and that Headley thought she might be good for me. Anyway, Scottie drew blank at both burrows and came home in a bad temper. Then he gave me a talking-to, but I wheezed at him and pretended to be semi-conscious. If you have got to have asthma, you may as well get some good out of it.

Anyway, I gathered one thing from the rather heated, one-sided conversation—that I should not be required to track Miss Le Fay Morgan to earth in the interests of abstract justice, a thing for which I have never been able to work up the slightest enthusiasm.

Scottie went back to the office nowise sweetened in temper by the interview, and, I rather fancy, made the office boy's life a burden to him. Anyway, the office boy got back at him in a very unexpected manner, and one that had far-reaching consequences in my affairs.

The office boy has the job of working the switch-board of the telephone extensions, and the trouble is that if you get a boy intelligent enough to manage the switch-board, he is intelligent enough to take an interest in the conversations, and this particular office boy had apparently been listening-in while Scottie and Miss Morgan had spat at each other, and had drawn his own conclusions as to the lie of the land. At any rate, when a lovely lady walked into the office next afternoon and demanded news of me, he did not refer her to Scottie in the inner office, but acted on his own responsibility, and told her everything he knew, and a lot he didn't. I shouldn't be surprised if half a crown changed hands, either. Anyway, the office boy played hookie from the choir practice that night and went to the pictures. This I know because the vicar asked my sister to ask me to speak to him, which I declined to do, it not being my business, and in any case a decidedly mean advantage to take of the kid. Neither my sister, nor the vicar, nor Scottie, needless to say, ever heard a breath of Miss Le Fay Morgan. That youth was a sportsman.

Now whether it was the half-crown or pure chivalry I shall never know, and it is not a question I should care to put, or one to which I should be likely to receive a true answer if I put it, but the office boy led the lovely lady down into the basement, and out into the back-yard, and through the shrubbery down to my abode. He put his head in at the kitchen window and called to Sally, as he was in the habit of doing when he brought my letters, and Sally unlatched the door and left him to climb down from the window and let himself in, as she was in the habit of doing with anyone like himself or Scottie whom she knew well; and in marched the youth, and up the stairs, and showed Miss Le Fay Morgan into my room without pausing to inquire whether I was suitably clad.

Needless to say, I wasn't, being in pyjamas and dressing-gown, though, thank God, I had shaved.

"As I am the person responsible for your illness, I thought I had better come and tell you how sorry I am," said Miss Le Fay Morgan.

I was so completely taken aback I could only stare at her. I had just had a shot of dope, and that is a thing that does not quicken the wits, though it may loosen the tongue under certain circumstances, as I was to find to my cost.

I started to get up off the sofa and do the polite, but she pushed me back again and covered me up with the rug, most motherly. Then she sat down beside me on the big pouf intended for my tray.

"Why aren't you in bed?" said she.

"Because I hate being in bed," said I. "I would much sooner get up and wander about."

Now theoretically I am entirely unconventional, but never having had anything to do with unconventional women, I was thoroughly off my stroke with her, and as prim as a curate. My head was also very swimmy with the dope, and I did not know exactly what I might be saying or doing next if I let myself go under the circumstances. Alone like this, with a woman whom I knew to be a Bohemian, I was like a teetotaller at his first cocktail party.

Miss Le Fay Morgan began to smile. "Is it against professional etiquette to make friends with a client?" she said.

"No," said I. "It is not against professional etiquette, but I think that a man is a fool who does it."

She looked taken aback, and the minute I had spoken I was damned sorry, and felt that I had thrown away such a chance as would never come my way again. For this was the very thing I had wanted to go to London for, and yet I couldn't break out of my shell and meet it half-way. I guessed it was the dope that was letting me down. Whatever is in comes out, apparently, under the influence of dope. I flatter myself I should have managed to be a bit more tactful than that if in my sober senses.

Miss Morgan looked at me pretty sharply, and I guess she saw I wasn't my normal self. At any rate, she took no notice of my rudeness and turned the conversation.

"What a charming room you have," she said.

I acquiesced gratefully.

"I have often wondered," said she, "what sort of houses people choose for themselves who know all there is to know about houses."

I thought that if she could see Scottie's abode, or our main building, for that matter, she would be disillusioned.

She began to walk around and look at my books, which made me squirm. I hate people looking at my books, they are too revealing. I especially hated Miss Morgan looking at them, for I was certain she was the last word in sophistication and culture, and I am not. My books are a most miscellaneous collection. I think she saw me squirm—she was a most perceiving person—for she turned away from my books and went over to the window and looked out. I am not responsible for the landscape, so I did not mind that.

Then she heard the voice of the weir.

"Is that the river down below you?" she said.

I told her it was.

"The one that comes out at Dickmouth?"

I told her that was so. "This is the Narrow Dick," I said.

"Where the Broad Dick is, I have never been able to discover. It is not marked on the maps."

"There is no Broad Dick," said she. "The original name of this river was the River Naradek. 'Narrow Dick' is only a corruption of it."

"How do you know?" said I.

"Because I am interested in such things, and I have looked it up," said she.

"Where did you get hold of it?" said I, for I was keen on the archaeology of the district myself, and thought I knew it pretty thoroughly, but I had never come across that before.

She smiled a queer smile. "If I told you, you wouldn't believe me, any more than you believe me when I tell you that I am Vivian Le Fay Morgan."

There was something startlingly familiar about the name that completely distracted my attention for the moment. I couldn't think where I had heard it before, or what significance was attached to it, and yet I felt sure it had a very vital significance if I could only recall it.

Miss Le Fay Morgan smiled again.

"I suppose you do not know it," she said, "but although you got my name right at Dickmouth, to-day you are calling me Miss Morgan Le Fay."

Then I remembered. Morgan Le Fay was the name of King Arthur's witch sister, to whom Merlin taught all his secret knowledge.

She smiled again. "I am part Breton, part Welsh," she said. "My father called me Vivian after Vivian Le Fay, the wicked young witch who beguiled Merlin in his old age in the forest of Broceliande. Perhaps he was right, I do not know. But Miss Morgan would never call me that; she hated it; and when she left me her money, she stipulated that I should take her name.

I wonder what she would have said if she had heard your version of it!"

It rubbed my fur the wrong way to hear her lying; I wasn't going to acquiesce, and I couldn't very well tell her to her face I disbelieved her, so I offered no comment and changed the subject.

"You still haven't told me your authority for the statement that the name of the Narrow Dick was once Naradek."

"Are you keen on archaeology?"

"On local archaeology, yes, very."

"Then perhaps you can tell me the whereabouts of the cave under Bell Knowle where the tide rises and falls."

For a moment I was about to answer her, for I knew exactly where the cave was; I had a perfectly clear picture of it in my mind's eye; it was in a particular fold on the side of the hill towards the old bed of the river, now dry save for a slender trickle of surface-water after rain. Then all of a sudden I remembered that the only thing I knew about that cave I had learnt in the curious dream I had had of the coming of the sea-priestess, and that the woman in front of me was strangely like the sea-priestess.

I raised myself on my elbow and stared at her. I couldn't speak. I was utterly bewildered.

She looked at me with a very curious expression in her eyes. I think she too was surprised. She hadn't expected such a reaction.

"Is there any such cave about here, or—any tradition of such a cave?"

I shook my head. "Not to my knowledge," I said.

"Then—why did you react so violently when I asked you about the sea-cave? What do you know about it?"

I was at a disadvantage. I could only roll over on my pillows and stare out of the window. She kept silent and waited. She knew I would have to answer sooner or later.

I was in that mood when I didn't care. Dope always has that effect on me. I rolled back and faced her.

"Well, if you want to know," I said, "I had a very curious experience recently, after I'd had an injection of morphia. I dreamed of the country round here as it must have been in pre-historic times, and there was a sea-cave then, though there isn't now, because the sea has receded and the river shifted, and the cave silted up. I have traced that cave, and it is probably there all right, though you can't see it. It gave me a queer turn to find the signs of it in a fold of the rock; but one can explain that by subconscious memory. But it gave me a much queerer turn to hear you refer to it, for I have never spoken of it to a living soul. Did you dream of it too? Or is it a thing that is known historically?"

"I did not dream of it, I saw it in a crystal."

"Good Lord," said I. "Where are we getting to?"

"That is what I would like to know," said she.

"Look here," I said, "I have got a load of dope on board. I think I had better keep quiet, I am only talking nonsense."

"Not at all," said she. "You are talking perfectly good sense, though I admit you would be wise to choose your audience."

I laughed. I think I was half tipsy with the drug.

"You wouldn't think I was talking sense," I said, "if I told you the whole of that dream, for I saw you in it. If you believe that, I'll believe that you are Miss Le Fay Morgan, or Morgan Le Fay, for the matter of that."

She looked at me, and her eyes suddenly glowed as they had done when she saw the effect she had on me when she put back her collar on that first day.

"I know you speak the truth," she said slowly, "for I saw you recognised me when I showed you my face."

"Yes, I recognised you all right," I said, and laughed.

"Don't laugh like that," she said, "you set my teeth on edge."

"I beg your pardon," said I. " 'It's a mad world, my masters.' "

"No," said she, "not mad, weak-minded. And you and I are just a little bit saner than most, and we are fortunate enough to have met each other. Let's put the cards on the table, shall we? I will tell what I know if you will tell what you know."

This was not a proposition to put before a house agent, especially one who had been trained by Scottie, but I was dead to the wide, and shot full of dope, and fed to the teeth with my illness, and I just didn't care at that moment if life went up in flames, or fell into the cellars, or blew to glory generally. That must be my excuse, if excuse is needed.

So I told her. It was very difficult to tell coherently, and of course I began at the wrong end, but by dint of questioning and patience she got it pieced together.

"You got the sea-priestess through the moon," she said, "for the moon rules the sea. They are not two separate experiences, but two consecutive parts of the same experience. And now— you have got me. I am the third part of the experience that completes it, you know."

I gently pressed the tender spot on my arm where Beardmore, our medico, had shoved in his needle. "I have had a lot of dope," I said. "I guess you are an hallucination."

She laughed. "Now I will tell you my half of the story," said she, "and then you shall judge."

CHAPTER VII

IT was certainly a startling tale Miss Le Fay Morgan told, and boiled down, it amounted to this.

Her ancestors had been a Huguenot family from Brittany who had settled in England at the time of the Revocation of the Edict of Nantes. They had married other French refugees, and later had intermarried with the English, and all had gone on quite peacefully until the last of the line, her father, had married a Welshwoman, and then the two Keltic stocks, the Breton and the Welsh, had reinforced each other and produced her.

"I am fey by nature as well as by name," she said.

Then her father died, and she was left to shift for herself, and had got on to the stage in the chorus of a provincial panto-mime, and thence worked her way up.

"My greatest success," said she, "was as the Demon Queen in 'Jack and the Beanstalk'."

I believed her. She must have made a magnificent female Mephistopheles.

Anyway, it was a precarious existence, and when she got the chance of a job with Miss Morgan through the good offices of a mutual cousin, she took it on.

Those were the days when table-turning was the vogue; old Miss Morgan was very keen on it and made her new com-panion lend a hand when she gave a table-turning party to some like-minded neighbours; and the table, which had hitherto only scraped its feet a little, suddenly rose on its hind legs and danced a jig.

Old Miss Morgan was thrilled to the marrow-bones, and so, for the matter of that, was Miss Le Fay, and they went at it hammer and tongs. The table proving unwieldy, they got a Planchette, and it was the Planchette that first talked about the sea-cave in Bell Knowle.

"If you find that," said the Planchette, "you will find the key to everything."

Naturally it gave Miss Morgan the Second a shake-up when she found I had learnt about the sea-cave in the way I had.

I told her all I knew about the archaeological point of view. Bell Knowle was really Bel, or Bael Knowle, the hill of the sun-god, where right down into historical times they burnt the Bale-fires on May-eve, the night of Beltane. Of recent years a dear soulful lady had revived the pretty custom, and even gone so far as to get the vicar to grace the proceedings. Little did he know what he was assisting at!

Planchette had quite correctly declared that the sea-cave faced on to the river and was filled by its tidal rise; but Miss Le Fay Morgan, who had been looking for it all yesterday, was not aware that the river had shifted its channel during the thirteenth century, and now came out on the opposite side of Bell Knowle from what it had originally done. Incidentally it had drowned out a prosperous monastery in so doing. Tradition declared that the monks were a rackety crowd, and one dark night, when they were throwing a party, the river shifted its bed and scoffed the lot. Miss Morgan's eyes shone like lamps again when she heard that, for one of the controls that had operated the Planchette had claimed to be a dead monk who had died of drowning. Being in an expansive mood, I told her that if she would come down when the neap-tides were at their lowest, I would take her out in a boat to have a look at the place, and she booked the appointment forthwith. That set me wondering how I would explain myself to Scottie and the family.

Apparently they got oodles of stuff through the Planchette, including the information about the River Naradek, which another control, who called himself the Priest of the Moon, said was so named after the original River Naradek in the Lost Continent of Atlantis by Atlantean colonists who had made this district their headquarters. He had also written out for them the words of an ancient hymn to the sun-god, that ended:

> "Waft thou my soul down the river of Naradek;
>   Bring it to life and to light and to love."

She threw back her head and sang it to me in a deep, humming, resonant undertone, half croon and half chant—and that was the end of me! She could do anything she liked with me after that. There was no need for her to say: "Believe it or not," for something had stirred in me, and I knew with a curious inner certainty that what she was telling me, though incomplete and unverifiable, was the truth.

And this was the story as told by Vivian Le Fay, onetime companion of Miss Morgan the First way back in the nineties.

They had persevered with the Planchette and made various friends on the Inner Planes. Later on, Miss Le Fay let me see the note-books, and they were certainly most convincing, for who in their senses would have perpetrated such a laborious fraud, and for what purpose? For they went on long after Miss Morgan the First had died and Miss Le Fay was in possession of her estate. Later on, Miss Le Fay abandoned Planchette for the crystal, and then, of course, her notes ceased to be evidential, save for the element of prophecy in their contents, which I must say was most marked.

Well, it seemed that the first communicator to avail himself of the line of communication opened up by Planchette was the drowned monk, very anxious to explain himself. He apparently wanted to justify what they had been doing at their abbey that had caused the sea to overwhelm them, and wished it to be realised that they had not been a rackety crowd, as tradition averred, but had been experimenting along original lines, and it was an experiment gone wrong, not commonplace debauchery, that had led to the catastrophe.

He said, and I could bear him out, that our district had been quite a centre of ancient civilisation, and that a certain brother, who I suppose nowadays would be called a psychic, had had a lot of queer dreams, aud on the strength of these they had gone exploring into the backward and abyss of time, where no Christian ought to go, and had got so fascinated and caught up with the whole thing that it was like taking to drink; and the old abbot was the worst of the lot—fairly mad on it. The little monk who came through was nobody in particular, just one of the rank and file and always thoroughly scared of the whole proceedings. In fact he would not talk about them more than he could help; all he wanted was to have masses said for his soul so that he could settle down and get some rest. So Miss Morgan the First arranged to have masses said for the whole party, finding the local priest unexpectedly sympathetic. Of course masses have to be paid for. But Miss Le Fay said it wasn't altogether that. He seemed to understand a good deal without having to be told very much.

They were not sorry to see the last of the little monk, as he burbled away about his sins and wouldn't tell them about the things they were really interested in, which I suppose, after all, were his sins, but not in the way he understood them. So they cleared the line and tried for someone else, and this time they landed a big fish that precious nearly pulled them in. At any rate, they landed the spirit who said he had been the one that had communicated with the old abbot through his mediumistic monk.

This individual called himself the Priest of the Moon, and believe me, he was a heavyweight. I met him afterwards, and I know. He, apparently, did not mind about sin, and was anxious to revive the old worship and get back to work again.

So these two good women undertook to lend him a hand. God knows why, with the example of that drowned-out monastery before their eyes; but these things have an extraordinary fascination like, as I said before, taking to drink; for here was I doing exactly the same thing myself, with the awful example staring me in the face equally.

Well, Miss Morgan was pretty ancient, and Miss Le Fay, by her own account at any rate, no chicken, and the old lady began to sicken for her last illness and had to be nursed day and night, so there was no chance for any more spooking for the time being; but old Miss Morgan made Miss Le Fay promise that she would carry on with the job as soon as she was free to do so, and left her her money on that condition, though of course it did not appear in the will. And then, thanks to my unlucky pater, there was no money worth mentioning to leave, so all the plans were hung up. Now, however, that things were improving, Miss Le Fay wanted to open up matters again, and wanted my help in so doing. She put it quite as a business deal; she wanted a property purchasing and putting in order, but I felt pretty certain she had got a few cards up her sleeve that she wasn't putting on the table at that moment.

So Miss Morgan the Second took her scanty pittance and went to live on the Continent, as many another old maid in straitened circumstances has done before her, living being cheaper there than here. But she took her Planchette with her, and presently purchased a crystal, and the Priest of the Moon apparently came along too. Anyway, the work went forward, in theory, if not in practice.

And then a queer thing began to happen. Miss Le Fay, or Miss Le Fay Morgan, as I suppose she ought to be called now, considering herself in the sear and yellow leaf, was in the habit of knocking about alone in these Latin countries in a way a young girl couldn't dare do; but presently she found it didn't pay. The local bucks began to make themselves an awful nuisance, especially after she had spent the evening with Planchette and the Priest of the Moon; and as soon as she began with the crystal, things became impossible, and she jolly well had to watch her step as if she were young and lovely.

It took her a long time to realise things, for she was wearing out Miss Morgan's wardrobe, but one day a dressmaker offered her a job displaying styles at the races, and you could have knocked her down with a feather. She took on the job, and had a high old time, and then she went back to the stage again. She never, she said, caught on in the Anglo-Saxon countries, where they like their chickens tender, but in the Latin countries, where they appreciate "It" for its own sake, she was Queen of the May. She was out in the Argentine at the time when it was opening up, and she was out in Mexico in the great days, and knew Diaz; and anyway, what with one thing and another, and I didn't ask too closely what they were, she got a bit of money put by, enough with what she had from the estate to save her from the need of working, and she had come home to London and settled down in the flat-cum-hayloft where Scottie found her, and got busy in good earnest. It was no wonder Scottie, being Highland Gaelic, took fright at that hayloft, for it was where she did her stunts.

Those were the bulletins up to date; and then cash began to come in in bulk, and she saw that the time was ripe for carrying out the original plan. She also saw, however, that

Scottie was in for a fearful attack of Calvinistic conscience, and to explain to him what she had explained to me was perfectly useless, and that if she couldn't straighten things out in some way, she was going to have trouble. She guessed however, having known the old man, that I might be a horse from a different stable, so had come down "on spec", also to spy out the land with a view to her forthcoming scheme, and found that I, all unknowingly, had crossed the same trail.

"And do you believe me now?" said she at the end of it all.

"Yes," said I, "I do. For if you were telling lies, you would tell better ones than these."

Then in came Sally with my tea, and looked as taken aback as if she had seen a ghost when she perceived that I had company. She hung havering in mid-air for a moment or two, not quite sure which way she was going to take things, for, as I remarked before, I had got the dog's job with her, and not even an old age pension kills out the Old Eve in the feminine breast. However in the end she apparently decided that the lovely lady would cheer me up, so she fetched another cup and cut some more bread and butter with a good grace. I was truly thankful for that, for if Sally had turned awkward, we had the makings of a mess.

CHAPTER VIII

THE arrangement was that as soon as I was fit again, I should ring up Miss Le Fay Morgan at her hotel at Dickmouth and arrange a house-hunting expedition. And believe it or not, I was as lively as a grig next morning, instead of my usual laborious convalescence. However, I lay doggo for a bit because I wanted to do some quiet thinking. I had, in fact, quite a lot to think about.

One of two things was obvious; either Miss Morgan was telling the truth, or she wasn't. And supposing she weren't, what then? Headley had already told us not to meddle in what was not our business, and given it as his opinion that we were unlikely to be involved if subsequent unpleasantness developed; at any rate, it was better to chance it rather than run our heads into an immediate hornets' nest, possibly get ourselves had up for libel, and lose business to a certainty. The latter argument appealed to Scottie, and he took a reef in his conscience. The worst that could happen to us, even if Miss Morgan the Third had murdered Miss Morgan the Second, was that the judge would give us a piece of his mind at the trial. No one was likely to go to jail over it.

Scottie simmered down after that, though he was always a smouldering volcano on the subject of Miss Morgan, whatever her numbering, for he thought she was very, very bad for my morals; and the spiritualism, of which he soon came to suspect us—though I swore it was archaeology, for I had to tell him a certain amount in order to make him keep quiet—he considered even worse for the soul, being unnatural, whereas flagrant immorality is natural. Anyway, what with one thing and another, it was a grief to Scottie, and we spoke of it as seldom as we could.

So as far as I could make out, even if Miss Morgan turned out to be a liar and a vamp and a general adventuress, I did not see that I could come to any very grievous harm at her hands if I did not part with any money, at least, not more than I could comfortably spare, for one expects to pay for one's fun within reason; and even if she were all Scottie said she was, I was going to have the time of my young life. In fact I was going to have the time of my young life if she were the half of what he said she was, and I thought I was due for it, having had a pretty lean season heretofore.

If, of course, what she said was the truth, as I more than half felt it to be, well, then we were in for big things. So I decided to have something on Miss Morgan both ways; I was entirely game for an adventure in the fourth dimension and if that did not materialise—if that is the right word to use in this connection—I was not averse to a reasonable amount of vamping.

So I got up round about noon next day, and crawled into the office, trying to look debilitated, for I had never felt so full of go in my life, and began to shuffle over the lists of suitable residences in the Dickmouth and Starber neighbourhoods that might fill the bill for Miss Le Fay Morgan. When Scottie learnt what I was doing, he sniffed portentously but ceased to rumble. Business is business in Scotland.

She wanted something isolated, with large rooms and a basement, that wasn't overlooked, and as near the sea as possible. In fact a sea-view from some windows at any rate was indispensable. I cursed when I thought of the white elephants I had practically given away with a pound of tea that would have suited her just nicely. Basements and isolation spell the servant problem in large letters, and you pretty nearly have to pay people to live in houses of that description. I had seriously thought at times of driving round the Morgan estate chucking cans of petrol and cigarette-ends through the windows. It would have been an economy in the long run.

Then I suddenly bethought me that we had the very thing she wanted, though Scottie cursed me for not letting sleeping white elephants lie and selling her someone else's property and making a bit on the deal, for in fact, not only we had it, but she had it. Out beyond Dickmouth, on the far side of the River Dick, was a big headland running right out into the sea for over a mile. At the end of it was a dismantled fort that the War Office had abandoned to the jackdaws as out of date and that my pater had picked up for the Morgan estate as a bargain. He had thought it would make a fine hotel, with a golf-links on the down behind it; but he omitted to inquire about the water supply before he bought it, and when he found that it depended on rain-water tanks, he knew it was a non-starter as a hotel. It might do for a couple of dozen Tommies who didn't wash over-much, but it was no use for the Grand Imperial Palace he had in mind. So he wrote it off as a total loss and did no more about it, except to let the rabbiting to whoever wanted it; and when the farm at the landward end became derelict, no one wanted it because it was too far from anywhere.

So I made up my mind to take Miss Morgan at her face value, plant one of her own white elephants on her, get a bit of fun out of life in general, and leave Scottie to pray for my soul if it needed it. I threw myself whole-heartedly into the adventure, feeling it was heads I won and tails I couldn't lose much, rang up Miss Morgan on the phone, told her that a special Providence was watching over her, which she seemed to believe, and that the Priest of the Moon had got his temple all fixed up and waiting for her; I asked her to get a luncheon basket from the hotel (for I did not see myself explaining matters to my sister, who would certainly have considered Miss Le Fay Morgan long past picnicking), and arranged to call for her next morning bright and early and take her to see the temple the Lord had provided.

But as soon as I set eyes on her I could have kicked myself for the way I had been thinking of her. Whatever she might or might not be when judged by conventional standards—and the friend of South American presidents was not likely to be very conventional—she was no fraud, I knew that. She was absolutely sincere, and if what she said wasn't true, it was not because she was lying but because she was hallucinated.

I was wondering how she was going to manage in her high-heeled shoes if I couldn't get the car all the way to the fort; but when she came out of the hotel I saw that she had changed them for a more substantial pair, which, though they looked useful, were nevertheless stream-lined. Apparently it was possible for a woman to get a workmanlike shoe that was not cut on the lines of a canal-barge, though my sister said it wasn't. She had also changed into a loose, blankety sort of coat of grey-green, with a big, fluffy, upstanding collar of light-coloured fur. Over the top of it one could just see her eyes, but no more. Apparently no one ever did see Miss Le Fay Morgan's face in the open street. There was a queer, unusual kind of smartness about the whole kit; I could see the loungers in the sun parlour watching her. I had never before had the experience of being the escort of a woman whom other men obviously coveted, and if there were any lingering languidness left over from my attack, it effectually tonicked it.

She was very charming and very friendly, but what with wanting to kick myself for the way I had been feeling, and pride of possession at being seen out with her, I was off my social stroke for the moment and very much the auctioneer, for which I could have kicked myself again with compound interest. But these things are like the asthma, the more you strain at them, the tighter they jam. Anyway, she took her cue from me, and drew in her horns, and I jumped to the conclusion I had wrecked the outing and shut up completely.

Although we could see Bell Head lying like a stranded whale on the far side of the bay, I had to drive nearly back to Dickford before we could make for it, for the ferry at the river-mouth didn't take cars. However presently we came to the swing-bridge that lets through the coasters bringing coal, and got across into the marshes.

Here the land changed, and with it my mood, for this was the country I had seen in my dream when I first met Morgan le Fay, if that were whom she really was, as I half suspected. At our backs lay the long ridge on the furthermost spur of which Dickford was built, taking advantage of the first firm ground and the lowest ford. All old towns have their situations chosen for them by necessity, and it amused me, going about the country as my work took me, to try and determine why a hamlet stood in a particular place or a road ran as it did. One could trace the end of the furthermost shelf of the ridge under the soil by the line of farms that followed the line of springs.

This part of the marsh was divided up by high dykes and water-cuts, and in the unwholesomely green grass cattle were grazing; but as we got further along, the dykes ceased and the land was given over to those it belonged to—the waterfowl and the old gods. Only the road was dyked now, and in the road-side ditches stood herons that didn't give a damn for us—they saw so little traffic they didn't know what it meant, and thought that if they froze as they were accustomed to, we couldn't see them any more than the fish could.

Suddenly the blue devils that were on me departed, and I

turned to Miss Morgan and said: "This was where I had to pilot you with fog-flares the first time you came."

I couldn't see whether she smiled or not inside her great furry collar, but her voice came all deep and golden:

"You remember that, then?"

"Maybe," said I, and concentrated on my driving, for I had stampeded myself with my own remark. Having so little to do with women, I am apt to be either crudely brusque or much too formal. Anyway, the driving needed concentrating on, for we were now on a narrow, grass-grown track carried on a ten-foot dyke, and I had no wish to join the herons.

Away on our left Bell Knowle rose in a perfect pyramid from the wide waste of the marshes. Fir-trees grew in the folds of its sides, but its crest was bare to the winds and rather noble, seen over that level land. I pulled up and pointed out the hollow that in my opinion held the old sea-cave, and from the vantage-point that even a ten-foot rise gives in those alluvial flats, I traced for Miss Morgan the shallow winding ditch marked by the gleam of standing water here and there in its bottom, which was all that was left of the ancient River Dick before it changed its course and drowned the monastery.

She naturally wanted to turn aside and inspect it, being a woman, but it was impossible to do so as there was no bridge over the water-cuts nearer than Starber, three miles further on, the next coastal town to Dickmouth, if town it could be called. It was really nothing but a fishing village these days. Once it had been a haven of some dimensions, and was listed in Doomsday Book as such, for the scour of the Dick kept the harbour open; but when the river shifted, the glory departed, and now only such boats as could be beached made use of it. Behind the town, however, were the traces of long lines of masonry that had once been massive quays but had long since been used as a quarry to build and pave the entire district, and only the trenches that marked the footings now remained. My father had bought up the last of them and built quite a lot of his white elephants out of the stone, and I well remember going out with him as a kid in his dog-cart, before motors had reached the likes of us, and seeing the enormous blocks being split with wedges before they could be handled. It was Cyclopean masonry all right, and the cement, wafer-thin, was of such tenacity that it was easier to split the stone than the join. If I knew the secret of that cement, I would make a fortune. We have nothing like it to-day.

I mentioned this to Miss Morgan, and heard her laugh.

"Do you know that Starber is Ishtar's Beere, or harbour? That was the place I was making for when you nearly let me run on a sand-bank because you were day-dreaming then as you do to-day."

"I'm frightfully sorry," I said. "I'm not half as loopy as I look, I'm not really, when you get to know me."

"Do you ever let anyone get to know you?" said she.

CHAPTER IX

THE embankment carried the road across the shallow groove of the ancient Dick, paying the tribute of a drain-pipe to that once navigable stream. Here we could see distinctly the remains of what had evidently been the old tow-path, trodden, I expect, by the feet of slaves when the unhandy sea-boats lowered their lateen sails and were towed up the winding water-way through the marshes to Dickford, where they met the tinmen from the hills behind the ridge. Taking advantage of the banked path, a narrow track turned off towards the sea, and this we followed, for it brought us by a winding way to the derelict farm at the foot of Bell Head, also Miss Morgan's property.

We looked at it over the fallen dry-stone wall that separated its narrow yard from the wide marsh. At some time it had been white-washed, as is the custom hereabouts, but the white-wash was gone, save for a leprous patch here and there, and the stones were as grey as the salt marsh grass.

The house was low and squat and boxlike, such as a small child that had no talent might draw on a slate. There were no signs of a garden, but a patch of ranker growth showed where the manure-heap had been, ominously close to the back door —you can tell the grade of a tenant by his sanitary arrangements better than by anything else—but the steep grassy slope that led up to the face of the rock behind the house showed the dints and ridges of cultivation. Bell Head was shaped like a couchant lion with his tail to the sea and the farm lay between his paws, getting what shelter it might from the

westerly gales. The slope that led up to the lion's chest had at
some time been terraced, though the plough of more recent
operations had gone over the terraces before all had been given
back to the thistles and slow-growing sea-down grass.

Miss Morgan remarked at once on the lion-form, and pointing to the terraces between its paws, said: "That was where
they grew their vines."

"Who?" said I taken aback.

"The people who used Bell Knowle as a temple. I will grow
vines there again if I come back here."

We came now into a road that was the work of the War
Department, and had been laid out by the simple expedient of
drawing a line on a map with a ruler and leaving fatiguing
Tommies to hack it out at their leisure. This line was carried
diagonally across the steep pitch of the landward end of the
Head on a ledge, and at the hairpin bend at the top I feared
the car was going to roll over backwards. I thought of the
Tommies toiling up here with their supplies before the days of
motor-lorries, and felt sorry for them.

After that one soul-searing bend the road ran straight again
for the full length of the headland till it dipped out of sight at
the point. Above us on the crest of the down were many
loose piles of stonelike cairns, in which Miss Morgan was
interested; but I would not let her stray off to look at them
then, but drove straight ahead through ten million skipping
rabbits till we came to the dip of the road and saw the fort.
Miss Morgan began to bubble with excitement at my side.

It was a small place, sunk to protect it from gun-fire, and
built of the local limestone by the same unimaginative architect
who had laid out the road with a ruler. The rotting gate was
off its hinges, and we drove straight into the forecourt. Behind
us were the barracks; in front, a semicircle of gun-emplace-
ments; ahead, a long tongue of half-tide rock ran out into the

water, and one had only to look at the popple and swirl round the point to know the way the tides ran even on a still day. In stormy weather I should imagine the waves made a clean breach of it.

Miss Morgan took one look round and pronounced the place her ideal. I thought of what life must have been like here for the poor God-damn Tommies, and carried the luncheon basket to a sheltered gun-emplacement.

Miss Morgan, however, would not settle down to lunch yet, but climbed up an embrasure and walked out to the end of the long razor-back spit that ran some fifty or sixty feet out into the water, and stood at the very edge of the oncoming waves, gazing out to sea. I was uneasy about her, for if she had skidded on those barnacled stones, nothing could have saved her, with the tide running like a mill-race, so I called to her to come and look at the bathing-beach. She did not answer, but stood there while I smoked three cigarettes, giving back a step at a time before the advancing waves, for the tide was rising.

In her grey-green blanket-coat she was exactly the same colour as the sea, hardly distinguishable from it as she stood there in the half-light of the grey day, the loose folds of her coat flap-flapping like a flag in the wind. Then she took off her hat, pulled a carved tortoise-shell comb out of her hair, and shook loose a flying black mane; I watched her, fascinated; much more fascinated than I ought to have been; I had never met a woman who behaved like this before. I smoked that second cigarette pretty fast. However, I had simmered down by the time I had smoked the third, and as I thought that she had stood there long enough, leaning up against the wind with her hair flying and her clothes blowing, I climbed down, intending to help her back up the rocks.

She turned and put out her hand. I thought it was to steady

herself for the climb back, so I took it—but no; she drew me down to stand beside her on the narrow point, and kept hold of me.

"Come and feel the sea," she said.

I stood silently beside her, leaning up against the pressure of the wind as she had done. It was not cold, but a warm and glowing wind that wrapped you round with strong pressure. At our feet there was a perpetual slapping of small ripples, and further out a steady boom-swish as the breakers hit the rocks. It was fascinating. The sea, deep and in its strength, was all around us save for that narrow knife-edge of wave-swept rock that stretched away back to the fort. I gave myself up to the glamour of it, standing there beside her.

Then I noticed a thing I have noticed before when listening to waves breaking on rocks—the sound of the bells in the water. It is, of course, an illusion produced by the noise; a kind of reverberation within the ear itself, fatigued by the rhythmical din. I can only compare it to the sound one would hear if the song of the sea in a shell had a throb in it. I listened fascinated; and as I listened it lost its elusive, wind-in-a-shell quality, and became a definite beat, and than a brazen clangour coming up from the very depths as if they were opening upon the sea-palaces.

Then I was suddenly aroused by a voice in my ear:

"My dear boy, wake up, or you will fall in!"

I turned, startled, to find Miss Le Fay Morgan beside me, still holding my hand.

We climbed back over the steep slippery ledges. I admit I looked over my shoulder to see if the sea-gods were following. It had seemed to me that at the moment when her voice interrupted me I had stood at the place where two kingdoms meet and the gates of the sea-kingdom were being opened to me. I suppose, in other words, that meant drowning, and I should have gone by that cold path to join the sea-people if Miss Le Fay Morgan had not roused me.

Then we had lunch, and I drove her home. I was glad she liked the place, for I felt that I had been a wash-out as a companion on an expedition.

As we parted outside her hotel, for I would not come in and have tea with her, she suddenly put her hand on my arm and said: "When will you realise that I have no ulterior motive in trying to make friends with you?"

I was so taken aback that I couldn't think of a word to say, and could not have trusted my voice to say it if I had. I muttered something ungracious and fled. I would have left my garment in her grasp, like the biblical gentleman, if she had hung on.

On the way home I was stopped by our local traffic cop, who said that if he had not known me, he would have run me in. He asked me what possessed me to drive like that, was it something the doctor had given me for my asthma? I said it might have been, and he advised me, as one man to another, to put up with the asthma.

CHAPTER X

I HAVE always been a notable exponent of what is called doorstep wit: that is to say, all the admirable things one thinks of as the door shuts behind one, and that might have been said with such telling effect if one had only thought of them earlier. I have the additional disadvantage that the mechanism does not work impartially with me, for when my temper rouses, I have a quick and bitter tongue, often to my lasting regret. But when I am moved emotionally, and would particularly like to respond, I am a dumb dog.

I could not expect Miss Morgan to persevere in the face of my boorishness. It was a most odd thing that the very companionship I had wanted to go to London to seek had sought me out here, after I had abandoned all hope of it—and yet here was I turning it down with both hands so persistently as to leave no possible doubt in anyone's mind as to what my apparent feelings might be, whatever were my real ones. I made up my mind that when next I expected to meet Miss Morgan I would have a couple of drinks, and see if that would loosen my inhibitions.

One consolation, however, remained to me—Miss Morgan had charged me with the task of transforming the fort into a human habitation, for the place where a pre-War government kept Tommies could hardly be reckoned as that. So in any case I must see her again, not once, but several times. I pinned my hope to the fact that I might get a little tamer as the novelty wore off.

I cast about for a firm to do the job. I did not want to use our usual contractors as I did not want gossip; finally I lit upon a quaint old boy well-known locally for church repairs, a highly specialised form of building, and one for which there is considerable scope round our way, for we have some lovely village churches.

This old boy, Bindling by name, used to load all his gear, his three old workmen, which were all he had, and his idiot son, into a huge hay-cart with a couple of hairy old horses to pull it, and set out for the job in any of four counties. They walked up all the hills, and they walked down all the hills, so they took some time to arrive after the contract was signed, and when they got there, they never hurried; but then, on the other hand, they never stopped; so in the end they got through as soon, and sometimes sooner, than more orthodox and up-to-date contractors. The idiot son was an inspired carver, and though they had to tether him to the scaffolding to prevent him coming down the quickest way when the whistle went, which consisted in stepping off into thin air, he was really the backbone of the business.

Old Bindling trundled out to the fort, arriving there in the course of a week or ten days. How he ever got up that Army road and round that hairpin bend, God only knows, but he did. The fort had been built to stand gunfire, so no structural repairs were needed, but of course there wasn't a pane of glass left in the windows or a door on its hinges, thanks to trippers, and there was something dead in the water supply. It turned out only to be a jackdaw in the end, but you would never have believed one miserable bird could have gone so far—or got so high!

I can do an architect's work, though I have never taken an architect's degrees, so I got the place measured up while Mr. Bindling and his party fished for the jackdaw—whom we were all convinced must be at least a sheep—taking turns at the job—one down, t'other come on, the idiot son standing the atmosphere best. He had some remarkable qualities, had that youth, for all he lacked in other directions.

I wanted to transform a place that looked like a jail into a temple for my sea-priestess, as I called Miss Morgan behind her back, lacking the nerve to call her to her face, though I am sure she would have liked it. I had not got an easy job on hand, for to stick ornamentation on that grim stone structure was useless, it would merely look like a tipsy deacon in a paper cap. I turned over many books dealing with architecture all over the world—Miss Morgan never knew how near she came to getting an Aztec temple to live in—and finally lit on one that struck the right note, and drew my inspiration therefrom. It was an old monastery in the Apennines that had become the villa of a rich American, and the architect had done his job well, retaining the original stark severity, but breaking it by the line of his windows and softening it with a pergola.

I roughed out my ideas, and saw that the fort would take to them kindly; then I worked up a scale drawing and sent it off to Miss Morgan, who of course had long since returned to London. She sent back a letter that made me feel warm for a week—

"I knew when I saw your room that you were an artist, but I did not know that you were such an artist as this."

Needless to say, I returned thanks on the office paper in the covering letter to an estimate. I would!

It was obviously impossible to follow my model slavishly and have a creeper-covered pergola. Any creeper except ivy would have gone out to sea the first wild night, and ivy would have taken a generation, possibly two, to cover a pergola in that situation. So I turned to and designed a stone-built pergola covered with carved sea-plants and queer sea-beasts. I nearly lost my life off the point of rock trying to fish up giant fucus to act as a model. Old Bindling, who caught me by the collar as I skidded towards deep water, told me that every place that is intended for a sacred edifice, even the humblest Little Bethel, always demands a life in its building. That is why he repairs churches, but won't ever build them. He little knew that he was preparing a temple for the sea-gods at the present moment, and that it was the second time they had come dashed near to having my life!

Uplifted by previous appreciation, I took a lot of trouble with the designs for the carvings on that pergola, and felt rather pleased with them when I finally packed them off to Miss Morgan by registered post where she was holiday-making on the Continent. But not only did she write back even more warmly than before, but she showed them to someone she knew, and they were reproduced in an art journal. Then she had them framed. She never knew it, but I had to do the dashed lot over again out of my head for the idiot Bindling to work from. Of course I did not do the second lot in as much detail as the first, and any way, it was a labour of love in which I worked off some of the libido that had got dissociated by the various bricks I had dropped in my dealings with her.

I had broken the grim line of the existing buildings by putting Gothic arches to all the windows. The entrance to the fort was by a most giddy-making plank bridge that spanned no end of a moat, a really efficient affair. I replaced the rotting timbering with a lovely little round-arched stone bridge copied from one in Cumberland that I had seen on a walking holiday before I had my asthma. Into the tunnel-like entrance that passed under the officer's quarters and gave access to the courtyard, and which I gothicked interiorly as I couldn't do it exteriorly without bringing the bally place down on our

heads, I put enormous double doors of oiled oak, copied from
the cathedral and decorated with some very fine wrought-iron
hinges, which I made with the help of our local blacksmith
from my own designs, and as nice a bit of genuine craftsmanship, if I may say so, as anyone could wish to see. Getting
this job done gave the show away to a certain extent, and my
sister was on to it like a hawk; but the special Providence about
which I had ragged Miss Morgan still watched over us, and
the hinges were borrowed for a local arts and crafts exhibition,
and then borrowed for a London one, so a slight cloud of glory
spread over the family, and my sister, who had no fault to find
with my goings-on, believing Miss Morgan to be rising ninety,
forgave me for telling her nothing.

"Has Miss Morgan still got all her faculties?" she asked one
day.

"She seems all right to me," I said, "but Scottie thinks she's
frail."

So he did, but not in the way they took it.

After that they became reconciled to my being more and
more out at the fort, going there nearly every day, in fact. I
found the sea-air was doing wonders for my asthma, which they
also observed, so altogether Fate was playing into my hands.
Not that I ever place too much reliance in that temperamental
goddess, for she has always had a knack of leading me on and
then giving me away. I suppose that is inevitable in a place
where everybody knows everybody, that is riddled with
poachers, and where all the courting is done under hedges;
what the poachers miss, the loving couples see, and as both
parties, owing to the nature of their activities, are obliged to
keep a sharp look-out, not much passes unnoticed.

I have finally come to the conclusion that frankness is the
better part of discretion in this district, though I have no con-
scientious objection whatever to telling lies to people who

inquire about what does not concern them. I suppose that
comes of being educated at our local academy for the sons of
gents, where the first thing one learnt, and the only thing one
learnt thoroughly, was to extricate oneself from difficulties
with the aid of the imagination. Being, as Miss Morgan said,
an artist, and in more ways than she knew of, I excelled at this.
Had I been a pukka sahib with an old school tie, it might have
been otherwise; but one needs considerable capital to achieve
honour without martyrdom, and all our capital was tied up in
the family business. It is a curious thing, however, that
though my sister has called me a liar times without number,
she has never caught me out, having always pitched on
the wrong thing owing to her limited knowledge of human
nature.

Recently I have not bothered so much whether they knew
things or not, my newly-acquired temper protecting me. All
my life long, till I developed asthma, I had been a mother's
boy. Then, with the coming of the asthma, I broke out. It is
said that the gods always make you pay the price for any great
blessing, but in my case, having sent me a pretty unmitigated
curse, they funded up handsomely in other directions. I can
honestly say, with my hand on my heart—what's left of it—
that if I had the chance to choose between being an asthmatic
or a mother's boy for the rest of my life, and having tried both,
I would choose to be an asthmatic. My family took it hard,
however, when I began telling them to go to hell. It was like
being bitten by a rabbit.

We worked on the fort all the summer, and I must say it
was a success. From the landward side it looked like the
remains of a ruined abbey, for it had the pointed windows, but
not the pointed roof. The roof was as flat as would throw off
the water in order to give minimum resistance to the wind, and
most of the slates having gone to glory long ago, I roofed it

with split stone like a Cotswold cottage, and it looked rather well.

The three gun-embrasures had shallow, semicircular steps leading up to them, and low balustrades, all carved with sea-horses and other queer beasts; and I had made a stair and path down to the point of the rocks, balustraded as far as I dare, for I had no wish to have Miss Morgan skidding off into deep water as I had so nearly done. I had also made a delightful, winding, balustraded balcony leading down to the bathing-beach, a little cove looking out to sea, just under the lee of the headland. It was here that drift-wood came ashore in surprising quantities; I did not think Miss Morgan would ever need to cart coal if she cooked with oil, as I expected she would. Whenever the idiot had nothing else to do, we put him on to fishing out the drift-wood to keep him out of mischief. If he were not kept busy, he was given to setting things on fire. I wanted to get a good stock of drift-wood well dried out against Miss Morgan's arrival, for I thought it would be rather nice for my sea-priestess to have a genuine sea-fire to welcome her, for the blue flame of the salt-soaked wood is so beautiful.

I put navvies to work on the hairpin bend and took the worst of the venom out of it, though it was still pretty tricky, and we got the furniture vans up without accident, though I admit there was plenty of cursing. Miss Morgan sent a man and his wife to take charge at the farm—Cornish folk, the square kind, as broad as they are long, and as thick as they are wide. I could see they both adored her. It was to be their job to look after the place.

They were to live at the farm, and to trundle out and do what was required at the fort, and trundle back when they had finished, and Miss Morgan told me to get them a car to trundle in as it was all of a mile and a bit over. The car for the job had to be considered carefully, as there were not the makings of a chauffeur in Trethowen—it was too much, I knew, to expect him to change gear—so although he had to have power to get up the gradient, I didn't want to give him a car that would get away with him. Finally I found an old ancient Ford of the original vintage that could shin up a telegraph-pole; a high, hump-backed two-seater with a hood, though they could never use the hood on that headland except in fine weather. It was the funniest sight you ever saw to see them trundling along in this, Trethowen and his missus in front, and all the brooms and brushes pushed in behind. He went bucketing along at a spanking ten, hooting at the rabbits. He loved hooting. I had to get him a new hooter, he soon bust the old one. He never went any faster, even on the flat; but then he never went any slower, even on the bend; to see him swing that hairpin bend at ten miles an hour was a sight to make your blood run cold.

They soon got the place more or less ship-shape, though of course the finishing touches had to wait for Miss Morgan. All my part of the job was done, and I was out at the fort for the last time, bustling old Bindling into his hay-cart, for Miss Morgan had wired to say she would be arriving that afternoon, and he ought to have been out the previous day; but builders have been the same since the Tower of Babel fell down on them through their stopping to talk.

There was only one train she could come by, which would get her into Dickmouth at 5.15, and then she would have an hour's drive out to the fort, so I reckoned I had ample time in hand to do my get-away before she was due, and was taking a last look round the place before leaving it. I had practically lived there all summer, bringing food out with me till the Trethowens arrived, and then they made my meals, and only sleeping at home—a God-sent relief.

Taking a last look at everything I had done, I felt like a mother whose child goes out into the world. I think that as creative artists, authors have the best of it, for an author does not lose his book when it is published, but an artist has to give up his picture to the purchaser, and even a composer is dependent upon the interpretation of the performer. As for an architect, poor devil, he puts his soul and infinite research into a period house, and the purchasers go and paint it pink!

I heard no sound to give me warning, and was mooning round at my leisure, saying good-bye to the sea-horses and other queer beasts I had brought into existence, when a little black sports car drove in under the archway, and there was Miss Morgan.

I was so taken aback that I simply grinned from ear to ear and said: "Hullo?" which is not the way the best house-agents greet their clients.

"Hello? How are you?" said she, smiling at me round her collar. I had been wondering all summer how she would manage about collars in the warm weather, and whether she would be driven to appear in public in her bare face. But not a bit of it, she had managed all right. She had got on a silk raincoat with a big stand-up storm collar that came to the tips of her ears, and a ragamuffin slouch hat was pulled down to meet it, so she was just as private and secluded as ever.

Luckily for me there was no need for any more effort at politeness on my part, for I had shot my conversational bolt with that one hullo. Out came the Trethowens, beaming a welcome; and then Mr Bindling had to be introduced, and the idiot son chased off. I took on the task of heading off the idiot son while the old boy did the polite, for the poor mooncalf was determined not to be left out of it, but as he dribbled profusely, and had other even less endearing traits, he could not very well be invited very far into it. However, the old foreman came to the rescue, and pressed a boathook into his hand, and put him to fish for drift-wood from the steps leading down on to the rocks, as the tide was high. The minute he saw the drift-wood he forgot all about Miss Morgan, so everybody was happy.

Old Bindling and I showed her round, and she was delighted and delightful. I saw him trying hard to peer under her hat, or over her collar, but nothing doing.

The fort consisted of the officer's quarters at one end, or whoever the person might be who was in charge of that God-forgotten detachment, and a great gaunt barrack-room at the other. Knowing that there would not be many days in that exposed spot when one could sit out in comfort, I had made the barrack-room into a sun-parlour by fitting it with shop windows right across the front. The barrack-room stove, when it was pulled up by the roots, left behind it a crevasse big enough for an ingle-nook, so I had fitted it accordingly, with a wide brick hearth and two seats in the angles. For burning drift-wood she wanted fire-dogs, not a grate, so I designed her a noble pair of fire-dogs and had them cast at a Bristol foundry. She hadn't commissioned them, but I hoped she would accept them as a present. Strictly speaking, I suppose they were not fire-dogs, being dolphins; fine, fat, pleasant-faced beasts, sitting up on their curly tails like a couple of cobras. My sister's Pekinese had been the model for the heads.

They were being duly admired, and I was addling my brains as to how I was to break it to Miss Morgan that they were a present and she didn't have to pay for them, and feeling hot and cold all over and wishing to God I had let well alone, when something caught the tail of my eye through the big expanse of plate-glass down one side of the room, and I turned to see the idiot Bindling, who had come off the steps where he had been left but not tethered, gaily galumphing on his shuffle-feet over the slippery rock. It was no time to explain things, so I just bolted.

But even so, I was not quick enough; for as I jumped down on to the rock I was just in time to see the youth's feet go from under him on the treacherous slope, and he sat down with a smack and went tobogganing down the steep pitch with a blissful smile on his foolish face and plopped straight into the sea, and we never saw him, nor his hat, nor anything belonging to him again.

I tore off my coat and started after him. It was an idiotic thing to do, for there wasn't the remotest chance of getting him. Luckily for me the foreman, who had sprinted up when he saw what was happening, threw his arms round me and stopped me.

"No good throwin' your life away for the likes o' he," he said.

The others climbed down and stood horror-stricken, gazing at the spot where the poor moon-calf had vanished and no trace left. Old Bindling slowly raised his hat, not in reverence, but in order to scratch his head.

"Well, I dunno what to say," he said at length, and slowly replaced his hat again.

"Maybe it's just as well," said the old foreman.

"Maybe 'tis," said the old father, "but blood's thicker'n water."

I was shaking all over, but Miss Morgan was utterly unmoved. She was very sweet to poor old Bindling, but it was a cold-blooded kind of sweetness that gave me a very queer feeling. I remembered the old man's words that a temple always demands a life in its building. Well, this one had had it. Three times the sea-gods had tried for it, and now they had got it. I also remembered that in my dream I had known that the sea-priestess had required many human victims.

Miss Morgan tried to find me a drink, but couldn't; and offered me tea, but I wouldn't stop. I wanted to get home.

I had had a thorough shake-up, what with the shock of the poor moon-calf, and my—I admit quite illogical—revulsion of feeling against Miss Morgan. It was no fault of hers the moon-calf fell in; if fault there were, it was mine, who hadn't fenced that rock more securely. All the same I had a queer feeling that it was the thing behind her that had taken him.

She did not press me to stop when she saw I really did not want to, but walked out with me to my car to see me off. And then the damned thing wouldn't start! We had been using the headlights to work by the previous evening, and the battery was down. These are the occasions to which swearing cannot do justice.

If I had had a grain of sense I would have called Trethowen to start her for me, but I am always forgetting I have asthma—though unfortunately the asthma never forgets it has me. I put my weight—what there is of it—behind the starting-handle, and gave her a couple of heaves, and then I knew I was for it. I leant up against the wing of the car and prayed; but it was no good, and I sat down on the running-board. Miss Morgan called Trethowen, and he and his wife came running. Fortunately he had seen my asthma before, and was able to reassure her, for what with me and the moon-calf, the poor soul was having an unpleasant afternoon. I am not a nice sight when I have these bouts, and I am always torn between a dislike of being watched and a dislike of being left alone.

They got me indoors and wanted to put me on the sofa, but I wouldn't; I can always manage better in a chair on these occasions. They put me in a huge arm-chair, whose legs Miss Morgan had not yet had time to saw off. I wondered how we should get on, for they were not on the phone and a doctor would be hard to come by. I reckoned I would have to make up my mind to thrash through without morphia. The actual attack itself, in its acute form, does not usually last more than a couple of hours with me, but they can be a pretty long two hours.

The Trethowens wanted to make Miss Morgan a meal after her journey, but she wouldn't have it. She just stood and looked at me; it was all she could do, poor soul.

"I wish I could help you," she said.

It was very sweet of her, and I appreciated it enormously, but as usual was unable to make any response, this time from physical causes. I heard her mutter: "This is terrible!" and realised she wasn't as cold-blooded as she looked.

She wandered about the big room and then came back to me.

"I would give anything to be able to help you," she said. But there was nothing to be done. I just had to go through with it.

Then, before I realised what she was doing, she sat down on the arm of the chair and put her arm round me and tried to take my head on her shoulder. But I wouldn't let her because I knew my perspiration would make a mess of her frock. She didn't press it when she felt me resist, and then of course I wished I hadn't, and felt damned sick with myself for missing my chances. But presently I reached a point when not only my pride went, but my shyness too, and I turned round and leant up against her, and very comforting it was. The only drawback being that it gave me a taste for that sort of thing, and whenever I have had an attack since, I have wanted her so desperately.

Presently, I don't know how—I think I was pretty nearly insensible towards the end, for there comes a point when Nature is her own anaesthetic—the attack wore itself out and I dropped off to sleep.

So Scottie's prophecy came true, and I slept with Miss Morgan, though not in the way he meant.

CHAPTER XI

THEY must have got me to bed, for I woke up there next morning, whacked to the wide, of course, but at peace. The attack having blown itself out quickly, my heart had stood up to it better than usual, and there were none of the after-effects of the various drugs to be reckoned with.

Miss Morgan had put me into her own room; I don't know where she slept, it being the only one that was ready. It was at the east end of the fort, and got the morning sun through a great window. I woke up at dawn and saw a glorious pathway of pale gold leading along the wave-tops.

There was something unearthly about the complete emptiness that one looked out on to through that window in the pale light of dawn. I could see no land from my bed, but only the glittering waves with the shadows still in their hollows, for the light was low.

And in that hour, freshly wakened from sleep, I saw things differently from what I had ever seen them before. I saw them, not as short chains of cause and effect, whose connections one could not see beyond a few moves, which is what life usually looks like, but as large tracts of influence into which one could enter or which one could avoid, and it was the bias of one's own nature which determined entry or absence.

It was rather romantic, to wake up at dawn like that in Miss Morgan's own room and take a look round. She had got it all fixed up in a curious shade of bluey-grey-green with a sheen on it that gave the effect of translucent sea-water. The head of the bed was carved to represent a wave curling over

ready to break; it was painted a dull silver, picked out with
iridescent blue-green, and in the half-light of dawn it gave a
very curious and a very realistic effect. All the gear on the
dressing-table was of dull beaten silver and shagreen, and there
were a number of odd-shaped bottles of bluish crackle-glass
with which, I suppose, Miss Morgan cared for her lovely skin.
It looked rather like a medieval alchemist's laboratory, only
needing an astrolabe and an athanor and a retort or two to complete the picture. The thing that particularly fascinated me
was the big scent-spray with its bulb concealed in a huge silk
tassel. I am very sensitive to perfumes, and I was determined
that the moment I could crawl out of bed I was going to investigate that scent-spray and find out what manner of scent Miss
Morgan was given to, for one can learn an awful lot about a
person from the scent they use. If my conscience would permit
me, and I thought it would, I also meant to snitch a drop or two
of that scent as a keepsake, for as I have said, scents mean a
great deal to me. Miss Morgan had also gone in for silk sheets
on her bed, and very large swansdown pillows. Who wouldn't
be a house-agent in such circumstances?

All the same, I was under no delusion that everything in the
garden was lovely. Sweet as Miss Morgan might be to me, I
knew with perfect clarity of inner instinct that the cult of which
she was priestess, the cold sea-cult of the primordial deeps,
required living sacrifices. I remembered what I had read of
the terrible Aztec faith, and how some unfortunate slave was
picked out from the people, and kept for a year in the lap of
luxury, and then sacrificed on their bloody altar by having his
heart cut out still living. That, thought I to myself, leaning
back on the down pillows of Miss Morgan's silken bed and
watching the dawn-light grow—is the part for which I am
cast if I don't watch out. And I asked myself if the life of
the body were of such great worth that one would refuse even

the most marvellous experience in order to preserve it? The
answer to that question is that it depends on the body. With a
body like mine, the answer is in the negative.

The realisation of the lie of the land solved several problems
that had been puzzling me a good deal. I could quite understand Miss Morgan trying to get hold of me and infatuate me
if she were a fraud, and needed my co-operation, or at least my
quiescence, in order to carry out her nefarious schemes; but
if she were what she claimed to be—a woman rejuvenated by
strange knowledge—I couldn't see why she was bothering with
me, for God knows I am no sheik. She herself was a woman
who would have been the centre of attention in any assembly,
not merely for her beauty, which was very remarkable, but by
the extraordinary magnetism of her, and her personality.
Moreover she was a highly bred and highly cultured woman.
Why then was she bothering with the product of an academy
for the sons of gents?

If, however I were designed for the rôle of sacrificed Aztec
slave, the whole situation was understandable. Of course she
would be charming to me. Of course she would take me up
and make a fuss of me. It was clear as mud. Twice I had only
escaped death on this blasted rock by the skin of my teeth.
If what she said were true, as in my bones I felt it was, the dog
was going to have his day, and then it was him for Battersea.
According to the ancient tradition, they always hacked out the
heart with a golden knife. I wondered how in the world they
got the gold to take any sort of an edge, and how they got
through the ribs with it if it didn't.

It was an odd feeling, to lie there, looking death in the face
quite placidly and comfortably. Life did not hold much for
me, but all the same I knew that when it came to the point,
I should cling to it tenaciously. After all, that was what I did
in every bout of asthma, at least, that was what it felt like,

for one seemed literally to be fighting for one's life. I knew from my experience with this last, unmedicated bout, which was the first I had ever been through entirely without dope, that as one lapses into unconsciousness, the spasm eases up. I suppose that is why they sometimes give me a whiff of chloroform.

The explanation of my placidity probably lay in the fact that in my heart I never really believed that Miss Morgan was what she said she was; that at bottom I was playing with the idea because that was the way my private inclinations went. Anyway, I made up my mind to take a chance on it. Everything that held any interest for me was bound up with Miss Morgan; the only alternative being to go home, and have asthma, and scrap with my sister, and sell dud houses to dud people.

I dropped off to sleep again after having taken that decision, and when I awoke next, Mrs Trethowen was in the room with a breakfast-tray. It is an odd thing, but asthma never spoils my appetite. I should get a lot more sympathy if it did, for my people can never understand that there is anything much the matter with a person who is not off his feed.

Miss Morgan came and talked to me while I fed. As usual, I had not got much to say for myself. Moreover I was as hoarse as a crow, and hadn't shaved, and knew I must have a pair of blood-shot eyes like an elderly bulldog—I always do after these bouts—and it seemed to me that I must appear so unattractive that I was in danger of losing my job as sacrificed slave. Presently she gave up trying to talk to me and got a book and sat and read, and I turned over and went to sleep again. Asthma is hard work.

She had sent Trethowen off with a telegram to tell my people where I was, and I knew they wouldn't worry; so I accepted her invitation to stop on over the week-end. I was incapable of putting one foot before another at the moment, and doubted if I would be able to drive a car with discretion for another twenty-four hours.

It was very pleasant up there in the sunny room, listening to the sound of the sea, and with Miss Morgan sitting there quietly reading, paying no attention to me, but nevertheless, very companionable. I liked having her there. On these occasions I seem to get the feeling of people's innermost souls and know exactly what they are thinking about, and how they feel towards me. I used to be perfectly aware of faithful old Scottie's profound good will; he is really very fond of me, I think, though I irritate him almost past bearing sometimes. I used to know perfectly well that my sister was fed to the teeth with me, although she did her best to hide it, at any rate when I was ill. I knew my mother was just sunk inside herself and didn't notice anything, and that she wouldn't have minded leaving the house a scrap, and my sister had engineered the whole job because she didn't want to have to shift her Friendly girls or occupy a house in a less commanding situation. As long as I was a leading business man in the town she had something of a position, but if I had cleared out and left her to it, she wouldn't have been anybody, and everyone she had ever offended, and their name was legion, would have had the opportunity to get back at her. So she had quietly torpedoed my one chance and now it was too late to do anything about it. I am afraid I have never wasted much sweetness on her from that day to this. She kept me with her all right, but I doubt if she found me pleasant company.

The feeling I got in regard to Miss Morgan as I lay dozing was of a curious steadiness. I cannot describe it any other way. She seemed to me to have the nerve of an operating surgeon. Everything was quiet at the moment, I knew that; but I was in the position of a patient whose strength is being built up for

an operation. Presently Miss Morgan would show her hand,
unless, that was, I hopped it first. But I knew I wasn't going
to hop it. I was going to have the time of my life till my year
ran out, and if it was then to be the sacrificial altar, well, so be
it. I wondered what form the sacrifice would take. I could
not see Miss Morgan chipping away with a golden knife till
she got to my vitals. I expected that I should be invited to
take a walk one moonlight night to the end of the reef, and
then a long wave would come and lick me off and she would
stand and watch me go. It is a curious thing that this knowledge, far from depressing me, gave me a curious sense of
exhilaration and power. I felt that, with this bit of information
up my sleeve, I could meet Miss Morgan almost on the level.
Morituri te salutamus.

So after I had had my sleep out I perked up and waxed
chatty. I could always amuse the barristers when I warmed
up and got going, so why not her? I told her tales of the
house-agent's trade—which has even less conscience to it than
horse-coping—till she giggled; and then I told her scandalous
yarns about the local notables till she guffawed. My rendering
of the local scandals is always in great demand at the club,
but I expect it will end by getting me shot from behind a
hedge; I have been promised hidings on various occasions,
but so far none of them have come off. It always gives me
great joy to gather round me the husbands of my sister's friends
and make them see the funny side of the things that their
womenfolk are taking deadly seriously. The vicar says I am
a very bad influence in the town, undermining everybody's
sense of right and wrong, for he does not find it easy to work
up a persecution of a wrong-doer after we have all had a good
laugh at his wrong-doing. Miss Morgan, having no more
social conscience than myself, thoroughly appreciated these
stories. Anyway, we waxed quite merry, and I forgot I had

ever had any troubles and felt so much better that I borrowed a dressing-gown from her—I was already decked out in Trethowen's pyjamas that his wife had made for him—and got up and wandered about the room to get the stiffness out of myself, as my custom is after an attack. Miss Morgan was a tall woman, and I am barely middle height and lightly built, so it was quite a satisfactory fit, which was more than could be said for Trethowen's pijjies. When Mrs Treth came in and saw me with apricot-coloured swansdown fluffles swathed round my unshaven chin, she blinked. There is one thing to be said in favour of being an ash-blond male—you have got to get him in a good light to see whether he has shaved or not.

So we gossiped, and time went by. We couldn't see the sunset from this room, but we watched its pink reflection gather on the clouds, and presently the moon rose, full and round, and for the second time that day I saw a path of light spread over the waves.

Now as I have said before, I was on rather intimate terms with the moon, and when I saw my old friend appear, I forgot my new one and fell silent and stared at her; and, as always when I communed with the moon, I became aware of the invisible side of nature. I knew there was a very intense kind of life in the sea, and that out here at the fort we were very closely in touch with it; for the sea so nearly surrounded us that we only just missed being an island, and the rock rose so slightly from the water that it was a sea-rock rather than a land rock, and in times of storm the over-carried spray swept clean across from bay to bay, running down the windward windows like rain, and great fucus was tossed down in the forecourt among my queer carved sea-beasts.

All the room was of a translucent, shimmering greyish-green, like sea-water in sunlight; even the dress Miss Morgan was wearing was sea-green, and round her neck was a string of star-sapphires that caught the light strangely. It was a queer dress, medieval, of shining satin, no trimmings, and moulded close to her figure, and she had a lovely figure. The neck was cut low and square in front, and pretty nearly to her waist at the back, but the sleeves were long, and tight to the arm, and ended in points like a fish's mouth that came down to her knuckles. She had not got her scarlet whore's claws to-night, but instead her nails were lacquered a pearly-white, iridescent, the effect very queer and inhuman.

Suddenly my meditations were interrupted.

"Wilfred, what do you know about the moon?"

I was so taken aback at being called by my Christian name that I nearly started another attack of asthma on the spot—I did really. In Dickford ladies even refer to their husbands as Mr So-and-so.

Miss Morgan saw my confusion, but she only smiled.

"If you think I am going to call any man 'mister' while he is wearing my negligée, you are very much mistaken. Tell me, Wilfred, what do you know about the moon?"

So I told her. I told her how I had got in touch with the moon when I was lying knocked out after my first go of asthma, and how I could feel her tides and knew just what the moon-powers were doing; whether they were waxing or waning; whether they were strong and in power, or ebbed far away like a receding sea on a level beach. And I told her that I believed the moon-tides influenced all sorts of things in a way we did not realise, and that although I did not yet understand this part, I believed that some day I should; for I should get enlightenment as I lay with the life gone out of me after a go of asthma.

She nodded. "Yes," she said. "It comes then. You get with asthma what I get with my crystal."

("Gosh!" I thought to myself, "I wish she'd swop!")

I told her, however, that I was afraid it was the drugs that did it. But she shook her head.

"You had no drugs last night," she said, "but you are in a strange mood this evening, quite unlike your usual self."

"You don't know anything about my usual self," said I. "This is me when I am normal, not how I am when I'm tied into knots."

"What ties you into knots?" said she.

"Trying to do my duty in the sphere where God has placed me," said I. "And I would greatly like to know why the All-wise so perseveringly knocks square pegs into round holes?"

Then I told her my idea that whereas the gods are always reputed to make mortals pay up for any great benefit bestowed, I, by virtue of my asthma, seemed to be running a kind of credit account with them. She agreed. And then she said:

"You are a very odd person; I never knew a man who could maintain such an animated silence."

For a moment I could not think what she meant, and then I realised that although I never have much to say for myself, I am doing some pretty lively thinking all the time. My silence is neither slow-wittedness, nor reserve, but the ingrained caution that comes from always living with people who disagree with you. I had learnt from bitter experience that the less everybody knew of my real thoughts and feelings, the better for me.

I told her something of this.

"But you feel you can talk to me, don't you?" she said.

I told her yes, that I had always wanted to talk to her, but that my conversation was so stiff in the joints from never being used that I couldn't get it to start, any more than the car would the previous evening; but as she could see for herself, I ran all right once I was warmed up.

She smiled. "In future," she said, "I shall keep my foot on

the starter until I hear sounds that show you are beginning to spark."

I wished her joy of the job.

"You can be very amusing when you choose," she said. "It is a pity you do not choose oftener, and keep your hand in."

I certainly enjoyed amusing Miss Morgan, and I think she enjoyed being amused by me, but it was not for this that I was being cultivated, unless I were very much mistaken. And then came the word, spoken perhaps idly or perhaps with intent— one never quite knew with her—that told me why I had been picked for the part of sacrificed slave, which with every hour that passed I felt more certain was my lot.

"Although you look a sick man, and I suppose you are a sick man, you are one of the most vital persons I have ever met."

I told her that whatever I felt like to her, I didn't feel like that to myself.

"And the curious thing is, that the more depleted you are, the more vital you become. You give off an extraordinary amount of a very queer kind of magnetism, Wilfred. I expect that is your trouble. You probably leak magnetism."

Now this was true, for in an odd way I always did feel very much alive as I lay absolutely flaccid after a bout. My mind would be extraordinarily alert and lucid, even when I could hardly hold a cup to my lips. It was at these times, in fact, that I had that abnormal lucidity that had enabled me to see behind the moon.

Miss Morgan suddenly leant forward and fixed me with her big dark eyes.

"You are like that now, aren't you?" she said.

"To a certain extent, yes. Not as much as I am sometimes, because I haven't had as bad a bout as I sometimes do, but— yes, I suppose to a certain extent I am lucid at the present moment."

"Then tell me what you know about myself—what you imagine, anything—so long as you tell me."

"Gosh, I don't know anything."

"Yes, you do. Go on, tell me. I'll sort it out afterwards."

I looked at her as she sat in a great high-backed, carved chair in that sea-blue room, lit only by the moonlight. The star sapphires round her neck caught the light in the strange way they have, and made a line of phosphorescent fire where neck joins breast. Her heavy black hair was wound round her head in swathes; her brow very white, and her eyes under it very dark. Yes, she was the sea-priestess whom I had seen gliding towards me out of the mist and the dusk in the high-prowed ship.

And looking at her as she leant towards me with her dark eyes fixed on me with an unremitting intensity, I seemed to slip out from this bourne of time and space on a smooth tide of dark water.

"Our land is being drowned because the sea is too strong for us," I said. "Our dykes cannot stand against it; and it is coming in and taking our land field by field. There is a malice in the water that we cannot cope with, and we have sent for a priestess, one with wisdom. There is our own arch-priest, who rules the sacred college here on the headland, but he says it is too strong for him; the moon-powers have got out of hand and there is malice in the waters. We must send for a priestess of the sea-peoples from the land beyond the sunset, the lost and drowned land of which so little now remains, just one or two mountain peaks to the south——"

"The Azores?" said she.

"Yes," said I, "the Azores, rising up from great depth, all that is left of that drowned land. And they sent us their last priestess, a sea-priestess, who was also a priestess of the moon, as she had need to be."

"Why had she need to be?"

"I do not know that yet.   But we shall know presently."

"And what did the sea-priestess do when she came?"

"She sacrificed."

"What did she sacrifice?"

"Men."

"Where?"

"In the cave under Bell Knowle."

"How did she sacrifice them?"

"They were bound alive to the altar-stone, and the tide came and took them.   She sacrificed till the sea was satisfied."

"Is that all?"

"It is all I know now.   Maybe there is more.   I do not know. I cannot think of it. Perhaps it will come later. I think, maybe, there is more to come.   I have always thought there is more to come."

Then I came back as one comes to the surface after a very deep dive, and found Miss Morgan staring into my eyes as if she would burn holes in the very brain inside my skull.

("Well," I said to myself, "you say I am a sick man, but I guess I'll be a dashed sight sicker man by the time you've done with me if you do this sort of thing to me often!")

CHAPTER XII

I BORROWED Trethowen's razor next day and had a shave, not without difficulty, for it was the old-fashioned kind that suicides use, and came downstairs and joined Miss Morgan in the forecourt. I felt curiously light, as if the ground were rising and falling under me like a ship, quite different from my usual leaden heaviness after a go of asthma. All the same, I did not fancy it was a particularly wholesome feeling.

Miss Morgan was very sweet to me, as always, and let me wander about a bit and stretch my legs, and then put me into a deck-chair, not the beastly canvas kind that catch you behind the knees, but the genuine P. and O. sort. When I denied I was beginning to tire she did not argue with me, as my sister does, but contradicted me flatly and took me by the arm and put me into the chair without asking me what I wanted. It is good for me to be bullied when in this state, for I am always very contrary after a bout, and insist on doing all the things that are bad for me, just as one bites on a sore tooth to spite it.

After I had been fed I was more amiable. Not that I actually snapped at Miss Morgan, though I probably should have done if she had been anyone else; for try as I will, there is a kind of fretfulness about me on these occasions which no one deplores more than I do. However, having slept most of the afternoon, I was practically back to normal by tea-time. I do not say that I wasn't still a bit weary, but mentally I was myself again.

We lay in our deck-chairs, and the sound of the bells of the little old church at Starber came to us across the still water; no air stirred, but on Bell Head the sea is never quiet, and a slow slight ground-swell came in from the west to wash over the rocks with a soft whispering. Presently a cold wind sprang up and drove us in, and Miss Morgan put a match to the sea-fire of drift-wood on the big hearth I had made for her between my two dolphins, and I sprawled on the enormous sofa, and she sat on a pouf with her elbows on her knees, and we watched the flames licking over the salt-soaked wood, all blue and mauve and golden and very lovely. The flames of a sea-fire are exactly like opals.

It was then Miss Morgan mooted her suggestion to me.

"What shall we do with these walls?" she asked.

I looked round the huge room where the Tommies had disported themselves—that is, if the poor devils felt like sporting at all on this rock. The southern wall of the room was one sheet of plate-glass, only broken by the slender supporting pillars of the pergola; at the back there were the narrow Gothic windows that broke the flat line of masonry to the landward side. The floor was parquetry, still smelling sweetly of the new wood, which is a smell I am very fond of, but the plaster stretched gaunt and bare, for I had not known what she meant to do with it.

"I should panel a big place like this, if I were you," I said. "That, or hangings. Wallpaper is no use to you."

"What about wall-paintings?" said she.

"What sort?" said I.

"Sea-scenes," said she.

It was a good idea, and I said so, but asked her how she proposed to fix the canvas to the wall in this sea-damp air.

"No canvas," said she. "Paint straight on to the plaster."

"You will have to get a fellow here to do it," said I. "Won't you find that an awful nuisance?"

"Not in the least," said she, "I'll be delighted to have you. Have you ever worked in tempera?"

"Never," said I.

"Oh, well," said she, "you live and learn."

Then I saw what she was driving at. ("Hell!" said I to myself. "Why doesn't she have the sacrificial cave under Bell Knowle put in order and be done with it?")

"Are you averse to the idea?" said she.

"Not in the least," said I.

When Miss Morgan said good night to me, she patted my hand and I never blinked an eyelid. I felt I had travelled a long way since I left Dickford last Friday morning.

It proved unexpectedly easy to satisfy my family concerning my sojourn at the fort. My sister had liked having my work in the art exhibition; she felt the family had gone up a notch on the strength of it; I was something a bit more now than a Dickford business man. Scottie's father-in-law, for instance, had never had any of *his* handiwork in an art exhibition. My sister jumped to the conclusion that Miss Morgan meant to leave her money to me in her will, and dashed out and bought me a new tie and some socks. Personally I should have thought she would have been more likely to leave her money to me if I wore my old tie and looked deserving.

My sister always kept a very close eye on my comings and goings, but Providence and my pals generally conspired to throw dust in it, and on the rare occasions when she was on the right track she knew so little of human nature that she never spotted it. Being a mother's boy has few advantages that I have ever been able to discover, but it does enable you to get away with pretty nearly anything, because nobody believes you capable of it.

Anyway, I felt pretty certain that in the present instance I could sail as near the wind as I chose with perfect impunity, and the worse my conscience might be, the less my sister would suspect me. As for old Scottie, having put no money into the business, he never feels entitled to throw his weight about in it, which is very decent of him; in the ordinary way I respect his wishes, but on this occasion I am afraid I took advantage of the position up to the hilt. He didn't say anything, but he drew down his long upper lip and sucked it till I thought of Kipling's story of How the Elephant's Child Got His Trunk.

The arrangement was that I should go out to the fort every Saturday, put in the week-end on the job, and come back to the office in time to deal with the correspondence on Monday morning. The town didn't give a hoot for the business, believing Miss Morgan to be rising ninety; except of course, Headley, in whom Scottie had confided, and who grinned when he saw me putting a suit-case into the car one Saturday afternoon.

I felt like a kid going off to the pantomime as I crossed the swing-bridge over the Dick, for the moment one crosses over into the marshes, the atmosphere changes and the Old Gods take charge. There are no farms among the marshes; the farmers who have the grazing take their beasts across by the swing-bridge and bring them back at night. Nor are there walls or any stone-built structure out on the levels, for they flood so frequently that no stone can stand. The road itself goes through them high-carried on a dyke, and I have driven along it when the floods were out and a sea-mist over them and one could see no land on either side, but only the narrow ribbon of road winding through the water : an uncanny experience. To-day, however, the heat-haze lay over the water-meadows where they were hay-making the aftermath.

I took off my coat, and rolled up my shirt-sleeves, and was jogging along quite cheerfully, intending to tidy up before I arrived, when who should I meet just beyond the farm but Miss Morgan herself, on foot. She said she had walked out to see Trethowen about planting vines on the old vine terraces, and she was very pleased to meet me as it would save her a hot walk back if I would give her a lift, for it was much hotter here, at the landward end, than she had suspected out at the fort.

She made me come with her up to the vine-terraces. I did not know how I was going to manage the scramble, but I went up like a bird, and we found Trethowen dubiously inspecting what looked to me like some very melancholy little vines done up in matting. Miss Morgan said they were Concord vines that she had had sent especially from America, for if they would stand the New England winters, they ought to stand ours. They looked like potential stomach-ache to me, and I could see that Trethowen had no high hopes of them either. A more attractive feature was the herb garden that was laid out on the highest terrace; we climbed up there, I taking my time and Miss Morgan appearing not to notice, for which I was grateful to her; I hate my infirmities being commented on.

Bell Head is a banana-shaped protuberosity with the concave side to the south. All that side is sheer cliff where the jackdaws roost, and I should think they grill on their shelves. The slope to the north is a grassy down in possession of the rabbits, with bracken in the hollows. At its foot is a beach of broken rock. The landward end, where the terraces are, inclines south-south-east. Fortunately for us a spur of the cliff gave shelter from the afternoon sun, and we sat down on a stone-built seat in its shade.

Behind us the grey breast of the rock rose a hundred feet or so to the top of the down, hung with ivy. A little below the top, the dark mouth of a cave opened on to a ledge, and Miss Morgan told me that from below with field-glasses one could clearly discern a series of cut-out steps and ledges by which an active man with a steady head could have climbed down to it from above.

"And," she said, "if you draw a line down the spine of the reef and along the down, following the lie of the strata, it passes exactly over the cave and ends on Bell Knowle. And it is my belief," she continued, "that on the longest day anyone watching in that cave would see the sun rise over the cairn on Bell Knowle."

Of course it was obvious the minute it was pointed out, that however the battering of the waves might have bent the coastline, the lie of the rock of the long sea-down was due east and west. In fact Bell Head, Bell Knowle, and the ridge above Dickford all represented the up-ending of the same long slab of strata. When the Dick altered its course it had slipped through the one gap in the ridge due to a fault in the strata caused by God knows what ancient upheaval, and had made the sand-dunes to the north around Dickmouth into a marsh, leaving the marsh to the south around Starber to dry out into sand-dunes. It was an interesting bit of country for the naturalist.

But our interest in it was not naturalistic. From our vantage-point up under the breast of the cliff I was able to point out to Miss Morgan the lie of the land and explain its significance. I showed her the line of mounds and hollows that marked the footings of the ancient quays behind Starber, now half a mile from the sea, showing that the land had risen. I showed her the line of the ancient Dick and its tow-path, and the patch of haze under the hills that marked Dickford, where the tin-men came down to meet the ships of the sea-people. I showed her the cleft in the steep slope of Bell Knowle that in my belief hid the sea-cave, now filled by the scour of ages.

She focused her field-glasses upon it and studied it carefully.

"Do you observe," she said, "that the bank of the Dick below it is straight and sharp? I believe the long grass hides masonry. It would be there I landed when I came to the cave."

THE SEA PRIESTESS 109

Then she put the glasses into my hands and bid me follow the coastline down to Starber. The opening of the ancient estuary was clear to see from this height, and in its jaws rose a rocky knoll, beyond all question the islet where I had waited to light the beacon that should guide the sea-priestesss in from the sea. My hands shook so that I could hardly focus the glasses. I swear that I did not know it was there!

Miss Morgan made no comment on my agitation, though I don't suppose she missed it. She didn't miss much, did that woman. We sat quietly for a while, till the sound of the rising tide on the shingle came up to us from below. All the ancient life of this hollow land was reconstructing itself before my eyes. I could see the Naradek rolling in silver flood among its reeds where now were bents and whin. I could see the dark line of the quays below the cave and the paved causeway leading up to it. Round the flanks of Bell Knowle one could still discern the winding line of the processional way going up to the cairn on top; but now I saw it no more as a cairn of fallen stone, split and broken by the weather, but a circle of standing stones, upright and with lintels, like a miniature Stonehenge. And I was sure that the pyramidal shadow of the peak would pass over the spot where we were sitting as the sun rose on the longest day, and that the first beam of the rising light would strike upwards through the high pylon of the sun-temple and fall upon the mouth of the cave above our heads.

To my eyes there appeared a come-and-go of white-robed priests, gold-belted and shaven-headed, on the processional way; and on the roads through the marsh I could see the common people, clad in russet and hodden grey as their custom is, kin to the earth they serve; I could see, too, the bright-dyed cloaks of the sailors and fighting-men and the flash of arms. The haze of the evening hearths hung over Ishtar's Beere, and along her quays lay the strange high-prowed sea-boats, decked stem and stern, and with their purple and blue and scarlet sails lowered over the midships to serve as an awning for the chained slaves that rowed them. The dark mouth of the sea-cave of Bell Knowle was clear to me now, so clear it seemed to fancy that I knew who was within, and that she was sacrificing. Then I came back to myself and found Miss Morgan watching me, and wondered how much of all this my face had shown.

She rose and led the way down. The shallow sloping earth of the herb-beds, held by stones, was so hot the hand could hardly touch it, and the grey aromatic herbs that love the sun-soaked soil gave off their sharp and spicy smell, and I thought of the scent that had wafted across to me the day in the empty house when Miss Morgan had opened her coat and revealed the smooth neck of a young girl.

I was not sorry to get back to the car, for going down was nearly as hard work as going up on those steep, irregular steps. When we reached the road to the fort, Miss Morgan suggested that we should leave the car and climb up on to the crest of the down and look at the cairns, but I had to say no, and give my reason, which made me sulky and miserable; and that upset Miss Morgan because she felt she had put her foot in it. No, I am not an agreeable person to live with. I don't wonder my family get fed up with me. When I get into these moods at home, I clear the air by provoking a row with my sister, never a difficult thing to do. I couldn't very well do that with Miss Morgan, but it showed me how I had deteriorated since I had had my asthma that I should treat a comparative stranger to my moods. This upset me still further, and when we got out of the car I followed her into the big living-room in a sullen silence, unable to find a word to say for myself.

She turned and considered me as I stood in front of her like a sulky kid, and then she took me by the shoulders and shook me.

"Wilfred, don't be a goose," she said, and smacked my cheek none too gently.

I could not have been more surprised if she had thrown a bucket of cold water over me. I have had my face smacked in good earnest by my sister many a time, and given her one on the jaw in return, but this was an entirely different matter, and I was upheaved to a degree I would not have believed possible, though in an entirely different way from what I had been. Miss Morgan saw it, and smiled. Then she went to take her hat off and left me to my own devices, and I subsided into one of her sawn-off chairs and tried to collect what was left of my wits.

I had just about enough of them left to wonder how I should be feeling when Miss Morgan finished with me and packed up and went back to London. And then something in me rose up and said: "After me, the deluge," and I settled back in my sawn-off chair, and stretched out my legs and lit a cigarette, and reckoned that next time Miss Morgan took me by the shoulders and shook me she would get kissed. Anyway, by the time she arrived back I was ready for any game she chose to play, and had begun to think out one or two of my own. But as soon as I saw her, I felt that I couldn't play games on Miss Morgan: she wasn't that sort.

Then, of course, I was badly off my stroke again, and in yet another direction; and she saw it, and patted my shoulder, and I caught her hand and kissed it, and that seemed to put things right in a way that I cannot describe. Anyway, I felt perfectly happy with her after that. There was something between Morgan le Fay and myself that made formality impossible. I did not want it; it would have spoiled everything. I admit there were times when I boiled up, being after all a male, but all the same, I did not really want it. It was from that time that I called her Morgan le Fay. I never called her Miss Morgan again, but on the other hand, I never came to call her Vivian, not to her face, anyway.

We went into the dining-room and had the first of the marvellous chafing-dish suppers that she used to make for me. It was most fascinating to watch her make them. There was a long, heavy refectory table in the dining-room, and at one end she had all her gear; Mrs Treth used to put it ready and then clear off, and we had the fort to ourselves, and for the matter of that, the headland as well. There was a big copper chafing-dish with a spirit-lamp under it, flanked by a "sluggard's friend" to keep things warm, and a trayful of all sorts of out-of-the-way flavourings, such as sweet basil and paprika and a sour white wine instead of vinegar; and with these Morgan le Fay cooked whatever she had to cook in cream, or in butter, or in a kind of bouillon. And there were various kinds of queer breads she had learnt to make in different parts of the world, not just one kind of bread as we have in England. Then she had made Trethowen grow all manner of odd pot-herbs, and taught me to eat raw seakale and salsify, and uncommon good they are. She could cook literally from China to Peru; and I learnt to eat crisp fried noodles without getting any in my hair, and to appreciate *maté*. All the same, she never looked domesticated as she stood up there at the end of the long table in her medieval dresses with a silver ladle in her hand, but rather like a priestess at an altar; and the dully gleaming copper over the blue flame looked like a witches' cauldron. The table was lit with very beautiful candles, tall and delicately tapering—lovely things, and outside we could hear the eternal beat of the sea. I used to sit and watch her, waiting for supper to be ready; luckily I had enough sense to know that this was a woman whom no one but a fool would try to domesticate; as well put a swift in a cage, for the beauty of a swift is in its flight.

It might be, as she said, that she was very old, with her youth marvellously preserved by strange arts; or it might be that she was a very clever woman playing some queer game of her own; I did not know, and had long since ceased to care. I only knew that she was Morgan le Fay, and there was no one like her.

Well, this was my first supper with her like that, and I put my elbows on the table where I sat at the end of it and rested my chin on my hands and watched her, and would have been content to watch her for hours. She knew the skilful use of alcohol, too, by which one tunes a mood, and I, being abstemious, got the full benefit of it. There was an old wine waiter at the "George" who used to amuse me enormously the way he got the barristers sozzled; he could make you drunk or keep you sober through a long evening, just as he chose, and if anyone didn't do by him as he thought a gentleman should, gosh, didn't he wake up with a head next morning! It wasn't so much the drinks he had had as the way they were combined. I used to buy the wine for the "George" at the auctions, and had many a consultation with the old boy, and when he saw I appreciated his artistry, he taught me a lot. It is a highly-educative thing to talk to a specialist in any line of business.

Morgan le Fay, who had been about the world a lot, used to have stuff sent over from all sorts of queer little châteaux and castles and estancias that produced uncommon good stuff but not enough of it to come on the open market, so it was only sold to local purchasers. Whenever she tasted anything she particularly fancied at any of the little country inns she was so fond of, she inquired where it came from, and traced it to its source, and made friends with the grower. There is an extraordinary thrill for a stay-at-home soul like me in looking at a snapshot of the vineyard while you drink the wine. Of course some of it did not travel well, and we poured it into the sea and chucked its barrel after it; but for the most part it was all right, for Morgan le Fay was a pretty good judge, and some of it was really wonderful.

Her cooking was entirely different from my old Sally's cooking, which also was good in its way. Sally relied on handling a thing so as to bring out its flavour, but Morgan le Fay looked on food as the raw material of cookery only. As for my sister's catering, it consisted in telling the cook what we'd have, and telling the butcher what he was to send, and giving both parties a rowing impartially on the principle that if they didn't need it now, they soon would; but she never put her hand to a pot, and would, I think, have been absolutely stumped if the cook had left. She knew as much about cooking as I did about ballooning, and cared no more; and yet she considered herself a good housewife on the strength of seeing to it that the steps were adequately whitened and the lace curtains clean, which are not things that I, personally mind about.

We strolled out to the end of the reef after supper to look at the moonlight on the water. I wondered whether a wave would rise out of the deeps and lick me off, and walked right out to the very point over the seaweed to see what would happen, till Morgan le Fay got quite agitated and called me back; but everything was dead calm and there was only a silvery whisper of ripples among the rocks and a faint wavy stir in the floating weed, for it was slack water and the tide was at uttermost ebb. Presently, as we watched, all the weed began to stream in one direction, and we knew that the tide had turned. Then we came in and sat by the fire, and my dolphins smiled at us, and I was absolutely happy.

CHAPTER XIII

NEXT morning I started roughing out the designs for the wall-paintings with charcoal on the wide expanses of none too smooth plaster. I had not bargained for wall-paintings when I had the plastering done—the War Department had considered white-washed brick good enough for its thin red line of 'eroes. Miss Morgan, however, had declined to let me have it gypsum-faced, so we compromised on a coat of size slapped on by Trethowen. Miss Morgan had a few things to say about size when next she saw me. I told her she ought to have known the fort in the days when the jackdaw was at large in the water-tank and then she would be thankful for small mercies. Size is only cows' heels. It is a perfectly wholesome smell.

The whole of one end of the big room was occupied by the fireplace and the book-shelves surrounding it. It is rather a nice idea, I think, to have one's fireplace framed in one's books. I have it in my room. Morgan le Fay, moreover, had her book-shelves made of cedar, and they imparted a most delightful smell to the books; I know, for I was always borrowing them. An old book has a fascinating smell anyway, and when it has been kept on a cedar-wood shelf it is a delightful thing to have in one's hand.

This left the spaces between the narrow Gothic windows and the blank wall at the far end to be dealt with. For the first of these I planned a wind-blown sky and an empty sea seen under fitful sunshine; the next should be drifting mist and oily dark water and things half-seen. Then came steel-grey, stormy weather and white, wind-blown crests. Lastly, a calm sea by moonlight.

These were all surface scenes; but for the end of the room where the wall was unbroken I planned a panorama of the deep sea palaces, with mermaids and what-not, and Miss Morgan herself as the sea-priestess for centre-piece. This was all approved, with the exception of the centre-piece, about which she was not told, so was not able to express an opinion. The draperies were what Kipling calls "harumphrodite" and the features a smear, which is as it should be in inspirational paintings.

For I had an idea that these paintings were going to be something more than my own composition. I knew that in the lights and shadows were going to appear faces half seen, as they do in some of the old puzzle-pictures such as we had in the bound volumes of antiquated magazines in the drawing-room at home. First one sees just an ordinary picture, and then one discovers that the lines make a picture within a picture, and one finds the jockey hidden in the horse. I believed that in some way, if I gave myself up to it, the life that was behind the sea would interpret itself in my paintings.

I managed to get the whole scheme roughed out in charcoal that first week-end, which was about as much as I expected to do, for I knew I should spend a good deal of time talking to Miss Morgan—and I did! On the Monday morning I departed with an armful of borrowed books in the back of the car and my head humming like a hive. Morgan le Fay was indeed strong meat for a Dickford bachelor. Clients found me a trifle absent-minded all that week, and Scottie looked at me with a sour eye. The office boy was openly sympathetic, for which I could have cuffed him, and I believe Scottie did.

Miss Morgan had talked of tempera, but when I came to

investigate it, I had my doubts of it in that damp sea-air, and anyway, it was a wicked ramp for such an acreage. So she was immensely amused to see me turn up next Friday with the back of the car full of tins of house-decorator's paints, and why not? You can't beat them for bold effects because they have body. I also obtained magnificent opalescent effects in both waves and clouds by slapping on the paint in sticky streaks and then combing it with an ordinary hair-comb in the same way as the edges of books are deckled. Miss Morgan was hugely amused when she saw me at work, but she admitted that the effect was fine. Anyway, I got results, and got them quickly.

Well, with all the groundwork roughed in, there still remained the finishing touches to give, and for this I had to await my inspiration. It was my intention to watch my chance, and commune with the sea in whatever mood she might be when I arrived, and then work on the corresponding panel, and the first mood she gave me was, appropriately enough, wind-blown space and broken light; so I went out to the end of the reef, although Miss Morgan made protesting noises, and there I communed with the sea-life all around me.

All sense of the land fell away from me as I stood and looked to the west where no land could be seen; a seagull or two sailed past and was gone; a spar went by on the racing tide; and then the sea and the sky were empty and I was alone with the waves.

The sun came and went in fitful gleams and light lay on the water in patches; here and there a wave was crested with white, but for the most part the sea ran without breaking in a short sharp swell that came cantering in and crashed on the rocks. The sea was not in strength to-day, but all the same it was not to be trifled with, and there was a darkness in the west that was more than the gathering dusk of an autumn afternoon. It was cold out there, and the tide was rising, and a wave got my ankles and made me wild; so I was glad to come in to where Morgan le Fay was sitting smoking, waiting to make tea beside her drift-wood fire. My feet were wet, and I had received no inspiration, and altogether felt rather cheap. However I cheered up, and we talked till late, and then I slept till late, and finally, resisting all temptations to go out to the reef again in the morning sunshine, I got to work on the first of my paintings.

Now I do not know what had happened out on the reef, or what had been the real significance of the wave that caught me round the ankles, but as soon as I got to work, I knew that there was power in my painting. And I saw in my imagination all the life that is behind the sea, and it seemed to me that there was intelligence behind it; a mind not unlike our own, but vaster, and vastly simpler. The life of elemental nature differed from our life in degree, but not in kind. It had the same kind of corporate being as a hive or a herd, which is not embodied, but overshadowed. And if I chose to see this life expressed by such lines as would express a similar life in a human face, why not? So I gave to the steep short waves shadowy lineaments; here a brow, and there a mouth, but nowhere a face complete; and each of these partial forms expressed the same way of life—a bright, inhuman, heartless animation. Quite beautiful in a rather petty way, but completely soulless, as are some young girls. One only, I think, gets great beauty where there is a mind behind it, as in Morgan le Fay.

And so all day I drew the sea-life of the smaller waves, such as had got me by the ankle. In the sunshine there was a sparkle like the gaiety of thoughtless young things, gay with their own vitality; but in the cloud-shadows one saw clearly that it was all pretty heartless. When it was finished, I was rather tired, and Morgan le Fay came and sat beside me on a stool and talked to me as I sprawled on the sofa before the drift-wood fire, for I was too tired to eat until I had rested; and she took off her necklace of star sapphires and gave it to me to look at, and I watched the queer cross of light shift and flash in the stones as they caught the flame, and there was a very curious magnetism about them. I have sometimes wondered why she used to let me hold her necklace and play with it.

That night I dreamt of the sea; and I also dreamt of Morgan le Fay, but I dreamt of her as a moon-priestess rather than a sea-priestess, and in some curious way I knew that the moon dominated the sea, and that Morgan was something bigger than a sea-priestess.

Next day I walked up with her to the top of the down to inspect the cairns. It was not such a scramble, going up along the spine of the down from the point, rising with the rise of the strata, as it was to go straight up among the rabbits from the road, and I managed it all right.

The cairns were interesting. I know of nothing more fascinating than trying to read the life of a forgotten people from the scanty traces of mound and cairn. It was quite clear to me that there had been here on the sea-down a college of priests. The ancients, placing their temples, always looked for impressive sites, something that would fire the imagination of the *hoi polloi*, and wherever you get anything striking in the configuration of the ground, it is safe to look for the traces of ancient worship. These it is not always easy to find if neither barrow nor dolmen mark the site, for a druid grove is no different from any other grove, and a cairn soon disappears.

Up here, however, on the bare and lonely down, no one ploughed the shallow soil and no one attempted to cart stones by that perilous road, so the cairns lay where they fell, and one traced them by the symmetrical plan of the patches of fallen stone on the arid grass. Two by two they marched along the spine of the down, and very fine they must have looked when they were all standing beside the processional way—white stone pyramids, built as dry walling is built, to the height of the reach of a six-foot man.

I guessed that they led from the point of the headland back to the spot where the perilous path took off that led to the cave of vigil; and sure enough, when I looked among the bracken and in the loose soil of the warrens, I found the white stones where I expected to find them. We were tremendously thrilled; I forgot all about my asthma and cantered about like a two-year-old. On the very crest of the down we found three great stones lying fallen, and guessed that they had been the two uprights and the lintel of a pylon; and as nearly as I could judge without instruments, one could sight through them to a similar pylon, or even a stone circle, on the crest of Bell Knowle, and gaze right into the eye of the rising sun on the longest day.

We also guessed that, as the line of cairns ran down towards the point, something special had stood on the site of the fort; but the War Department, blasting its way to perdition, had erased all that. However, I told Miss Morgan of my vision of the sea-pyre flaming at the uttermost ebb of the neap, and we wondered whether when the further rocks were laid bare we should find the traces we sought. It was a tremendous thrill, and Mrs Treth banged the gong three times before she could get us in to our dinner. That dinner!—being Mrs Treth's idea of what was becoming on a British Sabbath, we naturally slept after it.

While I slept, I dreamed. What I dreamed I do not remember, but something like a white-robed priest cleared off into the dusk as Mrs Treth roused us by throwing wood on the dying fire. We walked out to the point to look for the last of the sunset, but there wasn't any sunset that evening; everything was dull and cold and steely-grey, and we were glad to come in again.

Over the tea-cups I told Morgan le Fay of my dream, and she looked at me strangely; I had a kind of idea that she wasn't surprised, and that things were going as she hoped, and even better than she hoped. She rose and left the room without a word. When she returned she had in her hand a leather case. She opened it, and took out a large crystal.

"Would you care to look into this?" she said, and put it into my hands.

It was surprisingly heavy for its size, and I rested my elbows on my knees in order to get support for the weight, and gazed into its heart where strange lights shone, reflected from the fire.

It was icy cold when I first took it, but presently with the warmth of my hands it began to warm, and as it did so, it seemed as if the light within it grew brighter. Maybe it was only that the fire was burning up—I do not know. Then I noticed that the misty golden glow within focused to one sparkling point that, as I watched, was on the move. Afterwards I realised that it had moved in time to my breathing as the rise and fall of my chest altered the angle of my arms, and consequently the point of focus of the light within the sphere. But I did not realise this at the time, and watched the moving point fascinated, thinking that here were psychic phenomena in good earnest. It has been my experience that all the objective phenomena I have ever come across admitted of a naturalistic explanation, and that the real kingdom of faery is within.

Anyway, be that as it may, that moving point of light hypnotised me in the good old-fashioned manner, as I expect Morgan le Fay knew it would, and the warm golden glow of the crystal spread and deepened, and presently it flowed all round me and enclosed me in a golden cloud, and through the misty glow came the voice of the sea-priestess, commanding and asking questions.

And I told her what I saw. I saw the long line of the down and the cairns standing two by two, white pyramids of moon-fire. Here, where the fort now stood, was a stone-built palace, archaic, like the palaces of Knossos; and out at the point was a wide flat space with a hearth, and there they lit the sea-pyres when the tide was at uttermost ebb, and when the tide rose, the waves received the fire, even as I had seen in my dream. The pyre was built of sweet-smelling woods and was the sacrifice and tribute of earth to sea because the sea is the senior. Around the blazing pyre the white-robed, gold-belted, shaven-headed priests stood in a semicircle, waiting for the first long wave to lick the pile, and as the flaming brands fell hissing into the water they chanted the chant of the sea that makes peace between sea and land, and bid the sea remember that the moon ruled her and that she should be obedient thereto. They hailed the sea as the oldest of created things, older even than the hills, and the mother of all living. But they bade the sea remember that the moon is the giver of magnetic life, and that it was from the moonlight on the sea that living forms arose. For the sea is formless, but the magnetic moon is the giver of form to the life of the waters.

These things I said, and then I woke up and blinked, and Morgan le Fay took the crystal out of my hand and told me that it was enough for to-night. But having seen these things, I never lost them, and it was easy for me after that to reconstruct the forgotten life and see it all about me, moving in the ancient ways.

The effect of that experience was curious; for as I lay back in the great chair my breath came deeply and easily for the first time since I had started with my asthma. And this thing I knew beyond all gainsaying, that the gates of life were opening to me that I had thought closed for ever when I turned down the offer to go to London, and that for me life was once more on the move and progressing, and no longer turned back on itself in stagnation.

CHAPTER XIV

LIFE for me was a series of week-ends stuck together. The eyes of Scottie grew more and more sour, and the eyes of the office boy bulged more and more eagerly as I returned to work Monday by Monday, each time more muzzy and absent-minded. All the same, there was no more asthma for the time being, and I didn't care a hoot what happened to my immortal soul now that my body was becoming inhabitable. Even my mother, who seldom notices anything, observed my freedom from asthma, and remarked that she had always thought I should outgrow it. I have often wondered at what age my mother will consider me mature.

I was living in a kind of dream-world, and the only things that were real to me were Morgan le Fay and the fort. But by way of compensation something else was becoming real to me—the curious kingdom of the moon and the sea. Having once seen the faces in the water I could thenceafter see nothing else, and as the waves came rolling in I sensed their mood. Every rock for me had a personality, and presently I began to sense the moods of the winds; fire, of course, has a life of its own.

Getting in touch with the Unseen is like taking to drink —once you have started, you can't leave it alone. I found too that it was in my power to reconstruct the forgotten life of a place and see it as dream-pictures in a waking dream. With such toys to play with, was it any wonder that I turned away from the life that had yielded me so little nutriment and went exploring the secret paths of the Unseen?

With the development of this strange awareness came also an insight into the relationship between Morgan le Fay and myself. There was a very curious sympathy between us, and it meant a tremendous lot to me. I was not blind to the fact that I was fully prepared to fall head over ears in love with her if she so much as crooked her little finger, which was not a thing to be surprised at in a Dickfo. d virgin of either sex.

But although I was the only eligible bachelor in Dickford— that is, if you count an asthmatic as eligible—and had been pursued like an electric hare in consequence, I had always been mindful of the poem :

> "When I thinks of what I is and what I used to was,
> I thinks I throwed myself away without sufficient cause."

I admit I have done a certain amount of necking with little bits of local fluff, but my innate caution prevented me from ever getting myself mixed up with anyone who could reasonably expect me to lead her to the altar. My pater had played the fool over half the county, so I suppose one might say I was salted before I was born. To my credit be it said that my necking ended at the neck; though in some ways perhaps that is a pity, for love is like the measles—if one gets it at the proper age, it is a childish ailment, but taken late in life, it is a serious matter.

When I went down with the asthma my doctor asked me if I had been crossed in love.

"Well," I said, "you know Dickford as well as I do. Is it likely?"

And he agreed with me that it wasn't. Consequently, when I came within range of what could have been the genuine article, I was as susceptible as a nigger to the measles.

The breed of females round Dickford are, I fancy, quite exceptionally Itless. Districts are like that. One valley will be a mass of pudding-faces, and the next will have pretty girls on every bush—and behind them, too. Anyway, Dickford offered precious little in the way of temptation, and how my pater ever managed to do what he did is a mystery to me. I suppose I am my father's son to the extent that I have nothing much in the way of a conscience in these matters, my inhibitions, such as they are, being aesthetic, not ethical. If there had been anything doing with Morgan le Fay, I would certainly have done it; but I knew deep down in my heart that there wasn't, and that anything of that nature would have broken the magic and messed everything up.

I also knew, however, that Morgan le Fay did not mind my loving her, that it did not worry her in the least. Now in Dickford, if a fellow falls in love, he proposes; and if he is refused you do not meet again for a decent interval, someone going to stay with relations. Or if matrimony is not indicated, you go away together for a week-end or behind a hedge according to social position. In the literal meaning of the words I was week-ending with Miss Morgan every week of my life, and if anyone from Dickford had ever set eyes on her, the reputation of both of us would have gone to glory, so one might say that the arrangement had all the drawbacks and none of the advantages of a liaison.

All the same, I was getting something very definite out of it, though what that something was, it would be very difficult to say. There were times, naturally, when I wanted more than I got, and occasional upheavals and boilings-over in consequence, of which Morgan took not the slightest notice, in the same way as one shuts the family pet up in an outhouse upon occasion, and does not refer to the matter. The great thing was that she let me love her, quite naturally and without worrying about it. I suppose temperaments vary in these matters, and some folk placed as I was would have taken carving-knives to each other; I admit that I promised myself that when things came to an end with Morgan le Fay I would go in off the rocks on the point, for I did not see the fun of going back to my family and the asthma and Dickford. Meanwhile I had got something at last that made life worth living, and as I had neither illusions nor scruples, I developed no complexes. Our medico, yarning in my hayloft after he had attended me professionally, said that in these matters folk could be divided into sadists and masochists, which in plain English is the boots and the doormat. Sadists black their donah's eye or insult her in front of the butler according to social position, and masochists are never happy unless the lady just knocks plain hell out of them. Life is very odd. I think I incline towards masochism myself, though there is a limit to what I will stand in the way of hell.

Anyway, Morgan le Fay as remote as the moon was a lot more to my liking than she would have been mending my socks; for then I kept my dream of moon-magic and sea-palaces, and had for my love a princess of the powers of the air, and all this would have turned to dust like Dead Sea fruit had she degenerated into flesh and blood. Morgan le Fay, by letting me care for her without fear or favour, and by letting her woman's magnetism flow out towards me unchecked, gave me, though I never laid a finger on her, what is lacking in many marriages. Moralists talk of sublimation, but that is because they do not know what I learnt of moon-magic, out alone with Morgan le Fay at the fort. And so I think that to love as she let me love her is no bad remedy for sin, and a dashed sight better than the wrong sort of marriage; provided, of course, you are not of the type that blacks folks' eyes when you wax affectionate.

And so we got on very nicely, Morgan le Fay and I; and day by day the fort turned for me into a sea-palace, and Morgan

le Fay into a sea-priestess, and I lived more and more in another
dimension where I had that which I knew I should never have
on earth, and I was very happy, though possibly a little mad;
but anything was better than Dickford and the asthma.

And so the weeks slipped by—just a series of week-ends as
far as I was concerned. Something new had entered into life
for me with my friendship for Morgan le Fay; I borrowed her
books, and she cooked me the most amusing meals, teaching
me to appreciate food as I had already learnt to appreciate
wine, and talking to me of life as she had known it, and incidentally of her philosophy of life, which was exactly what my
own would have been if I had not been carefully brought up.
All that I had always regarded in myself as original sin I found
elaborated into a code of morals by Morgan le Fay. There
was no question whatever about it but that my asthma improved enormously.

But there was something else that improved also with what
I can only call, to borrow a term from our medico, the breaking down of my ethical adhesions. and that was my capacity
for creative design. I remember once hearing the story of one
of the greatest of modern painters. When he was young he
was a good young man and minded his mother and painted
like lids for chocolate boxes; but one day when he was on holiday he dived off a rock, and cracked his skull, and became a
great artist—but he no longer minded his mother.

I was indubitably beginning to slosh the paint on to Morgan's walls in style. There is one thing to be said for modern
art, you can make up your own technique as you go, and do
not have laboriously to learn a tradition so long as you get your
results. The fact that I splashed house-decorator's paints on to
rough plaster and combed them with the comb I used for my
hair was nothing against me as an artist—in fact with some
folk it was something in my favour. I must say, however,

that I had behind me the laborious draughtsman's training, for I should have been an architect if my father had not died prematurely and thrust me into a position of responsibility before my time. Consequently, when I massed my waves or my clouds, it was with the architect's innate sense of proportion, and I knew better than to try and do figures.

And so, as I say, the weeks went by. I got all the donkey-work done in the designs, if that is the correct term for it, but I had to wait for inspiration from the mood of the sea before I could work in the half-seen forms that showed forth the innermost spirit. I had finished the panel of the calm shallow sea, and Morgan was thrilled by it; but I knew that it was only the beginning, and that there was more to come.

And presently it came. I got up one Saturday morning and looked out of the window and couldn't see the opposite chimney-pots.

"Well," said I to myself, "if it is like this here, what will it be like on the coast?"

As soon as I saw that blinking fog of course I began to wheeze, though I had slept peacefully all night while it was banking up; which shows how mental asthma is, though it doesn't seem to make the slightest difference to know it.

I came in to get some clean shirts which my sister was supposed to be mending but hadn't, being concerned with higher things, and she heard me wheeze and wouldn't give them to me, saying I wasn't fit to go out to the fort in that fog. So I went round to the Co-op. in my dressing-gown and bought some navvies' back-raspers, and had them put down to the housekeeping account, and brought them back over my arm unwrapped-up. That larned her! She never tried that trick again. People who value public opinion are at a very great disadvantage in dealing with people who don't.

Then I went round to Beardmore, our medico, and got him to shoot me full of dope.

"You aren't fit to drive," said he to me when he saw the car outside.

"That needn't worry you if it doesn't worry me," I said.

"But what about the other folk on the road?" said he.

"To hell with the other folk on the road," said I.

"That's just what I'm afraid of," said he.

It was not too bad going through the town, and one could see the sun like a tarnished brass disk sailing overhead through the fog-wreaths; but as soon as I crossed the swing-bridge into the marshes it began to coal up in good earnest. I don't suppose I could see more than a dozen feet; luckily the road was straight, and there is never anything on it except an occasional cow; but I took the car along pretty carefully, for there were deep water-cuts on either side and she was a saloon, and a saloon can drown you in three feet of water.

I toiled along at about ten miles an hour for an eternity, and presently I came level with the farm, and Trethowen, hearing me, came out. He said he hadn't been able to take the car out to the fort that morning, and Mrs Treth had had to leg it, and he begged me not to try; but I knew I couldn't make it on foot, with that pull up the gradient of one in four, so I told him that what would be, would be, and he sighed and gave me the milk. Morgan, it seemed, was living on tins at the moment.

I got up the gradient all right; one couldn't very well help that, for it was well banked on the side of the drop so that one slid along in a kind of slot; but I very nearly over-ran the hair-pin bend, and it was only the banking that saved me. Even so, I butted a good bit of it down, for I was grinding along in bottom, and she shoved like fury. I always run a high-powered car so as to avoid gear-changing as much as possible when I am seedy.

However, I survived, and came out on to the crest of the down. Then I got the full brunt of the fog in my face. There was a slow cold air moving, and the fog came sliding along in big banks; it got on to the inside of the wind-screen as well as the outside, which was a thing I have never seen before; I switched on my big headlights that I use for fast driving at night and that everybody hates me for, but it was just a waste of battery, and I switched them off again and continued to nose my way foot by foot; it would not have done to run off the road, for one stood a very good chance of rolling over and over into the sea. I couldn't see a thing, in fact I could hardly see the end of the bonnet. However, we toiled along, the radiator boiling like an urn at a school treat, what with coming up the hill at a foot-pace, and now this rake's progress. As for me, I thought I was never going to breathe again.

Presently I felt the road dip towards the point, and thanked God for it. I honked to announce my arrival, and Morgan came out and opened the great gates for me, of which I was glad, for I cannot manage them when I am short of breath. If ever anything looked like a sea-priestess, she did, standing there in the fog in her sea-green gown with fog-dew on her hair.

She wanted me to come in and have some coffee by the fire, but I wouldn't, for this was the mood of the sea I wanted to catch, so we went out on to the rocks of the point and stood still and listened. It sounded dead quiet at first, but as soon as you listened, the air was full of sound. Away to the south the Starber lightship moaned on two notes that earned it the name of the Cow and Calf. Out to sea two or three ships called and replied, and an invisible fishing-smack rang a bell. The slow slight heave of the sea swashed and swashed among the rocks and the fog kept on the move the whole time. It wasn't as still and quiet as it seemed by any means.

I told Morgan le Fay that this was the sea-mood I wanted to

catch, and begged her to leave me alone and go in and make the coffee. She murmured a bit, for she was never too fond of my going out on to the point; but the tide was up, so I couldn't go far, and she agreed to go in. I watched her pass through the fog, almost invisible in her pale draperies as she moved graceful and sure-footed over the rocks. Then she was lost in the mist, and I was alone with the sea.

The smother closed in around me and everything disappeared except the weed-grown rock just under my feet. The fog passed over my face with a curious, soft, impalpable touch like the feel of fur. The big ships mooed and hooed, and the smack moved slowly away, ringing its bell like a lost sea-leper.

Then a sudden rift opened in the fog and a patch of pale sunlight shone down it, and I saw the sea for the first time. It was a pallid silvery-grey as if diseased, and rose and fell with a slow, languid, sickly heave; yes, it was a very sick sea, believe me; fog did not agree with it. Then the fog closed in again, and the faint far moaning went on, and a sea-gull cried from the rocks like a wandering soul. I had had enough of it, and turned to come in.

But as I turned, I skidded, and before I knew where I was, I was into the rising tide up to my knees. It didn't matter, as I had plus-fours on, and could take off my shoes and stockings and dry them in front of the fire, Morgan having calmly taken the shirt off my back for the same purpose on another occasion; but it gave me a curious turn to feel that each time I communed with the sea out on the point it seemed to make a clutch at me, and each time it got hold higher up. First the ankles, and now the knees; by the time I had finished the last panel, would its cold clutch rise to my throat?

Morgan le Fey was upset when she saw I was soaked to the knees, for I think she had the same thing in mind. They had never recovered the body of the poor moon-calf; he was gone for good. The channel deepens suddenly just hereabout, and whatever does not float on the surface slides off "to the cod and the corpse-fed conger-eel", and gets eaten before it can bloat and rise. However, Morgan gave me coffee, and I changed into dry gear and felt better. My asthma had disappeared completely. I know of nothing like a shock to clear it. I once fell downstairs during a bout, and felt absolutely normal as I sat on the mat at the bottom.

Dusk closed in early, and by three in the afternoon we had to light the lights. Morgan put camphor and cedar and sandalwood oil into her paraffin, and her lamps smelt sweet as they burnt. I had brought some muffins with me, and we toasted them at the drift-wood embers and they picked up the curious iodine tang of the sea as well as the delicious flavour of woodsmoke. Morgan le Fay had taught me that things cook quite differently over different kinds of fire, and that a gas-oven can never take the place of bright wood-embers that diffuse a soft lambent heat instead of the dry harshness of gas. Then, she said, there were different kinds of woods, and for some dishes nothing but coals of juniper would serve, and told me the old rune—

> "Take two twigs of the juniper tree.
> Cross them, cross them, cross them.
> Look in the coals of the Fire of Azrael——"

and we forgot all about the cold clutching hands of the sea and the poor moon-calf who was gone to come no more.

She asked me if one day I would like to look in the coals of the Fire of Azrael, and I asked her what it meant; and she said that one made a fire of certain woods, and gazed into the embers as it died down and saw therein the past that was dead. We would do this, she said, one day, and then we would see all the past of the high sea-down and the hollow land of the marshes reconstructing itself. When this happens, I thought to myself, the sea will get me round the neck. *Morituri te salutamus.*

We had a wonderful meal that evening, even if Morgan were killing tins with a can-opener. She cooked me clams as the Americans cook them, in butter and bread-crumbs. She had brought back recipes from every land she had ever travelled in, and she had travelled in a good many. It was fascinating to sit and watch her cook and hear her talk. The spirit-flame burnt blue under the great copper chafing-dish, and all the little bottles caught the light; I felt as if she were compounding for me the elixir of life, and to tell the truth I fancy she was.

For a woman like Morgan le Fay, who knows the arts of the moon-magic, can compound a very curious elixir for a man's drinking. There is a virtue in her hands that passes into the food. I would fire a cantankerous cook even if I had to live on dog-biscuits for the rest of my days, for everything she touches she poisons for a sensitive person.

Next day I awoke at dawn and went out on to the point and saw a marvellous sight—I saw the fog roll back as the sun came up. A light fitful wind came in from the open sea and pushed it back in great wreaths, and the sun shone down out of a cloudless sky of palest autumn blue and caught the little waves that followed in the wake of the wind. All the sea was a-sparkle with pale gold, and the fog, snowy white, lay along the coast in a bank that hid the land. It was as if all the world had sunk in the sea and only the high sea-down remained.

I climbed to the crest of the down where the three fallen stones of the pylon lay, and watched Bell Knowle slowly emerge from the haze. And I thought of the vigil kept day by day in the landward-looking cave high up on the breast of the cliff, and wondered if I had ever kept it, coming down by the perilous way along the ledges before first light, or watching by a fire of drift-wood through the long darkness. I promised myself that Morgan le Fay should soon have her fire of sweet woods. I knew where I could lay my hands on cedar logs, for one had blown down near us in a summer storm; sandal-wood was to buy at a price, and juniper grew on the hills behind the town. Yes, we would light a Fire of Azrael before we were very much older, and I would look into its coals and see the past. Then I came back to breakfast and found Morgan le Fay with her eyes starting out of her head, for she had made up her mind I had gone in off the point.

All that day I worked on the second panel. I painted the rift in the mist and the pale sun coming through, and the sickly silver sea that heaved so slowly. And down the sea-lane thus opening came the shade of the *Flying Dutchman;* a ship of antique shape; her sails hanging aslant; her ropes trailing in the water; and on her high forecastle a great barnacled bell that had been sunk long centuries in deepest ooze. Slow swirls of water followed her forefoot, and through them showed the faces of drowned mariners who clutched at her stem as she went by. And some of them had no faces, for like the poor moon-calf, they had gone down into deep water and been made one with the sea-snakes.

Morgan le Fay did not altogether like these things. She said—had she got to live with this picture, for it was terrible? And I said:

"You have chosen to live with the sea, Morgan le Fay, and the sea is terrible. Perhaps some day I who love you will be like these things without faces."

She looked at me strangely, and I said:

"But meanwhile I have to-day."

CHAPTER XV

THREE woods were wanted by Morgan le Fay for her Fire of Azrael. Two of these I knew where to lay hands on, but the third had to be sought.

On the opposite side of the little canyon in which ran the river Dick, a cedar had blown down during a thunderstorm last summer, to my great grief, for it was a noble tree and left an ugly gash in the greenery. So I crossed the river by Bridge Street, and turning left into a maze of alleys, set to work to try and trace the house in whose garden it must have stood, in the hopes that I might be able to lay my hands on a few logs, honestly or otherwise.

This was the oldest and meanest part of the town and had been condemned by successive generations of sanitary inspectors, but as the owners were all town councillors, nothing ever came of it. I suppose local government is much the same wherever you go, and it is nothing to write home about, what I have seen of it. Anyway we had got as nasty a little slum as you could want, tucked away in a bend of the Dick at Dickford.

It seemed unlikely that any of these unlucky ones would run to cedars, but I persevered, and presently I came to a high wall of ancient brick, mellow and old, like my stable, with most of the mortar out of the courses, and wild snapdragons and mulleins and the remains of wallflowers clinging to the crevices. This looked promising, for that mellow red brick-work went with cedars.

I followed the alley that ran under the wall, and presently

came to a tumble-down dwelling of some dimensions that
presented its backside to the public gaze, as was the custom of
Queen Anne. I rang the bell, and was answered by the caretaker, a doddering old dame like my Sally Sampson gone to
seed. I told her what I wanted, and she told me that the old
lady, the last of the line, was dead, and she was caretaking for
the distant heirs; half a crown changed hands, and the cedar
was mine. I found out who were the distant heirs, for I guessed
that the old place would go for a song owing to the slum
around it. But, thought I to myself, if, having bought it for a
song, I cannot ginger up the town council into doing something about the slum, I'm a half-wit. Thus does the worthy
house-agent make his humble living.

I went out to view the corpse. It was a Lebanon cedar and
I reckoned it would do very nicely, so arranged to have it
sawn up and carted out to Trethowen at the farm, whence
he could haul it in penny numbers in his chug-cart along with
Mrs Treth and the brooms, for I had no mind that any Dick-
fordian should set eyes on Morgan. I had got to live in the
blasted town.

The house was full of Benares brass, and foxes' masks, and
unskilful water-colours of ships of the line in full sail, very
correct as to nautical details, and assorted swords all up the
staircase; so one could see just the sort of family it had been,
serving king and country for generations, and dying out in
consequence, till only one old lady was left, and as she couldn't
serve her country she survived to be ninety.

There were a number of faded sketches of the Lebanon and
its cedars, and the old dame told me that the fallen cedar had
been grown from seed brought home by a son of the house.
It was a curious thought that here in English soil had grown
the seed that had ripened under Arabian suns, and that dead-
alive Dickford had a living link with the ancient East. The

old dame showed me a picture of the tree that was the ancestor of their tree, and I think it must have remembered the Crusaders, or—more agreeable memory—Saladin.

So I left her to arrange with her agricultural offspring to saw up the logs, they being glad of the job, and took the car up on to the hills behind Dickford where I knew juniper grew, juniper being a plant of the chalk. It was a clear day, and as I drove along the road on the ridge I could distinctly see the farm at the foot of Bell Head, freshly whitewashed by Trethowen; but the fort I could not see, for it was hidden by the bend of the down, which, as I have said before, curves like a banana. I was glad of this, for distant as it was, I did not wish either Dickford or Dickmouth to overlook the sea-palace of Morgan le Fay. Starber, humble little fishing village, was a different matter, I do not know why.

Presently I saw beside the way an ancient gentleman repairing the dry-stone walling. Him I accosted and explained my desires. He said juniper burned very badly, with sparks and sputterings. I said it didn't matter. He said he had never heard of such a thing as cutting and carting juniper for burning. I said that didn't matter either. He shook his ancient and infested head and said he didn't think it could be done. I asked him why, and he didn't know, but continued to shake his head. What a country to die for!

I drove on a little further and came to a camp of gipsies; so I thought I would have a word with them, and see if I could persuade them to steal the old gentleman's juniper as he wouldn't part with it honestly. Needless to say they did not need much persuading. Then an old dame crawled out of a tent and wanted to tell my fortune. I agreed, for I have a weakness for gipsies; they have broken away from the haunts of men as I would like to do. So she produced a pack of cards as ancient and tattered as herself, and bid me take one, which

I did gingerly, glanced at it, and found that I held in my hand the portrait of Morgan le Fay as I had seen her sitting on the high stern-poop of the ship that brought her to Ishtar's Beere. There she sat, in her great carved chair with a book on her knee; and behind her were strange fruit, pomegranates, I think, and under her feet the moon. It gave me quite a turn; the old girl saw it, and asked me to take another. This I did, and it proved to be the Hanged Man—a knave hung up by the heels to a kind of gallows, with a halo round his head and a tranquil expression on his face. I crossed the old dame's palm with silver, and she told me that there was a woman in my life who would sacrifice me for her own ends.

("Tell us something we don't know, mother!") thought I to myself.

Then I had bread and cheese and beer at a pub at the cross-roads, it being far enough away from Dickford not to upset my sister's Band of Hope, and went on to Bristol.

Bristol is a peculiar port, and one for which I have a great affection, for the ships come up into the town in an intimate and agreeable manner, and one can walk under a bowsprit that only just gives sufficient clearance for the trams. So I left the car on the quay and hopped over the cobbles seeking sandal-wood.

Now sandal-wood sawdust is easy to get but darned hard to burn; what I wanted was sandal-wood chips, or better still, bits of board that could be broken up. I was looking for a curiosity shop, and presently, between establishments where they sell oilskins and save souls, I found it.

It was a genuine bit of old Bristol. I only just missed going through into the cellar. The small-paned window was packed so full of undusted junk that it was impossible to see what was there; and it was all unpriced, save for some picture post-cards, very vulgar, and in my opinion, very dear, being twopence each. We have much ruder ones in Dickford for a penny.

I went in, and some stones in a cocoa-tin tied to the door-handle announced my entry. Out came a great obese spider of a man from the room behind the shop, whose half-glass door was carefully curtained. His eyes brightened when he saw me, thinking I wanted post-cards, or what they stood for. I told him my needs, and he registered disappointment in human nature in general and mine in particular. However, I gave him a bob, and he sent me down the street to knock at the door of a tumbledown warehouse; the whole street, in fact, looked as if it were in imminent danger of falling into the dock, which in my opinion was the best thing that could have happened to it.

A Eurasian youth admitted me, and ushered me into a little office where I found myself face to face with a Mongolian of some sort, but not, I think, a Chinaman. There was no difficulty whatever in obtaining what I wanted here, and I was immediately supplied from stock with neat little packets of sandal-wood done up like kindling, and I don't fancy he charged me more than the proper price for them, though they were not cheap. I wondered greatly who burnt this expensive wood, and why? Also what he imagined I meant to do with it, for he expressed no surprise and asked no questions.

Then I drove home and had the hell of a row with my sister over the dinner. If there is one thing that lays me out quicker than another it is pork in the evening, and yet she will give it to me. This pork was under-done, too. Then I went out to the "George" to seek something edible, and called in at the butcher's on the way, and told him if he delivered any more pork at my house I would close the account and buy foreign. He grinned. There are times when I even surprise myself.

I had a very good evening at the "George" in the commercial

room, and made up my mind I would dine there in future, and have a glass of wine with my dinner in peace—and may God have mercy on the Friendly Girls, and the Band of Hope, and anything else that needs it. The idea of setting a good example has always been a very odd one to me, and I could never understand why we did it; for we do not dispense charity lavishly, so why should anyone take any notice of us? Personally, I never found they did.

The next three days I was at a sale, not auctioneering, which I hate, but buying on behalf of a big Bond Street dealer, which I enjoy. On the third day he turned up in person, after the pictures, which I won't tackle, and I dined with him when the sale was over in a private room at the "George". They do you well at the "George"; the proprietor's mother does the cooking and I choose the wines. Mind you, it is stodge; plain roasts and boileds and fruit-pies and such-like, but it takes a lot of beating because the family live with the business. There is some very fine linen-fold panelling in the private room, too, which my pal wanted to buy, but they wouldn't part. We could hear grandma from the kitchen saying they weren't to. We knew it was no use then. After dinner, I took him round to my place and tried Morgan le Fay's personally-imported wines on him, and helped him home as it got light. After that I took the day off, too, and then it was the week-end again.

CHAPTER XVI

WHEN I drove out to the fort on Friday evening my car smelt like an Eastern temple, for all the sandal-wood was in the back. Mr Treth I found very indignant, with his hair full of juniper and a black eye. Knowing gipsies, I had not paid them for the juniper, but given them a note to Treth telling him to pay them the agreed price and I would settle up with him; and they had had a shot at altering the figures and made a mess of it, resulting in a blot which no one could decipher. So he assessed the job at his own price, and told them to take it or take their load home. His price was considerably less than the one that had originally been on the chit, and they felt injured. So they knocked him down and tipped the juniper on top of him and it was only his spouse's zeal that had saved him from being smothered. She was applying a bit of steak to his eye when I arrived.

I helped him shove the juniper in the chug-cart, and the procession started. A good deal of the cedar had already gone out, and I saw by the state of the road how the old boy had laboured. A cedar goes a long way when cut up, but I found it difficult to believe that all those logs came from one tree, and have a suspicion that the caretaker's enterprising offspring had been buying up all the cedars in the district. The inside of an agricultural labourer's head is often a lot smarter than the outside along his own line of country.

Morgan put her nose inside the car and snuffed up the sandal-wood and was ravished, and said it reminded her of Kashmir, and that my pseudo-Chinese was probably a Tibetan. Anyway, we had high hopes of the Fire of Azrael, and she cooked me the steak that was left over from Trethowen's eye. We walked out arm in arm to the point and considered the sea, which was calm; and then we came in and she made me coffee, and I played with her star sapphires by fire-light, watching the change and stir of the star of light within them.

We spent Sunday morning strolling over the down to the sound of the bells of Starber, getting the lie of the land well into our heads in preparation for the great event.

Bell Head sticks straight out into the sea, pointing towards America, and when the wind is westerly the great Atlantic rollers come driving in without let or hindrance, which is why we have such heavy seas on the point. It is formed of cocked-up strata, lying slab-like one upon another; this gives a steep drop along the exposed edges of the strata, forming a ledged precipice. The top is weathered fairly flat, and rises whale-like to the highest point above the precipice that faces the land. Then there is a narrow neck of detritus connecting what was probably once an island with the mainland, beside which lies the ancient channel of the river Dick, now a runnel in wet weather and dry at other times, being fed from no source.

About five miles to the north is Dickmouth, and three to the south is Starber. All between the two is a marsh filled with tidal channels. In the middle of the marsh rises Bell Knowle.

By the crying of gulls over the water and the cackle of jackdaws on the ledges we judged that the weather was due for a change. That evening Mrs Treth cleared the ashes of driftwood off the hearth and we laid the Fire of Azrael, invoking the dark Angel of the Doors that he would permit egress.

Cedar is a lovely-burning wood, and sandal takes the flame well, too, but we soon saw why juniper was not recommended as fuel. It was fascinating, however, to watch the flame creep from twig to twig and see the flying shower of golden sparks as the sap-filled cells burst with the heat. But as the fire died down it cleared, and the juniper produced a curious pale charcoal of its own, the ashes of the twigs lying in fine golden lines among the redder embers of the other woods. It was a fire of great beauty; no one has yet done justice to the artistry of fires.

Then we settled down to look at it, Morgan le Fay with a note-book in her hand to record what we saw.

I gazed into the heart of the caves of flame, now flickering into redness and edged with grey ash, for a fire of juniper burns out quickly, and in their glowing folds saw the palaces of all the kings of earth. But it was not the sea-palaces I saw, which disappointed me. Then, a whiff of the sandal reaching me, I saw the immemorial East and heard temple bells and soft gongs and singing. I thought of the Tibetan who had served me, and wondered what he was doing in far-away Bristol, and who was the West Country woman he had married who had given him a Eurasian son.

And from him my mind went to the high plateau of his home, which had always interested me, and of which I had read; and I saw the cliffs and chasms surrounding that shattered land, tossed by the hands of the gods at the birth of the earth and unchanged ever since, where, some say, is the birthplace of the human race, and from whence the great rivers come down, along whose ways travelled civilisation. The men of the high bleak plateau are less changed since the dawn of time than any other peoples, and it may be that they know more of the mind of the gods than most. It pleased me that I had bought sandal-wood from a Tibetan in Bristol.

Every people believes that its high hills are the thrones of the gods, but in snowy Himalaya are the thrones of the gods that made the gods. It was meet that for the work of our magic we should have a link with the high plateau through the far-wandering Mongol who had sold me sandal on the Bristol water-front. There is something in these links, I am certain.

But we did not want to go back to the birth of the world, and I recalled my mind from the ancient East, returning by high Pamir down the Oxus, as they say the first wisdom of men travelled West with the Magi; and I saw all earth laid out below me as a map, for I was well away on the wings of phantasy, having passed out through the flaming caves of the Fire of Azrael into another dimension.

And I saw the city of Babylon between the twin rivers, where the maidens of Israel hung their harps upon the willows and Belteshazzar learnt the wisdom of the stars. And I came still towards the West, following my star, which shifted and glowed in the great sapphire on the breast of Morgan le Fay. I came to the land of the people who worship the stars, to whom the Pole Star is holy as the centre of heaven. Their god is the Lord of This World, the Peacock Angel. Then I saw the black tents of the wanderers of Chaldea, whose fathers had known Abraham and whose flocks still pasture in the valleys where the kings had fought, four against five—Amraphel, king of Shinar; Arioch, king of Ellasar; Chedorlaomer, king of Elam and Tidal, king of nations. I remembered also who came to meet them, bearing bread and wine; and then I saw the immemorial cedars of high Lebanon, where it may be his foot had passed.

I remembered that Morgan had told me that here was the fountain-head of the wisdom of the West, only less ancient than the gods of Himalaya. But senior to both was the sea-wisdom of Atlantis. And I voyaged in vision by the peaks of Atlas and the high hills of Thessaly, famous for witches, across the Baltic barrens whence our race came, to our own land at last, and then I saw the juniper twigs pale and bright amid the embers of cedar and sandal.

Now the juniper is of more ancient lineage than the yew, and belongs to the chalk whence civilisation arose in these islands. It is the tree of the old gods, more ancient than oak or ash, the Nordic hawthorn or the Keltic mistletoe, for it was a sacred tree to the people of the river-drift, who were older than the people of the flint. To them came the far-voyaging Atlanteans, and they it was who worshipped the Mother Goddess. And I knew that the fires that burnt at uttermost neap were Fires of Azrael, lit for vision as well as sacrifice, and that they were of juniper.

Then there awoke for me the ancient civilisation in all its glory, and I saw first the mountain like a truncated cone on which was built the City of the Golden Gates of the island of Ruta in the lost land of Atlantis, and it put me in mind of Bell Knowle.

I saw the great cone burst once again into flames, for it was a volcano; and all Atlantis went down in one fiery death—all the temples where they worshipped themselves and gave their slaves to unnamable evil; all the golden-roofed city of wisdom and abomination, more wicked than Babylon, shining like a jewel in the dawn with its roofs of aurichalcum which is like pale gold. And I saw in that last dawn of the ancient world three great tidal waves sweep in and swallow all; and far out to sea, riding them, was a narrow sea-ship, high-pooped, high-prowed, with a crimson dragon embroidered on its purple sail, its prow set towards the east by the golden pathway of the dawn upon the waters; chained rowers toiled at the oars in the morning calm, and over lost Atlantis with all its wickedness and wisdom the waters closed for ever, for the gods hated it for its abominations. Nothing remained save a few floating things and those that clung to them, more luckless than the others for whom death had been speedy, for when the high gods call it is best to go swiftly. Then Morgan le Fay aroused me, saying it was enough.

The Fire of Azrael had sunk to grey ash, but the night was mild, so we went out again on to the point to look at the sea by moonlight, for the sky was clear overhead though dark clouds were massing in the west and slowly moving up and masking the stars. Then we went in to bed and slept very sweetly, for there is a deep peace after these experiences, shot through with faint shadows of reflected dreams.

On Monday morning I went back to Dickford and had the hell and Hades of a row with my sister over taking my meals at the "George"; and I went all round the town, and stopped all credit at all the shops, and gave her five pounds a week and told her to pay cash and manage on that, for it was all she'd get, and if she couldn't behave decently, she wouldn't get that. Tuesday morning she blew up again, so I took back ten bob and left her with four pound ten. After that she was quiet. All the same, I had asthma for the rest of the week and my mother said God was displeased with me. Perhaps He was, for old Sally was ailing too, though why God should concern Himself in these matters I have never been able to understand. Why couldn't He leave us to fight it out among ourselves? I refused to meddle when the office boy cut choir practice. It has always puzzled me, too, how God finds time for it all. And anyway, if He must interfere, why doesn't He interfere effectually, instead of pursuing a policy of pin-pricks?

CHAPTER XVII

M Y asthma bothered me a lot all the week without actually laying me up, and when I drove out to the fort I was feeling rotten. I had hardly set foot in the place before I started up a row with Morgan le Fay, saying that if she didn't like me well enough to marry me, we had better part and be done with it, for we couldn't go on as we were, at least, I couldn't.

She sat down on the low stool by the sofa on which she had put me, and took my hand, and began to talk to me quietly; when she had finished I understood a lot of things I had not understood before; some of them were sweet, and some of them were wonderful, and some of them were very bitter to me.

She told me how, through her acquaintance with the Priest of the Moon who had come to her in the crystal, she had learnt a strange lore, lost since the world grew wise, or thought it did. This was the inner, intuitive wisdom of the ancients and of primitive people to this day. She said how the soul was of ancient lineage, coming to earth again and again, learning the lessons of earth and finally winning to freedom; and there were some souls, that, having no more need of the lessons of earth, came not to learn but to teach, and she believed that she was one of these. They were not, she said, of ordinary birth, but magically incarnated, biding their time till conditions were right and then slipping in. It was the mingling of Breton and Welsh that had made the conditions wherein the strange soul that was hers could come, for she believed that she had actually been Morgan le Fay, King Arthur's witch sister, and that Merlin had been her foster-father.

The mother of Arthur, Uther's queen, was a sea-princess of Atlantis, so she told me, married to a brutish husband for the sake of trade, so that the ports of the Tin Islands might be open to her father's people. Merlin, who was of the priest-hood of Atlantis, came to Britain with the tin-ships to conduct the worship, and Bell Knowle, being like the sacred mountain of the mother state, had been adapted to their purpose. After the death of Uther the sea-princess had gone back to her own people, and had married a man of the sacred clan and borne a daughter.

Now this daughter, as the custom was among them, had been taken to be trained in the House of the Virgins; for all children of the sacred clan were brought to the great temple at the time of the winter solstice in the year in which they attained the age of seven, and those that were deemed worthy were taken into the temple precincts to be trained; those that were not so chosen were handed back to their families till they attained the age of fourteen, and then the males were made scribes or warriors as they should choose, and the maidens were given in marriage to the men of the sacred clan; and it was death for one of the sacred blood to mate outside the clan, and death by torture for him who took her. Very strictly did they guard the sacred blood, for it held the power of vision.

But the priestesses were not married to any man, but mated with the priests as was required for magical purposes.

And Morgan le Fay told me how she grew to womanhood in the House of the Virgins, tended and guarded as a queen bee is guarded, knowing herself to be set apart, and that the joys and ties of human life were not for her; and when she was reborn as the child of Breton and Kelt the memory remained with her, and no human ties held her. There were times, she said, when as a young girl she looked for love, but her destiny forbade it; and presently she realised her destiny and accepted it, and then life was easier. But it could never have been very easy, I think, for she was in this life, but not of it.

Then, with the coming of the power of vision came awakening memory and the return of forgotten knowledge. She knew herself for a priestess, with the powers of the priesthood latent in her soul. But there was none to teach and train her, none to awaken her powers, save the Priest of the Moon who came in the crystal, and he was not of this world.

Little by little she learnt and built, always handicapped by the fact that the moon-magic requires a partner, and partners were hard to find.

So, thought I, I was right when I felt I was cast for the part of sacrificed slave; and I wondered whether Morgan was like the surgeon who spoilt his hatful of eyes in learning to operate for cataract.

I asked her point-blank what was the exact job of the sea-priestess's partner, and what became of him in the end, and was he sacrificed?

She said, in a way yes, and in a way no, and that was all she would tell me. The sea-priestess it seemed, was a kind of pythoness, and the gods spoke through her. Being a pythoness, she was negative, passive; she did not make magic herself, but was an instrument in the hands of the priests, and however perfect an instrument she might be, there was no use in her if there were no one to use her.

"Then what you need," said I, "is a properly trained priest as impressario."

"Precisely," said she.

"Where are you going to find him?" said I.

"That is my problem," said she.

Then I knew why she wouldn't marry me.

"But I am not worrying," said she. "In these matters the road opens before you as you advance. Take the next step, and the next one becomes plain."

"And what is the next step?" said I.

"The next step," said she, staring into the fire and not looking at me, "is to complete my own training."

"That being——?" said I.

"To make the magical image of myself as a sea-priestess."

I asked her if I were to do the carving, and if so, how? for I could no more do figures than I could fly.

She shook her head. "A magical image does not exist upon this plane at all," she said. "It is in another dimension, and we make it with the imagination. And for that," said she, "I need help, for I cannot do it alone. If I could, I would have done it long ago."

"Are you counting on me for that?" said I.

"Yes," said she.

It was on the tip of my tongue to ask her if I should see about getting the sea-cave of Bell Knowle opened up, the cave where the tide rose and fell to receive its sacrifice; but I kept silent, knowing that was the way to learn most, rather than by showing that I had guessed anything.

"For me to make a magical image by myself is auto-suggestion," said she, "and begins and ends subjectively. But when two or three of us get to work together, and you picture me as I picture myself, then things begin to happen. Your suggestion aids my auto-suggestion, and then—then it passes outside ourselves, and things begin to build up in the astral ethers, and they are the channels of forces."

"Gosh!" said I, to whom all this was Greek, "do you need anything more from me than I am already giving you?"

"Not a great deal," said she. "The magical image has built

up rapidly since I have known you because you believe in me, and because you are willing to make sacrifices."

I asked her what she meant, and she told me that these magical images are built up by the imagination; when I thought of her as a priestess, she became a priestess.

"And what has sacrifice to do with the business?" said I, wondering in what manner the blow would fall when the time came.

"It gives off magical power," said she. "You can do nothing in magic without it."

"What exactly do you mean, Morgan?" said I, hoping it was sheep she used and that I was not being asked to participate in a crime; for although I thought very highly of Morgan, I knew there was not much she would stick at.

"It is difficult to explain," she replied, "for different kinds of sacrifices have to be made to different kinds of gods. You have to give something of yourself along whatever line it is."

"Oh?" said I, more relieved than I cared to admit, "Then we don't sacrifice someone on the altar and use his gore?"

"No," said she, shaking her head. "No one can sacrifice for another. We each sacrifice ourselves, and thereby gain the power to give magical help to each other. I can't put it any clearer than that, because you wouldn't understand; but you will see how it works out step by step in practice, even in spheres where we have no control.

"We have travelled some distance already," she added, "you have already made a priestess of me, for you have given me a great deal, Wilfred, perhaps more than you know, and I shall always be grateful to you, however things may turn out."

I hastily changed the subject, for nothing embarrasses me so much as being thanked.

"Wasn't it this making of magical images they got drowned for in lost Atlantis?" I asked.

"It was the abuse of this power," said she. And she told me how the making of the magical images was originally the prerogative of the priesthood and they being all dedicated to the gods and free from all ties and desires, never were under any temptation to use their knowledge for selfish ends. But boys would be boys in old Atlantis, the same as here, and some of the young priests in each generation went over the garden wall by night, and the same thing occurred as happened when a misguided maiden lady introduced her dachshund among the terriers of Kerry. In the end the gods drowned Atlantis, which I believe was what the men of Kerry had to do with their terriers.

Now, thought I to myself, since she wanted me to build the magical image, and the magical image is now built, what is the next item on the programme? For, all assurances to the contrary, I felt perfectly certain the golden knife was coming my way in the end. So I put the question point-blank, and asked her if she had any further use for me when once her sea-palace was finished and her magical image in working order.

"There will always be a welcome for you here," she said. "I do not drop old friends."

"That is very kind of you," said I.

"I am beginning to sympathise with your sister," said she.

"Try my life for a bit, Morgan le Fay," I said, "and see if it sweetens the temper."

"Well, what *do* you want?" said she.

"What every normal human being wants," said I. "Fulfilment. To feel one is getting somewhere—doing something with one's life. Ought I to be content with supporting my mother and sister?"

She looked into the fire for a long time without speaking.

"Is life dear to you, Wilfred?" she said at length.

"About as dear as the wife of one's bosom," I said. "We lead a cat and dog existence, life and I, but it would be a wrench to part."

"I could use you," she said, "very ruthlessly, very riskily, and after I had finished with your life, there mightn't be very much change left to hand back to you. But if you care to take the risk, I could, I think, give you fullness of life for a short time: after that—I do not know."

"And I don't care," said I. "Anything is better than the way we are going on at present, which is the half of nothing."

"Then you would like to try it?"

"I'll try anything once," said I.

She smiled. "You certainly won't try this twice if it isn't a success," said she.

She took the poker in her hand and pushed the flaming driftwood to either side, and in the hollow centre thus left she piled the woods of the Fire of Azrael. Then we sat and watched them take the flame.

"This time," said she, "try to find and follow the ship you saw leaving Atlantis."

I watched the flame and waited, and presently the coals grew clear and in the hollows appeared the whitish glow of lambent heat that comes from the fierce-burning juniper as it dies down. I watched it, and gradually it turned to the golden light of dawn upon the waves, and there was the long sea-ship with the dragon sail. I watched her as she travelled towards the east, and saw the sun rise over her and sink behind her and saw the stars wheel through the heavens. Then I saw the steep high peak of Teneriffe, as I had seen it in pictures, and the sea-ship lay at anchor below it.

Then the scene changed, and I saw our marsh around Bell Knowle, much as it is to-day; but behind it, where now are farms, was open moor. Then I saw the difference. The

shallow channel of the Dick was full to brimming, and beside
a stone quay a long sea-ship was moored.

I knew then that I was back in the old days, and that this
vision was different from the other visions, for I was not an on-
looker but part of it. I knew that I had been down to the shore
to light the beacon for the guidance of the incoming ship, and
that the fascination of the strange priestress, glimpsed for that
passing moment in the mist, had caused me to follow her boat
inland till it came to the quay below the cave of Bell Knowle.
I followed it against my better judgment; but this was a
woman like no woman that I had ever seen, or ever hoped to
see. I had heard the tale of the sacrifices the sea required—
sacrifices of men; and the eyes of the priestess were cold yet
desirous, and I thought that in passing they had noted me. I
knew that I should be wise to keep away; that it was not good
that those cold bright eyes should see me again; nevertheless
I went, following the sea-boat up the winding river to the quay
below the cave, where I saw the priestess land, stepping ashore
with the same lithe, balancing grace with which Morgan le Fay
walked over the rocks, and I knew that they were one and the
same woman.

Then the scene changed to night, and I was among those
who gathered around the mouth of the fire-lit cave to watch
what was going on within. The sea-priestess was seated at a
high table, and around her were shaven-headed men—her
priests, and some other men, bearded and armed, that looked
like fighting men or chieftains; and they, I thought looked
unhappy and more than half afraid, for there was something
sinister about all these shaven, pallid, parchment-faces, with
cold eyes and cruel resolute lips, like men accustomed to terrible things. The sea-priestess looked at them with indiffer-
ence, as if inured to the terrors of their cult, and the bearded
chiefs watched her covertly and with fear.

I knew that these chiefs, at the bidding of the priesthood of
Bell Head, had sent for the sea-priestess in order that she might
offer the terrible sacrifices which alone could appease the sea;
and now they dreaded what they had done, for they had let
blood loose in the land and none knew where it would end;
for there is a blood-madness that comes upon men, and once
they start to kill they cannot stop; and these bearded men,
inured to wounds and war, nevertheless dreaded the calm pas-
sionless killing of the priests. I knew, too, that such as I,
young men in their strength who had not known women,
would be the acceptable sacrifice that the cold sea-priestess
would choose, and that the bearded chiefs were wondering
each one whether he would be called upon to offer up a son
or sons, for the best in the land must be given to the gods. And
as I stood there in the crowd about the cave-mouth, I met the
eyes of the sea-priestess once again, and it seemed to me that
by such a woman it would be good even to be sacrificed.

They were dining at the high table, and when the meal was
finished and the débris flung to the dogs, as the custom was,
a great bowl was carried in and placed in the centre of the
table; it was not of the bright gold such as we know to-day,
but the pale aurichalcum that was used in Atlantis, and it was
richly wrought with waves of the sea, and strange fabulous
beasts and dragons; and around the rim was a band of precious
stones, cabochon-cut, that caught the light. I knew that this
was a sacred Cup, the prototype of the Graal. Into it from a
high ewer of similar workmanship was poured a dark and
aromatic wine; then a brand was flung in that set it alight,
and the surface burned with thin blue flickering flames. They
ladled the blazing liquid into golden cups, and as the flames
died down, the company drank. This wine, I knew, was made
from the small, black-graped vines that grew on the vine-
terraces under the breast of Bell Head, and in it were infused

aromatic herbs that were grown upon the topmost terrace where the breast of the rock reflected the heat upon them and drew out their volatile oils.

Then the scene changed again, and I was along the quays of Ishtar's Beere in the sunlight, marvelling at the dark, far-travelled mariners with curled beards and golden rings.

Down the crowded quays there came a small band that moved in military formation. Half a dozen spearmen, and a captain with a short, broad, leaf-like sword, and an elderly shaven priest with a parchment skin and dark, bright, lashless eyes under his hairless brows, for it was part of their religion to remove all hair from the body.

People fell back respectfully to give them passage; but while no one actually fled before them, the crowd melted away down alleys and byways till none were left but the staring sailors and a few beggars and hucksters. The crowded quays became empty as the small band went by.

But swiftly as folk slipped away, they did go so swiftly but that the priest had time to look them over; and here and there he raised a finger and pointed, and the soldiers advanced and closed round one or another and returned with him to the band. There was no protest, no struggle; once a woman cried out as her son was taken, but her cries were quickly stifled by those around her. Folk slipped away if they could, but if they could not, they went quietly; for this band of the high priest was picking up the sacrifices for the sea, and it was an evil omen if a man resisted, and would bring the wrath of the sea upon the whole people. Moreover, the man who was chosen was extraordinarily fortunate, for he went to an eternity of bliss in the sea-palaces, where the fairest of the sea-women were his, and the pearls of the sea and her gems, and richest food and finest drink in all abundance. Moreover, all his kin were blessed unto the second and third generation, and the king rewarded them with grants of land and gifts of jewels. Yes, it was indeed a very fortunate thing to be chosen as a sacrifice, and those so chosen were greatly honoured, and each one could ask for what he would on the eve of his death, and it was granted him. There was only one thing that was refused him, and that was mercy.

Now I know not what madness possessed me, but it seemed to me, having seen this priestess, that there was no other under the sun that could be a woman to me; and as the band of the high priest went by, I put myself in their way, and in a fever of anxiety, even as those who strove to avoid his notice, I sought it. His dark bright eyes met mine, and with as much eagerness as one who seeks for a reprieve, I saw his finger raised. The guards closed round me, and I joined the band.

Then the scene changed again, and I was back once more in the cave under Bell Knowle, lit by the fires, but this time I was seated at the high table, I and two others, and facing me was the sea-priestess in her great carved chair, and upon her right was the high priest, parchment-faced and shaven, and upon her left the high king, bronzed and bearded; and between them she sat and smiled at me, and she was even lovelier than I had thought, so that I felt well repaid for my sacrifice. I feasted and drank with joy in my heart, though those upon my either hand made no pretence at eating. And when the flaming wine came round I pledged the priestess with such joy that all present looked at me strangely, and the priestess smiled her slow, amused smile that had no feeling in it, for she had seen very many men die as I was about to die.

Now it was ordained that no man should know the hour of his death till it came, lest, it was thought, his last hours should be clouded, for the sea liked her sacrifices in the full vigour of their manhood. Therefore each night three dined at the high table, and of these three, two should go free and one should

die, therefore all had hope, so that the life ran high in them.
None knew who should die, not even the sea-priestess; for
three cups were prepared and filled with the flaming wine,
but in one was a pearl, and whoso received the pearl was the
one to die. Upon either side of me the men sipped slowly,
hardly able to swallow; but I flung down the wine at one
draught, and upon my lips I felt the pearl. I turned down the
empty cup, and cried "I am the sacrifice!" and the pearl fell
out upon the board and rolled towards the priestess, and her
red lips curled in a smile as her hand closed over it.

Then all present held out their cups towards me and hailed
me as chosen of the sea. And the chief priest and the high
king together asked me my last wish, pledging themselves that
it should be granted—and I asked for the priestess!

Then there was confusion among them, for such a thing
had never been known before. Men asked for lands for their
family, or for their wives to die with them, or for vengeance
on an enemy, but such a thing as this had never been heard
of and they did not know what to do, for she was of the sacred
clan and the punishment for taking her was death by torture.

But I smiled and said that that was my wish, and were it
not granted I would carry ill tales of them to the sea-gods to
whom I was going; and the priestess smiled also, and I judged
that she was not ill content. But the high priest was white
with wrath, and I know not what he would have done if the
king had not struck his hand upon the board and said that a
pledge was a pledge, and must be kept, else should I go free.
But the high priest said that they dared not deny the sea-gods
the sacrifice they had set their seal upon, lest worse befall the
land than had already fallen; die I must, and die I should.
It is in my mind that the high king was well pleased of an
opportunity to humiliate the priesthood and maybe put a
check upon the bloody worship he had let loose in the land.

Then the high priest, smiling grimly, said that the law of the sacred clan decreed death for her who mixed the blood, and death by torture for him who took her.

"So let it be," said the high king, looking well content that he would see the last of the sea-priestess and her sacrifices. But the high priest looked mad with wrath, for he had no mind to destroy his priestess; but he put a good face on it, and smiled his smile, which was more terrible than other men's frowns, and said that it should be as I wished, the pledge would be kept. I should possess the priestess till the tide rose, and then I should see death coming with open eyes, instead of drinking the drugged wine as was the custom; for it might justly be reckoned that a death by slow drowning was a death by torture if one went to it in full consciousness, and so both laws would be fulfilled. And turning to me, he asked me was I willing, and would I pledge myself not to disgrace them all by going to the sea-gods struggling? And I swore that I would.

Then from the centre of the cavern they turned back the rich carpets that covered the stone, and revealed a great ringbolt set in a flag of the floor; two slaves passed a bar through it and raised it, disclosing a stair; and the priestess, still smiling, took a torch in her hand and descended, I following.

We went down a winding stair of steps roughly cut in the rock till we came to a natural cave, low of roof and floored with sand, and I guessed we were at the river level, for the sand and the walls were wet and weed-clad. In the centre was a rectangular block whose length was twice its breadth and whose height equalled its width; this was the altar of sacrifice whereon the one who was given to the sea awaited her coming. But whereas they that had gone before had lain thereon so drugged that they knew not who came, I was to await the water open-eyed, for this was my punishment for my presumption.

And in those hours while the tide rose there were delivered to me things whereof but few have dreamed and fewer still have known, and I learnt why Troy was burnt for a woman. For this woman was not one woman, but all women; and I, who mated with her, was not one man, but all men; but these things were part of the lore of the priesthood, and it is not lawful to speak of them. And through my bliss I heard the wash of the waves coming closer. Then when the water reached our feet the priestess kissed me and left me. And presently the water rose over me, and I fought for breath between the ripples till finally I breathed no more.

And as the vision darkened into death, I awoke, and as I woke, I knew the asthma had me by the throat.

CHAPTER XVIII

I SHALL never forget that attack so long as I live. I have never had one like it, before or since. Morgan le Fay, who knew by previous experience what to expect, got straight into her car and went for a doctor. I had made her open the windows before she left me so that I could get as much air as possible, and as I lay alone I heard between spasms a curious low moaning note in the sea that I had never heard before. I knew that the barometer had been falling rapidly all day, and I wondered whether this sound heralded the storm. A gust of wind bellowed in the chimney, setting the ash dancing on the hearth, and there began a high shrill whistling overhead; then the first of the rollers struck the rocks with a boom and I heard the over-carried spray come pattering down in the forecourt. I realised that there was trouble afoot of a kind we had never weathered before out at the fort, though we had already been through some pretty good blows. I wondered whether Morgan would be able to get back to me, and whether the doctor would be able to make it, and got into a sudden panic at the idea of being left there alone and unhelped all night.

I lay fighting for breath and listening to the steadily growing thunder on the rocks and the pelt of the spray in the forecourt. Presently it sounded to me as if something more solid than spray were coming over. From where I lay I could just see out through one of the big windows, and all of a sudden I saw the gleam of water outside. I don't suppose it was more than ankle-deep in the forecourt, but the sight of it threw me into a complete panic. I felt it was impossible for Morgan le Fay to get back, and that I should be alone all night. I got to my feet and struggled across the room to the window, and stood leaning against the pillar and looking out into the night. It was pretty dark, but in the light that shone out from the room I could see the foam going high up in the air as the breakers hit the rocks. It was a terrific night, and every minute it was getting worse.

I had made up my mind it was impossible for Morgan le Fay to get back to me, and that I had got to stick it out alone, when I saw a beam of light come wheeling into the forecourt, and knew that it was the headlights of her car. The din outside was such that I did not hear her enter the room, and the first thing I heard was her cry as she discovered the empty couch and made up her mind that I had gone out into the storm. I came out from behind the curtains looking like my own ghost, and she called my name and rushed at me and caught hold of me, to my very great surprise, for I had no notion she felt like that about me, and was almost forgetting my asthma in wondering what it meant, when another paroxysm came on and reminded me. Then, over her shoulder I saw the doctor, who looked as if he too were wondering what it meant, and between them they got me on to the sofa.

I do not think that any of us who went through that night out at the fort will ever forget it. It was, in any case, one of the worst storms that ever swept England, and the wind was just a point or two south of west, which meant that the waves came on to the fort with the whole force of the Atlantic behind them. It was like a bombardment. Even lying on a bed upstairs I could feel the jarring thud as the tremendous combers hit the end wall. The storm rose with the tide, and towards midnight it was at its height. There was no question of the doctor getting back; here he was, and here he had to stop.

The forecourt was swamped, but, thank God, it was only the wind-blown crests and not the solid body of the waves that was coming over; and the windows held, which was lucky, for the pergola went to glory and I was afraid that chunks of it would get thrown at them by the force of the wind.

The din was indescribable. There was the high shrill screeching of the gale, every pinnacle of rock and point of the building whistling its own note; then there was the general roar of the sea all round us, and the thundering bang, bang, bang, as the breakers hit the point broadside on; there was a furious rushing sound as the broken water raced up the rocks, and the smack and spatter of the crests of the waves coming over into the forecourt. I have never heard anything like it in all my days.

There is something shattering about very loud noise anyway, even when there is no actual danger; but we did not know what was going to happen out there on the point, for if the sea had once succeeded in knocking a gap in any of the embrasures, there was a very good chance of our being drowned out, like lost Atlantis. And it came pretty near doing it, too, as I discovered when I climbed round the footings a week later and found the underpinning pulled out in half a dozen places.

So there we were, out on the point in the din and the darkness, and then, to add to the gaiety of nations, my heart began to give out. I had the best of it after that, for I slipped into unconsciousness, leaving the other folk to get on with it.

It was then I met the sea-gods. It seemed to me that I was out of my body, floating upright and clad in a shroud. I was hung in mid-air over the fort, and though the din and uproar of the storm were all around me, I did not feel its force, for I was of another dimension to the warring elements. There was a fitful moonlight coming and going amid the wind-torn clouds; when it shone, I could see rank upon rank of white-crested billows driving in from the Atlantic, rising and falling in long regular lines like galloping cavalry; then, off the point, where the currents and tides took charge, everything broke up into a welter of foaming, roaring water, with squirts and boilings where the sunk reefs checked the rush. Then the moon would disappear behind jagged masses of cloud and in the darkness the roaring and thundering sounded louder than ever; then out she would come again as the driving gale swept the sky, and I could see the reef and all the sunken rocks roaring and spouting like fountains.

Then I noticed that in all the din there was a rhythm, and my ear began to pick out the tremendous orchestration of the storm; I could hear the deep-toned roar of the surf under the cliffs, and the clangour of the waves on the outlying rocks of the point, and the tenor of the roaring gale and high piccolo notes of the wind round the buildings. Through it all came clarion-calls and bells, which I suppose, if the truth were known, were the drugs singing in my head, but which I thought were psychic phenomena. In my delirium I rode the gale as a sea-gull rides, balancing against the pressure of the wind.

And then the faces began to appear in the waves, and out of the wind-whipped foam and the shadows forms built themselves up, and I saw that the white horses had riders.

Some had winged Viking helmets and armour, and some had wild flying robes and hair, and these last were the Choosers of the Slain, who caught up to their saddle-bows those whom the charging white horses rode down and bore them away to Valhalla; and behind these flying outriders, as the great surge follows the surf, I saw the sea-gods come, moving with an irresistible momentum, not rising into the air as the riders rose, but deep in their own element, unhasting, unresting; for the power of the sea is in the weight of the waters and not in the wind-blown crests. These Great Ones rose with the tide, and like the tide, nothing might withstand them. Their faces were vast and calm; they were the rulers of the great waters and in their realm their word was law. By their grace and not otherwise life moved on the surface or lived at the tide-mark, and only those might live who knew this.

And I saw with clear eyes the folly of men who thought they might master the sea. For only by grace of the sea-gods does man live upon the face of the land, for if they gathered themselves together in wrath they could drown the earth. And I saw that man's life is spun like a thread between irresistible forces that with a breath could destroy him, but that nevertheless, from them he draws his strength.

For there is in the earth a reservoir of elemental force, just as there is a fountain of life beyond the far stars, and from the violence of the sea the violence of man's own nature draws its energy even as he draws breath from the air, for all things are but one thing at the last analysis and there is no part of us that is not of the gods.

That within me which answered to the sea was awakened by the storm, and I knew that there can be in man a dynamic force that bears down opposition by sheer momentum; but this can only be in a man when he is as cruel as the sea and cares nothing for destruction or self-destruction, for the twin poles of this force are courage and cruelty, and there is a nobility about it that the world has forgotten in the cult of love.

With the turn of the tide the sea began to go down, and at peep of day the Dickmouth medico went off in his car and got a Bristol consultant on the phone, and likewise Beardmore, and in due course the whole party met at the fort and held what looked like being the beginnings of a post mortem on me. The Dickmouth man had got all sorts of fancy degrees and went by the book; old Beardmore had got the least that enabled him to sign a death certificate and went by human nature, and they wrangled over my body like a couple of hyenas. Beardmore was in the habit of shooting me full of morphia and chancing my dying on him, doing as he would be done by in like circumstances; the Dickmouth gent said that this was not according to Hoyle; then they began to reproach each other bitterly anent the Dangerous Drugs Act and I started to stop breathing. The consultant intervened then, and saved my life by agreeing with both parties impartially and shooting a squirtful of his own patent dope into me without telling them what it contained, and I slept till the following afternoon and woke up greatly cheered. I knew what that syringe contained all right, for you can't fool anyone who has once had morphia, but I kept my mouth shut. I had been nearer eternity than I quite fancied.

As always, I had a quick pick-up when Morgan le Fay was about or in the offing, for I do not get the ghastly depression that usually follows an attack; and Morgan was having tea with me, and I was reviving nicely, when suddenly we heard a commotion to the landward side of the fort, and shrieks of fury from Mrs Treth. Morgan went down to see what the fuss was about, and returned with Scottie. I could not understand why Scottie had caused so much excitement, and demanded further information, for I could see that Morgan was trying hard to stifle her smiles.

It transpired, in response to my questioning, that Beardmore had informed the family of my predicament, and my sister, with that martyred air I knew so well, had proposed putting aside her parish work and coming out to the fort to help nurse me; but Beardmore, whom may God reward, said she ought not to leave my mother and he would get Scottie to go instead.

Now Scottie did not run a car of his own, as I always tooled him about in mine whenever he wanted to go anywhere, and to hire a car to take him out to the fort would have cost a quid, which Scottie grudged greatly. So he hit on the bright idea of asking his father-in-law to run him out. Now Scottie's father-

in-law, as I think I have mentioned before, is the local undertaker, and he does not keep a private car either, but runs a
kind of pre-hearse in which he takes round the coffin and the
layers-out, and it was this thing, with a mute at the wheel, that
he and Scottie drove up in, for the old boy elected to come too,
though whether for the sake of the drive or with an eye to business, I do not know. So it was no wonder that Mrs Treth went
up in the air when she saw them arrive.

As soon as I heard old Whittles was there I made him come
up, for I like old Whittles. He came in, looking rather embarrassed, for he had never met a client at my stage of development before, and didn't know quite what line to take with him;
deprived of his tape-measure, he was at a loss. To put him at
his ease, I asked him what he generally did when the corpse sat
up and winked at him, and he said it depended entirely on
who it was—some folk he screwed down quick. Morgan gave
him a cocktail, and he settled down to cheer us with tales from
the tomb. I have never laughed so much in my life. An undertaker off duty and abreacting his repressions is really awfully
good fun. We could hear roars of laughter from the kitchen,
too, where the Treths were entertaining the mute. Then, in
the middle of it all, the Bristol consultant turned up again,
anxious to see what effect his injection had had on me, and
when he saw Whittles' equipage standing at the door, concluded he had polished me off, and got a most fearful wind up,
seeing his reputation going west. However, Morgan led him
in and soothed him with a cocktail, and then he too joined the
party upstairs, and there were more cocktails all round, and my
convalescence progressed by leaps and bounds.

It seemed that Whittles's grandfather, who founded the business, had started life as a body-snatcher. You should have seen
Scottie's face when this bit of information came out! However
the Bristol specialist put everybody at their ease by volunteering

the information that his grandfather had been a butcher. Not to be outdone, I told them of my ancestor who had been hanged for house-breaking. Then we had more cocktails all round and discussed the Mendelian theory of heredity. Finally, when the party broke up, Whittles and the specialist were such pals that Whittles offered to show him the short cut through the marshes, and they departed with Whittles's pre-hearse in the lead and the specialist's luxurious limousine following behind, which was a reversal of the usual order of things.

CHAPTER XIX

THE specialist had advised that owing to the state of my
heart I should not be allowed to get up for a week, a piece
of advice which I, in view of the state of that organ metaphorically as well as literally, was nothing loath to accept, and
a very enjoyable week it was. I won't go so far as to say that
I lay flat on my back for seven days, but anyway, I had a very
good holiday.

For the first couple of days I was naturally pretty glad to be
in bed, and I lay and listened to the swell that followed the
storm pounding away at the rocks like artillery; then there
came the most marvellous halcyon days, which I have noticed
often follow a gale, and I lay out in the forecourt in the sun
and listened to the gulls having the time of their lives among
the huge piles of wrack washed up by the surf. There was one
piece of fucus whose stem was as thick as my arm and that
measured twenty-eight feet from root to tip; there were also,
tragic relics, bits of blue and white and scarlet board that could
only have come from a lifeboat. We had, too, the most marvellous sunsets, as if the Fires of Azrael had been lit in the
west, and the moonrise over that heaving sea was a thing I
shall never forget.

Then, too, Morgan sang to me. I never knew before that
she could sing. Her singing was like nothing else that I have
ever heard; it was half-way between folk-song and jazz, rising
and falling by quarter-tones, and very rhythmical. And her
songs were not like any other songs, either, being hymns to
the old gods and the chants of priests. Moreover her pitch was

not the modern pitch at all, but in between, so that at first it sounded curiously flat and out of tune; but as one's ear became accustomed to the strange intervals, one realised that it was true music after its kind and that it spoke direct to the sub-conscious.

And she sang it, not with the full singing voice of the concert singer, nor yet with the wail of the crooner, but with a mantric chanting, not loud, but of a pure resonant tone that to me was very beautiful, and the rhythm in it was like the beat of the sea. And there were times when there came into her voice a strange inhuman timbre, curiously metallic, and when this came there was a change of consciousness, and she was someone else.

Then it was that I learnt something of the secret of the magical images and their use, for borne away on the wings of her song she became that which she had imagined herself to be in the making of the magical images. Then I saw the sea-priestess of Atlantis standing before me, Morgan le Fay, the foster daughter of Merlin, learned in all his lore.

I said to her one evening after she had been singing to me:

"Morgan, you have become that which you have imagined."

She smiled, and said: "That way lies power."

Then I told her of my vision of the sea-cave of Bell Knowle, and said: "Supposing I too play that game, Morgan le Fay? Shall I have power?"

And she smiled again, and said: "Why not?"

Then I told her that in my vision she had not been herself, but all women; and I had not been myself, but all men. I could not put it clearer than that, for I did not know what it meant. And she looked at me strangely and said:

"That is the key to the sea-cave of Bell Knowle."

"Morgan, what do you mean?" said I.

"Do you not remember," said she, "that in Atlantis the

priests and priestesses did not marry for love, but as the rites required?"

"You were more than a priestess to me in that cave," I said. "I thought you were Aphrodite herself."

"I was more than Aphrodite," she said, "I was the Great Mother."

"But the Great Mother is an earth goddess," said I. "How can you be her priestess as well as the priestess of the sea?"

"Do you not know the Mystery saying that all the gods are one god, and all the goddesses are one goddess, and there is one initiator? Do you not know that at the dawn of manifestation the gods wove the web of creation between the poles of the pairs of opposites, active and passive, positive and negative, and that all things are these two things in different ways and upon different levels, even priests and priestesses, Wilfred?"

"Then," said I, "if you cannot love me as a man, Morgan le Fay, will you work with me as a priest?"

She smiled her curious smile. "Certainly," she said, "that is what I have been aiming at."

"Good Lord!" said I. "You've got a nerve!"

Then Morgan le Fay began to tell me about herself, and how things looked from her point of view; it was a curious experience, for I had never dreamt there could be such a viewpoint for any human being. She told me that those whom the gods chose were dehumanised and semi-deified.

"For that remark," I said, "you would have been burnt in the good old days, and quite right too."

"What are the gods?" said she.

"God knows," said I.

"I think they are natural forces personified," said she. "So to be made one with the gods is to become the channel of natural forces. And that is not as rare as you might think."

And she told me that devout men of all faiths had held that it was possible to bring the soul to a single-pointed focus by adoration and meditation and dedication; and that when this took place, the god came down and possessed the worshipper, and the power of the god shone out from him like light from a lamp. She told me, too, that the ancients had known things of which we moderns had only touched the fringe.

"When the Priest of the Moon came to me in the crystal," she said, "he asked me if I would like to learn these things, and I said that I would. And he told me that to do this I must give myself up to them; and I said that I would do this also. Then he said he would teach me, and little by little he has taught me.

"He taught me that there is but one priesthood, which is the service of the One, whence all life proceeds and to which all returns, and It is Unmanifest, and no Man at any time hath known It, or ever shall know It. Only in Its works is It known to us, and from these we deduce Its nature, and Its nature is Nature. Primitive man personified Its powers and called them gods; modern man depersonifies them and calls them forces and factors. Both are true," said she, "but neither is the whole truth; for the gods are forces, and the forces are intelligent and purposive, being expressions of the nature of the One.

"And as It is, so is creation, for creation is the expression of Its nature; for as the Chaldean Oracles say, 'The wise man looketh upon the face of Nature and beholdeth therein the luminous countenance of the Eternal.' And human nature," said she, "is a part of Nature, and you learn a lot about both Nature and the gods if you study it."

Then she told me the idea the ancients had of priesthood—that it was mediumship; but it was not the personified god that spoke through the possessed and inspired priest or pythoness, for the personified god is the form under which man represents these potencies to himself, and the real god is far otherwise—but that the priest, overshadowed by the god, put forth his powers; that which was latent in him was released, and he became for a time what all men would be when perfected.

"Then that being so," said I, "what are the gods?"

"God knows," said she. "But we know that by doing certain things we get certain results."

"And what do you propose to do?" said I.

"I will tell you," said she.

And she told me that each man had it in him, by virtue of his manhood, to be a priest; and each woman by virtue of her womanhood had it in her to be a priestess; for the Source of All Life created the worlds by dividing Its Unmanifest Unity into the manifesting Duality, and we that are created show forth in our beings the uncreate Reality. Each living soul has its roots in the Unmanifest and draws thence its life, and by going back to the Unmanifest we find fulness of life.

But because we are limited and imperfect beings we cannot show forth the Infinite in Its totality; and because we are imprisoned upon the plane of form we can only conceive the Formless as far as minds habituated to form can imagine it. "And that," said Morgan le Fay, "is not very far, and the mathematicians go furthest. But we who are men and women, Wilfred, and who want to know God as He manifests in Nature—we see the luminous countenance of the Eternal in the beautiful forms of the gods. And in that way," she said, "we learn more, and can do more, than if we strive after abstract essences that elude us."

She told me how the Priest of the Moon. who instructed her, had bidden her go back to the Great Unmanifest and dedicate herself to the One, leaving aside all lesser manifestations; and having made that dedication and won that realisation, and found the roots of her being, he bid her see the One Life manifesting itself in all things, and in herself too.

And he taught her that the manifesting Life had two modes or aspects—the active, dynamic, stimulating—and the latent and potent which receives the stimulus and reacts to it. He showed her how they changed places one with another in an endless dance, giving and receiving; accumulating force and discharging it; never still, never stabilised, ever in a state of flux and reflux as shown by the moon and the sea and the tides of life—ebbing and flowing, waxing and waning, building up and breaking down in the dance of life to the music of the spheres. And he showed her how the passing of the sun through the starry belt of the Zodiac makes the greatest of all the tides.

"And these Zodiacal tides," said he, "are the illuminations of faith. And to-day the sun is passing over into Aquarius, the Sign of the Man, and the old gods are coming back, and man is finding Aphrodite and Ares and great Zeus in his own heart, for that is the revelation of the aeon."

Morgan le Fay told me that she had chosen for her part the cult of the Great Goddess, the primordial Mother. And this goddess was symbolised by space and the sea and the inmost earth. She was Rhea, and Ge, and Persephone, but above all she was Our Lady Isis in whom all these are summed up; for Isis is both corn goddess and queen of the dead—who are also the unborn—and the lunar crescent is upon her brow. Under another aspect she is the sea, for life first formed in the sea, and in her dynamic aspect she rose from the waves as Aphrodite.

And Morgan le Fay, pursuing these things, had studied the symbols of cult after cult, for all worshipped the same thing by different names and under different aspects, till at last she found that to which her own nature was attuned. And it was not the austere Egyptian faith, nor the radiant gods of Greece, but the primordial Brythonic cult that had its roots in Atlantis, which the dark Ionian Kelt shares with Breton and Basque.

"For this," she said, "is older than the gods of the North, and there is more of wisdom in it, for the gods of the North are mindless, being the formulations of fighting men; but the Great Goddess is older even than the gods that made the gods, for men knew the function of the mother long before they understood the part played by the father; and they adored the Bird of Space that laid the Primordial Egg long before they worshipped the Sun as the Fecundator.

"They conceived all being as coming forth from the sea, and they were right, for there was a time when the waters covered the earth, as both Scripture and the rocks bear witness. Then came the time when they learnt the part of the father, and they looked in Nature for the fecundating father of all, and perceived it to be the sun. So they adored the sun as well as the sea; but the cult of the sea is older, for she is the Great Mother.

"But in my dedication to the moon and the sea," said Morgan le Fay, "I had chosen the part that was passive, and I had to await the coming of the fecundator, and I still await it."

"Might it be," said I, "that I should play that part to you, Morgan le Fay, for I love you?"

"It might be," said she. "We can but try. And it does not matter whether you love me or not if you can bring through that power."

"It matters very much to me," said I.

"It does not matter to me," said she, "for I am a dedicated priestess; and if it matters to you, you will not be able to bring it through."

I did not understand what she meant then, but I knew later.

"How many men have you tried this with, Morgan le Fay?" said I.

"A very great many, Wilfred Maxwell," said she. "And from all I have got something, but from none have I got everything, and I was beginning to think that it is not to be had, when I met you."

"But surely," I said, "I, with my bad health, have less to give you than most?"

"On the contrary," said she, "there are possibilities in you that I had not realised before."

And she told me that in every being there are two aspects, the positive and the negative; the dynamic and the receptive; the male and the female; and this is shown forth in rudimentary form even in the physical body. In normal folk one of these is dominant and one is recessive, and this determines the sex; but though the recessive one is latent, it is nevertheless there, as is well known to those who study the anomalies of development and disease—and as is still better known to those who study the anomalies of the soul.

But the ancients did not concern themselves with anomalies, but said that the soul was bisexual, and that as one or the other aspect manifested in the world of form, the alternative aspect was latent in the world of spirit; and if we look into our own hearts we shall see how true this is, for each of us has two sides to his nature—the side that is forth-flowing by its own dynamism, and the side that lies latent, awaiting inspiration, and that comes not forth unless it is evoked. "And this," said she, "is the greater side of each one of us; and in a man it is his spiritual nature, and in a woman it is her dynamic will."

Then she told how in some the two sides of their nature came near to equilibrium, not in any physical or instinctual anomaly, but in temperament; for an anomaly is due to the repression of the dominant factor, whereas in that of which she spoke it was the two-sided soul that was finding expression through the higher self, and this was due to the work of initiation in past lives.

"I learnt these things in Atlantis, when I was one of the sacred clan," said she, "and the memory was reborn with me, and I have always known it. But you, I do not think, were ever of the initiated priesthood; but by the trick you played upon the high priest of Bell Knowle you got something, though how much I do not know, and it remains to be seen."

"At least I forged a personal bond with you," said I.

"Priestesses have no personal bonds," said she.

"Anyway, it served to bring us together," said I, but she did not answer, and that angered me.

"There is another way of looking at it all," said I. "It may have been that my dreams and my visions all sprang from the same thing—sex-repression and wish-fulfilment, for God knows, if any man ever had a subconscious full of frustrations, I have."

"That, of course, is an alternative theory," replied Morgan, quite unmoved.

"And it may be, Miss Le Fay Morgan, that both your priesthood and your inheritance under our client's will are—magical images?"

"'What is truth?' asked jesting Pilate."

"And I suggest that you stop playing the fool with me lest my partner and I inquire into your antecedents in good earnest."

Morgan laughed. "Whether my priesthood is a magical image or not, it has been effectual to wake the manhood in you, Wilfred Maxwell."

That was an unanswerable argument, and I succumbed to it.

Then she said a thing for which, in the mood I was in, I could cheerfully have hit her.

"Do you realise, Wilfred, how much of the woman there is in you?"

"Fifty per cent," said I. "Same as other folk. My mother was a woman."

"I don't mean that. I mean in your temperament."

"Yes," I said, "I suppose I am being catty. But it is no use arguing with me after I've just had a go of asthma, for there is no sense to be got out of me."

"I don't mean that, either. I mean that your nature is predominantly negative."

"Not as negative as you think, Morgan le Fay. Having lived all my life with women, I have learnt to assume protective colouring. I may pursue circuitous routes to save trouble, but I generally arrive where I want to get in the end. Moreover, I live and carry on my business in a very conventional town, and if I were suspected of being unconventional, I should lose business. So when I want to kick over the traces, as at the present moment, I come outside the three-mile limit, my dear."

"And I don't mean that either. You are a beast, Wilfred. I know you are nothing like as mild as you look, and your slyness is the thing I like least about you. I mean that you are not positive and dynamic as most men are."

"Well, my dear girl, I haven't got the physique for the job. You can't be a husky he-man under eight stone, you only get yourself thrashed. And what you are pleased to call my slyness is really tact and diplomacy. Why go out of your way to stir up avoidable trouble when there is so much unavoidable trouble?"

"Then if those are your principles, why not live up to them? Why go out of your way to pick a quarrel with me?"

"Why go out of your way to pick one with me, Morgan? Do you expect any man to like being told he is half a woman? And the truer it is, the less he likes it. And if any man ever asks you if you have played this game before, you swear you haven't, see?"

"I thought you would be a little more understanding than this."

"Then you thought wrong. I know in the good old days the priests of the Great Mother castrated themselves in her honour, but I'm not doing that. To hell with you, Morgan le Fay."

"There is a commonplace relationship which you can have with any female of the species, and there is a subtle, magical relationship that is very rare. Which do you prefer?"

"Have I any choice? Shan't I have to be content with what I am given?"

"Yes," she said, "I am afraid you will, but I am sorry you take it like that, for I could give you so much."

"Why are you taking all this trouble over me, Morgan le Fay? I am certain it is not for my own sweet sake, quite apart from your repeated assurance that priestesses have no preferences in these matters."

"Because, Wilfred, if you and I can do this thing, we break trail for those who come after us, and we shall bring back into modern life something that has been lost and forgotten and that is badly needed."

"That something being—?"

"The knowledge of the subtle, magnetic relationship between a man and a woman, and the fact that it is part of a larger whole. Do you remember how you felt in the cave—that I was all women and you were all men? Do you remember how our personalities stood aside and we were just channels of force—the positive and negative forces out of which creation is built? And how, when this happened, primordial powers rushed through us straight from the Unmanifest, and it was a tremendous thing? This was what was aimed at by the temple-trained priestesses and the hetærae, and it is what is lacking in our modern understanding of these things. You can see dozens of marriages where there is an annual baby and occasional twins and yet something is lacking; and you can see curious companionships where they can't marry that yet fulfil a great need—and they don't necessarily go week-ending either, Wilfred. People think that sex is physical and that love is emotional, and they don't realise that there is something else between a man and a woman which is magnetic in just the same way as the compass turns to the pole; and it isn't in them any more than it is in the compass, but it is something that passes through them and uses them, and it belongs to Nature. It is the thing that has kept me young, Wilfred, when I ought to be an old, old woman, and it is the thing that is making you, who used to be a mother's boy, as quarrelsome as a cock on a midden."

"Then in that case it is surely a thing that I am better without, for I was a good young man until I met you."

"You will be a better young man before I have done with you," said Morgan le Fay. "But you do understand, don't you, Wilfred, why I won't marry you? Physically I may be a comparatively young woman, for they say a man is as young as his arteries, so I suppose a woman is as young as her endocrines; but mentally I am an old, old woman, and the sort of thing you need has no meaning for me, and I don't want to tie myself up in marriage; and if I did, I believe I should suddenly become the old hag I really am. It is not in me to love you, Wilfred, but I am exceedingly fond of you, and with what you will learn from me, I believe you will be able to love some girl very much indeed."

"Morgan le Fay, having known you, do you suppose that I will ever love anyone else?"

"Yes, I hope so, Wilfred. If I do my work rightly, you certainly will; for what I want to study with you is the way in which these magnetic channels can be opened and the power brought through."

"It is a cold-blooded proposition," said I, "but I suppose I must be thankful for small mercies; in fact, I ought to be used to them, for they are all I have ever had."

I knew now the kind of golden knife that Morgan le Fay had been getting ready for me, and that history was repeating itself to perfection; and that like the Aztec slave, I would have my year during which I was royally treated, and then would come the end, and it would be slow and painful.

Next day I got to work on the panel of the stormy sea, and I worked up from the foam of the white-capped waves the battle madness of the galloping sea-horses and their riders; and in the indigo hollows behind were the bleak, calm, ruthless faces of the greater gods.

CHAPTER XX

THE following Monday I was still far from well, and thoroughly edgy and nervy, so Morgan drove me down in her little coupé to Starber and I phoned Scottie and arranged to stop on at the fort for another week. He said he could carry on all right, and would fix things with my family. I didn't think they would take much fixing, as my sister certainly wouldn't spend a quid on a car for the pleasure of my company, and Whittles swore he wouldn't take her anywhere, except in his official capacity. It was exceedingly decent of Morgan to keep me on, and I don't know why she did it, for I was as fractious as a spoilt child.

When we got back from the Starber trip, after fixing everything up, my mood changed again, and I said I was going to pack up and return to Dickford forthwith; it was in my mind that I had had enough of all these upheavals, and would break with Morgan le Fay. She said I must do as I liked, which made me wild. She suggested, however, that I should have a meal before I left, as I would land in too late for lunch, and she had brought something special back from Starber for me. Being a male, I fell for this, and I then knew that nothing would induce me to chuck Morgan till she finally chucked me.

The last of the swell that followed the storm had died away, though the halcyon days went on and the hunter's moon sailed in a cloudless sky over the sea by night. One calm and perfect evening we strolled up on to the crest of the down, passing between the fallen cairns of the ancient worship till we came to the place where the overthrown pylon lay on the grass. We

183

sat down on the fallen lintel and watched the moon rise behind
Bell Knowle. She came up a queer dull orange, for there was
mist over the marshes; but presently she cleared it and rode the
cloudless sky like a ship in full sail, little light wisps of cloud
going the other way lending her the appearance of speed. It
was a strange thing to watch that great silver moon that looked
so near and went at such a pace; if anything could, it gave one
the realisation that there was more in the universe than our
earth.

Everyone knows nowadays the effect that sunlight has on
health and vegetation, but Morgan told me that there was an
ancient, lost knowledge of the power of the light of the moon—
how it affects vegetation in a way we do not realise with our
uncertain island climate; but in places where the sunlight is
constant they know the effect of the moon, and are careful to
sow seed and cut timber according to her phases. She told me,
too, that the moon had a profound effect on mental states and
moods, as is well known to any who have to do with the mentally sick; and even we who consider ourselves nominally
normal are more affected than we choose to believe.

"Perhaps that is what is making me so cantankerous," said
I, glad of the chance to find something to blame it on.

"Yes," said Morgan, quite seriously, "it probably is. The
moon intensifies everything and brings it to its crisis. Have
you never noticed how many crises take place round about the
full of the moon?"

"What crisis are you expecting now?" said I.

"The crisis of you and me," said she, and took my arm and
walked with me to the end of the down that looked towards the
land. I said nothing, for I had nothing to say.

The mist that rose from the marshes gave the illusion of
water where the moonlight fell upon it, and Bell Knowle rose
like an island out of a misty sea.

"The land is drowning," said I, "as it was when they sent for you, Morgan le Fay."

She smiled. "Is it not strange," she said, "that men think they can keep back the sea by anything save observing her ways?"

"I suppose it is the same with all natural forces," I said. "We try it on with what we are pleased to call our morals, and get drowned out."

We strolled slowly back over the dew-soaked grass with thousands of rabbits feeding all round us. The dew was the only water-supply they had, but they did not seem to mind.

We came down to the fort, and then strolled out over the rocks to the point. The tide was very low to-night, for the moon and the sun were making common cause for once.

"Wilfred," said Morgan le Fay, "shall we light a sea-fire out on the point?"

I looked where she pointed, and saw that a large, flat, table-like surface of rock, obviously artificial, was slowly coming up through the ripples. It was the uttermost end of the ebb, and in another half-hour the tide would be turning, so there was no time to be lost. Morgan and I worked hard, despite her lovely gown of sea-green silk, and we raised a pile of juniper boughs with cedar and sandal-wood mingled among them; we made it pyramidal, for that was the ancient custom, and then, just as the hair-like weed on the edge of the rocks slowly turned round and began to stream the other way, we put a match to the pile.

It took the fire well, as juniper does, the flames leaping from twig to twig and throwing off the showers of sparks that characterise burning juniper; in the heart of the flame the cedar and sandal glowed with a fiercer heat and the scented smoke went rolling over the sea.

Presently a shallow silver ripple came washing over the level surface of the rock and met the burning base; a furious hiss replied to it and a line of inky black cut the perfect circle of flame, making the pyre look like a gibbous moon. The sea thought better of it, and kept quiet for a bit after that. Then, with the rising tide behind it, the ground-swell sent another ripple across the rock. Furious hisses and clouds of steam rose from the angry fire; and then we saw a curious sight—the crest of the pyramidal pyre went on burning, crowned with flame and plumed with scented rolling smoke, but all around was water.

Slowly the tide rose higher, but the crest burned as fiercely as ever; not easily could the sea accept the sacrifice and devour its prey. Then finally, its base undermined by the working of the tide, the whole fiery pyramid collapsed into the dark creeping water in a shower of sparks and flying, burning brands that sank hissing through the softly waving weed, and I smelt again, as I had smelt in my dream, the acrid odour of burning wood extinguished by salt water.

And there came to me a vision of the sea as the source of all things. I saw her lay down the sedimentary rocks and withdraw and leave them land; I saw the slow process of the lichens and the weather that broke down the rocks into soil; I saw the sea rise and take them again as primordial slime, and in that slime arose the first life. And I saw life come ashore from the slime and grow feet and wings. Then I knew why Morgan worshipped the sea, for it is the first of created things and nearer to the Primordial than anything else.

That night I could not sleep, and I sat up in my bed and smoked cigarette after cigarette and watched the moon-set. She went down a dull copper as she had risen, for a haze had gathered over the waters and I thought the weather was in for a change.

It may be that watching that shining disk had hypnotised me, for I began to see back into the beginning of things with a great clarity. I remembered the Greek tag, "panta rhei", and that the mother of the gods was Rhea. I looked out into the measureless depths of inter-stellar space and saw arise a fountain out of which water like liquid moonlight poured in boundless abundance. This, I thought, is the First Begetting. I watched the liquid light gather into a great pool in the deeps of space. I saw currents arise in the pool, and presently it began to swirl, and out of its swirling motion arose the suns. And I knew that water had two moods—the flowing and the still, and not until it is still can life arise in it. And learning as I had that the beginning of things is reflected through all their nature, I reckoned there must be in us this flowing of our energies and their gathering into a deep pool, and that these things might be under the moon-rhythms. And I recognised that it was a man's nature to be predominantly dynamic, like the First Outpouring; and that it was predominantly a woman's nature to gather into a deep pool wherein life can form. But I knew also that there must be an alternating rhythm in these things, and that maybe it is this rhythm we have forgotten.

Then I began to see where I stood with Morgan le Fay, and why she had seen in me possibilities that she had not found before in other men with whom she had been friends. It may have been my upbringing by women, or it may have been my bad health, or it may have been that I was the child of my parents' old age, but in me the physical dynamism is low; I am never really virile unless I am in a tantrum. Morgan, on the other hand, was an extraordinarily vital woman. Then I saw why there must be priestesses as well as priests; for there is a dynamism in a woman that fecundates the emotional nature of a man as surely as he fecundates her physical body; this was a thing forgotten by modern civilisation which stereotypes and conventionalises all things and forgets the Moon, Our Lady of Flux and Reflux.

Then I saw what Morgan was playing at with me—that she was trying to discover the manner in which this lost force worked. Most men wouldn't let her do it, for it is the male convention to keep the initiative at all costs. But behind our conventions there is primordial Nature, and I saw why vamps have such a success and the kind, unselfish woman gets left on the shelf; for men do not love the women who give and give, but the ones who make demands on them and so call out their strength. It is women like Morgan le Fay, who will not give themselves to any man completely, who are best-loved, not the women who give their all. Love is one of those things in which to travel hopefully is better than to arrive.

I wondered what the hell Morgan thought she was driving at with me, and where she expected to land. As far as my experience of life went, we could only land in a mess. But she seemed to have other ideas. And as the only alternative open to me was to go back to Dickford and be a decent citizen, and I could not see myself doing that, I decided to give Morgan her head and let her get on with it, that is, so far as the option was mine; I had a shrewd suspicion that we had reached a point by now when it mightn't be.

Having arrived at this decision, I was considerably more amiable next morning than I had been for the last ten days, and I settled down to watch Morgan and see what she would do. I was also able to settle down and paint the last of the panels— the still and moonlit sea; and in the lights and shadows of water and cloud the face of Morgan le Fay appeared from every conceivable angle.

CHAPTER XXI

THE moon was two days off her full and the barometer was falling, so I knew the halcyon days could not last for ever. After the evening meal we went out on to the point and watched the shadow of Bell Head shorten over the sea as the moon rose higher and higher. One could only go out along the rocks in single file, and Morgan was on ahead of me; she was paying no attention to me and I saw she wanted to be alone with her thoughts, so I did not follow her out to the end, but sat down on the remains of the balustrading, smoking and watching her.

She stood for a long time looking out over the moonlit sea till the shadow of the down drew in to her feet; then she turned and looked up at the moon with the moonlight full upon her. She was like a statue, so still and so perfectly formed. Then she raised her arms to the sky till they looked like the horns of the moon, and began to sing one of her strange songs that she had been singing to me on and off for the last few days, and that had, I think, contributed not a little to my restless and disturbed state, but this time she was singing with the power of evocation—

> "O Isis, veiled on earth, but shining clear
> In the high heaven now the full moon draws near,
> Hear the invoking words, hear and appear—
> Shaddai el Chai, and Ea, Binah, Ge."[1]

Impelled by what power I do not know, I rose and walked

[1] Pronounced Eeah, Beenah, Ghee.

189

towards her, and as I got close enough to see her face in the
moonlight, I saw that it was not Morgan le Fay at all, and that
the eyes were strange and wide and inhuman, not even the
eyes of the sea-priestess, but of the sea-goddess herself. She
raised her arms like the horns of Hathor and she sang to the
moon and the sea—

> "I am she who ere the earth was formed
> > Was Ea, Binah, Ge
> I am that soundless, boundless, bitter sea,
> Out of whose deeps life wells eternally.

> "Astarte, Aphrodite, Ashtoreth—
> Giver of life and bringer-in of death;
> Hera in Heaven, on earth, Persephone;
> Levanah of the tides and Hecate—
> All these am I, and they are seen in me.

> "The hour of the high full moon draws near;
> I hear the invoking words, hear and appear—
> Isis Unveiled and Ea, Binah, Ge,
> I come unto the priest that calleth me."

And I knew that whether I liked it or not, I was cast for the
part of Priest of the Sea.

Morgan's arms came slowly down from the sign of the horns
of the moon till they were horizontal, and then they began to
work backwards and forwards with a curious stroking motion
to which the long loose sleeves lent the appearance of slowly-
beating wings. The wailing, humming rhythms, rising and
falling by quarter-tones with their recurrent rhymes, held me
as the bird is held by the snake, and step by step I came towards
her till my outstretched palms were pressed against hers and I
suddenly realised that I had not got a woman's hands in mine,
but the two poles of a powerful battery.

The vibrations of all the ancient rituals by which men have
ever invoked the gods had awakened in that strange singing

voice of hers, and I knew that with the touch of her hands she had indeed brought something down from heaven that passed from her to me and so to earth. The tide was rising and the ground-swell was washing softly over the rock where we stood, touching the foot, touching the ankle, threatening danger. A cloud passed over the moon and we were in darkness. A cold breath of wind from the north-west came soughing over the water, and I knew that the weather had broken. Following the wind a wave ran in and broke on the rocks, and another and another. I saw Morgan's drapery afloat on the water, and drew her towards me, she following like a sleep-walker. It was a risky business bringing this blindly-moving woman through ankle-deep water over the broken rocks in the dark with the waves breaking white behind us and the wind rising; but foot by foot I did it, and got her safely to the steps. I was too busy thinking about our mutual safety to think about myself, but as I got her down into the forecourt, where the light of the windows shone out and we could see what we were doing, she suddenly opened her eyes and looked at me like one aroused from deep sleep, and I knew that something very strange had passed between us.

Next day it all seemed like a dream. Morgan le Fay did not refer to it, and neither did I. There are some things that are broken if one speaks of them. The wind rose and cold rain fell and we did not go out on the point or up on the down all that day, but sat over the fire and read and had very little to say to each other.

But towards bed-time, as we were sitting over the dying fire, I had a sudden impulse to take the reading-lamp that stood at my elbow and go down to the far end of the long room and study the design I had roughed in across the wide expanse of plaster broken only by a door in the corner.

The design was that of the deep sea-palaces, with their

iridescent domes like bubbles in the foam and the crests of the waves curled over them for a sky; sea-snakes twined around their pillared porticoes and the treasure of sunk galleons lay scattered about their courts. In the centre, seated on the throne of the kings of the sea, was a figure in silvery drapery like breaking waves. which I had planned should be Morgan le Fay when the inspiration came to me to paint her face. But it had not come yet, and only the shadowy outline of features was faintly indicated.

But as I stood there, holding the lamp in one hand and picking over my brushes with the other, I knew that the time had come when I could do that face. Morgan le Fay was half asleep over her book at the other end of the big room, paying no attention to me, and I got to work, holding the lamp in one hand and painting with the other in the uncertain wavering light as best I might. I needed no model, for I knew her so well, every line and curve of her.

But as I painted, I saw that it was not the face of Morgan le Fay that was taking form under my brush, but a man's face— fine-featured, ascetic, not of this world; and the eyes were the most marvellously living eyes that I have ever seen on canvas, although I painted them myself. They looked straight at me, and I looked straight back at them. Then, I know not what impulse possessed me, but I painted Morgan le Fay's great crystal between the hands. A crystal is a very difficult thing to paint, but I did it, and it caught the light as if it were lit up from within.

As I finished and stepped back to look at the result, not knowing what to make of it, I heard a sound behind me, and there was Morgan le Fay. She looked at what I had done for a long moment, and then she turned to me and said:

"That is the Priest of the Moon!"

CHAPTER XXII

IT is very difficult for me to convey any idea of what it meant to me to get into touch with the Priest of the Moon. I have already told of my experience in contacting the invisible reality behind appearances, which is to their outward form as the personality of a man to his body. I have told of the power that had come to me to see the past living again. It is not for me to deal with the metaphysics of these things; I only know that they were experiences like none other I have ever had, and that they had far-reaching effects on my life. It is by this last I judge them, and not by the arguments that can be advanced pro or con. That they represent the workings of the subconscious I am quite prepared to agree, for they are entirely beyond the range and scale of the normal scope of consciousness. That they are such stuff as dreams are made of, I am equally prepared to agree, for they are more akin in their nature to the life of sleep than the life of action. But having said this, have we written them off as a bad debt? Have we not still to define what we mean by sleep and subconsciousness? I am not prepared, not in these pages, anyway, to say what I mean by them, because I do not know; to me they are finger-posts, not labels; when I am satisfied that I have got the soul safely done up in brown paper with a bit of string round it, then I will tie a label to it, but not before. Until then, I think sign-posts are safer and less likely to let one in for foolishness; for they point the direction, which is helpful, but set no limits, which is a futile thing to do in the present state of our knowledge.

I will therefore be content to describe, and leave it to other folk to classify according to taste. There was an old dame near us who for many years replied to all inquiries about her son that he was in Bristol Infirmary. Finally someone got suspicious, and asked her which ward he was in, and elicited the information that he wasn't in a ward at all, but in the museum. So I can at least serve as a specimen, if not as a tutor, instructing by what I am rather than by what I say.

I have seen a lot of inspirational pictures in my time, and they are all right as long as the artists stick to clouds and drapery, but as soon as they try and do figures and faces, it makes one pin one's hope to total extinction. Knowing this, I had the sense to keep my figures shadowy, for say what you like, the soul cannot transcend the hand when it comes to craftsmanship. The features of the Priest of the Moon were therefore but dimly seen, and the imagination had to build up the completed picture. I did not represent my priest, but evoked him. There is a whole theory of art in that, but it is not my business at the moment. The outward eye saw coloured shadows; it was out of one's knowledge one completed the picture. If one knew nothing, one saw nothing. If one knew something, one saw a lot. It is not for me to judge my pictures. They have interested competent judges, we will leave it at that. Old Whittles said it was a pity I did not finish them. The vicar said they were depraved. My sister said they were silly. Scottie said he wouldn't have one if you paid him. My Bond Street pal wanted me to go in for painting professionally, but it is too much like hard work to suit me, and one cannot take a partner.

Whatever may be said of my pictures, and they always evoke violent partisanship, it has been a liberal education to paint them.

But the thing that mattered was not the aesthetics of the

business, but what came of it.   Through those pictures the
Priest of the Moon came into my life, and he was a very
curious person to know; even more curious than Morgan le
Fay, and God knows, she was odd enough.   It may seem a
strange thing to say, but for the shadowy figure that had come
up to the surface in my drawing I had the same kind of feeling
that I have for any dynamic personality.   I have not met a
great many in my life, Dickford not being prolific of such, or
if they appear, driving them to drink and the devil early in
their career.   I have met one or two among the barristers, and
some of the old judges must have been pretty potent in their
day, though the kick has usually gone out of them by the time
they get to the bench.   My Bond Street pal was a personality in
his way.   My sister, too, in her way, if you call it a way.   Those,
I think were all.   No one else I ever met could see much beyond
the next meal.

I judge a personality not so much by what they say, or even
by what they do, but by the way they affect you.   For a person
may do a lot in the world by virtue of the start he has been
given in life, or because he has got something that is wanted
at the moment, but that does not constitute a personality as
I use the word.   A personality fetches a reaction out of you of
one sort or another, and it need not necessarily be a pleasant
reaction—anything more unpleasant than my sister you would
go a long way to find; and I stir up a good deal of dislike too,
especially locally, because I go my own way and pay no attention to anybody, and a country town hates that.   A personality
stimulates you—whether to save your soul or lose it is imma-
terial to my definition.

The Priest of the Moon had personality in a very marked
degree, and if he was the product of my subconscious, I am
proud of it.   There were times, not infrequent, when I used to
wander what he was, and whether I was deluding myself, or

whether I was loopy; but each time I met him afresh I knew what he was, beyond all doubting, and he left his mark on me.

At first I thought he was the sea-priest who had been so wroth over my impertinence when I was being sacrificed; and I was scared because I reckoned that an enemy had picked up my trail; then I began to see that this was not so, but that he was something altogether bigger than that. It seemed to me that this was the priest who was behind Morgan le Fay, who had brought her away from Atlantis when his knowledge told him that the final catastrophe was due.

I could see the scene clearly, as if it were a picture vividly stamped on memory—the sacred city built around the mountain that had been a volcano, just as Pompeii and Herculaneum were built within historical times. I could see the wide alluvial plain that stretched away to a far range of mountains—land laid bare by the receding sea just as the marshes stretch towards Dickford and the hills behind; and at the very verge of land and water rose the great cone, as it might be Bell Knowle. The cone was flat on top, not pyramidal, because in some previous cataclysm it had blown off its crater, as volcanoes do. And on this level crest were the white buildings of the sacred clan—the great sun-temple with its open court paved with the black and white of alternate marble and basalt, and its two pillars that were the twin gnomons of a time-dial vast as the court, one for the sun, and one for the moon, and calculations were made upon the way the shadows crossed the squares. It was the prototype, Morgan told me, of the Temple of Solomon the King, and all other temples of the Mysteries take after it.

Around the temple were buildings with porticoes and colonnades, beam-spanned, for the Atlanteans, though they knew much wisdom, had not got the secret of the arch any more than the ancient Egyptians had; these were the houses of the priests and scribes that served the temple, and beyond them was the

House of the Virgins, built around a court, with no windows looking outwards. It was there that Morgan le Fay grew to womanhood.

Within were courts leading one into another and surrounded by rooms and colonnades. And there were sunken stone tanks, with steps leading down to them, where the sacred lilies grew; and over them leant trees not unlike mulberry trees, ancient and gnarled, from whose bark oozed the fragrant resins they burnt in the temples. The young priestesses sat under the trees spinning with the spindle and whorl that are more ancient than the wheel. I think that they had not the use of the wheel in Atlantis, any more than they knew the arch.

From the House of the Virgins an underground way led to the temple, and priests from whom all passion had gone watched over the up-bringing of the young priestesses in the care of the wise women. By this way they were brought into the temple as occasion required, never setting eyes on the outside world nor any undedicated man; and by this way they returned when their work was done, not always virgin.

Beneath the temple a way led by the path of the lava to the very heart of the ancient volcano, and herein was hollowed out a crypt where a rising jet of flame burnt continually, telling those who had eyes to see that the mountain was not dead, but sleeping. This flame, lit by the Earth herself, was to them the symbol of their faith, for all fires are one in nature, though after three kinds—volcanic, solar and terrestrial. It was the leaping of this flame that warned the Priest of the Moon that the catastrophe long foretold was at hand.

Now the Priest of the Moon was other than those who served the flame, though as a young man he had been taken and trained as they had been. He had seen that the worship had fallen on evil days, and had gone back, as men must, to an older and purer faith, tracing the river to the rill till he came to the pure source; and he worshipped the Great Mother under Her forms of moon and sea, and in this he was wise, for with Her are hidden the secrets of human life, though with the All-father are the keys of the spirit.

In his prime he set out to seek a land where life might be lived unsullied by the decay of a dying race, and he travelled with the tin-ships to the Islands of the Sea, where the marts of the sea-kings' trade were established—far marts, where men brought strange things, the blue and the purple dyes, and medicinal plants, and silver.

And when the time came that the leaping flame gave warning, the ancient Priest of the Sun, too feeble for that far journey yet knowing what drew near, prepared to die with his temple. And he gave into the hands of the younger man the secret scrolls and sacred symbols. And they went by night by the underground way to the House of the Virgins, and looked at the young girls as they slept in the moonlight, and chose one who had been prepared to serve their purpose, and roused her and led her away wrapped in a dark cloak while the others slept.

And she saw for the first and last time by moonlight the wide spaces of the plain where the spearmen and javelin-throwers learnt their skill and horsemen rode the two-toed horse; and she went down the winding processional way to the shore, and so to sea. And the land-wind, blowing at dawn, filled their sails and they went swiftly. For a day and a night and a day they went, the rowers toiling till they met the trades. Then, upon the third morning, in the hour between dark and dawn, three great billows heaved their ship as the sea-floor shook, and when the sun rose they saw a dark pillar of smoke and cloud where once was Lost Atlantis.

And the Priest of the Moon, travelling by way of "thrice-vexed Bermoothes" and the Azores, brought the young girl who was to be his priestess to a place he had prepared in the Holy Isle that is off the Isle of Druids, looking towards the Isle of Saints, which is Ireland. And there he left her in the care of wise women, to be trained in the terrible discipline of the priesthood, he himself coming and going about the wild land, watching its ways, men calling him Merlin.

And when the time came that the summons was sent, they brought the young priestess, now grown and trained, to the priests who had their sacred college on Bell Knowle. And there befell that of which I have already told, so that the sacrifice was in vain, and the sea came in and took the land. And by all the water-ways of the marshes the tide rose, and meadow and field fell back to the sea, and men that had ploughed and sown became fishers and hunters again, living in huts on piles among the reeds who had known stone-built forts and timbered palaces. And Morgan le Fay, priestess of the sea and half-sister of the king, sat in her palace in the island valley of Avalon and watched in the magic well the things to come unfolding.

And she saw her brother the king betrayed by his faithless queen; and the wise Merlin led by the young witch Vivien; and all the evil that comes to lands and men when the sacred hearth-fires die untended.

CHAPTER XXIII

I TOLD Morgan all these things, but she would not say very much; all I could get her to say was:

"Your dreams march with mine."

"Morgan," I said, "what *is* the truth?"

"You are not the first man to ask that question," said she.

"I think I'll go and have a wash, the same as him," said I, seeing there was nothing to be got out of her.

When I got back she was busy making supper, dressed in a long flowing dress of wine-coloured velvet, the big wing-sleeves looped back to her shoulders and showing their silvery lining, leaving her arms free for what she was doing among her copper pots and casseroles. She had lovely arms, rounded, firm-muscled; the skin smoothly, opaquely white; the hands not small but long-fingered, and supple and eloquent in a way she had learnt among the Latins. I sat down in my usual chair at the far end of the long narrow table and watched her. She was making a fanciful French dish that is supposed to catch fire as it cooks, and presently it blazed up and we sat down to our meal.

There was no chance of talking while she was doing this, for it was a tricky business and she took her cooking seriously, a lot more seriously than I took my painting, or even my house-agenting; moreover, Morgan would never talk to a man until she had fed him, a rule she had learnt among the South-American presidents, who are quick with their guns.

But when I was fed, and was smoking and drinking my coffee, she suddenly said to me:

"What is truth, Wilfred?"

"That was what I have just been asking you," said I, "and you snubbed me."

"No, it wasn't," said she, ignoring my innuendo. "You asked me what was the truth concerning a certain matter, and I am asking you what is truth in itself? We cannot deal with the particular until we have dealt with the general. What is truth, Wilfred?"

"God knows," said I, "what it is in general, but you know all right what it is in this particular instance, whether you choose to tell me or not."

"I am not so sure that I do," said she. "What do you imagine to be the truth about me, Wilfred?"

"Sometimes I think one thing, Morgan le Fay," said I, "and sometimes I think another. It just depends how I happen to be feeling at the moment."

She laughed. "I expect that is about as near to the truth as we shall ever get," she said, "for that is exactly my position too. Sometimes I think one thing about myself, and sometimes I think another. As long as I believe in myself I find I can do certain things. If I ceased to believe in myself, I think I should just crumble into dust, like an unwrapped mummy. There is more than one kind of truth. A thing that does not exist in our three-dimensional world may exist in the fourth dimension and be real in its way."

"And what may the fourth dimension be?" said I.

"I am incapable of the mathematics of the matter," said Morgan, "but for all practical purposes I take mind as the fourth dimension, and I find it works. That is good enough for me."

"It isn't good enough for me," said I. "I want to understand things a bit better than that before I am prepared to trust them."

"You will never understand things until you trust them, for you inhibit what you doubt."

"And you will never know if the ice will bear unless you get on to it, and then, if it won't, you go through."

"And you will never make custards without breaking eggs."

"And what's to be done about it?"

"I don't know what you mean to do about it, but I know what I mean to do."

"What is that?"

"Take my precautions and take my risks."

I offered no comment, and she asked for none. She knew that when it came to the point, where she led I would follow, she being her.

"I can show you things that I can't tell you, Wilfred," she said. "Very curious things. I don't pretend to understand them, but I know that they work. Leave them alone for the present, because the moon will be waning by next week-end; but come back to me at the next full moon, and I will show you."

CHAPTER XXIV

MORGAN'S instructions to keep away till the next full moon meant that I did not see her for a month. It was the first time I had missed my week-ends since she came to the fort, and a very long month it seemed. It taught me pretty unequivocally what Morgan meant to me, and the part she played in my life, and what life would be like without her. By the end of that month my mother and sister were seriously considering my original offer to set them up in a separate establishment. What Morgan did during that time I do not know, but when I came out again there was a curious, subtle difference about the fort that I cannot define, and the smell of cedar and sandal had soaked into it till the whole place was redolent. The fort felt like a harp that had been tuned ready for use; and every now and again, like an aeolian harp, faint sighing sounds came from it spontaneously. I shall never forget the curious tense expectancy of the atmosphere and the all-pervading odour of the incense-woods.

There was something curious about the sea, too, that is not easy to describe; it seemed as if it had come much nearer to us and could at will flow in and fill all the rooms. And yet it was not a drowning and alien element, for a kinship had been established between us and the sea, and we would be able to breathe in its waters as if we were amphibian. I cannot put into words the curious sense I received of being made free of the sea : as if no wave would ever sweep me off the point, but I could walk down into the depths as I would walk out into a fog—conscious of a denser medium but not of an alien element.

Morgan gave me a very odd supper. There was almond-curd such as the Chinese make; and scallops in their shells; and little crescent honey-cakes like marzipan for dessert—all white things. And this curious pallid dinner-table was relieved by a great pile of pomegranates in an earthenware dish in the centre.

"It is moon-food," said Morgan, smiling.

"And if you eat the pomegranates," I said, "you never come back," and I took one.

We didn't do anything that night, but just sat over the fire; I tried to amuse Morgan with anecdotes of Dickford, but it wouldn't work, the atmosphere was too tense, and we went early to bed.

I went early to sleep, too, or at least I think I did, and I dreamed a very curious dream.

It seemed to me in my dream that I was standing in the big living-room downstairs, and that all the pictures on the walls were real, and not painted plaster, and the Priest of the Moon on his throne was real, too, and he came forward and stood beside me in his strange high head-dress, like the crown of Upper Egypt. I looked into his eyes, and he looked into mine, and I felt a more perfect confidence in him than I have felt in any living being.

We went out together, moving with the floating movement of sleep. The glass of the great windows offered no impediment to our passage, and we passed on to the point where the poor moon-calf had perished, and so out over the sea.

And then I found myself on that high tabular peak of Atlantis where the sacred college had stood, though whether it was sunk in the Great Atlantic Deep or high in air, I do not know. My guide had gone, and before me were two figures veiled in misty light. I could see neither face nor form, but only the shadowy sweep of the robes and great folded wings behind them. What they said to me, or I said to them, I shall never know, for nothing remained in memory save that I knelt on the knee before them upon the rock of the plateau and iridescent, opalescent light played all around me, and there was in my soul a reverence so profound and awe so great that ever afterwards life has been to me a sacrament.

Then I found my guide beside me again, and we were far out over the sea; and presently I saw the rocky point of Bell Head below, and we passed over the place where the poor moon-calf had died and were back whence we started, and I woke up in bed.

That is all there is to tell. It might have been a dream; but it was a dream like no other dream that I have ever had, and it changed my whole life. One thing, and one thing only had I brought back with me through the veil that was dropped as I returned—I knew that my dedication had been accepted, and that I was chosen of the sea-priestess to be sacrificed to provide power for whatever ends she had in view, whether the land were to be saved from the sea, or whether the sea were to regenerate the land.

I started to tell Morgan of my experience when I came down next morning, but she held up her hand and stopped me.

"I know everything," she said. "Do not talk about it."

I was glad of this, for I felt that to talk about it might cause it to vanish.

After our usual belated breakfast we went up over the down for a walk, and I saw that the white moon-pyramids, two by two, had been reconstructed, and the processional way stood as it did in ancient days. I wondered what the natives made of the great pylon that showed up against the sky-line on the crest of the down. However, there weren't many natives to

make anything of it, only a stray crab-catcher or two along
the rocks, and thatchers cutting reeds in the marsh. I offered
no comment on the state of affairs, and Morgan didn't either,
and we walked along the ancient way as if we were making
pilgrimage. There is a curious power in silence when you
think alike without word spoken and each knows the other's
thoughts. As long as nothing is said, the thing you are thinking remains in another dimension and is magical, but as soon
as you speak it, you lose it. It is the old story of the jewels
bought in the goblin market, which you must only look at by
moonlight or you find them to be a handful of dead leaves.
There is more than one kind of reality, and they won't mix.

We passed through the great pylon, and I felt as Caesar must
have felt when he crossed the Rubicon. Something was sealed
with our passing, and sealed irrevocably. Yet nothing was
said as we walked over the short grey sea-down grass, with
only the sound of the waves below us and the crying of the gulls
overhead. It is very curious, that power of silence in another
dimension, and very potent.

We came to the end of the long sea-down, and below us the
weathered limestone of the cliff-face fell away in broken but-
tresses to the steep slope where Trethowen was trying to grow
vines. Far down below I could see the narrow beds banked
with stone to hold the shallow soil, and edging them the grey
aromatic herbs that were infused in the sacred wine, and that
Morgan le Fay used to make into the stinking incense she
sometimes burned; why, I never knew.

Morgan walked down the steeply-sloping, treacherous turf
that fell away to the sheer drop. I have not got too good a
head for heights, and felt horribly gone in the knees. But I
followed her, and we entered a shallow fold of the ground
that deepened into a gully as we advanced and took us down
on to a high and giddy ledge that clung like a balcony to the

cliff-face. It bore the mark of tools and sloped evenly, a yard wide, and presenting no difficulties to a reasonably steady head provided one did not set foot on a rolling stone; for it was a very long time since tools had been used on that high and perilous path, and the weathering limestone had dropped down on to it in detritus, and although the overhang had caused the heavier stuff to fall clear, enough had remained to demand careful walking, and it was no place to come along in the dark. I wondered whether Morgan had risked her neck here, watching the moon-rise.

The way sloped down at a steeper pitch than even the War Department had dared to use for its road; but we had not far to go, and presently I saw what I had been expecting to see— the narrow cave-mouth set obliquely in the rock that we had once seen from below as we sat on the vine-terraces in the heat of a sultry summer afternoon. Then I had been in my shirt-sleeves and Morgan in blue linen, and now I was clad in a Burberry and Morgan muffled up in furs. It amazed me to remember that then I had been so shy with her that I hardly knew how to address her, and now I was so intimate that I could bicker with her like I did with my sister when she rubbed my fur the wrong way. There is no greater test of intimacy than to be able to have a row with a person without quarrelling with them.

We went down a short flight of rough but regular steps as we entered the cave, and in the centre I saw a rectangular table of solid stone that had evidently been made by cutting away the natural level of the floor—hence the steps leading down from the entrance. Round the walls that had been shaped to a semicircle a low stone ledge had been left to serve as a seat; and in the centre, facing the entrance and in line with the table-stone, was a higher block that looked as if it might serve for a throne, or the seat of the priest. Whether the stone table was an altar, or a couch, or a slaughtering-slab, I could not tell, and Morgan did not tell me. The place had been, I thought, recently swept, for there was no débris of ages in here like there was on the path that led to it. Then I noticed that on either side of the entrance stood two braziers such as road-men use, and in a recess was a heap of coke. The ceiling was darkened by the fumes, which I guessed found their way into the long rift in which it terminated. From the degree of the blackening of the ceiling I judged that Morgan le Fay had been here a good deal.

She offered no explanation of anything, but let me look all round at my leisure.

Then I saw that near the entrance stood a small portable electric battery with a coil of wire beside it, and the wire went up and terminated in the rock overhead.

"What is that for, Morgan?" said I, unable to contain myself any longer, for I knew the use of batteries like that and their tamped-in wires.

"That is how I shall shut the door when my work is finished," said she.

"And which side of the door shall I be when you shut it?" said I, wondering if this were the substitute for the rising tide.

She smiled. "You will be outside, and at a safe distance," said she. "Don't be alarmed, Wilfred, I don't intend to make a living sacrifice of you. I want you alive, not dead."

"That is very sweet of you," said I bitterly.

Then we walked back by the way we had come. The wind was cold. I turned up my coat collar, Morgan snuggled her furs about her, and we walked fast. We were glad to get within the shelter of the forecourt of the fort, where the banking of the gun-embrasures kept off the wind.

"Morgan," said I, "when are you going to let me get to work on the repairs?"

For after the storm we had simply cleared the court by chucking the debris over the wall into the water, reconstructing nothing, and the place looked a bit battered.

Morgan did not answer, but walked on towards the point. A sudden flash of knowledge told me that she did not mean to reconstruct it.

"If you don't have that underpinning attended to, the end wall will come down in the next storm," I shouted after her. She went on without answering, and I turned and went into the house and tried to warm myself by the huge fire of drift that blazed between my beloved dolphins, for I had suddenly realised that the cold wind had penetrated to my very bones, and getting chilled through is not the best thing for asthma.

Being upset, I was sulky, and when she came in, Morgan saw it. But she did not say anything, and neither did I; for I had realised that every time either of us spoke, something went wrong. We ate our Sunday dinner, and then slept it off, and it was dusk before anyone was stirring.

Morgan went out on to the point again, but I did not offer to stir from the fire.

"The wind has dropped," she said when she came in.

"Glad to hear it," said I.

"Moon-rise at midnight," said she.

I said nothing, for I had nothing to say on the subject.

We had a kind of high tea, the ideas for which Morgan had borrowed from Yorkshire in the course of her travels. It was pretty exotic according to Dickford standards, where the proper thing for Sunday supper is cold beef, beetroot, and blancmange. I had provided crumpets, which I thought were appropriate moon-food, being white and flabby.

Morgan smiled her strange smile and removed the sausage rolls out of my reach before I had had my second.

"To-night's the night," she said.

I knew it was, but I never felt less like anything esoteric in my life. I reckoned I should be a wash-out as a dancing partner, or whatever it was she wanted me for.

Round about ten, as I was beginning to get sleepy, she began to get active. She produced a kind of kimono made of the coarse white shantung which I fancy is native-woven and native-bleached. Anyway, it has a certain roughness of texture and is not dead white. On to my feet went a pair of pliable rubber sandals such as bathers use, only painted with silver paint, and on my head by way of head-dress went a large loose square of silver lamé. After she had arranged it in the appropriate folds, the effect was vaguely Egyptian. Then she handed me an enormous cloak made of heavy curtain velvet in dark indigo blue. It was perfectly circular, and came right down to my heels and had a hood, and there must have been fathoms of material in it—I know it weighed a ton—but I was pretty glad of it before the night was out. It was held at the throat by a massive silver buckle on which was a three-pronged trident, the sea-gods' sigil.

"I want you to go out to the cave," she said, "and sit there in meditation till the moon-rise, and then come back to me here."

"What am I to meditate on?" said I.

"Whatever comes to you," said she.

"Won't that be a pretty barren performance?" said I.

"No," said she, "I have been meditating there for the last month; it will not be a barren performance. Try and see."

She gave me an electric torch.

"Keep it under your cloak as you go down the path over the cliff-face. I don't want anyone to see the light from the coast, for no one suspects the existence of the path to the cave."

I went out. As she said, the wind had dropped and it was no longer cold. The moon had not risen yet, but there was

clear starlight from a cloudless sky. I went slowly along the
down between the two rows of sentinel cairns, and it seemed to
me that there was something alive about them and that they
were watching as sentinels watch. To me it was: "Pass, a
friend!" but I would not have envied any stranger my job of
going up between those silent watchers. It might have been
my imagination, or it might have been the effect of straining
my eyes in the obscurity through which they loomed half-seen,
but each appeared to glow towards the apex and to be crested
with a faint white flickering flame.

But when I approached the rebuilt pylon there was no question about it but that here was something odd and out of the
ordinary. I could not actually see anything, save its dark bulk
against the stars, but my heart began to beat as I drew near
and there was a most extraordinary sense of electricity in the
air. I cannot describe it better than that. And a sort of heat
that was not heat. I passed through, and it was like entering
and coming out of a tunnel from one dimension to another.
East of the pylon was another land, an older land, where things
were real that are hallucination with us.

I noticed that there were no rabbits about. They had all
disappeared. It was their feeding-time, and they should have
been there in thousands, but not a rabbit was to be seen. Maybe
the sentinel cairns had put the fear of God into them the same
as they had into me.

I found the fold in the cliff-face easily enough, being guided
thereto by the cairns. It was not as bad by night as it was by
day, for I could not see the drop beneath me. I got down on
to the path all right, and picked my way pretty cautiously over
its uneven surface. Then I saw a dull red glow among the
rocks, and knew that the cave was there, and that it was lit up.

I passed through the narrow slanting entrance, and found
that the glow came from the two big braziers that were alight

and stoked to the brim with coke. It was pleasantly warm inside, and the fumes disappeared up into the lofty crevasse of the roof and gave no trouble. A curious rug of Morgan's, made of the skins of white Samoyedes, lay over the throne-like stone, which I took to be the seat of the priest, and on this I sat and commenced my vigil. I remembered that dogs are sacred to Diana, who is likewise the Moon, ruler of the tides of flux and reflux. I wondered what the tide was doing, and wished I had noted. I fancied it was going out.

Except for the faint crackling of the burning coke there was no sound in the cave, for the wind had dropped and no traffic moved among the marshes at night. Then I heard, faint and far off, the lowing of a calving cow. And in some odd way it was not inappropriate, for Luna is also Isis, who is also Hathor under another form, and the horns upon her brow are interchangeable with the crescent moon. The cow lowed intermittently as the birth went on and then was quiet, and I guessed that there was a new life in the world. After that there was nothing but the crackling of the coke, and I sank deeper into meditation.

I felt very much the priest, sitting there on the curious stone throne with the dark folds of my heavy velvet cloak about me and my silver sandals showing under the hem. I had thrown back the hood, and the folds of the soft silvery stuff of my head-dress fell down straight on either side of my face. I laid my hands along my thighs after the manner of the gods of Egypt and gave myself up to meditation.

I could tell at once that much magical work had been done here, for the images rose and flowed with spontaneous ease and abnormal vividness. Incense had been scattered on the coke, and as the fire worked its way through, a scented smoke began to rise and take on curious shapes as it eddied in the draughts of the cave, and I saw faces in it as I had seen the faces in the waves. I had an odd feeling that the other cave in Bell Knowle was all lit up and that vigil was being kept there also, although, with my rational mind I knew that it was long since filled with the fallen earth of ages. But my rational mind was in abeyance that night, and things were real to me that I would normally have called illusion, and all my mundane life had ceased to be. I was the priest keeping vigil, and I was concerned with things that are not of this world.

With what was left of my intelligence I pulled myself together and tried to do my duty by the meditation. I visualised the country stretched out below the cave as I had seen it in the previous visions, and tried to project myself back into them. But it wouldn't work. The memory-pictures had none of the vividness of vision, but were dead and in two dimensions only, without depth, like painted canvas. I saw that the conscious effort was a mistake, and sat still and let the pictures form as they would.

The marsh and its water-ways faded and were replaced by the deep blue of the night sky, and it was starless. A faint silvery haze appeared at the centre and began to spread, and formed into bands like the rings of Saturn. Then long shafts of light like wheeling searchlights cut the sky, and everything began to swing round and round and to revolve upon itself. And as I watched, stars and suns swung into being, keeping station like ships in line. And I heard the machinery of the universe take up its marvellous rhythm—synchronised, synthetised—and through all moved the station-keeping stars.

And there were harp-notes in it, sweet arpeggios, and strong gongs calling through the deeps of space as the stars spoke one to another. And I waited and listened for the shouting joy of the sons of God that should have rung out over all; but there was silence, and I knew that something was lacking—something to which Morgan and I held the keys.

To each sphere of the heavens is assigned a vision, so Morgan had told me, and to the Sphere of the Moon is assigned the Vision of the Machinery of the Universe, and this, I thought, is what I must be seeing.

I watched that vast machine working like a dynamo, more organic than mechanical and with the sensitiveness of a living thing. And I saw life begin; and the tides of life that move like water and have no form; they swept backwards and forwards like the tides in the estuary off Bell Head, and it seemed to me that the beginnings of form streamed in them like the seaweed streams in the sea.

I felt that this peculiar tidal rhythm was in all things, like a great breathing. And I remembered that the Moon was called Our Lady of Rhythm and the Ruler of the Tides of Life. There rose to my mind one of Morgan's songs with which she had plagued me with an all too sweet torment:

> "I am that soundless, boundless, bitter sea.
> All tides are mine, and answer unto me.
> Tides of the airs, tides of the inner earth;
> The secret, silent tides of death and birth.
> Tides of men's souls, and dreams, and destiny—
> Isis Veiled, and Ea, Binah, Ge."

Isis Veiled, I knew, was Our Lady of Nature, just as Isis Unveiled is the Heavenly Isis. Ea was the soul of Space and parent of Time, older even than the Titans. Binah, the Dark Sterile Mother of All, was the Great Sea whence life arose, the female principle and pre-matter. And Ge herself was the magnetic earth that is like an aura to our globe and in which move the tides that the Easterns call the Tattvas. These things I knew, for Morgan had already told me, and I realised that I was now watching them.

How long I would have waited and watched, I do not know, but the rim of the rising moon cut the edge of Bell Knowle and the first beam of the moon-dawn fell full on my face as I sat on the throne of the priests.

I rose, and went up by the giddy way that clung to the eaves of the cliff, and along the down where the sentinel cairns stood white in the light of the moon. There was no wind and I could hear the sea below me, and I knew by the sound of its far-off voice that it was at ebb, and calm.

CHAPTER XXV

A S I came down towards the point I was surprised to
observe that a haze of light hung over the fort such as
one sees over a city. There was no doubt about it; I saw it quite
distinctly, but I have never been able to account for it. The
great gates stood ajar for my entrance, and as I came through
them I met a curious fresh slippery coldness, like wet seaweed,
yet with no sense of chill in it.

As I had guessed, the tide was going out, and the rocks of
the point were slowly coming up out of the water as the languid
wash of the ground-swell heaved the weed. The rising moon
had not yet cleared the down, and the fort lay in shadow
though the water was silvered; one could see the wide faint
furrows of the slowly-moving swell coming in from the
Atlantic, and it was very like the traces of the plough that
remain when arable land goes back to pasture. The sea was
not like sea that night, and the land was not like land, but they
seemed to be one thing, even as they were before the Spirit of
God moved upon the face of the waters.

I called to Morgan, but got no answer, and seeing the big
room lit up, I went in there to look for her.

She sat silently, calm and aloof, and she might have been
asleep save that she was bolt upright. She was clad in a close
silvery robe, and her cloak was of indigo gauze, and she looked
just like the moon in the night sky amid light cloud. On her
head was the horned head-dress of the moon, which is also the
lunar crescent of Isis. At the far end of the room was another
raised dais, and I took my seat on it. Immediately behind me

was the shadowy outline of the Priest of the Moon in his painted sea-palace. In the centre of the floor was the altar of the double cube, draped in silver, and upon it a crystal bowl filled with water, and Morgan and I sat and faced each other across it, the length of the room away.

Then I became conscious of a curious thing. It seemed to me that the painted pictures on the walls were no longer pictures but actuality, and that the sea stretched away level with the floor, even as I had painted it; and it was just as real as the sea outside that I could see through the gap we had cut in the embrasures where the path led out to the point. And it suddenly occurred to me that the Priest of the Moon behind me might have become real also, but I did not dare to turn my head to look.

Then Morgan rose, and her cloak of dark gauze floated out from her shoulders like wings and the silver robe shone through it. She struck a bell beside her, and its soft note filled the room with humming overtones that died slowly away. She raised her hand:

"Be ye far from us, O ye profane, for we are about to invoke the descent of the power of Isis. Enter her temple with clean hands and a pure heart, lest ye defile the source of life."

I thought of the dome of light that had been built to enclose the fort, and reckoned that here we could wake the ancient forces, unprofaned and safe from all intrusion.

"The temple of Isis is built of black marble and hung with silver, and she herself sitteth veiled in the innermost. She is all goddesses that men's hearts have worshipped, for they are not many things, but one thing under many forms.

"Those who adore the Isis of Nature adore her as Hathor with the horns upon her brow; but those who adore the celestial Isis know her as Levanah, the Moon. She is also the Great Deep whence life arose. She is all ancient and forgotten things wherein our roots are cast. Upon earth she is ever-fecund: in heaven she is ever-virgin. She is the mistress of the tides that flow and ebb and flow and never cease. In these things are the keys of her mystery, known only to the initiated."

Morgan struck the bell again; its vibrations sank to silence once more, and we sat in stillness for a while. It seemed to me that we were on a low rocky islet surrounded on all sides by the sea, and upon it was the black and silver temple of Isis, through whose arched portico we looked out on the water.

Then Morgan rose again, and lifted her arms to the moon as the women of ancient times had done before her.

"O thou most holy and adorable Isis, who in the heavens art the Supernal Mother, and upon earth Our Lady of Nature, and in the airy kingdoms between heaven and earth the ever-changing Moon, ruling the tides of flux and reflux upon the earth and in the hearts of men. Thee, thee we adore in the symbol of the Moon in her splendour, ever-changing. And in the symbol of the deep sea that reflects her. And in the symbol of the opening of the gates of life.

"We see thee crowned in silver in the heavens, and clad in green upon the earth, and in thy robe of many colours at the gates. O heavenly silver that answerest to the celestial gold! O green that risest from the grey! O rainbow glory of living!"

The soft bell-tones sounded again, and taking her note from the bell, Morgan began to sing the song of which the snatches had plagued me for weeks past:

> "O thou that wast before the earth was formed—
> Ea, Binah, Ge.
> O tideless, soundless, boundless, bitter sea,
> I am thy priestess, answer unto me.

> "O arching sky above and earth beneath,
> Giver of life and bringer-in of death,
> Persephone, Astarte, Ashtoreth,
> I am thy priestess, answer unto me.

"O golden Aphrodite, come to me!
Flower of the foam, rise from the bitter sea.
The hour of the full moon-tide draws near,
Hear the invoking words, hear and appear—
        Isis unveiled, and Ea, Binah, Ge!
I am thy priestess, answer unto me."

Morgan sat down, but the rite went on. But now I had no need to turn my head to know that the Priest of the Moon was behind me, for I heard his voice.

"Learn now the secret of the web that is woven between the light and the darkness; whose warp is life evolving in time and space, and whose weft is spun of the lives of men.

"Behold we arise with the dawn of time from the grey and misty sea, and with the dusk we sink in the western ocean, and the lives of a man are strung like pearls on the thread of his spirit; and never in all his journey goes he alone, for that which is solitary is barren."

The voice ceased, and there was silence; and in the silence I could hear the sound of the sea murmuring among the rocks and knew that the windows stood open to the night.

Then the voice spoke again, and it had gathered a strength that dominated the room :

"Learn now the mystery of the ebbing and flowing tides. That which is dynamic in the outer is latent in the inner, for that which is above is as that which is below, but after another manner.

"Isis of Nature awaiteth the coming of her Lord the Sun. She calls him. She draws him from the place of the dead, the Kingdom of Amenti, where all things are forgotten. And he comes to her in his boat called Millions of Years, and the earth grows green with the springing grain. For the desire of Osiris answereth unto the call of Isis. And so it will ever be in the hearts of men, for thus the gods have formed them. Whoso denieth this is abhorréd of the gods.

"But in the heavens our Lady Isis is the Moon, and the moon-powers are hers. She is also the priestess of the silver star that rises from the twilight sea. Hers are the magnetic moon-tides ruling the hearts of men.

"In the inner she is all-potent. She is queen of the kingdoms of sleep. All the invisible workings are hers and she rules all things ere they come to birth. Even as through Osiris her mate the earth grows green, so the mind of man conceives through her power.

"Let us show forth in a rite the dynamic nature of the goddess that the minds of men may be as fertile as their fields," and from behind me came a bell-note where I knew there was no bell.

"Be ye far from us, O ye profane, for the unveiling of the goddess is at hand. Look not upon her with impure eyes lest ye see your own damnation.

"The ignorant and impure man gazeth upon the face of Nature, and it is to him darkness of darkness. But the initiated and illuminated man gazeth thereon and seeth the features of God. Be ye far from us, O ye profane, while we adore God made manifest in Nature."

The voice fell silent again, and the sea outside answered with a slow soft wash on the rocks that was like the beating of muffled cymbals.

Then Morgan slowly rose, all her silver draperies a-shimmer, and stood upright in the rigidity of Egypt; she raised her hands from the bent elbows till the palms faced me, and there was power coming from those palms. I saw that her face had changed, and was almost negroid about the mouth, though the still, calm, Nordic breadth of brow remained. Then a voice spoke that was not Morgan's voice, curiously inhuman and metallic.

"I am the Veiled Isis of the shadows of the sanctuary. I am

she that moveth as a shadow behind the tides of death and birth. I am she that cometh forth by night, and no man seeth my face. I am older than time and forgotten of the gods. No man may look upon my face and live, for in the hour he parteth my veil, he dieth."

Prompted by I know not what power, I spoke.

"There is one man that looketh upon thy face. Behold, I am the sacrifice. I part thy veil and die to the birth."

And behind me came the voice of the Priest of the Moon:

"There are two deaths by which men die, the greater and the lesser. The death of the body, and the death of initiation. And of these two, the death of the body is the lesser. The man who looks upon the face of Isis dies, for the goddess takes him. They that die thus go by the path of the well-head that is beside the white cypress."

And I answered:

"I will take the path that leads to the well-head beside the white cypress."

And the voice of the Priest of the Moon replied:

"He that would die to the birth, let him look upon the face of the goddess in this mystery. Be ye far from us, O ye profane, for one goes forth by the path that leads to the well-head beside the white cypress."

I felt a strange feeling stealing over me as if I were going into trance; and I saw that Morgan's hands were no longer upheld, but stretched out and parallel, palms facing; and between those outheld palms my very life was being drawn in. I felt myself becoming passive, neuter, unresisting, like a man drugged into sleep. Then I heard, as if from very far off, the sound of Morgan singing.

"I am the soundless, boundless, bitter sea;
All things in the end shall come to me.
Mine is the kingdom of Persephone,

> The inner earth, where lead the pathways three.
> Who drinks the waters of that hidden well
> Shall see the things whereof he dare not tell—
> Shall tread the shadowy path that leads to me—
>   Diana of the Ways and Hecate,
>   Selene of the Moon, Persephone."

It seemed to me as if death were calling to me out of the great deep, and my life ebbed away from me like a man bleeding to death. If ever man died, I died then; but I heard the voice of the Priest of the Moon speaking to me through the gathering shadows:

"The daughter of the Great Mother is Persephone, Queen of Hades, ruler of the kingdoms of sleep and death. Under the form of the Dark Queen men also worship Her who is the One. Likewise is she Aphrodite—and herein is a great mystery, for it is decreed that none shall understand the one without the other.

"In death men go to her across the shadowy river, for she is the keeper of their souls until the dawn. But there is also a death in life, and this likewise leadeth on to rebirth. Why fear ye the Dark Queen, O men? She is the Renewer. From sleep we arise refreshed; from death we arise reborn; by the embraces of Persephone are men made powerful.

"For there is a turning-within of the soul whereby men come to Persephone; they sink back into the womb of time; they become as the unborn; they enter into the kingdom where she rules as queen; they are made negative and await the coming of life.

"And the Queen of Hades cometh unto them as a bridegroom, and they are made fertile for life and go forth rejoicing, for the touch of the Queen of the kingdoms of sleep hath made them potent."

I knew the time had now come that I had foreseen from

the first, when my life should be poured out on the altar to give the goddess power; but I had thought of that sacrifice as a bloody rite, violent and terrible; but this was a slow ebbing away of strength and a sinking down into nothingness that was only terrible because it was the end. I felt sleep rising over me like a tide as the sea rose over the rocks outside, taking back again that which belonged to it, lent for an hour to the air. I was returning to the nothingness whence I had come, and life was ending as it had begun, in sleep.

I remembered the words of one of the wise—"Or ever the silver cord is loosed, or the golden bowl is broken——" I felt the golden bowl of my soul lifted up and poured out upon the cubical moon-altar; but it must have been that the silver thread was not loosed, for I still lived, though I came as near to death as a man might and yet return.

With the eyes of vision I saw the stars moving in the heavenly spaces and tides in the earth-soul following them as the tidal wave of the earthly seas follows after the moon. Then through my vision I heard the voice of the Priest again.

"Our Lady is also the Moon, called of some Selene, of others, Luna, but by the wise Levanah, for therein is contained the number of her name. She is the ruler of the tides of flux and reflux. The waters of the Great Sea answer unto her, likewise the tides of all earthly seas, and she ruleth the nature of woman.

"But there is likewise in the souls of men a flowing and an ebbing of the tides of life, which no one knoweth save the wise; and over these tides the Great Goddess presides under her aspect of the Moon. She comes from the sea as the evening star, and the magnetic waters of earth rise in flood. She sinks as Persephone in the western ocean and the waters flow back into the inner earth and become still in that great lake of darkness wherein are the moon and stars reflected. Whoso is still as the dark underworld lake of Persephone sees the tides of the Unseen moving therein, and knoweth all things. Therefore is Luna called the giver of visions."

The voice ceased, and I thought it was the end. Then I saw that in the utter darkness light moved like a tide, and knew that even death has a manner of life of its own. It seemed to me that I looked out over the dark lake of the underworld to where Persephone, who was also Morgan le Fay, sat on her throne awaiting my coming. I remembered that in my sea-cave vision I had been required to swear that I would go to my death without struggling, for the sacrifice must be consummated by the unreserved surrender—and I willed to cross the dark water and come to her.

I found myself in the strange, highprowed boat called Millions of Years wherein Osiris voyages, and I was Osiris. Beside me were the gods that travelled with me, that were also my other selves. Horus, hawk of the morning, was look-out in the bow, and Toom, god of the gathering dusk, sat silent in the stern; and at my feet the Kephra Beetle, symbol of the sun at midnight, held in his claws the emblem of time that is past. And so we travelled over the dark waters of the lake of the underworld to come to the Queen of the Dead, my magical bride. And as we drew towards her the light increased till it was the light of the room at the fort, and at the far end I saw Morgan sitting.

And as I looked, I saw her begin to change from silver into gold, and a glowing aura of all the colours of the rainbow sprang out around her. Her sleeping eyes opened into an amazing animation of life, and she glowed with life like a glorious dawn. Then the tide that had flowed from me to her turned and flowed back from her to me, and I felt my life returning to me, but different, for it had been made one with the life of the Goddess.

Then she sang, and I knew that this was Isis, unveiled and dynamic:

> "I am the star that rises from the sea—
>   The twilight sea.
> I bring men dreams that rule their destiny.
> I bring the dream-tides to the souls of men;
> The tides that ebb and flow and ebb again—
>   These are my secret, these belong to me—
>
> "I am the eternal Woman, I am she!
> The tides of all men's souls belong to me.
> The tides that ebb and flow and ebb again;
> The silent, inward tides that govern men—
>   These are my secret, these belong to me.
>
> "Out of my hands he takes his destiny.
> Touch of my hands confers polarity.
> These are the moon-tides, these belong to me—
>   Hera in heaven, on earth, Persephone;
> Levanah of the tides, and Hecate.
> Diana of the Moon, Star of the Sea—
> Isis Unveiled and Ea, Binah, Ge!"

And all the while she sang her weaving hands stroked my soul and drew it out.

Then slowly, with no stir save the flutter of her draperies, Morgan moved towards the window. I did not follow her. I was incapable of movement. She went out into the forecourt; the moon had risen higher now, and the fort was flooded with the moonlight. She stood still for a moment among the remains of sea-beasts that the storm had shattered, and in the changing light as thin cloud crossed the moon they all came alive and wriggled. Then she moved on down the steps that led to the point. The balustrading had gone in the storm, and there was nothing between her and the sea; the moonlight fell full on her and made her robe glitter, but against the brighter glitter of the sea she was almost invisible. She went on down the point out to the very end, where the flat table of rock lay just below the surface, for it only appeared at the neap.

"God!" I thought, "she must be knee-deep in water! Supposing she over-steps the edge?"

But I was powerless to move, being as one bound.

I could only just see her now, for her silver robe was almost invisible against the treacherous glitter of the water. Then a cloud crossed the moon, and when it had gone I saw that a light mist was coming in from the sea in long drifts, and I could no longer distinguish her through its uncertain haze.

My first instinct was to go after her and see if she were safe, but a strong inner compulsion prevented me. I knew that I must not do this, and that all was well with her. So I sat in my chair and waited.

And as I sat, I became conscious that I was not alone. There was no stir or sound of breathing behind me to reveal that someone was there, but nevertheless I felt a presence, and gradually there came upon me the sense of awe and stimulation that one feels in the presence of a very dynamic personality—one of the great of the earth. I waited and listened, holding my breath between each breathing in an effort to hear the least movement from what was behind me, but kept as if hypnotised from turning my head.

Then a voice began, clear to my physical ears, resonant, measured and calm—the voice of the Priest of the Moon, no longer a disembodied voice, but fully materialised. It went on and on like the sound of running water, and in the pauses I heard outside the wash of the waves on the rocks as the tide rose, covering the point. And as the voice went on there arose before my eyes the images it created, and I knew why it was that the Mystical Gospel says that all things were made by the Word, for the Word moved like the spirit of God upon the face of the waters. I saw the sea of space and time, indigo-dark in the Night of the Gods, as I had seen it in the beginning. And over the dark of the sea I saw the silver light and the gold light coming and going in long undulant pulsing beams. As the resonant voice went on, I listened; and some I understood, for it explained what had happened; but some I did not understand then, for it explained what was to come later.

"Thrice-greatest Hermes graved on the Smaragdene Tablet: 'As above, so below.' Upon earth we see the reflection of the heavenly principles in the actions of men and women.

"All the gods are one god, and all the goddesses are one goddess, and there is one initiator.

"In the beginning was space and darkness and stillness, older than time and forgotten of the gods. The sea of infinite space was the source of all being; life arose therein like a tide in the soundless sea. All shall return thereto when the night of the gods draws in. This is the Great Sea, Marah, the Bitter One, the Great Mother. And because of the inertia of space ere movement arose as a tide, she is called by the wise the passive principle in nature, and is thought of as cosmic water, or space that flows.

"She is called by many names by many men; but to all she is the Great Goddess—space and earth and water. As space she is called Ea, parent of the gods that made the gods; she is more old than time; she is the matrix of matter, the root-substance of all existence, undifferentiated, pure. She is also Binah, the Supernal Mother, that receiveth Chokmah, the Supernal Father. She is the giver of form to the formless force whereby it can build. She is also the bringer-in of death, for that which has form must die, outworn, in order that it may be born again to fuller life. All that is born must die, but that which dies shall be reborn. Therefore she is called Marah, the Bitter One, Our Lady of Sorrows, for she is the bringer-in of death. Likewise she is called Ge, for she is the most ancient earth, the first-formed from the formless. All these is she, and they are seen in her, and whatsoever is of their nature answers unto her and she hath dominion over it. Her tides are its tides, her ways are its ways, and whoso knoweth the one, knoweth the other.

"Whatsoever ariseth out of nothingness, she giveth it; whatsoever sinketh down into nothingness, she receiveth it. She is the Great Sea whence life arose, to which all shall return at the end of the aeon.

"Herein do we bathe in sleep, sinking back into the primordial depths, returning to things forgotten before time was, and the soul is renewed, touching the Great Mother. Whoso cannot return to the primordial hath no roots in life, but withereth as the grass. These are the living dead, who are orphaned of the Great Mother."

All this meant little to me at the time, save that there rang in my ears the words of the Smaragdene Tablet—"As above, so below"—but later, little by little, the things that were said returned to me as life explained them. For indeed in that deadly little town—walled about with conventions and paved with dust and ashes—were we orphaned of the Great Mother; and I had to die before I could be reborn, and the Great Goddess was indeed to me the Bitter One. Like many a better man before me, I was to drink what passes in civilisation for the waters of Lethe. But these things were still to come, and I did not know then.

I heard the voice of the Priest of the Moon, speaking to me by name: "My son, I go now, but will come again. The work is not yet finished."

The voice ceased, and I sat silent in my chair, awaiting the return of Morgan. But although the voice spoke no more, I knew that I was not alone, but that the Priest of the Moon bore me company in my vigil.

Dozing there in my chair between sleeping and waking, the understanding of many things came to me. I knew that Morgan had performed with me a rite that was also an experiment, but I could not divine its purpose or see what it led to or how it was to go on. For I could not conceive that we had come so far to stop suddenly short. The rite we had performed, I was convinced, was the prelude to something, but what it was I could not discern. And yet there was about it a curious sense of finality as if it were also an end; and this I could not explain either, though I was not long before I found out.

So I dozed in my chair and waited for Morgan to come back to me, and towards dawn I fell asleep. But she never came back. I never saw her again.

CHAPTER XXVI

ROUND about eight Mrs Treth came into the room. I saw by her eyes she had been crying, but suspected nothing. She told me that Morgan wanted me to go home now, and that she would write to me. There was nothing else to do but go. Mrs Treth gave me my breakfast, and I got my car and drove off. I noticed that Morgan's little black sports car was not in the garage.

Going round the hairpin bend one does not usually take one's eyes off the road, but I risked it, and looked up at the cave where I had kept vigil, and was startled to see that a mass of rock had fallen, leaving a white scar on the grey weathered surface; and I knew that Morgan had fired the shot and that the door of the cave of vigil was closed for ever. But still I suspected nothing.

As I passed the farm Treth came out and insisted on shaking me solemnly by the hand. As it was only a few days from Christmas I thought he had his eye on a Christmas-box.

Then I drove home. They were suprised to see me back so early, but very glad, as Scottie had gone down with the flu. I sat down at his desk to tackle the morning mail, and his secretary, with embarrassed apologies, laid a letter before me which had been opened by mistake, not being marked personal. It was from Morgan.

"By the time you get this," she wrote, "I shall be gone. Never mind where. You will never see me again. You must make up your mind to that. I am sorry, for I am very fond of you.

"The work I had to do has been done; and I would like you to know that it was by your help I did it.

"I took a big risk with you, Wilfred, but if I have done my work rightly, you will not be broken. I have arranged for my star sapphires to be given as a wedding present to your bride when you marry.

"All my property is now in a trust, of which you and Treth are the two trustees. You will find him very shrewd and absolutely trustworthy. At my death it is to be divided equally between you. Until such time as you can legally presume my death you are to pay over the income from my estate to my bank, keeping one tenth for yourselves. The farm I have made over to the Treths and the fort to the National Trust. All my manuscripts and books are yours by deed of gift, the manuscripts are in cases at the farm.

"I have had a very perfect friendship with you, Wilfred, my friend; I have never known any man to give so unreservedly. The name of friend is not one I use lightly, but I give it to you.

"Myself I could not give to you, for it was not in my power. Remember old Atlantis and how they trained them there.

"Good-bye till we meet again, which will not be on this side of the Gates of Death."

It did not matter how much work there was to do at the office, I got out my car and drove straight back to the fort.

Or rather I set out to drive straight back. I thought the sky looked a bit odd as I came out of the town, and as I crossed the bridge into the marshes a flurry of snow came up and caked on the wind-screen, and before I knew where I was I was butting into the teeth of a blizzard.

I could hardly see the end of the radiator, and I was driving on a ten-foot dyke. However, there was a kind of grass kerb at either side, and when I felt my tyres scraping along it, I

straightened her out. The Treths did not appear surprised to
see me back. I wanted Treth to come straight out with me to
the fort, and rated him like a pickpocket when he wouldn't,
till Mrs Treth threw her apron over her head and came out to
me in the snow and made me come into her kitchen and sit
by the fire till I quieted down.

They told me that it had been pretty nearly as much of a
shock to them as it had to me. Morgan had always said that
this was the way she would go when her time came, but they
had never suspected that her time was now till they arrived
in the morning and found a note on the kitchen table. I asked
Treth whether he thought she had gone in off the point or had
shut herself up in the cave. He said he had no idea. I wanted
him to climb up and see if the wire and battery were outside
on the cliff path, but he said they wouldn't be; for if Morgan
had fired the charge from inside, they would be inside with
her, and if she had fired it from outside, she might have pulled
the wire out of the débris and taken it away. So we should be
none the wiser, and to climb down that path in this howling
gale was to risk one's life. If Morgan were in that cave, she
couldn't possibly be alive, and in any case, all her arrangements
had been made most carefully so as to prevent any disturbance
or inquiry over her passing, and he for his part meant to respect
her wishes, and he hoped I would do the same.

Then with a sudden start I remembered that Morgan's car
was gone from the garage, and asked them if they had heard
her go by in the night? But they said no, she had not gone
by. The car had been removed some days before. She had
done that, she said in her note, so that if any questions should
be asked, they would be cleared. And she had left them a
second note, to show in case anybody raised trouble for them,
in which she said that she had made an early start, and all letters were to be sent to her London flat. I asked Treth when

he had seen the car last, and he admitted that he had not seen it all that week, not having had any occasion to go to the garage. I asked him whether, as he slept at the back of the house, he could be sure of hearing Morgan if she had driven past with the engine off, letting the slope of the road take her; and whether he had examined the road for wheel-marks before the snow came? He shook his head.

"She's dead to you, sir, anyway," said he. "Better leave it be."

"How do you know?" said I.

"Because it is what we have been expecting. It was what she always intended. Me and my missus was young when we came to her, and we have grown old, but she hasn't. She always told us she would go this way when the work was done that she had to do. Anyway, you had better leave it be, sir, for if she is alive, she would never forgive us for interfering."

I wondered if she were lying injured in the cave, but he shook his head.

"Nay," he said, "I set that shot for her, and I'm an old quarryman. She's not lying there injured. She's lying there buried. But to my mind it is more like she went in off the point, for she always had a feeling for the sea."

"Or gave us all the slip and went off in her car," said I.

"I'd leave it be if I was you, sir," said Treth.

After a bit more persuasion I turned the car round and drove back to Dickford. If Morgan were alive and did not choose to have anything more to do with me, she was as good as dead to me. But somehow, I did not feel she was alive. I have always believed that she never returned when she walked out on to the point. But then, who fired the shot? And why the curious financial arrangements of the trust? Treth and I have never been called on to give an account of our stewardship, so whether Morgan died that night, or whether she still walks the ways of men in all her beauty and strange power makes no odds. I learnt a lot about death when I lost Morgan. It has always puzzled me why folk bother to prove survival; for if your loved ones cannot come to you, what good does it do you to know that they survive? For my part I would sooner understand the whence and whither of the soul in its aeonial evolution. "Behold, we arise with the dawn of time from the grey and misty sea, and with the dusk we sink in the western ocean. And the lives of a man are strung like pearls on the thread of his spirit." Those words of the Priest of the Moon kept recurring to my mind as I drove back across the marshes. The snow had let up for the moment, but looked like more to come, and a howling gale did its best to push me off the dyke. I have had some penitential drives in my time, but never such another as that, in the oncoming dusk and snow over those bleak saltings. I was too dazed to do any real thinking. I couldn't believe that Morgan was dead, and yet I was pretty sure she wasn't alive, and my brain was just going round inside my head, and how I ever got to my journey's end alive myself I do not know.

I don't know how much of Morgan's letter Scottie's secretary had read before she discovered that it did not concern the firm, but she looked very surprised to see me back so soon. Then she brought me a large cup of strong tea, of which I was very glad. I also found she had tackled the correspondence on her own initiative, and had all the letters ready for me to sign, which was just as well, for signing them was about as much as I was capable of doing.

It was an amazing thing to me that the asthma did not take me by the throat then and there, but I think it was just about as stunned as I was. They wouldn't let me see Scottie for fear of infection, but I gathered that he was pretty bad. Thank God all the quarterly accounting had been done the previous week, and we had a few days breathing-space over the holidays.

On Christmas Eve I drove out to the farm to take the Treths a turkey. It was a pretty ghastly drive, and I wished I hadn't undertaken it, for all the time I kept on having to remind myself that I should not be going on to the fort and seeing Morgan. Ovid is quite right when he says that the only remedy for love is to clear out. But the turkey was a promise, and they would have been let down over their Christmas dinner if I had failed them.

Treth came out to me when I pulled up at the farm, and asked me if I would run him out to the fort as there had bee. the devil's own blow and he was a bit uneasy as to how things might be out there; he knew as well as I did that the end wall wasn't all it might be after the last storm, and Morgan had refused to have any repairs done to it. Although he did not admit it, I could see that he funked going out there alone.

I think the same thing was in both our minds as we drove up the familiar way. Was Morgan sleeping her last sleep in the cave, or had she walked out into the sea from the point? And if so, were the cod and the conger at work on her strange beauty or had she gone living to the sea-gods, as tradition averred the priestesses did?

There were a lot of unsolved problems in this business that have always remained unsolved so far as I am concerned at any rate. Was Morgan a fraud all along, and had she slipped away in her car after misleading the Treths? And if so, what was her motive? Was she sincere but self-deluded, going to her death in all good faith? Or was she right in her faith and was her life-work crowned with success? I suppose one chooses one's explanation according to taste; and although one's theory may explain nothing about Morgan, it tells a good deal about oneself.

As soon as we got round the hairpin bend we saw that all the cairns were down, and the pylon too. After all, they were held by nothing but their own weight, and it had been blowing a full gale out here. The fort looked all right from the landward side, but when we tried to open the big gates we could not manage it, so we knew that something must be down on the other side that was blocking them. Treth did a hair-raising fly-crawl round the end of the rocks, and presently I heard him shoving lumber about on the other side of the gate, and in a few minutes he got it open just wide enough for me to squeeze through sideways, and I saw what had happened.

The end wall had come down as I had prophesied, its underpinning having been pulled out and never repaired, and the waves had made a clean sweep of everything. The courtyard was knee-deep in sea-wrack and fucus. Everything I had done in the way of ornamentation had gone as if it had never been, and the fort was practically as it was when I first saw it. I went into the big room to see what was left of my pictures, but the place was a wreck—all the plaster off the walls; the ceiling down; the windows out; all the furniture smashed to bits at the far end, and nothing intact save my two dolphins, still *in situ* in the fireplace, surveying the wreck quite unperturbed.

Treth and I looked at each other, and without a word we went up to Morgan's bedroom, but as we opened the door we recoiled, for the floor had fallen in, and the end wall had fallen out, and blue water was under our feet.

Treth waited in the courtyard while I went out on to the point. There was a pretty heavy sea hammering at it after the storm; the balustrading had gone, every scrap of it; just here and there was the socket of an upright to show that anything had ever been. I went out along the crest of the slabs, a precarious scramble without the balustrading, and got out on to the extreme end where the surf was roaring and crashing and frothing like suds all over the rocks. As my ears became accustomed to the din I could hear the high shrill crying of the gulls above it, and I remembered the old legend that the souls of the drowned mariners became sea-birds, and wondered whether Morgan was there, changed from woman to bird of the sea, but lost to me for ever.

I thought of the poor moon-calf, sacrificed for the building of the temple, who had gone to his death with a smile on his face as a sacrifice should, and of the poor old father who had loved even that parody of humanity.

Then I thought of Morgan as I had last seen her, disappearing into the glitter and the mist, and I spoke to the sea and told it that it could have me too if it wanted me. I waited a bit, but nothing happened, and I turned round and came back. Treth was gone from the courtyard, and I stood for a moment or two and looked round. The place felt as empty as an unused coffin.

Then I knew that Morgan was gone from this world and that her experiment had succeeded.

When I got back to the car I found Treth busy loading the dolphins into it.

"I reckon her would have liked 'ee to have 'em," he said. "They bain't no use to the Trust."

We drove back in silence, neither offering any comment on what we had seen, but I think we both thought the same thing. In some curious way the trip to the fort had settled our minds. We had accepted the situation. We were no longer in the midst of it, but had begun to put it behind us. I presented the turkey to Mrs Treth, had a cup of tea with them, and started for home.

And then as I went over the marshes in the winter dusk there came to me a vision sudden and blinding as the vision of

Paul on the road to Damascus, and I saw the Priest of the Moon standing before me in the way. Too dazed to pull up, I drove right over the place where he had appeared. I was too shattered, too absorbed in my grief for Morgan, to wonder what his appearance meant.

When I got back to Dickford the bells were ringing for the Christmas Eve service. We have very fine bells at the parish church, the only ones that beat them being those of the cathedral. I pulled up the car in a narrow lane behind the north porch and listened to the organ playing the Christmas hymns; and why I do not know, but my mind went back to the vigil in the cave when I had heard the calving cow out in the marshes and known that she was Hathor. And I thought of a curious little statuette I had seen of Isis suckling Horus; and that the Great Deep whence life arose is also called Marah, the Bitter One; and that Our Lady is called Stella Maris, Star of the Sea; and I remembered the saying of the Priest of the Moon that all the gods are one god, and all the goddesses one goddess, and wondered what it meant. This was the last I was to see for some time of the dark side of the moon. Everything relating to Morgan and the sea-magic closed down as if it had never been.

Then I drove on, and seeing our office still lit up, turned in there, and found Scottie's secretary doing a final clear-up before the holidays; and remembering what a decent kid she had been all through the difficulties, I went off to the sweet-shop and got her a box of chocolates as a Christmas present.

Exchanging the compliments of the season with the damsel behind the counter, who looked longingly at her bunch of mistletoe, the memory came into my mind of the synthetic charmer who had been the downfall of my old dominie and who had presided behind that very counter, and I wondered how well her peroxide charms had worn, and whether her lover had stuck to her, or, more problematical, whether she had

stuck to him. Then I ran the car into the garage, and leaving
the dolphins to their own devices overnight, for they were
weighty, took my parcel back to the office, and made a solemn
presentation to Scottie's blushing secretary, whose name I did
not know. After that I went home and Sally put what was
left of me to bed; next day, being a Christian family, we saluted
the happy morn with the Hell and Hades of a row because I
wouldn't get up and go to early service, my sister being quite
determined that even if I didn't get up, I shouldn't sleep.

CHAPTER XXVII

IF there is one thing that is worse than another, it is Christmas when you aren't feeling festive. Not being officially in mourning, I was not entitled to any overt display of grief, so had to bottle it all up inside me as best I might. Sally, I think, guessed, but I could not discuss it with her because there was so much I could not tell her, and so little the simple old soul would have understood if I had. Scottie was sick, and anyway he wasn't sympathetic. So I went round to the "George" and told the wine waiter that I had been crossed in love and had he anything in the cellars that would console me? I woke up there next morning, and Sally collected me, saying that Christmas often used to take her old man the same way.

That evening my sister had a party for the Friendly Girls, and insisted that I should lend a hand. I tried to get out of it and go to bed, for I was more dead than alive, but she kept on at me, and finally the worm turned and I agreed. I kissed the bloody lot under the mistletoe till my sister had hysterics in the study and phoned for the vicar; then I shoved brandy and champagne in the temperance shandygaff and cleared off. By the time the vicar arrived, the girls had drunk the shandygaff. I found bits of mistletoe all over the house next morning. I bet it was some party! He must have found them genuinely friendly girls for once, to judge from the distribution of the mistletoe.

I was very glad to get back into harness next morning. I had had enough of holiday-making and Christmas revelry, and so, I think, had my sister. Sally was seedy, too; she had been

Christmassing at the house of a married son and it had disagreed with her. In the small hours of the morning she was taken with a heart attack to which I had had to minister with what was left over from the shandygaff. As I went out to the bank, I saw cylinders of oxygen being taken into Scottie's house. So altogether it was some Christmas.

But the fun hadn't finished yet. I was received at the office by Scottie's secretary, whose poor little countenance was decorated with a carefully camouflaged black eye. Blushing and squirming, she asked me if I had meant to give her what I had given her. I began to wonder whether, amid so much battle, murder, and sudden death, poison had got into the chocolates, and asked her what was amiss. She asked me if I knew what I had given her. I told her that I had bought them as chocolates. She said that it wasn't chocolates at all, but jewellery.

Then I knew what had happened. Treth had given me Morgan's star sapphires to put in the bank till the extremely unlikely event of the clause in Morgan's will becoming operative, and in the dark of the garage I had taken up the wrong parcel out of the back of the car where I had dumped all the dunnage. The chocolates were safely in the strong-room at the bank and Scottie's secretary had the sapphires.

I apologised hastily and abjectly for my mistake, and explained that the sapphires did not belong to me, but that I was responsible for them, and must ask her for them back. She looked as if about to expire with mortification, and explained that she hadn't got them; her stepfather had taken them from her and was hanging on to them. That, I thought, explains the black eye. She had probably gone counter to parental authority in her honesty. If she had said nothing, the chocolates would have stayed at the bank till they mummified and she would have got away with the sapphires. Of course star sapphires are not worth as much as the unflawed kind, but even so, Morgan's set would have represented a small fortune to a girl in her position.

Blushing very self-consciously, the girl tendered me a letter. "This was inside," she said. "That was how I knew they were not for me."

I took the envelope, and saw that it was addressed to the recipient of the sapphires.

"If you don't mind my mentioning it," said Scottie's secretary, "I think you ought to seal it up again, and not read it till you give it to the person it is meant for."

So then and there, in her presence, I sealed it up.·

Then I asked her who her stepfather was, as I now had the task before me of recovering the sapphires from his hands, and to judge by her eye, he was heavy-handed.

When she told me who he was, you could have knocked me down with a feather, for he was Muckley, the lowest pork-butcher in the town. He hung out in the bend of the river where our local slum was, that I have spoken of before, and he had a fourteenth-century house that would have been all right as Ye Olde Tea Shoppe, but was damned insanitary as a butcher's. I had been getting a move on about that slum, having bought the house the cedar came from, and Muckley was organising the opposition. He would. He was that sort.

It amazed me that a refined, educated girl like Scottie's secretary should have come out of that awful pork shop, but then I remembered that Muckley was her stepfather and not her father.

I asked her what her name was, and she told me Molly Coke. The name woke memories, and I asked her if she were any connection of my old schoolmaster, and she told me she was his daughter. Then I remembered her as a little dark-eyed, pale-faced thing, who used to play in the playground when we were in school, and come in when we came out. I wondered what had become of the lovely for whom my late dominie had deserted his wife and family, and incidentally his means of livelihood, for since his wife had remarried he was obviously dead, divorces being beyond the means of the likes of them.

So leaving Molly Coke in charge of the office, I went round to interview the amiable Muckley and make him disgorge the sapphires. His beastly shop wasn't open, but there was a terrific screeching coming from the back premises, so it evidently soon would be. I saw the Cruelty to Animals man craning his neck out of a top window down the street, trying to get a line on what was happening; he had a down on Muckley, who was popularly credited with omitting to kill the pig before he started making the sausages.

I waited till the screeching died away in a wail, and then began to hammer on the door. After a bit this elicited Mrs Muckley, late Coke. I remembered her as a quiet, neutral sort of creature, who seldom spoke but contented herself with waiting on her flamboyant husband, and was probably, if the truth were known, the man of the family. I certainly should not have know her. Her hair was quite white, and she looked to me as if she hadn't got much longer in this world. I told her my errand, and she flushed nervously and went to fetch her husband. I could hear his voice booming away out at the back, and he didn't sound amiable.

The place smelt too awful for words, having been shut up and unaired over the holidays.

Presently he appeared, covered with pig and offensively hearty, whereas I had expected, from the "noises off" that I would be lucky if I didn't get my own eye blacked—and proceeded to do the finest lying I have ever heard, and an auctioneer and estate agent is a connoisseur of lying.

"Yus," he said, "I told Molly she'd have to hand back them stones, they wasn't for her. But it's no good her saying I've got 'em because I haven't. She's got 'em. You make her hand 'em back, Mr Maxwell, the thievin' little huzzy."

"So she's done the snitching, has she?" said I.

"Yus," said he, "she's done the snitching."

"And did she do the eye-blacking too?"

He gave me a nasty look.

Then I set to and told him what I thought of him. He looked surprised. He hadn't expected anything like that from Mr Wilfred Maxwell, the only son of his mother, and she a widow. He went and fetched the sapphires, meek as Moses. All the same, I wondered what sort of a reception poor Molly Coke would meet with when she got home. He would have to do something to restore his deflated *amour propre*.

When I got back to the office I told her the line Muckley had taken with me; I also gave her a bowdlerised version of the line I had taken with him, and said she was to let me know if she had any trouble with him and I would call round again and say it with flowers; but she never complained, so I concluded that she had nothing to complain about, beyond, of course, what anyone would have to complain about who had to associate with Muckley

We shuffled along for the next few days, I picking up the threads of the business as best I could with Molly Coke's help, for I had been leaving everything to Scottie. We had half a dozen assorted clerks and clerklets, but no one had any head worth mentioning except Molly, Scottie believing in keeping everything in his own hands as being the best way of ensuring efficiency and honesty. So it may be, in normal times, but any disorganisation hits you hard.

I had to take the weekly auctions in the cattle market, than which I hate nothing more, and had some nastiness with Muckley over a very dud lot of pigs he put in, and that I referred to the sanitary inspector. He and his farmer friends tried to bounce me with their superior knowledge of pigs, but I exercised my rights as a licensed auctioneer and rode rough-shod over them. I mayn't know much about pigs, but I know a lot about Muckley, and there must be something pretty wrong with any pigs that he wouldn't risk sausaging. I was right, too, for the whole party were tubercular.

Well, things were beginning to look up a bit with me, and I was getting my sleep back, when the next blow fell. I came down one morning, and wondering why I hadn't heard Sally stirring, went up to her room and found her lying dead in her bed. Poor old soul, I suppose it was merciful; she had been ailing a lot lately, and getting very tired, and nothing would induce her to have help. It was the way I should wish to go when my time comes, if I have the choice; but I don't suppose I shall have. Asthma wears you down, it doesn't knock you out. I can never see why we mourn for the dead; it is much more rational to mourn for the bereaved.

I owed a lot to Sally, she was a real good soul. My sister was annoyed with me for being so upset over the loss of a servant. Said it was undignified. She would soon find me another. I said, what about a Friendly Girl? I had taken rather a fancy to them, and she was always trying to get them nice, refined jobs. That settled her. She would have nothing further to do with the matter after that, which was what I had intended. So I asked Molly Coke to see what she could fit me up with. But it wasn't as simple as it seemed, apparently. The municipal elections were coming on shortly, and parish relief was being doled out in dollops, so chars were hard to come by. She said I would have to make shift with the office cleaner till she had time to search out something for me. So she sent over a horrible cross between a slattern and a virago. I had always thought the offices looked pretty dingy, and now I knew why. I asked Molly why we didn't fire the creature, and she said that Scottie's wife took an interest in her. I said it would be much more helpful if Scottie's father-in-law took an interest in her, and for the first time in my experience Molly laughed.

Mrs Leake's deficiencies did not matter so much when I was up and doing, as I fed at the house, but it was a different matter when I went down with one of my goes of asthma. Benger's food, on which I rely on these occasions, is by no means foolproof, and Mrs. Leake was a fool.

"I thought you wanted slops," she said sulkily when I complained.

"Yes," said I, "but not bedroom slops."

She must have repeated my remark, which I admit was not in the best of taste, for Molly appeared to see what was amiss, and took away that loathly bowlful and made me some that was decent. Then she fetched her pad and took my letters, and we carried on like that till I was better, Mrs Leake doing the cleaning, and Molly doing my food. I gave her Sally's key, which I wouldn't trust Mrs Leake with, for although she might be honest enough, I was pretty certain her husband wasn't. He worked for Muckley as general roustabout and did any dirty work that was going, and there was plenty going in that firm, believe me.

My asthma was changing its form. Instead of the acute attacks with gaps between, it was becoming less acute and more chronic. I wheezed pretty nearly all the time now, but the attacks were less severe. I don't know which form of asthma I prefer. I suppose the one I don't happen to have at the moment. Scottie's influenza had turned to pneumonia, and they were very anxious about him. So what with one thing and another, we were a party of crocks. They say that troubles never come singly, and I reckon they are right.

I was beginning to get over the acute phase of the loss of Morgan. Time is a great healer, and does its job whether we want it to or not; but there was nothing, either in time or eternity, that could fill the gap that was left in my life or make Dickford existence tolerable to me. If the truth were known, I was drinking a dashed sight more than was good for me, but I did not think that anyone but the wine-waiter at the "George" knew, and he used to talk to me like a father, and bring me a lager when I ordered whisky, and pretend he had muddled the order.

The loss of Sally was a heavy blow, quite apart from the fact that she had been a dashed good soul. Mrs Leake was a poor sort of creature; any bed she made was a rag-heap, any fire she laid wouldn't light; she was always forgetting to fill up the coal-scuttle, and if there is one thing I can't do, it is lug coal-scuttles. I couldn't very well get Molly round to cart coal, and I couldn't sit in a fireless room all evening, so I used to go round to the commercial room at the "George' and that got me drinking still more, for you can't very well spend the evening in a place like that and not pay your footing. So altogether I was making a mess of things when the curtain rang up for the grand finale.

I was over in my quarters after lunch when my sister sent the maid down with a message to say there was someone at the house who wanted to see me. I went over, quite unsuspicious, and found my sister entertaining Muckley. I felt pretty surprised, for the natural thing was for him to have come to the office if he wanted to see me, not go intruding on the house, for he could hardly expect to be on calling terms with us. My sister was looking exactly like the Wolf in the pantomime, getting ready to eat Little Red Riding Hood. I saw she was fearfully pleased about something, and wondered what in the world was afoot. I couldn't imagine what Muckley could have made her a present of that had pleased her so much. She soon explained however.

"Mr Muckley has come here to speak to us about his daughter."

"Stepdaughter," I corrected.

"He says you've seduced her, Wilfred."

"Good God!" said I. It was the only thing I could think of. I was so completely taken aback.

"Do you deny it?"

"Of course I do. There's not a word of truth in it."

"You have been having her over in your rooms a great deal," said my sister, for which I could have kicked her, for it was the last thing she ought to have said under the circumstances, but she had too little sense and experience and knowledge of the world to know it.

"She has only been taking my letters while I was laid up," said I.

"You seem to have had a lot of letters lately," said she. "Especially late in the evening."

As a matter of fact, Molly had been coming over and doing my supper for me, and generally settling me for the night. As Mrs Leake was there too, I had thought we were all right, but my sister was simply making Muckley a present of the situation without realising in the least what she was doing, and there was no way of stopping her, short of knocking her insensible, when once she started on this tack.

I mentioned Mrs Leake.

"Yus," said Muckley. "It's what Mrs Leake 'as bin telling us wot put me and my wife on your track."

Then I saw what was afoot. I wondered whether Molly was a party to it, but instantly acquitted her. She was not that sort.

I referred him to Beardmore as a witness that it was physically impossible for me to meddle with the girl when I had asthma.

"I don't see what he can know about it as he wasn't there," said my sister. "And anyway, you men always stick up for each other."

There was a knock at the door, and in came Molly, note-book in hand.

"I am sorry to have been so long," she said to me, "but there was someone on the phone for Mr Scott."

I guessed my sister had sent for her in my name as if the message had come from me. She looked at Muckley, and by the way she looked at him I saw that although she was surprised to see him in our drawing-room, she knew what was afoot all right. I could see her square her shoulders and brace herself to meet it. She was a good-plucked kid.

"Miss Coke," I said, "your stepfather has been complaining of my conduct towards you. Have you any complaints to make about it?"

"None," said she.

"They never 'ave," said Muckley. "All the same, she's lost 'er reputation, even if there ain't more unpleasant consequences, and me and 'er mother 'ave got to live it down. Wot about it, Mr Maxwell?"

"Yes," said my sister. "What are you going to do about it, Wilfred?"

I knew what was coming all right, even if she didn't, and nothing would suit me better than to get Muckley to make his demands in front of witnesses, if I could possibly lure him into that trap.

"What do you want me to do about it?" said I to Muckley.

"Are you willing to marry 'er?" said Muckley.

"Yes," said I.

It was the last thing they expected. A gasp went round

the room, and was echoed from the hall, where the servants were listening.

It was also the last thing Muckley wanted. He never thought for a moment I had been up to any hanky-panky with Molly, I am perfectly certain, and wouldn't have cared if I had; so it spiked his guns nicely, as he couldn't very well claim compensation in the face of that.

My sister's reaction was too funny for words. She had been all on the side of the angels when it was a question of immorality, but she went straight up in the air at the idea of righting the wrong. I don't suppose such a possibility had ever entered her head. She is extraordinarily obtuse in some ways.

"You can't possibly do that, Wilfred," said she, very tartly indeed.

"Why not?" said I.

"You can't afford it," said she.

"Can't we economise?" said I, pulling her leg.

"No, we can't," said she.

"You'll have to, if I dock your allowance," said I.

She glared at me as if she could have killed me. I always expect she will, some day.

"Do you expect me to share my home with *her*?" she said, with a theatrical sweep of her hand towards Molly, who stood still as a statue beside the door.

"Certainly not," said I. "I shouldn't dream of asking my wife to share her home with anybody."

"Well, you can't afford to keep two homes going, Wilfred, that's quite certain."

"I shall have to during mother's lifetime," I said.

"You'll get into debt."

"You will have to economise here."

"I shan't do any different from what I've always done."

"You will get a pound a week and the push if you give any

trouble," I said. "I am willing to look after mother, but I'm not obliged to do any more than keep you off tne rates."

I have never seen anything look as mad as my sister outside an asylum. It has always amazed me that I put up with her nonsense so long and never used the power of the purse over her before.

Muckley was obviously enjoying it all hugely; what poor Molly was feeling over this fracas, I do not know, for her face was like a mask. It was impossible for me to throw Muckley out, as he was a great bruiser of a brute, twice my size, so I thought that as my sister had let him in, she could jolly well get rid of him. I don't lay any claims to chivalry where she is concerned. She twisted my tail too hard and too often when she had the upper hand.

I walked across the room and put my hand on Molly's shoulder. "Come along," I said, and opened the Joor and pushed her out in front of me. Pushed her right into the arms of the cook, in fact, who, together with the parlour-maid and a little sort of between-creature, were all outside on the mat, for the last thing they were expecting was for the interview to break up so abruptly.

"Take a month's notice, the lot of you," I said, and still shoving Molly ahead of me, went down the passage that led to the offices.

She sat down at her desk, and I sat down at mine, and we looked at each other.

"That's torn it," said I.

"Yes," said she. "He can't do anything in the face of that. But if you don't mind, Mr Maxwell, I'd like to get off as soon as you can spare me."

"You mean you want to leave?" said I.

"Yes," said she. "I can't possibly stop on. The maids heard everything, and it will be all over the town."

I put my head in my hands. I was absolutely sick at heart.
I felt that not only had I messed things up for the girl, but I
had let Scottie down so horribly. I ought to have had more
sense than to let her come over to my quarters at all. It had
seemed to me so obvious that when I was in such a condition
that she or Mrs Leake had to hoist me up on my pillows when
I slipped down, I couldn't be suspected of wanting to do anybody any harm. I wondered how in the world I was to face
Scottie—coming back after an illness to this mess-up. For I
knew from the way Molly had all the threads in her hands that
Scottie must have relied on her tremendously; as for me, I
shouldn't know where to look for a thing without her.

And there was the domestic problem of my bachelor establishment. Bad as Mrs Leake was, she was better than nothing;
she would certainly have to be fired for this day's work, and
then there would be nothing. If Molly had not been able to
find me another woman to replace the unsavoury Leake creature, it was improbable I should be able to find one for myself.
It seemed to me that life was an all-in wrestling match without
a referee. It had fairly got me down. I felt deadly ill, too, for
my heart was bothering me owing to the row we had just been
having.

Then I heard a kind of suppressed squeak and looked up,
and there was Molly weeping.

I went over, and sat down beside her, and put my arm
round her. It was all I could do; I was just as done in as she
was.

Then the town-hall clock struck three, and I got up in a
hurry, for I had an auction on at the Assembly Rooms at three.

More haste, less speed; I had got up too quickly and now
couldn't get my breath, and could only lean up against Molly's
desk and fight for it. Molly looked at me, and then she took
up the telephone and rang up the other auctioneers in the town,

and asked them if they could arrange to take the auction for me. I couldn't argue because I couldn't speak.

"We may as well be hung for a sheep as a lamb," said Molly when the worst of the attack was past, and took me by the arm and walked me slowly over to my own quarters and put me to bed. Then she got Beardmore to me, and Beardmore doped me.

CHAPTER XXVIII

I WOKE up next morning still feeling pretty rotten. It was getting on for eleven; I had overslept, having no Sally to call me, and Mrs Leake had very wisely not shown up. I rang up the office to see how they were getting on. One of the clerks in the outer office answered me, and said they were getting on all right. I asked if Miss Coke were there, and he said, yes, she was there, dealing with a client.

I got into some clothes and ambled round to the "George" and had brunch. I thought I should catch Molly at the office, as she always left after the others, but when I got there she had cleared out with the rest. I wanted to have a word with her and see how she was faring, for I thought things might be a bit sticky for her at home, and I reckoned that if a fiver would unstick them, it would be money well spent. It was Saturday, so she wouldn't be back at the office after lunch; but I knew that Muckley would be at the local dog-races, which started at three, and at which he was a leading light, so I went back to my place to wait till he should be out of the way, and then I reckoned I would drop round and have a word with Molly and her mother, and tell them how awfully sorry I was about everything and see if there was anything I could do towards straightening things out.

When I got back to my own quarters they were, of course, exactly as I had left them when I rolled out of bed that morning, so I went back to the empty offices, but the fires were out there, too, by now. So I went on to the "George" and had a drink or two in the saloon bar to kill time till Muckley would have gone to the dogs. Thus does a lot of trouble start in towns like ours. Muckley wasn't the only one who was going to the dogs.

When I knew by the cheering that things had got going at the greyhound track I left the bar, only to find that I had taken more than I meant to. I don't say that I couldn't walk all right, but I certainly would not have cared to drive a car. So I decided to stroll about a bit till the church spire had straightened out and steadied down before going to call on Molly and her mother; I also indulged in the good old deacon's remedy of a penn'orth of peppermints. This brought me in touch with the synthetic charmer in the Bon-bon Box, where my old dominie had met his doom, and before I left I had pulled her peroxide curls and promised her a run in my car. When I got out into the fresh air I spat ceremonially in the gutter and decided that I had better not stroll around the town any more in case worse befell me; I fetched from the office the key of the house the cedar came from, and decided I would occupy my idle hands by inspecting my property.

All the furniture was gone, save some of the choicer bits I had bought at the sale, and which stood disconsolately along the walls, irregularly spaced out by the gaps left by their departed comrades. In the centre of the floor in the downstairs rooms were various bits I had picked up at various other auctions and that I had dumped in here for storage, having in mind some dim idea of making the place into one of those antique shops which imitate a dwelling-house and that are fashionable nowadays; or perhaps, if the truth were known, from sheer jackdaw acquisitiveness, for there were some nice bits among them that nothing would have induced me to part with. The inside of the windows was stuck up with newspaper to keep out the sun, and in the dim light the rooms looked like the scenes of those traditional card parties that end up in a murder and are then locked up for years for fear of the ghost.

I soon had enough of looking round the house, and went out into the garden.

The sky was just getting pink in the west for the early winter sunset, and the low light came through the tops of the leafless trees into the rectangular walled garden that Queen Anne considered the correct thing. I had not thought it a particularly promising garden when I had seen it all overgrown with weeds and greenery at midsummer, but now in its leafless bareness it revealed all sorts of treasures that had been smothered then. There was yellow jasmine against the mellow brick, and bushes of wintersweet scenting the whole garden, and to my immense surprise, parties of little irises among their grass-like leaves, palest mauve, deepest blue, and a velvety black and green. They were the nearest thing to orchids I have ever seen, and looked as if their proper place were a hot-house; but here they were, braving the January day and getting the best of it, too, from the looks of them. So I picked a bunch for Molly and her mother, together with some wintersweet, which I thought might be acceptable on Muckley's premises.

Then I went round to make my call. Mrs Muckley opened the door to me, looking, I thought, very surprised to see me. I wondered what version of the affair had been given to her. I tendered my floral offering, and she asked me in and took me through into the living-room-kitchen behind the shop, apologising for not taking me up to the drawing-room on the ground that she couldn't manage the stairs. I replied that I wasn't particularly good at them either, and then we swopped symptoms for a few minutes, and got acquainted.

I broke the ice by putting my foot through it in my usual jerky manner, and told her that I was glad to have a chance to see her alone, as I wanted to talk to her about Molly, and asked her if she knew what was afoot? She said she did. I asked her would she accept my assurance that Molly and I had behaved ourselves. She said that she was quite satisfied on that point, but that we had been uncommonly foolish and had only ourselves to thank for what had happened.

"And I blame Molly more than you," she said. "For you were ill and perhaps did not realise things, but I warned Molly over and over again of the risk she was running, but she would do it."

Then I realised, what I had not realised before, that Molly had not blundered into things blindly, as I had, but had taken her risk with her eyes open rather than leave me stranded, and I should have been very badly stranded if she hadn't done so, as nurses were unobtainable owing to the influenza epidemic that was going on. I told Mrs Muckley this, but she offered no comment, and a silence fell between us in which I did some pretty rapid thinking.

"Well now," said I to her at length. "What is the position with regard to your daughter? I told your husband I was willing to marry her if she wanted me to, but does she want me to? She has given me no indication of her attitude in the matter."

"Molly did not take your words seriously, Mr Maxwell, and she would be the last girl in the world to hold you to them if you did not mean them."

"Well, has she got any other views for herself? How is she placed? How, for the matter of that are you both placed since I have been capsizing things for you?"

"I have got cancer, and it cannot be very much longer now. After that, Molly will be homeless. She cannot live on the twenty-five shillings a week Mr Scott pays her."

"My God!" said I. "Is that all we pay her? Why, she runs the business!"

"Yes, she could have got much better posts than that if she

had been willing to take them; the *Argus* would have given her three pounds a week, but she wouldn't take it."

"Why ever not?"

Mrs Muckley did not answer.

"I will certainly see she gets a living wage," I said, "but she was saying yesterday that she wanted to leave."

Mrs Muckley still kept silence.

"Well, Mrs Muckley," I said, "I'll marry her if she wants me to, but I shouldn't have thought I was any catch. She could do a dashed sight better than a wreck like me, old enough to be her uncle. Hasn't she got anyone else in view? We have got some very decent lads in the office, and they treat her like a queen."

"There has never been anyone except you, Mr Maxwell, since you gave her a pink sugar mouse when you left the school."

"Good Lord!" said I, in a state of utter consternation, and then Molly herself walked in and looked as if she could have gone over backwards at the sight of me.

I looked at Mrs Muckley, and Mrs Muckley looked at me, and her eyes had the curious expression that I have seen before when people are getting ready to cross the Great Divide, as if they could see right into the heart of things and knew at last what was worth while and what wasn't. I went up to Molly and took her hand.

"I have come round to see what your mother has to say to me, Molly," I said. I had never called her anything except Miss Coke before.

"I have no more to say to him than I have already said. You two must settle things between you," said Mrs Muckley, and rose and left the room with her slow, painful, stooping walk and I was left alone with Molly.

Molly loosened her coat and sat down in the chair her

mother had vacated and looked at me questioningly. I felt that frankness was the only thing. It was no use beating about the bush, even if I had any talent in that direction, which I have not.

I asked her how old she was. She told me twenty-four. I told her I was thirty-six. I also told her that I had been pulling my sister's leg over the question of expense, and that I could perfectly well afford to marry if I wanted to, provided everybody was willing to be reasonable.

"But," I said, "there are certain things you ought to know before you come to a decision," and I started to tell her about Morgan.

I knew it was going to be difficult, but I had no idea it was going to be as difficult as it was; and I got in a most fearful muddle, and made Morgan sound like a harlot through trying to keep the supernatural element out of it, which I thought Molly wouldn't understand. Then everything began to come back to me through talking about it, and I forgot who my audience was, and told Molly the blinking lot; and everything I had bottled up got loose, and I ended up by breaking down completely. It was an odd way of proposing.

Then Molly did what Morgan had done, and came and sat on the arm of my chair and put her arm round me.

"I know you love her," she said, "but I think you need me, so I'll marry you."

Then a tremendous hullabaloo started up outside as Muckley came home unexpectedly and Mrs. Muckley tried to head him off from the living-room. I reacted into one of my tantrums, and went out and told him exactly what I thought of him in most unparliamentary language, and he put himself in a fighting attitude and dared me to hit him.

"Of course I daren't hit you," I said, "and I'm not such a fool as to try. But I can hit your business, and will, too, if I have any trouble with you," and I told him, clearly, concisely and conclusively exactly where his back premises contravened the building laws, and what it would cost to bring them into line with requirements if someone laid an information. He shut up and cleared out, and I have never had any more trouble with him from that day to this. I may not be one of the bulldog breed, but I am a pretty good hand at a cat-fight.

Then I returned in triumph to the living-room, where Molly and Mrs Muckley were all of a doo-daa, thinking I'd be murdered, or at least badly knocked about. Frankly, I can't think why I wasn't, for Muckley had that reputation. I was feeling distinctly pleased with myself, for it was no mean achievement to throw a brute the size of Muckley supperless out of his own house; and what with that, and having got my trouble off my chest to Molly, I was feeling better than I had done since I lost Morgan.

So I kissed Mrs Muckley, and was officially accepted as prospective son-in-law, and we all sat down to supper, and I told them some of my yarns, including the one about the Friendly Girls and the temperance shandygaff, and they loved it. It was only after I got home that I remembered that I had forgotten to kiss Molly.

While we were having supper I noticed a kind of moaning, wailing noise that had apparently been going on for some time, but I hadn't paid any attention to it amid all the alarums and excursions.

"What in the world's that?" I said.

"It is the calves in the slaughter-shed," said Mrs Muckley. "My husband ought not to have left them over the week-end. They have to be fasted before they are killed."

"I'll go and give them a drink," said Molly, "perhaps that will quiet them."

It did for a bit, but presently the poor little beasts started off again. I wasn't sorry to get out of earshot when I said good night and set off for home, leaving Molly to put her mother to bed.

As I walked back through the frosty starlight I thought of the conditions under which that girl lived. She had all the housework to do now her mother was helpless, and got up God knows what time to do it before she came to the office. At midday she went home and gave the demon Muckley his dinner, and then she came back and put in overtime for Scottie, who worked her like a black. Then she was up with her mother every hour or two through the night. At week-ends she did Muckley's books and a bit of extra housework. Muckley came home drunk fairly frequently and knocked them both about impartially; and week in, week out through-out the year, with never a holiday since Mrs Muckley had married him, they lived amid the sights and sounds and smells of the slaughter-yard. She had married him for the sake of a home for herself and Molly, and he had married her for the sake of the little bit of capital that came from the sale of the school, and that had set him up in his beastly business. My old dominie had hanged himself with his braces in a common lodging-house in Bristol when his synthetic charmer left him after his money came to an end. She had something to answer for, had that girl.

Then I fell to wondering why old Coke had abandoned a decent job and a decent wife to go off with the flamboyant creature from the Bon-bon Box, whom even we youngsters had thought pretty awful. He was an Oxford B.A., and when he wasn't in a bad temper his manners were those of a gentleman. But evidently his tastes weren't, or he wouldn't have cottoned on to the Bon-bon Boxer.

By this time I had arrived at my own door, and I reckoned the best thing I could do was to go straight to bed and shut my eyes to the Augean stables till the morning, and then shift my digs to the "George" till Molly was ready to marry me. But when I got upstairs, I found that everything had been cleared up, and the fire lit and banked with slack, and I knew why it was that Molly had been out when I called. I reckoned that it wasn't Molly who was getting the best of the bargain in the forthcoming marriage, even if I had been the well-to-do eligible I was popularly supposed to be, but which anyone who had inside information knew I decidedly wasn't.

Next morning when I arrived at the office, there was Molly at her desk as usual, ready to take my letters. I went over and patted her on the back (I was too shy to kiss her in cold blood) and gave her my signet ring so she would have something to show for her engagement. She thanked me and put it on her finger, and we tackled the correspondence.

I told her of my plan to move to the "George", and she said no, it was a very bad one. I asked her why, but she would not give a reason. She said that her mother and she hoped I would come and have supper with them whenever I wanted to, as Muckley was never in in the evenings. I asked her what about coping with the housework, and she said that four servants was a ridiculous allowance for a house the size of ours, and they ought to do it on their heads or explain the reason why; and that I was the master of the house, and it was for me to give my orders. It had never struck me that way before, and I thought it rather a bright idea. So I went down to our kitchen premises and rounded up the staff. I found that my sister had re-engaged those I had sacked, and they were very saucy in consequence, all except the tweeny, who was an orphan from an orphanage, and didn't know whether she stood on her head or her heels.

They told me that they worked for my sister, not for me. I told them that they could work for her as much as they liked, but that there would be no wages for it unless they minded their P's and Q's when I spoke to them. Then I re-re-engaged the tweeny and led her off, dustpan in hand, and handed her over to Molly.

I went round to have supper with Molly and Mrs Muckley that evening. As soon as I set eyes on Mrs Muckley I saw there was a change in her. I couldn't define what it was, but it seemed to me as if she had kind of sat back and let go, now that she knew that Molly would be cared for. I felt certain she wasn't going to last long.

While Molly was out of the room seeing to the supper, Mrs Muckley called me over to her, and took my hand in hers, and asked me if I would promise her to stop drinking. I nearly dropped. I had no idea that anyone except the wine-waiter at the "George" knew I was doing it.

"Do you imagine you can do what you are doing in a town like this, and no one know?" said she.

I felt deadly sick about it. I don't care twopence about public opinion in the ordinary way, because the public opinion of a place like Dickford is too futile for words; but letting Scottie in for a scandal at the office and giving way to drink were two things I was genuinely ashamed of, and it got me on the raw that they should have come out.

Then in came Molly with the supper, and she saw that something had upset me, and she went for her mother like a tigress. Said she wouldn't have me scolded; that I wasn't in a fit state to stand it; that she had got me well in hand and could manage me perfectly and there was no occasion for anxiety. And all this from Molly, who had never said anything except "Yes, Mr Maxwell," and "No, Mr Maxwell," to me at the office!

I told Molly she needn't worry. I had given her mother my promise, and would keep it. I did too, but it gave me a pretty thorough scare when I found how hard it was to keep it; if

Molly had not taken me round to Beardmore and made me take him into my confidence, I doubt if I should have kept it. I asked Molly about every two hours for the next few days if she still wanted to go on with the marriage, and she said that if I jilted her she would sue me for breach of promise, and made me stick it. Not having been on the booze very long, I got off comparatively lightly, but I am sorry for the poor devils who are experienced inebriates.

As I had foreseen, Mrs Muckley went downhill rapidly, and one evening when I was there she sent Molly out of the room, and asked me when the wedding was to be, and where I proposed to put Molly after I had married her. I said that I proposed to make our home at the Cedar House, and leave my mother in possession of the old house during her lifetime, even if it meant going into capital a bit. She asked me how long it would take to get the Cedar House ready, and I said I thought about three months. She said that was too long for her, couldn't I take Molly sooner? I said I'd take her any time she liked if she didn't mind camping out in my quarters. Mrs Muckley said that was a great weight off her mind, and could I get her a letter for the hospital, as she couldn't hang on any longer. I asked her when she wanted to go. She said that wasn't for her to say, she'd have to go when there was a bed. I told her to leave it to me; if she could be ready to-morrow morning, I'd see to the shifting of her. She said she didn't see how I could be sure, but she'd be ready in case.

Next morning I came round with my car bright and early as arranged, and took her to the nursing-home, where I had got a room for Molly too. So she ended her days in comfort. She was a sweet soul. Muckley we left to wrestle with the local servant problem that we had already found so intractable.

Mrs Muckley died that day fortnight. Molly and I were both with her when she went. She said she died happy, leaving

Molly in my care. I thought that if she knew what I was going through, trying to keep off the whisky, with Molly hanging on to me to keep me from doing something desperate, she would have thought the boot was on the other leg.

It gave the town a turn to see me in topper and tails riding with Molly and Muckley and a mouldy aunt in the front coach at the funeral. They had been perfectly ready to believe the scandal, but had never credited the rumours of the engagement. As we passed our house I noticed that the blinds of my sister's room were down, as well as those of the rest of the house, which had been drawn by my orders. I thought this was a sign of grace, but I learnt afterwards that she had developed a sick headache out of pure chagrin when she learnt that I was attending the funeral as one of the family, and had vomited her dinner; rather a left-handed tribute, but nevertheless, a tribute.

I took Molly to see my mother, and mother mistook her for a Friendly Girl, and asked her if she had been confirmed and whether she was willing to go into service. However, she was quite pleasant to her, and she mightn't have been if she had known that she was the prospective daughter-in-law, so all's well that ends well.

Then I went and saw the vicar. He was High, and disliked the idea of a wedding in Lent. I asked him did he expect us to live in sin till after Easter? Anyway, we weren't going to, and if he wouldn't do the job, we'd patronise the rival show at the registry office. So he climbed down, and said he didn't mind so much if it was quiet. I said he could bet it would be quiet under the circumstances. He said that in his opinion I was treating my sister exceedingly badly. I said it was a free country, and he had a perfect right to his opinion.

The matron of the nursing-home insisted that the wedding should take place from there, and the nurses fairly spread themselves, for they all loved Molly. We had an awfully funny mixed bag of guests. My mother was not expected, as she had not been out of the house for years. My sister was asked, but wouldn't say whether she would or whether she wouldn't. We hoped to God she wouldn't, and in the end she didn't. I asked the Treths, and Molly asked the mouldy aunt and a couple of girl friends. The wine-waiter from the "George" turned up at the church and we took him back with us to the wedding-breakfast at the nursing-home. Scottie crawled out very shakily to be best man at the risk of his life, and went straight back to bed again after the service. He was awfully pleased about it, to my immense astonishment, for it meant he would have to break in a new secretary.

I took Molly to the Grand at Dickmouth for a week-end for the honeymoon, which was all that could be spared from the business in the absence of Scottie, and went down with a go of asthma almost as soon as I set foot inside the doors. Some honeymoon for the child! I brought her back as soon as I was fit to move, perhaps a bit sooner, if the truth were known.

In order to get to my quarters, where we were to live till the Cedar House was ready, we had to go through our hall. Now our house is a long, two-story, double-fronted affair, with the offices on the right of the front door, and the living quarters on the left. The street door stands perpetually open, and the real front door is just inside the hall, facing the door leading into the offices.

As we drove into the square I saw our chief clerk on the corner signalling to me, so I pulled up to hear what he had to say. He told me that my sister was simply raising hell. Said he thought she was off her head. The clerks had wanted to give us a welcome home, but he saw that there was going to be trouble, and he had judged that the most humane thing he could do was to shut up shop, and clear everybody off, and leave us to wash our dirty linen as privately as might be. I entirely agreed with him, and ran Molly and him round to his little house to wait till the row was over. Then I went back to tackle my sister.

As soon as she heard my key in the door, out she came and let fly. Called me a thief and a liar; called Molly a common prostitute and said I'd catch v.d. from her. Didn't I thank God Molly wasn't there! I am never in the sweetest of tempers after a go of asthma, and I hit Ethel a back-hander across the mouth *à la* Muckley, and knocked her flying. Then I fetched a bricklayer and bricked up the door and brought my bride home in peace. However, it wasn't a peaceful night, for I had more asthma and a heart attack, as I always do after a row. Some home-coming for the child! My sister had to shift the ash-bins and use the back door and explain herself as best she could to visitors. I never spoke to her again.

Next day the solicitor she and my mother always go to, a gentleman for whom I have no use, sent for me to come and see him. It seemed that my sister had allowed the servants up from the kitchen to see the fun, so there were witnesses to the assault. Ethel had a cut lip. (For the matter of that, I had cut knuckles.)

Then he asked me what settlements I was prepared to make on my sister now I was married. I said, none. They could go on as they were during my mother's lifetime, and then I would give Ethel three pounds a week to live on anywhere except at Dickford. He said she wouldn't accept that. I said she could take it or leave it, and if she made any trouble she wouldn't get that. He offered me a document to sign in which I settled the house on her, all the furniture, and half my interest in the business. Lying beside it on his desk was an application form for a summons. I told him to go to hell.

Next day I was served with a summons for assault. My sister had me up in front of the local beaks along with the other drunks, and folk who had been riding bikes without lights, and keeping dogs without licences. The servants gave their evidence with the greatest gusto. According to them, I had knocked my sister down and kicked her. The only difficulty was that they could not agree where I had kicked her. Neither could she produce any footmarks, and if what they said was true, she ought to have looked like a human Dalmatian. So the magistrates discounted the foot-work, though they said, and quite rightly, that I had undoubtedly socked her on the jaw. So I was bound over to keep the peace.

With the exception of a few of my pals, the town took sides with Ethel. In addition to which, Muckley sedulously spread a story of an enforced marriage. So we were sent to Coventry, Molly and I. Now I had stopped drinking there wasn't much for me to do at the club or the "George", and Scottie carefully kept me away from clients lest they should feel their houses were polluted. The only person who stuck to Molly was the mouldy aunt; even the two girl friends faded away after the assault. The mouldy aunt stuck closer than glue because we helped her a bit. I don't know that she deserved it, but she certainly needed it, and perhaps that is the best claim that anyone can have.

CHAPTER XXIX

SO Molly and I settled down to our married life, I in my usual quarters, and Molly in Sally's, downstairs, for there was no question of sleeping with me; no one who wasn't chloroformed would have got a wink; for I breathe like a bulldog such times as I am asleep, and such times as I am not, I walk about. The Moon side of things had faded as if it had never been.

The reconditioning of the Cedar House moved slowly; it needed a lot doing to it. Not that I could grumble at that, for I had given next to nothing for it. Moreover, there was a strike in the building trade that held up materials. Perhaps if the truth were known, I lacked the energy to chase the builders as builders needed chasing. Then I wanted to furnish altogether with Queen Anne stuff, and it had to be picked up gradually. I am afraid I wasn't taking as much interest in the business as I might have done; and so things dragged along till the autumn, and we were still over at the stables; and then the weather held up the work on the house.

There wasn't much to do for an active girl like Molly in my bachelor quarters, especially as she had the tweeny for a maid, and the tweeny shaped up well; so she offered to lend Scottie a hand when he crawled back to work after Easter, so that he wouldn't have to break in a new secretary while he was feeling rotten. And somehow or other she stopped on. The only difference from her pre-nuptial days being that he paid her no salary and she no longer called me Mr Maxwell. As a matter of fact, she never called me anything. The circumlocutions she used to avoid addressing me or speaking of me as Wilfred were too marvellous.

Of course living conditions were better for her than they used to be. I didn't knock her about like Muckley did; nor did I get her up as often in the night as her mother did. Nor did my profession require me to kill things on the premises, not with an axe, anyway, though I dare say we shortened a good few lives indirectly. Scottie would have let a grid in Hell as an eligible residence. Molly read a lot, and we were both keen on the wireless; we even used to turn it on at meal-times. Personally, I think that the thing that saved the situation for Molly was keeping on with her work. The thing that saved the situation for me was Mrs Muckley. There is something about a promise to a dying woman whom you respect that is very binding. I had no wish to turn up at Heaven's gate with a bottle-nose and account to her for my dealings with Molly.

I had hoped there would be kids to amuse us, but the outlook in that direction did not appear very bright. It is an odd thing that when folk are without benefit of clergy, kids appear at only one remove from spontaneous generation; but when the best thing you could do would be to raise a family, nothing comes of it. And if you try to bludgeon Brother Ass in these matters, it only starts him backing.

I believe Molly was happiest when I was having my attacks. Sometimes she would take my hand in hers and look at me with a very strange expression on her face. I couldn't ask her what she meant because I couldn't speak, and that is not the sort of thing you can ask in cold blood afterwards. At least I can't. I was horribly shy, and Molly was very reserved, and progress was consequently slow. The condition we settled down to would have been all right for Darby and Joan on their golden wedding-day, but was a dashed thin deal for a girl like Molly. "Spring, mishandled, cometh not again." I was damned sorry for her. I had had my own youth mishandled and knew what it felt like, but what could I do? The cupboard was bare.

I knew from my experience with Morgan what the relationship between a man and a woman could be. Nothing had ever come of my love for Morgan, and I had known all along that nothing ever could, and yet it had lit up my whole life; and for all the pain that came of it, I wouldn't have missed it. There was something that ought to come across in marriage that was lacking between me and Molly, and yet we had done nothing that we ought not to have done, and left undone nothing that we ought to have done according to the Prayer-book, and it is pretty explicit. The thing, as I said before, had never lit up. Yet from the very moment I laid eyes on Morgan it had not merely lit up but had given off sparks. It was not a thing of the body, and it was not even a thing of the emotions; it had nothing to do with the intellect, and it certainly wasn't spiritual. Then what was it?

I could understand now why old man Coke had gone off with his synthetic charmer. I was in the Bon-bon Box one day, getting some sweets for Molly, and the girl said to me: "I suppose our little trip in the car is off now, Mr Maxwell?"

"You must ask my wife that question," I said, and she giggled.

All the same, she hadn't been far out; and although I would have cut her throat, and my own too, before I would have done any such thing, for I had an enormous respect for Molly, I reckoned she had spotted my state, as her business was. It was an odd thing that although I thought so much of Molly, she left me absolutely unmoved, yet synthetic charmers affected me. It was a mystery to me why this should be so. It was certainly the last thing I expected.

It is easy to see how, in the animals, Nature uses them. We

like to think that we are not only of more worth than many sparrows, but constructed upon entirely different principles, which we are not. You have only got to watch a cock-sparrow to see that. Nature shoves us from behind, and we call it romance. We talk about falling in love, as if love occupied a position in space, like a duck-pond; whereas the springs of love are in ourselves and we overflow when the pressure reaches a certain point, not always with due regard to the suitability of the recipient; and for the resulting tragedy we blame everything except Nature. There is a dashed lot of Nature in human nature, as Freud pointed out.

Old man Coke had tried to supplement his rations at the Bon-bon Box, and the social side of his marriage had gone phut in consequence, as anyone but a fool must have known it would. I, on the other hand, without ever laying a finger on Morgan, had had my soul fertilised. We know that there has got to be give and take on the physical plane if the ovum is to develop into an infant; but there are apparently some queer things that have to go on in the subtler planes if a marriage is to be a success.

I addled my brains to try and make out what Morgan had been driving at. I knew she had had in her mind a perfectly clear-cut idea of what she meant to do, and that she regarded her relationship with me as the crux of the whole matter. It had been a pretty grisly bit of vivisection so far as I was concerned, but I knew from her last letter to me that Morgan thought it had gone off all right.

Morgan had deliberately made me fall in love with her, that was clear, anyway. Not that it had taken much doing, Dickford having few counter-attractions; but Morgan could have dodged it if she had wanted to; it was odd to me that she had not wanted to, for she was kind, and would never have done what she did out of idleness. I had a feeling that she had deliberately steeled herself to hurt me because she had some very big end in view, just as the Priest of the Moon had had when he took her from Atlantis.

.   .   .   .

Our first Christmas was approaching, and I was dreading it. It was the anniversary of Morgan's passing—I cannot call it her death for I have never known for certain whether she was dead or not—and the Christmas bells and carols were all associated with that time in my mind. Moreover I had got to do something festive for Molly. We were completely outcast in the town. I did not mind that in the ordinary way, and neither, I think, did she, being used to it, first for her father's sake, and then for her stepfather's; but round about Christmas you feel these things, seeing everyone exchanging peace and goodwill and being left out of it yourself. I think if my sister had asked me to the Friendly Girls' party that year I should have attended. But not she! She could never forgive me for not having gone to prison for assaulting her.

I went into the bank to get some cash for the festive season, and the cashier told me that the manager wanted to see me. I wondered what in the world he wanted me for. Had my sister let me in for an overdraft? She was quite capable of it.

He popped his head out of his sanctum and said:

"Look here, Max, whatever it was you put in the strong room has gone mouldy. I wish you'd clear it out, or at least clean it up."

I went down with him to the nether regions, and there, sitting on a shelf, was the brown paper parcel I had deposited with him that night a year ago. It had gone mouldy all right. It was sitting in a little pool of its own perspiration wearing a complete set of grey whiskers.

"What in the world is it?" said he.

I told him. He roared.

"What has become of the sapphires?" said he.

"I suppose they are kicking around at the office in a cardboard box," said I. "Unless, of course, Muckley has called while I have been out. I shall have to take a look for them."

Then the caretaker fetched a shovel and shovelled the carcass into the furnace.

I went back to the office to look for the sapphires, and turned out both our desks and the safe, and began to think Muckley must have been calling, when they were discovered on the shelf where we keep the tea-things. I took them home and gave them to Molly for a Christmas present. I didn't know what in the world to give her. I had given her so many chocolates I thought she'd be sick if I gave her any more; besides, I had made up my mind to cut out synthetic charmers as well as whisky. I did not wish history to repeat itself.

I did not want to see Molly open her parcel, which she, not recognising it, was busy doing, so went over to the window and looked out. I could tell by the voice of the river what the tide was doing away on the bay; it was at uttermost ebb and just on the turn, and I remembered how the seaweed would be slowly swinging round on the rocks of the point and streaming the other way as the tide set up-channel. Then I heard Molly's voice.

"Have you read the letter?" said she.

"No," said I.

She came over and put it into my hand. I continued to look out of the window.

"Read it," she said. "You've got to, Wilfred."

It was the first time I had ever heard her use my name, and it woke me up. I looked at the letter. There was no mistaking the writing. Hadn't I seen it on receipts and instructions ever since I came to the office as an angular adolescent when Molly's father closed the school by bolting? I began to read.

"To the one to whom these sapphires are given.

"The soul of a man came into my hands; it is now passing into yours. In order to achieve a certain thing, I sacrificed this man. If I have done my work rightly, the burden of humanity is perhaps a little lighter; the road will not be quite so difficult for those who come after. But that does not help this man.

"If you can make yourself a priestess of the great spiritual principle which is behind womanhood you will be able to help him. Meditate upon the Moon. She will awaken your womanhood and lend you power. May the Great Goddess bless you and help you."

"Do you understand it?" said Molly.

"Partly," said I.

She took the letter away from me and gathered up the sapphires and cleared off to her own quarters, leaving me still gazing out of the window. I wasn't upheaved, and I wasn't sulky, I had just given life up as a bad job; there was nothing I could do about it. The only thing I was worried about was Molly. I was deadly sorry for her. As for me, I had just gone like perished elastic. "Spring, mishandled, cometh not again."

I drove Molly over that afternoon to the carol service at the little old church at Starber. It was our first Christmas and we had to do something about it. I did not particularly fancy going to Dickford Church and being glared at by the vicar.

As we drove along the road through the marshes we could hear the sound of bells before and behind us—the Dickford bells gradually dying away and the Starber bells gradually coming clear. Bell Knowle rose up on our left with a bit of mist round its crest, and a haze lay over the levels.

Molly broke the silence—I don't talk when I drive. I don't talk much at any time, for that matter.

"You will never do any good as long as you stop at Dickford," she said.

"I can't very well leave it, Molly," I said. "It's my bread and butter."

We drove on in silence again after that. Away on the right, between us and the sea, was the raw earth ramp of the new coast road that the county council was building. I must say I resented that raw scar across the marshes, breaking their ancient peace. I supposed that ribbon-building would now string out all along here from Dickmouth.

We called in on the Treths and gave them their Christmas turkey. They were surprised, not expecting it, and had stood themselves a pheasant. I told them they were to regard it as an institution. Treth shook his head.

"We shan't be here next year, at least I hope not," he said. The place was too isolated for them. Mrs Treth wanted to be near the shops and a cinema. They had decided to go back to their old home in Truro, where all her relations were. He had been meaning to come and see me as soon as the holidays were over, and get me to put the farm on our books. It seemed to mark the breaking of the last link with Morgan, but somehow I did not mind. I did not mind anything much nowadays, which I don't suppose was a very wholesome symptom.

Driving back from Starber through the dusk, Molly said to me:

"Why don't you open a branch at Dickmouth? There isn't really enough for you and Mr Scott to do at the office. Dickmouth is the coming place."

"Filthy hole, Dickmouth," I said. "I hate the place. All asphalt and lodging-houses and pierrots in the summer and wind in the winter."

"Why don't you buy the farm from the Treths and let us live there? You could get into Dickmouth very easily from there when the new road is through."

"Don't you like the idea of living at the Cedar House?"

"I don't mind. I can be happy anywhere. But you would be happier at the farm."

"How do you know I would, Molly?"

"I have been talking to the Moon, and she told me."

What Molly had been saying to the Moon, or what the Moon had been saying to Molly, I do not know, neither party confiding in me; but if it was the half of what the Moon said to me when I first made her acquaintance it must have been illuminating.

I owed Molly so much, and there was so little I could do to repay her, that on the rare occasions when she asked me for anything I felt I ought not to refuse, though I must say I dreaded the idea of the farm. I thought it would wake all sorts of memories; moreover it meant going out of the hands of Beardmore, who was liberal with the morphia, into the hands of the Dickmouth medico, who wasn't. However, I reckoned I'd thrash through somehow. I always had, so far. I dare say it wouldn't be so bad after I had settled down to it.

So I bought the farm from the Treths, and Molly saw to the move. It reminded me of taking Mrs Muckley to the nursing-home. Molly got the new offices, and engaged the new clerks, and saw to the advertising, and chivvied the furniture removers, and even succeeded in making old Bindling trot up the hills, though not down them, in going out to the job. He wasn't the same man since he had lost his son, but his foreman pulled him through, same as Molly did me. Finally all I had to do was to drive the car from Dickford to the farm, with Molly beside me and the irises in at the back. For Molly had dug up half the garden at the Cedar House and we were taking it with

us. Strictly illegal of course, for I had sold the Cedar House to
Muckley of all people, he having married a rich widow, God
help her. But he didn't know any more about real estate than
I knew about pigs. All the same if he had known as much
about human nature as I did, he would have kept an eye on
Molly when she was looking after my interests.

Molly was quite right, I must say I felt a sense of relief as
soon as I arrived at the farm; it was as if a weight had rolled
from my shoulders, and the asthma was easier immediately.
I had spent all my life at Dickford, never getting away from it
for more than a fortnight, and all my repressions and frustrations had accumulated around me in a kind of psychological
midden. I believe there is a town in Tibet which is supposed
to be the dirtiest town on earth. Everybody has chucked their
garbage into the street till the muck-heap is higher than the
houses. That was how it was with me at Dickford. I have
seen farmers in the fields moving the chicken-coops so that the
chicks shall have a fresh run. Molly had very wisely moved
my coop.

It was really rather nice at the farm. The two spurs of Bell
Head between which it lay sheltered us from the prevailing
winds and left us open to the sun and the south. Treth had
already planted a quantity of silvery poplars that throve like
weeds in the sandy soil and would soon be giving shelter from
the summer sun; and there were quick-growing cypress hedges
dividing the garden up into plots to give shelter from the wind
in winter. The day was one of those spring days when the first
touch of strength is coming into the sun, and altogether the
effect was rather pleasant. I made Molly leave her unpacking
and stroll with me up to the vine-terraces to see how the little
vines had fared through the winter, and whether they had lived
up to their reputation for hardihood. Poor child, she was
pathetically pleased; God knows, it was little enough to be

pleased about, but I believe I had never done anything like that before with her, so I suppose it meant a lot.

The little vines were all tucked up in matting, without even their little noses showing, so we couldn't see how they were; but the grey, aromatic herbs are much the same summer and winter, and we picked and crushed in our hands the leaves from first one and then another, and sampled their savour, aromatic and sweet and lemon-scented. Then we sat down on the seat in the angle under the cliff and I told Molly how, in the days when our island climate was hotter than it is now, the terraces on sunny slopes were used to grow vines; and I showed her how one could tell those terraces from the ones that fringed bare downs and were used to keep off the wolves. She loved it. I don't know that she was especially interested in archaeology, but she loved to hear me wake up and talk. I so seldom did it with her, poor child.

Then, I don't know what possessing me, I told her why the grey aromatic herbs were grown along with the vines, and how they were infused in the mulled wine; and she said she would like to try that recipe when the little vines matured, and would I write and ask Mrs Treth for it, and I said I would; though privately, I thought that my promise to Mrs Muckley to refrain from fermented liquors might come in uncommon handy.

Then I began to tell her what the land had been like in ancient days, and traced the line of the original Dick for her by the gleam of standing water. And she too, as Morgan had done, remarked on the straight, hard line of the quay among the winding water-ways, and I told her of the cave of Bell Knowle, and the priests, and the sea-sacrifices, and all the ancient worship, and she listened like a two-year child. I wasn't in the least upheaved, though this was the last topic I would have got on to in cold blood if I had realised where my conversation was taking me, but was immensely interested in it all, and woke up and became my old self again, like I used to be with Morgan. And all my old enthusiasm came back, and I told Molly that Morgan had left me a whole roomful of books and papers that we must tackle as soon as we were settled, and there would probably be a lot of awfully interesting stuff among them that we should find when we come to sort them. I told her how I had seen the cave of Bell Knowle in a vision and Morgan had seen it in her crystal; and I showed her the fold in the flank of the hill that I thought hid the cave. She was frightfully thrilled, and said couldn't we buy it and excavate? I said no, better let sleeping dogs lie; I had had enough of that cave, and told her of my untimely end therein.

Then I felt I had dropped a brick, though I don't think Molly, dear generous soul, looked on it in the least in that light. And I explained to her how the sea-priestess had been to me not a woman at all, but all women. A sort of impersonal representation of the woman-principle that men idealised as the goddess.

Molly looked at me strangely.

"That was what she said in the letter. She said I ought to think of myself as that—the impersonal representative of the woman-principle."

"So she did," said I, thinking hard.

Then we heard the luncheon gong from the farmhouse far below us, and started to go down, and Molly skidded on the loose steep surface and I tucked her under my arm to steady her, and we slid down together.

"My, don't the sea-air suit Mrs Maxwell!" squeaked the tweeny when we arrived back at the house.

"Don't it just!" squeaked I.

I think that if I hadn't been so abominably shy I should have kissed Molly, she looked so sweet as she presided over the first meal in her new home. However I managed to pat her on the back quite spontaneously and apropos of nothing in particular.

Later in the evening I made a start upon Morgan's papers. For over a year they had lain locked up in one of the attics the Treths did not use, and I had never been able to bring myself to touch them. But now I was eager to be at them, for they no longer seemed reminders of an irreparable loss, but communications from a friend. And among them I found the words of the songs she had sung to me. Also the words of some songs she had not sung to me. I showed all these to Molly, and told her about the strange ceremony Morgan had performed before she had gone out and passed away, and sang her what I could remember of the tune she had used for her chanting. It was an odd tune, on a very limited range of notes, rising and falling by quarter-tones. Just a few short monotonous musical phrases, repeated over and over again in different pitches, and it got you! Kipling speaks of "Scientific vivisection of one nerve till it is raw", and this was it! It was mantra all right —Western mantra.

We sat up talking till nearly one that morning. I started to tell Molly of ancient Atlantis, and the way they trained the priestesses there, and how they paid no attention to their inclinations, but paired them off as they saw fit; and that had been Morgan's attitude in the matter—that she did not consider the personality the important thing, but the force. I told her that I hadn't reached that point myself, and didn't suppose I ever should, but that I could quite see that the force counted as well as the personality. I had enough tact not to mention it to Molly, but in the light of our talk I realised that the pinchbeck Aphrodite in the sweet-shop was a transmitter of the force all right, though she very decidedly wasn't a lovable personality; whereas Molly was a very lovable personality but wasn't a transmitter of the force. It struck me as an odd thing that the second generation had been within sight of getting left on the shelf of the Bon-bon Box.

It was Molly herself who voiced the thing.

"I think I have been too nicely brought up," she said. "It was not until I read *her* letter that I had any idea that you could do anything for a man except love him and look after him.

"It is a great drawback," she added with a sigh, "to be too well brought up."

Then I had my clue. The Bon-bon Boxer, who from the looks of her must have been thoroughly badly brought up, knew how to deliver the goods, and Molly and her mother didn't. For the mother obviously hadn't known any more than Molly, for she hadn't been able to hold her man; therefore she hadn't been able pass on the tricks of the trade to her daughter, and the kid was what Havelock Ellis calls erotically illiterate. These things may come by instinct, like mousing in kittens, and I believe they do; but if you train a kid away from them the whole time, you produce a state of chronic virginity that nobody can do anything with, and folk like old man Coke bolt into the Bon-bon Box, and we call them wicked. But after all, he'd had his problems as well as her. What was really needed was a course of Mae West on the pictures for the old grandmother; but then that wasn't a practical solution.

God knows I hold no brief for the pictures; I would just as soon sit in the back kitchen and read penny novelettes as go to them, but they have certainly raised the standard of feminine immorality.

It began to dawn on me that the same thing applied to Molly, as Morgan had said flat out and made no bones about—that emotional initiative should rest with the woman, and that a modest woman is one that has no emotional initiative. It is, of course, her protection when she doesn't want attentions, but the woman who is permanently modest is a non-starter in the matrimonial stakes. It was, I think, George Robey who spoke of the kind of woman you could leave on a bench in Hyde Park after dark while you went to have a drink, and find her there waiting for you when you came back. Now what sort of use is that woman to anybody? What use is she, poor soul, to herself? After all, you can hire a cook, you can engage a housekeeper, and you can phone up the Co-op. for a nurse: why marry them?

I couldn't for the life of me see how I was to put all this to Molly, and yet it needed putting; but she must have had an inkling of it, for she said to me:

"What effect will it have on me, Wilfred, if I meditate on the Moon?"

I said I didn't know. She had better try and see, and I would do anything I could to help her.

I began to see now the value of a classical education. Old man Coke, though a B.A. himself, had given us a strictly modernist curriculum, which was considered to be a great advantage in Dickford, as all the lads that were sent to him might expect to have their livings to earn in illiberal walks in life. I had only picked up Latin enough to be able to gather the drift of the footnotes to Gibbon, which, though illuminating, are not uplifting. Whereas if you learn to read the ancients in the original, you get a viewpoint which is a very valuable corrective to what passes for ethics in places like Dickford. I sometimes think in this connection of the "ca' canny" strikes on the railway, which consist in observing literally the "safety first" rules, with the consequence that all the trains run late and some of the goods trains don't run at all. There are some codes that can only be honoured by breeching them.

So I turned Molly loose on the Loeb Library and left her to get on with it, and she changed most remarkably in the course of the next few weeks.

They were pretty strenuous weeks, for Molly had been quite

right about there being an opening for a house-agent at Dickmouth. I had not much of either time or energy to give her,
but we were much happier together, and I let her dig among
Morgan's papers and books, for I trusted her utterly.

What she found she did not say, and to tell you the truth,
I forgot to ask; for I was up to my eyes in trying to persuade,
cajole, blackmail and intimidate the Dickmouth town council
into applying the Town Planning Act to the place before it
developed bungaloid growths in every direction. Then they
turned the tables on me by cajoling me into standing for the
council, and before I knew where I was, I was a city father.
Shades of the black sheep of Dickford! I had never worked
so hard in my born days. I had no time to attend to my asthma.
It had to fend for itself.

Things were much better with me. I was looked upon as
the coming man instead of the black sheep; all the letters of
lodgings and takers-in of boarders seemed to want someone to
give them a lead in building up the place and seeing that its
prosperity did not spoil it, and they seemed to think that I was
their man. It was even suggested in a rash moment that I might
stand for Parliament in the Socialist interest, though why I
should be suspected of Socialistic tendencies I do not know,
save that I used to pull the vicar's leg, and if anyone does that
in a country place, he is credited with leanings towards anarchy.
It was for that reason I had probably been made a member of
the Labour Club at Dickford; that, and because I am incor-
rigibly hail-fellow-well-met with all the wrong persons. As a
matter of fact, I have no tendencies of any sort.

It made an enormous difference to be in good odour for once
in my life. I had not realised, until I got away from it, what
a brake on the wheel a general atmosphere of antagonism and
disapproval can be; until I kicked over the traces I was always
considered more or less of a half-wit. My family were respon-

sible for that; they were convinced that I never would, and never could, grow up; and unless they held me one by either hand, I would sit down with a flop in the nearest puddle and spoil my pants. I think there must have been something pretty tough in me somewhere to have kept alive my self-confidence despite the fact that no one else had any confidence in me. If the whole town sits down round you and says steadily: "Every day in every way you get worse and worse," it is bound to affect you if they persevere. At any rate, that was the way they got results at Nancy. People realise the possibility of psychotherapy, but they don't realise what you can do by psychologising people backwards, which is, in my opinion, on a par with putting poison down wells.

So altogether things were a lot better with me in every way. My asthma was better, consequently my temper was better, and therefore things were easier for Molly. She had no time to listen to the wireless nowadays, for when I came home she had to listen to me.

I had got over the terrible sense of loss and frustration and emptiness that had simply knocked me flat when I lost Morgan, though I still missed the things she stood for in my life. But although things were going quite decently between Molly and myself, they had never lit up as they had between me and Morgan. I often used to talk to Molly about those days; they had been well worth having, even if they hadn't lasted long. She wasn't in the least jealous of Morgan, which I thought was rather marvellous, and she used to encourage me to talk because she said it gave her ideas. Once started, I did not need much encouragement. I saw that Molly was taking it all in, but I had no idea what she was making of it.

CHAPTER XXX

THEN we came round to midsummer, and Molly and I got up early on Midsummer Day and went up on top of Bell Head to see if the sun really did rise over Bell Knowle and could have been sighted through the pylon; and we found sure enough that it could, and the alignment, if prolonged, went right over the point; and I took Molly out on to the point for the first time, and showed her the flat table of rock where the sea-fires were lit, just visible through the shallow water as the level light came over the down. Then we discovered that two of the casemates were still full of the cedar and juniper, and I said I would have it carted back to the farm and we would burn it. Molly asked if it did not now belong to the National Trust? I said it might, but what the eye did not see, the heart did not worry about. Morally it was mine, and I was disinclined to spend time or money on legal arguments, having heard so many. Then we went home to breakfast, which by now we needed, and I went off to the office, and found myself, in my capacity as city father, let in for a dreadful kind of carnival, and got a lot of confetti down my neck, which made me wild. The charmer who threw it was just such another as my Bon-bon Boxer, but I felt no inclination whatever to follow the matter up, but went down a side-street and took off my collar and shook myself, so I had evidently come on a lot since the Dickford days.

Then, being fed to the teeth with the general foolishness, and no business being likely to be transacted in the midst of it, I shut up shop and ran over to Bristol, where a decent sobriety hangs permanently over the town like a fog, and got a further con-

signment of sandal from the Tibetan. I asked him where he
hailed from, but he only smiled. I asked him if he came from
the hills, and his eyes lit up and he nodded. Then back to the
farm, and Molly frightfully intrigued by the sandal-wood. She
was a business-like young woman, and had got hold of a farmer
and had the other stuff hauled already. So when the evening
chill came off the sea we made a little Fire of Azrael in the
living-room, and sat together to watch it, and Molly told me
of what she had been doing all these weeks while I had been
too busy to attend to her, and perhaps, if the truth were known,
too full of myself.

She had been communing with the Moon, as Morgan had
instructed, and she had got a lot, but had found, like I had,
that it was too abstract to be of any practical use. I told her
the trick of the magical images, and how they enabled one to
get a purchase on things, and though they might not be essential they were uncommonly useful. She said, weren't they
hallucinations? I said yes, they probably were, but that was
nothing against them so long as they did their job. Then we
talked of the Priest of the Moon, and I found myself speaking
of him as if he were as real as Morgan and the Treths. He
might be a hallucination, but he was on the job all right. We
both felt him as we talked of him. Molly asked if he would
flop letters on our noses, like the Mahatmas did with Mme
Blavatsky, and I said I hoped not; I had had enough things
thrown at me for one day. I judged from her remark, however, that she had been making use of her time by reading
Morgan's books.

Then for the first time since Morgan's passing, I took pencil
in hand and began to draw. I drew the Priest of the Moon
for her as I remembered him in my sea-picture, sitting on the
throne of the sea in the deep sea-palaces; and the eyes came
alive, even in black and white, in just the same way as they

had done before. But somehow I could not do the curling waves that had arched over like a sky, but instead there stood up on his either hand the two great pillars of polarity that are at the porchway entrance of King Solomon's temple—the Black and Silver pillars—and upon their capitals rested the terrestrial and celestial spheres.

The Fire of Azrael burnt low on the hearth and fell apart in caves of flame as it had in the days of Morgan le Fay, the pale ash of the juniper gleaming golden in the midst. Its incense odour drifted over the room, and I thought of the fort, and caught myself listening unawares for the sound of the sea working among the rocks, unresting as ever out there on the point. But instead there came to me through the open windows another sea-voice that I had not heard before—the patter and rustle of light surf on the shingle as the tide closed round the narrow neck of land where stood the farm.

It was all different here from the fort, and yet it was taking on a life of its own. There was more of earth and less of sea here than out on the point, just as there was more of earth in Molly than in Morgan; yet it was cosmic earth, and I remembered that the Great Goddess ruled both moon and earth and sea. Molly would never be a sea-priestess, like Morgan, but there was awaking in her something of the primordial woman, and it was beginning to answer to the need in me.

Molly in her selfless, tireless, courageous giving was the eternal mother, and the eternal child in me went out to her. It was a beginning, but it was not enough. I should never have been faithful to her without a struggle if that were all there were to it. But there was something more than that, and although we neither of us knew quite what it was, we were feeling our way towards it.

But there seemed to be a great gulf fixed between us and the invisible realities we sought, and unless we could cross it I felt that we were doomed to perish; and I think that Molly felt it too, for she spoke of these things with a sort of desperation that reminded me of a starving fish in an aquarium hitting its nose against the glass. And we sat and talked in the dusk as the fire sank lower. Something was needed to swing us across that gulf, but what it was we did not know, and we fell silent in the gathering dark and sat and looked at the fire.

Outside the sea was working among the shingle, for the tide was high to-night. We could hear the soft crashing and rustling of the breaking waves coming nearer and nearer. They had never sounded so close before; it seemed as if they must be right under the garden wall. I was on the point of getting up and going out to see what was happening when I heard the bells in the water, and knew that this was no earthly tide we were hearing.

A long ray of moonlight came through the open window, uncurtained to the mild night, and the blend of moonlight and firelight was very strange, and dazzled the eyes. The moonlight fell on the fire and made it look like an opal amid its grey ash; the curling smoke and its shadows took on the appearance of squirming creatures rising out of the coals, and I re-remembered the medieval tales of salamanders.

The odour of the incense woods kept on coming to us in wafts, and it seemed to me as if the fire must be smoking a good deal; meanwhile the sound of the sea filled the room till it hummed like a shell. Something uncanny was afoot, and Molly knew it just as well as I did.

Then suddenly we saw that where the moonlight fell upon the smoke a form was taking shape; the smoke no longer rose in slow eddying whorls, but hung in folds like drapery. I watched it rise in front of the chimney-breast as if the fire were smoking; and then out of the formless soft grey we saw a head and shoulders emerge, and the Priest of the Moon stood before us as I had so often seen him with the mind's eye, with his shaven head and ascetic hawk's face. The eyes were dark and sparkling and very much alive. The moonlight and smoke were amorphous, but the eyes were not.

Then he began to speak as he had spoken in the rite out at the fort. Whether we heard with the inner ear and saw with the inner eye, or whether it was the eyes and ears of flesh that apprehended him, I do not know; it was more like a waking dream than anything else, and yet it was as clear-cut as a diamond.

I saw it was to Molly that he was speaking, and that I was a mere spectator; and I remembered that in most ancient times, when Great Isis was worshipped, it was the women who were dynamic, and it was not until corruption came upon the pagan world that the priests took all the power.

And as I sat there, listening to the voice from the shadows and watching Molly listen, I thought of the House of the Virgins in lost Atlantis, and how the ancient priests must have talked like this to the young girls sitting at their feet under the incense-trees in the walled courts around the lotus-tanks, telling them what was expected of them, and how it must be done, and why; and then of the cloaked journey by the underground way to the great temple; the young girl taken silently from beside her sleeping comrades, going and returning without wakening them; and I wondered which was the more sacred way of dealing with sex—that, or the way of the nuns.

I heard the voice of the Priest of the Moon going on and on, talking to his young priestess, and it seemed to me that I was sinking back into the same state I had been in when I travelled in the Boat of the Dead over the underworld waters, and I wondered whether, on my return, I should see Molly glow all golden as I had seen Morgan do.

The rhythmical speaking of the priest set something vibrating within me; I wondered what Molly was making of it all as she lay in her low chair, gazing up with rapt attention at the shadowy form standing over her, luminous with its own light, with dark sparkling eyes amid the shadows; for this was·a thing of which one understood much or little according to the knowledge one brought to it.

"And even as the Queen of Hades is the daughter of the Great Mother, so from the Great Sea riseth golden Aphrodite, giver of love. And she also is Isis after another manner.

"Equilibrium is fixed in inertia until outer space oversets the balance and the All-father pours forth to satisfy the hunger of space. Strange and deep are these truths; verily they are the keys to the lives of men and women, unknown to those that worship not the Great Goddess.

"Golden Aphrodite cometh not as the virgin, the victim, but as the Awakener, the Desirous One. As outer space she calls, and the All-father commences the courtship. She awakeneth Him to desire and the worlds are created. Lo, she is the Awakener. How powerful is she, golden Aphrodite, the awakener of manhood!"

The voice paused, and I thought of the travesties of golden Aphrodite who rule as divinities in bars and Bon-bon Boxes, and remembered the words of the Smaragdene Tablet: "As above, so below," and thought how creation and procreation mirror each other.

Then the voice began again:

"But all these things are one thing. All the goddesses are one goddess, and we call her Isis, the All-woman, in whose nature all natural things are found; virgin and desirous by turn; giver of life and bringer-in of death. She is the cause of creation, for she awakeneth the desire of the All-father and for her sake He createth. Likewise the wise call all women Isis.

"In the face of every woman let man look for the features of the Great Goddess, watching her phases through the flow and return of the tides to which his soul answereth; listening for her call.

"O daughters of Isis, adore the Goddess, and in her name give the call that awakens and rejoices. So shall ye be blessed of the Goddess and live with fullness of life."

He was speaking to Molly as if he stood again in the courts of the Temple of the Sun and she were a virgin preparing for the ordeal that should make her a Moon-priestess.

"Now this is the rite of the worship of Isis. Let the priestess show forth the Goddess to the worshipper. Let her assume the crown of the underworld. Let her arise all glorious and golden from the sea of the primordial and call to him that loveth her to come forth and come unto her. Let her do these things in the name of the Goddess and she shall be even as the Goddess unto him, for the Goddess will speak through her. All-powerful shall she be in the Inner as crowned Persephone, and all-glorious in the Outer as golden Aphrodite. So shall she be a priestess in the eyes of the worshipper of the Goddess, who by his faith and dedication shall find the Goddess in her. For the rite of Isis is life, and that which is done as a rite shall show forth in life. By the rite is the Goddess drawn down to her worshippers; her power enters into them and they become the substance of the sacrament."

He fell silent and stood looking at Molly, as if wondering how much she had understood, and how much she could or would do; for she lay back in her chair dazed and helpless, and only her eyes answered him.

Then the moonlight faded and a shift of the shore-wind silenced the sea and we were alone in the darkness, Molly and I, for the Priest of the Moon had gone; and in the darkness we sat together silently for a long while.

From that silent, formless communing we came back knowing many things. And I took Molly in my arms in a way I had never done before, and something suddenly flowed between us like warm light; it encircled us in a single aura so that our lives mingled and interchanged and stimulated each other and then flowed back to us, and I was reminded of the flow and interchange of force that had taken place in the rite I had worked with Morgan. We just stood there silently in front of the fire, now sunk to a dull red glow; neither could see the other; we were almost unaware of each other; then suddenly I felt the thing that Molly was letting flow out to me so unreservedly in her giving, and knew that it was the same thing that Morgan had invoked deliberately by her strange knowledge, and that it was using ignorant, innocent Molly because the conditions of her soul were right for it, she being a woman, and in love.

CHAPTER XXXI

THERE were two things that I saw clearly as the result of that night's work—firstly, that the Priest of the Moon meant to come to us as he had come to Morgan le Fay when she was Miss Morgan the First's companion; and secondly, that he meant to use Molly as they used the Moon-priestesses in Atlantis; and I wondered how Molly, who had been brought up by Mrs Muckley, would take to this, and hoped to God she had had her fair share of original sin before education got in its work upon her.

Our conventions have so stereotyped the polarity between a man and a woman that it has got stuck and no one knows how to shift it. But what we want in the part of marriage that is behind the veil is the dynamic woman, who comes in the name of the Great Goddess, conscious of her priesthood and proud of her power, and it is this self-confidence that the modest woman lacks.

These are vitally important things, and we have forgotten them, and I think it was to bring them again that Morgan le Fay and the Priest of the Moon were working. But it was not enough that Morgan le Fay should do them, for she was not, I think, of our evolution or epoch, but one sent to us from another place; it was needed that those of our own age and race should do them, and someone had to break trail for those that came after. Someone had to find in marriage neither an animal function nor a remedy for sin, but a divinely instituted sacrament for the bringing down of power, and in this sacrament the woman must take her ancient place as priestess of the rite, calling down lightning from heaven; the initiator, not the initiated.

And to this end I, being a man, had to learn to receive, which is not easy for a man, for he will not admit his need, wishing to be self-sufficient unto himself and always the giver; but God knows, he isn't! If there is one thing on God's earth he isn't, it is self-sufficing. We had to reverse the conventional polarity in our inner relationship, had Molly and I, before our marriage would light up for us. She had to become the priestess of the Goddess, and I, the kneeling worshipper, had to receive the sacrament at her hands. This a man can readily do when he has reverence for a woman as well as being passionately in love with her, for then to him marriage with her automatically becomes a sacrament.

For there can be no greatness of any kind that is purely personal and an end in itself. When the body of a woman is made an altar for the worship of the Goddess who is all beauty and magnetic life, and the man pours himself out in worship and sacrifice, keeping back no part of the price but giving his very self for love, seeing in his mate the priestess serving with him in the worship—then the Goddess enters the temple, roses in her hands and her doves flying around her, called down by the faith of her worshippers. It is because we have no faith that we do not see the Goddess behind all womanhood and thereby invoke her; and it is because they do not realise the sanctity of Great Isis that women have no respect for the gifts they bring us.

For if marriage is a sacrament, as the Church avers, it is so by virtue of being the outward and visible sign of an inward and spiritual grace, but that grace is not the grace of the Crucified, but of Great Isis, giver of life on earth. We blaspheme when we call it a remedy for sin—it is a rite of evocation and the power evoked is Life. It is the rite of the adoration of Beauty

which, together with Wisdom and Strength, form the Three
Holy Pillars that support high Heaven. For there is a mysticism of Nature and her elemental powers as well as a mysticism of the spirit; and these are not two things, but two aspects
of one thing, for God is made manifest in Nature, and Nature
is the self-expression of God; and when we deny the natural,
we deny the gift of God, which is to our use and His glory.
How can we better worship God than in the sanctity of the act
of creation that hands on His gift of life?   And shall it be more
holy as an animal function and remedy for sin than as the
evocation of all beauty in the soul of man and the expression
of his love?   These are not things that it is particularly safe to
say, but they are things that need saying.

Day by day, as the moon-power got in its work on her, I
watched Molly change from a little, quiet, staunch, faithful
thing, very sweet, but entirely Itless, into a pocket edition of
Morgan, with the same vitality and magnetism, and the same
lithe grace and bell-like tone of voice, for these, it seems, are
the things the moon-power brings to women.

And I saw, too, the change of the moon-tides in Molly, ebbing and flowing like the tides of the sea, never twice alike; and
learnt why it is her right to summon to the worship as priestess
in charge of the shrine, for she alone knows the set of the tides
of the moon; for a man's tides are the tides of the sun, changing
only with the seasons, and under civilised conditions changing
so slightly as to be negligible.

In those days there were not two at the farm, but three, for
Molly and I constantly felt the coming and going of one who
came to us from another sphere. And in the dusk, when the
moonlight fell on the wood-smoke, we saw, or thought we saw,
the shadowy figure formulate; we built it out of our imagination in the shadows as one sees faces in the fire, as Morgan had
taught, and to our eyes it took on life and spoke, for we were

not imaging a phantasy, but the shadow of the real, and the real came down and ensouled it. Thus, I think, have the gods always manifested to their worshippers.

And night by night, called down by faith and phantasy, the Priest of the Moon came to us as he had come to Morgan le Fay when she was an ageing and penurious woman—bearing the bread and wine that turned to strange life and vitality. For this was the work he had set out to do, and these were the secrets he had brought from lost Atlantis in those forgotten ages when he came to the Islands of the Sea with the Sea-king's ships—the secret of generation and regeneration by the wine of life, which is the moon-wine, the Soma.

He told us of ancient Atlantis and its lost and forgotten arts, and the knowledge that, perverted to evil, was destroyed by a cataclysm that the earth might be cleansed. He told us how, foreknowing the coming of disaster, he had travelled to the Islands of the Sea, bringing with him his books, and that this was the origin of the Graal legend, for as the custom was, a Christian dress had been given to the old tradition.

But the hearts of men becoming evil once more, the knowledge was withdrawn lest the tragedy of Atlantis repeat itself; but now it might be that the knowledge should come again if a way could be found; and he had found it in part through Morgan and had made a start with his work and carried it as far as he might.

But Morgan, as I had always known, was a strange being, both man and woman at heart, as the higher adepts are; and for that reason she could not surrender herself to the mating; and although she fetched the Graal from Mount Salvatch and bore it to the shore, she might not walk the ways of men, but remained a sea-priestess for ever, coming to the water's edge at the uttermost ebb of the neap, holding out her Graal and waiting. Till at last her call was heard, and one came down,

and she placed the Graal in his hands and went back to the
sea again. I remembered how Morgan had always veiled her
face, like the Great Goddess whom she worshipped, whenever
she had occasion to visit the mainland, and only revealed her
features out on the sea-girt down, the best part of a mile from
the coast.

Night by night, as the wood-smoke rose from the Fire of
Azrael, we built up the form of the Priest of the Moon in the
drifting shadows till he was as real to us as we were to each
other; and though we knew his form was such stuff as dreams
are made of, there came through that form the touch of mind
on mind, and that was the thing that counted, and no one who
felt it could think that he was hallucinated.

Now it was the touch of mind of the Priest of the Moon
on ours that made everything possible. Without him, we
should never have succeeded in bringing anything within
reach; he gave us the start that enabled us to get going, and
for that I shall be eternally grateful, and to that I shall never
cease to bear witness in spite of scepticism and discredit.
Mme Blavatsky talked of her Masters, and her words have the
ring of sincerity, though the flopping of letters on to folks'
noses has not, and was done, I think, to impress the *polloi* who
were exceedingly *hoi* in her days. We had no phenomena,
had Molly and I, but we had the sense of the touch of mind
on mind and of the presence of power. After all, if telepathy
is a fact, and survival is a fact, there seems no reason why the
survivors should not telepath, even if the letter-flopping is open
to question. As for me, I would sooner have that sense of the
touch of mind on mind, with its tremendously stimulating
influence, than any amount of objective evidence.

But the Priest of the Moon could no more cross the gulf to
come to us than we had been able to cross the gulf to go to
him. Some device had to be found whereby we could meet

half-way in the abyss of air, and that device was the art of the
magical images whereby we visualised the form before the
inner eye in the inner kingdoms and he projected therein the
life by the power of his mind; and so we felt the touch of
mind on mind where no man was, and heard the words where
no one spoke, for the thing came across the gulf on the wings
of phantasy; for phantasy is the ass that carries the ark, as they
said in the ancient Mysteries.

Now it is a very odd thing that I, who could visualise the
Priest of the Moon at will till he seemed to stand out like an
image in a stereoscope, always felt him to be a shadow thrown
by some other reality; whereas Molly, who couldn't visualise
him at all, was perfectly sure of his presence and actuality, and
seemed to commune with him interiorly with as much certainty
as if he were on the telephone. He taught me, and I learnt all
manner of things from him about Atlantis and the ancient
ways in Britain. But he did not so much teach Molly as change
her; I watched her changing before my eyes, until finally the
Priest of the Moon seemed to belong to her rather than to me,
who had introduced her to him.

Then one day Molly told me a strange thing; she said that
there was something else as well as the Priest of the Moon; that
just as we had made the Priest of the Moon real to ourselves
by thinking about him, so he was making a goddess real to her
by visualising her, and the goddess was Great Isis in whom all
womanhood is gathered up. · Then I sat back and left Molly
alone and watched her, for it was her turn now.

And just as she had confidence in the Priest of the Moon,
though she did not understand the psychology of him, so she
had confidence in Great Isis, though she did not understand
the metaphysics of Her; and it was this confidence that made
Her real and brought Her through, as my enlightened
mysticism never could have done.

For Molly, in her own eyes at any rate, was becoming something; and the result of it was that she was becoming something in mine also. She liked to think of herself as a priestess of Great Isis, and presently I found that I was thinking of her as a priestess of Great Isis too, for her feelings affected me more than I realised. And I began to understand what Morgan had said about my belief in her as a priestess making her a priestess. But hang it all, it wasn't just belief, for Molly was functioning as a priestess and bringing through the power!

As the days went on she became more and more sure of herself as she saw my reactions, and began to feel that she as priestess had the right to invoke the goddess, and finally she dared to do it.

There was a sea-fog that night that wrapped all round the narrow neck of land where stood the farm between the salt marsh and the tide-water. Save for the shadowy bulk of Bell Knowle the land had disappeared and the high sea-down had vanished like lost Atlantis. All that remained of it was a hollow echo verberating and re-verberating as the melancholy two-tone call of Starber lightship struck the hollow rock. We were cut off from the land and only the sea remained open to us as an occasional shift of the drift of the wind opened long sea-lanes in the fog down which the moon shone, for she was low and near her setting. It was strange to see a sea-lane open thus, with the water all silver in the moonlight and the fog standing up in walls on either hand, like the cliffs of a phantom fiord. It was such a sea-path as this down which the oldest gods might travel, coming from the moon and that which is behind the moon—most ancient time and space when earth and moon were both etheric, not yet solidified into dense matter and not yet parted one from another.

The tide was coming in. I had begun to notice that with the rising tide Molly always seemed to wake up, unlike Morgan, who came to her power when the tide was at uttermost ebb. But then she was a sea-priestess, and Molly was a priestess of corn and hearth and garth, which is another aspect of the Great Goddess whom they both served after their different ways.

With the rising tide to-night Molly grew restless, and was constantly looking out of the window into the fog, and opening the window and letting the fog into the room till I protested, for I was wheezy. Then she went out into the porch and shut the door behind her so that the fog should not inconvenience me.

She was gone so long that I got uneasy and went after her. She was not in the porch, nor in the narrow front garden, marked off by its low loose wall from the wide marsh, and I had a sudden panic lest she had answered the call of the sea-gods as had Morgan, and I dashed out of the gate and down through the fog to the beach, calling her frantically. Then I heard her answering call in the fog, and the tremendous sense of relief taught me something that it was very good for me to know.

I found her down there in the grey half-light where the waves were breaking, and she put her little warm hand in mine and I was most frightfully glad to feel it there; and I put my arm round her and wanted to march her back to the house to make sure of her. For I was taking no more chances with the sea-gods. Morgan had never in any sense been mine, and I had no right to protest when they called her, but had to bear it as best I could; but Molly was mine, and no mistake about it, and I was standing no nonsense from sea-gods or anybody. I was prepared to fight for Molly, and defy high heaven if necessary; which was a very great surprise to me, just as great a surprise as it was when I realised the hold the Bon-bon Boxer had got over me. I do not pretend to understand these things. They are very odd.

But Molly wasn't having any. She kept tight hold of me and made me stop there where the water was breaking, asthma or no asthma, for she had got something afoot that was bigger than my temporary well-being, and like Morgan, she could harden her heart. I saw that upon the line of dry seaweed that marked high water she had built a little Fire of Azrael, pyramidal, according to tradition, and was awaiting the approach of the water to light it. I saw too that she was dressed in shadowy drapery, and that Morgan's sapphires gleamed on breast and wrist. Molly was doing the thing properly.

And because it was real to her it became real to me and infected me with its emotion. I forgot my asthma and became absorbed in what was afoot, watching the slow creep of the oncoming waves up the sand and the line of foam at their lip coming further and further up the beach as the tide rose, pushing the languid, fogbound rollers in front of it, for they seemed too flattened and stifled by the thickness of the air to move of their own volition.

Presently the first shallow, spreading wash of a breaking wave ran up to the edge of the weed, and Molly put a match to her Fire of Azrael and we watched it take the flame, the dry and resinous woods rapidly turning into a pyramid of fire after their year-long storage out at the fort. The seaweed burned too, with an odd iodine smell that seemed to have the ancient essence of all sea-beaches embalmed in it, and I thought of the far-travelled mariners with their gold ear-rings and curled beards, who had drawn their high-prowed sea-ships up on Ishtar's Beere.

Then the cold drifting draught that is in every fog opened a sea-lane that led right out to the moon, and we saw the slow heave of the sea running all black and shadowy as the tide made up-channel. But even as we watched, the sea felt the call of the moon, and the water became flickering silver as the turn of the tide broke the rhythm of the waves, and we watched the water that had come far up the land turn again to the great deep. The waves had respected Molly's fire, and just lipped it and made it hiss before they turned again, sinking slowly back, leaving a belt of wet sand and fresh weed to mark their path.

Molly raised her arms in the sign of the horns of the moon and invoked the Great Goddess as I had seen Morgan do. The moon was low in the west towards her setting, and at Molly's feet was the red-lit Fire of Azrael, and beyond it the silver pathway stretched out over the sea toward lost Atlantis. And it seemed to me that at her call came the gods of the past and their priests and worshippers, for she was waking the old worship once again. I could see them come in a long procession over the sea, an army with banners, called by her from the Great Atlantic Deep where their land was sunk. I saw them come as they had come of old, winding up the processional way to the temple on the crest of the sacred mountain, for a priestess of the true lineage called them to the worship.

They passed around us, dividing on either hand, and went on over the marsh to where Bell Knowle raised its mist-crowned head to the night and the stars. And Bell Knowle received them; they passed within to the great chambers of the caves where the worship was held, and Molly and I were left alone with the moon and the sea to do the greater worship that is held out there in the silence and darkness, close to nature.

The Moon sank lower; the sea cut her disk and the mist of the sea banked about her in a golden nimbus. Then Something seemed to formulate in the darkness and come over the sea towards us through the mist, moving by the pathway of silver light upon the water; and It was vast, so that Its head met the stars, and It was all veiled and swathed and shrouded. Only we saw the silver Feet upon the sea, and they were like moonlight over water.

And so She came, She of the Sea, to the place where sea meets land, and we awaited Her coming. She paused at the edge of the line of the breaking foam, Her feet in the water and Her head among the stars, star-crowned. There was no Face to see, for She is for ever veiled, but there came to us the great exalted awe which some say is the gods and none other.

This tingling fear took me by the heart and by the throat and by the eyes, gripping like a hand. And my hands began to burn and tingle with a pulsating force, and from behind my eyes it seemed to come out like a beam. And I broke out in that heavy sweat of the heat of the gods, which Morgan had told me always heralds their passing; and my breath was taken short, but not with the asthma, and I grew rigid and shook like a man in a fever-fit. I looked towards Molly, and saw that she stood on tiptoe, reaching up towards her Goddess as if floating between earth and air like a frozen figure of dance, immobile, tense and effortless.

Then slowly Great Isis turned, and drew Her veil closer about Her; and She went down the long sea-lane out towards the west, the fog closing in behind Her.

The sea drew back with the falling tide and bared the place of Her passing, and on the sand we saw silvery pools that might have been the marks of eddies but that we knew were Her foot-prints. And so She passed away as silently as She had come, but the place where She passed was holy, being filled with power. Something had touched our souls to awe, and we chose to call it the passing of the Goddess.

Then we knew that what we called Great Isis had deigned to answer the invocation of Her priestess, and that the altar fire was lit in the sanctuary that Molly had swept and garnished and tended with such fidelity—the empty shrine of the loveless home to which I had brought her in my sorrow and loneliness and sickness, and to which she had come for the sake of the greater love that seeks not its own but is fulfilled in the good of the beloved.

We had, perhaps, in these things the making of magical power; for in magic, as Morgan said, there is no power save there be sacrifice, just as the sea-gods had tried for me and got the poor moon-calf before they would accept the fort as their temple. So Great Isis had demanded of Molly that she should lay herself on the altar of sacrifice, and then, like the fierce tribal fetish that Abraham propitiated with the offer of Isaac, had kept the life but returned the form of flesh. So Isis had taken Molly, and Molly had let Her.

A horrible pang of fear shot through me lest once again I should be called upon to sacrifice to the sea something that was becoming very dear to me. And I told the sea flat out that if it took Molly I should come after her. And it seemed to me that somewhere among the stars I heard faint laughter, silver laughter, and I knew that the Goddess was glad and this was the sound of Her joy, for I had offered the acceptable sacrifice without which no mating can be consecrated to the Great Goddess. For in every union the woman makes this offer, for she goes down to the gates of death to open them to the incoming life, and shall not the man, in common justice, match her giving? For without the shedding of blood there is no redemption whether in childbed or upon the field of battle, both crucifixions after their kind, and both of redeeming power when made sacramental by an ideal.

Then we turned to go home; and the earth under our feet glowed and felt warm like the flesh of a living thing, as it surely is, for is it not the body of a goddess?

The mist rolled back with the turning tide, for a breeze sprang up off the land and swept it out to sea. And the breeze freshened and veered, and as we walked up the steep sea-beach we heard the crisp crash of waves on shingle. The stars came out in the indigo night of the sky, for Great Isis had set, sinking below the waves on Her way to Atlantis, where maybe She took counsel with Her priests, sitting in circle in the deep-sea palaces, and told them concerning the coming to earth again of Her ancient wisdom by way of a man and a woman who in spite of many difficulties had come to love each other.

The sea behind us sang like a choir, the waves of either bay beating against the narrow neck of land where our home stood, like the two parts of a choir calling and answering across a cathedral. The pyramidal height of Bell Knowle rose dark against the stars, a sentinel guarding the marshes, and the long bulk of Bell Head stretched out to sea. The lights of the ships going up to Bristol city moved slowly between sea and sky, and in the clearness following the fog a low glow hung on the horizon from the seaport towns of Wales.

And there came to me the great tragedy of all these moving lights of toiling men and the glow of the crowded towns set on the narrow strip of land between the iron coast and the iron hills with their valleys of harsh toil, where Aphrodite Pandemos walks the sordid streets and the Little Bethels preach half a god to half a man.

CHAPTER XXXII

L UCKILY for all concerned, the next day was a Saturday. The Great Goddess, true to tradition, had come upon the day sacred to her—Friday—so called after Freya, the northern Venus. There not being much doing at the office on a Saturday, I stopped at home and nursed my asthma, which had not been improved by breathing sea-fog in bulk.

The day was sparkling and sunny after the fog, and the bay was full of little dancing waves, very blue. I thought, as we strolled over the level sands left bare by the tide, what a magnificent place it would be to raise kids, if we ever had any. I did not like to voice my thoughts to Molly for fear of hurting her feelings, but I had a feeling, from the way she was looking out to sea, that she was thinking of the same thing.

I looked at Molly, as she wasn't looking at me, and it struck me as odd that I should have known her all this time and never seen in her what I saw now, and wondered whether the change was in her or me—perhaps a bit of both, if the truth were known. The Priest of the Moon had done his work well; what he had taught was certainly putting Molly and me on our feet. It struck me that it would put a good many other folk on their feet, too, if they knew what we knew.

We climbed slowly, for I was rather breathless, up to the vine-terraces, and sat there in the sun on the seat under the breast of the down, for sun does me more good than anything else when my asthma is bothering me. The little vines had long since shed their winter wrappings, and their funny little woolly buds had developed into pretty, yellowish leaves on their long whipcord stems. All the same, they looked to me melancholious little plants, but Molly had hopes of them, and she and the tweeny nursed them as if they were kids.

We looked out over the hollow land of the marshes. It was barely above the level of the spring tides, and only the dykes prevented the sea flooding it when there was an on-shore gale. But to-day there was no gale, only a soft breeze, and we watched the uncut hay rippling like water as it passed. The place was stiff with larks, and their songs came up to us as we sat under the breast of the cliff. I told Molly how I had seen as a boy the footings of the ancient quays, left behind by the receding sea.

The marshes had changed but little since those days, and the ancient life seemed all about us in the warm breathing air and sparkling sun. I became very conscious of the continuity of life in the land, passing down from father to son in the slow ways of husbandry that never change at heart. Life goes on, the life of the race, and we are but parts of a larger whole. For the life of the race itself is a part of the life of Isis.

And I thought of the days when men worshipped Her as giver of life to the race and warden of its continuity, naming even their seaport after Her, and wondered what things they had known that we had forgotten, to which Morgan had given the clues and then left us to puzzle out. There was a lot in the old pagan worship, I was convinced. The vicar could never have steered Molly and me through our difficulties in the way that the Priest of the Moon had done. I could picture his face if he had been consulted on the subject! He would have gone out through the roof of his confessional like a scalded cat.

It was very pleasant up there under the shelter of the warm grey rock. The heat of the sun made the herbs smell, and it was like incense. Far below the little waves broke whispering and silvery on the shingle and the song of the larks rose through them. I took off my coat and rolled up my shirt-sleeves, and the sun cooked me to a crisp, and I felt very lazy and very amiable. Out across the marshes we could see the new road, with the cars sliding backwards and forwards on it like beads on a string. Down below us was the thatched roof of our home, with blue smoke rising from the chimney, and a waft of the wind brought up to us the smell of baking bread. Set in the masonry beside the hearth in the living-room was an old-fashioned bread-oven in which you lit a fire of peats, and when it had burnt out, raked out the ash and put in your loaves. Molly insisted on using it, and I must say it baked champion bread. In some odd way we seemed very much a part of the life of the marsh because we burnt its peats and thatched with its reeds. As soon as I found myself among the water-cuts and willows I felt at home, long before I got to the farm. Bell Knowle and Bell Head were our two watchmen, keeping the land and the sea-ways that led to us.

Then we went down and had lunch in the garden, the cupressus hedges, that grew like Jonah's gourd in that sandy soil, being already big enough to break the breeze off the sea the blows on even the hottest day across that neck of land. We were glad of it, for all afternoon the farm baked in the shimmering heat that danced on the levels, till towards evening the shadow of the down fell across it as the sun sank in the sea.

I ran Molly out to the fort to watch the sunset, and it was very fine that night. The sea was one sheet of palest gold; along the horizon lay low masses of purple cloud looking like a mountain range, and behind them was a rose-pink sky. As the sun sank, curious green beams of after-glow shot up from below the sea-line and the sea turned violet-purple. I drove back as the dusk closed in, and as we came up over the crest of the down and all the levels lay spread out beneath us, we saw a wonderful second sunset like dawn in the eastern sky, reflected from the sun below the sea. Then down the steep way along the cliff in bottom gear, and so to our home.

We built a small Fire of Azrael, June though it was, for it is always cool out there on the coast as soon as the sun has set; and we sat over it and gossiped very happily, quite forgetting what Fires of Azrael are for, till a curious sense of the gathering of power in the room reminded us. I had thought we had had enough excitement for one full moon, but apparently the gods thought otherwise.

Nothing came of it, however, but perhaps that was because high tide would be an hour later that night, and Molly chased me off to bed, saying the gods could call us if they wanted us.

So we went to bed, Molly to her quarters and I to mine, for no one in his senses wants to share its kennel with a bulldog, faithful and affectionate animal though it is. My nocturnal habits were too much even for Molly.

Upstairs the faint sweet smell of the juniper, cedar and sandal was very noticeable; I even saw a faint haze of blue smoke drifting along the passage, and concluded that there must be some cracks in the old chimneys and that Bindling had not done his work too well.

My room was at the seaward end of the house, and as the moon got towards its setting, its light came streaming on to the bed. I would not have it shut out, though Molly thought it helped to make me sleep badly, and I lay and watched the moon pass slowly across the window and thought of the other moon-sets I had seen out at the fort; and the silver pathway that led to the gods of the sea; and my trip to Atlantis in the company of the Priest of the Moon, and what it had meant when I was told that my dedication was accepted, and what was going to come of it. And then and there, in my heart, I renewed the dedication. But somehow it seemed vague and ineffectual. And so I sat up in bed and raised my arms in the sign of the horns of the moon and renewed it again out loud, and the outward and visible sign felt as if it were effectual, though the unspoken one had not.

The smell of the aromatic smoke from the Fire of Azrael was coming upstairs very strongly now, and I began to get rather worried, and wondered whether the defective chimney was going to set the house on fire; but then I remembered we had only left a handful of ash behind us when we had gone to bed, and there was something about that smoke that no terrestrial fire could account for. I began to wonder what was going to happen. I held out my hands to feel the air, and see whether it was developing that slippery coldness that had come at the fort when Morgan worked her rite, but on the contrary it felt surprisingly warm for that hour of the night, and with a curious dry heat, like the hot room of a Turkish bath, and the temperature was rapidly rising. I began to wonder whether the house had gone on fire in good earnest, and what in the world was going to happen next, and whether I had better get up and see.

Then the door opened soundlessly and Molly entered. She had never come to my room of her own accord before unless she had heard me moving about and knew I was seedy, and I wondered whether she had come to rouse me with the news that the house was on fire. But she did not speak, though she could see me sitting up in bed in the moonlight and knew that I was awake. She took up her stand at the foot of my bed with the window behind her and the moonlight streaming through it. Molly always wears flowered voile nighties which she makes herself, and very pretty they are, too, but no use when the light is behind her. She looked just like an antique statue, a pocket Venus, and she held out her arms towards me in the strange stiff attitude of the ancient gods, like Hathor when she is a hawk, and I saw that about her neck and on her wrists were Morgan's sapphires.

Then she began to sing. She used Morgan's tune, but the song she sang was not one that Morgan had ever sung to me.

> "I am the Star that riseth from the sea,
>   The twilight sea.
> All tides are mine, and answer unto me—
> Tides of men's souls and dreams and destiny—
>   Isis Veiled and Ea, Binah, Ge.
>
> "Lo, I receive the gifts thou bringest me—
> Life and more life—in fullest ecstasy!
> I am the Moon, the Moon that draweth thee.
> I am the waiting Earth that calleth thee.
> Come unto me, Great Pan, come unto me!
> Come unto me, Great Pan, come unto me!"

The low room faded under the magic of the singing, opening out into a vast and moonlit plain of bare black basalt, barren and volcanic, and I thought of lost Atlantis after the cataclysm, and the mountains of the moon. In the centre of the plain was a moon-temple of open black columns set in a circle like a slender and graceful Stonehenge of Doric pillars. Silhouetted against it were the lovely lines of Molly like a Tanagra figurine in her shadowy shift, and I knew that she was exercising her ancient right and giving me the mating-call in the name of the moon, far truer to Nature than any convention of duty and modesty. And I knew why Morgan had said that on the inner planes the woman is positive and should take the initiative, for the Astral Plane is ruled by the moon and woman is her priestess; and when she comes in her ancient right, representing the moon, the moon-power is hers and she can fertilise the male with vitalising magnetic force.

And the answering power awoke in me from the very deeps of my being, far deeper than the overflow of desire that comes from a physical pressure; for she called up from me the reserves of vital force and brought them into action—the reserves that the law of our nature guards against the great crises when we fight for life itself—the things that give the madman his strength and the poet his creative frenzy. Not until these things are called up by the call of the beloved can we be said to have mated to the depths of our being. They are not called forth when the man wooes the woman because he feels like it, but they are called forth when she comes to him in the name of Great Isis and bids him worship the goddess with her and through her.

The dark plain with its pillared temple grew clearer and clearer as if I saw it at the moon-rise; the low-ceilinged room of the farm-house had disappeared, and overhead was a high clear sky; Molly remained, however, a silvery figure in the silver moonlight—Isis Unveiled, come down from heaven to me, for she was made one with Her.

We had passed out into another dimension—the dimension of the things of the mind, and that which was between us had taken on a significance which was no longer personal but part of Life itself—of Life going on in the eternal becoming. Molly was to me not a woman, but the thing which is woman. And because I saw not her, but what was behind her, life came in with such a rush that we were whirled away like leaves in the wind. The barriers of personality went down, and we were made one with the cosmic life—not one with each other, for that, I think, can never be, and we miss the turning when we seek it—but one with a larger whole; and as things which are equal to a third are equal to either, losing ourselves in the larger life we found each other. It is a thing difficult to explain, and a matter of experience. I have put it as clearly as I can. I do not pretend to understand it. There is something beyond comradeship to be found in marriage; something that the

personality of the beloved cannot give; it is this magnetic something that begins to flow when we reach out beyond the
personality of the woman towards her essential womanhood;
it is, I think, this essence, this vital principle that creates the
form through function, which was what the ancients personified as the Great Goddess Isis, veiled in heaven and unveiled
in love.

And through all the ecstasy of the experience, like the muted
orchestra accompanying great singing, went the sound of a
voice as clear as a bell, and I knew that the Priest of the Moon
was presiding over the rite as they did in ancient Atlantis when
the Virgins of the Sun were brought into the great temple. It
was an ordered rite, corresponding to processes in Great Nature
herself.

"Learn now the mystery of the ebbing and flowing tides.
Isis of Nature awaiteth the coming of Her Lord the Sun. She
calls Him; She draws Him from the place of the dead, the
kingdom of Amenti, where all things are forgotten. And He
comes to Her in His boat called Millions of Years, and the
earth grows green with springing grain. For the desire of
Osiris answers unto the call of Isis, and so will it ever be in the
hearts of men, for thus the gods have formed them. Whoso
denieth this is abhorred of the gods.

"But in the heavens our Lady Isis is the Moon, and the moon-
powers are Hers. She is also the priestess of the silver star that
rises from the twilight sea. Hers are the magnetic moon-tides,
ruling the hearts of men. In the Inner She is all-potent. She is
queen of the kingdoms of sleep. All the invisible workings are
Hers, and She rules all things ere they come to birth. Even
as through Osiris Her mate the earth grows green, so the mind
of man conceives through Her power. This secret concerns
the inner nature of the Goddess, which is dynamic."

As the sound of the voice went on I seemed to find myself

inside the circle of slender black pillars that formed the temple
of the moon in the midst of the burnt-up, barren plain, and in it
the moonlight was concentrated, leaving all else in darkness;
and there was silence for a while, and I heard the great tides
of the skies come up and go by in their rhythm of musical
colours. Each had its beat and its note and its periodicity.
They were like the notes of an organ, and they were like wheeling beams of light. One could conceive them as forces, or one
could personify them as angels and see the great Forms go by
on strong wings, singing as they went, and glimpse the half-
seen Faces.

We were alone now, were Molly and I, in the open temple in
the empty plain, with only the moon above us and the whirling
earth beneath, for all sacraments end in silence. Even the Priest
of the Moon withdrew and left us alone with the Moon and
the Earth and Space.

And then we heard far off the sound of a rising tide, the
soft silvery beat of light surf on shingle; and we knew that the
waters were spreading over the earth at the end of the aeon.
And the voice of the Priest of the Moon came again as the sea
drew nearer.

"Consummatum est. Those who have received the Touch of
Isis have received the opening of the gates of the inner life. For
them the tides of the moon shall flow and ebb and flow and
never cease in their cosmic rhythm."

Then the moon-temple and the wide plain faded, and
through the open window we heard the surf of an earthly tide
upon the shingle as the moon passed to her setting.

We were back in the low ceilinged room of the farm, but
still the voice of the Priest of the Moon went on.

"The great sun, moving in the heavenly houses, has left the
House of the Fishes for the House of the Water-bearer. In the
coming age shall humanity be holy, and in the perfection of

the human shall we find the humane. Take up the manhood into Godhead, and bring down the Godhead into manhood, and this shall be the day of God with us; for God is made manifest in Nature, and Nature is the self-expression of God."

The Society of the Inner Light, founded by the late Dion Fortune, has courses for those who wish seriously to pursue the study of the Western Esoteric Tradition. Information about the society may be obtained by writing to the address below. Please enclose British stamps or international postal coupons in your letter if you wish a response.

The Secretary
The Society of the Inner Light
38 Stelle's Road
London NW3 4RG, England